The Department

Jacqueline Faber

OCEANVIEW PUBLISHING
SARASOTA, FLORIDA

ISBN 978-1-60809-634-3

Published in the United States of America by Oceanview Publishing

Sarasota, Florida

www.oceanviewpub.com

10 9 8 7 6 5 4 3 2 1

THE

DEPARTMENT

Advanced Reader's Edition:
This is an advanced reader's edition from uncorrected proofs.

CHAPTER 1

NEIL

Now

What can I say about Phaedra Lewis except from the moment I met her, I wanted her. I remember the early days, sitting at the bar, burning down cigarette after cigarette like we wanted to inflict real damage. Gin and tonics on the counter, swiveling on our stools in the dim orange light.

"Why are you here?" she asked me one night.

"Like, here at the bar?"

"Here at school." It was our first year as grad students in philosophy. I was already wasted, but I finished off my gin.

"Um," I said, as "Guns of Brixton" came on the jukebox and a group of girls stumbled in. "I think because I watched a woman die once." I had never uttered the words out loud before.

Phaedra's eyes widened, and I felt her lean in. "That is *not* what I was expecting." Wisps of her blonde hair floated like strands of a spider web in the blurred bar light.

Truth be told, most of my memories are fragments. Broken bits, cut glass. But this one—this memory of the woman drowning—was different.

It was summertime. I must have been six years old. My brother, Ethan, only four. Our family had piled into my dad's Oldsmobile Cutlass, and we'd driven across the country from Indiana to California. Rows and rows of crops, sun-scorched fields that touched the sky. My comic books spread across the back seat. Motels and fast-food chains. Then, one day, we sat on a beach in Los Angeles—hot sand beneath us, waves crashing, seagulls overhead—like we'd been cast in a commercial for something that looked like real life but wasn't.

Ethan and I dug a trench that filled with water when the tide came in. My mother was lying on a towel, a T-shirt draped over her face to block the sun. From somewhere down the beach, someone started shouting. We all leaped up. My mother grabbed our hands and held on tight. The sun bounced off the ocean, and I could see a woman swimming out past the breakers. One minute, her head was bobbing, the next, it slipped below the waves. It was like a video game. There, gone, there again.

Up and down the beach, people ran into the water, but no one dared to swim out. The riptide was too strong. When help eventually came, they carried her body out of the surf and laid her in the sand. They did chest compressions and affixed a breathing apparatus. But even I could see it was too late.

Ethan and I stood in front of our trench, the water filling and draining, while the dead woman lay on the beach.

"You know what I think about all these years later?" I said to Phaedra. "The quietness. All of us just standing there."

She looked at me, a sheen to her eyes. "You think someone should have done more?"

"I don't know." I smashed the butt of my cigarette into an ashtray and tugged another from the pack. "Later, we found out that the woman's husband was on the beach. And her kids. Two boys—same ages as me and Ethan."

"Jesus," Phaedra said. "That's horrifying."

It was then that she told me about the Kitty Genovese. In 1964, a young woman was raped and stabbed to death in Queens, New York, while 38 people watched from the safety of their apartments.

"I mean, what does that say about who we really are?" she asked. "Thirty-eight sets of eyes. You know how many called the cops? None." Phaedra shook her head. "We all think we'd be different. That we'd be the ethical one."

Five years later, I would be married to Phaedra Lewis and writing my dissertation on bystander apathy. Kitty Genovese, the center of my work.

Even now, all these years later, it's hard for me to separate the smell of gin, Phaedra's beautiful face, the drowning woman, and Kitty Genovese. All those pieces seemed to find each other that night, and I felt certain of only two things in the entire world: I was falling in love with this beautiful girl, and I would never be a bystander.

***

Thirteen years later, I sat in Paul Rutger's office, my palms slick with sweat, my leg jittering. I wondered what I must look like to Paul. The bags under my eyes. The weight I'd packed on. The general decrepitude. A man already washed up before middle age. Paul took a breath, leaned forward, and steepled his fingers.

"I'll be honest with you, Neil," he said, "I'm not entirely sure how to proceed here."

I nodded. My leg bounced. I needed a smoke so bad my hands were shaking.

Years ago, when Phaedra and I landed our teaching jobs, Paul had taken us out for celebratory drinks. "I'm just so damn glad to welcome you both," he'd said, whiskey-breathed and beaming. "You're exactly what this department needs!"

At the time, Phaedra and I felt like luminaries, like bright, shining stars that would never burn out. Now, Paul eyed me like he was trying to find some trace of that promising young professor beneath the sad sack of shit that I'd become.

"I wanted to check up on you," he said. "To see if there are any . . . updates?" Paul avoided the word "tenure," but it hung over our conversation, leaden and airless.

"I'm on the judiciary committee," I offered.

"Okay," Paul nodded, as if to a child. "That's good. That's a start."

He leaned back in his chair. Behind him were shelves of trinkets, objects he'd picked up on his travels. Figurines of sparrows, an angel from the German Erzgebirge, iridescent globes of glass. Paul once brought back garden gnomes for everyone in the department. Phaedra and I didn't know what to do with ours, so we wrapped scarves around their necks and laid them on the lounge chairs we'd dragged up to the roof of our loft.

Back then, everything was smooth. I had a teaching job I loved. I was married to the woman of my dreams. My work mattered. Then, one Wednesday afternoon, I read an article. Apparently, a documentary was coming out about Kitty Genovese, the woman who had been killed in New York while 38 people witnessed in silence. Turns out, those witnesses weren't so silent after all. Some had called the cops. One had held Kitty in her dying moments, blood smeared on the stairwell next to her.

Oh, I remember thinking. *Okay.*

From an ethical perspective, this was obviously good news. But on a personal level, it gutted me. My work sputtered. My book stalled. Everything was grounded in that number. Those 38 negligent bystanders. Those 38 assholes who didn't do a thing.

But as devastating as the Kitty Genovese documentary was, it was a mere paper cut compared to the full-scale disembowelment that was coming.

Paul removed his glasses and exhaled.

"Listen, Neil, you know I'll do everything I can to support you, but there needs to be some—some movement—so they know you're still kicking."

I looked around. It felt hard to breathe. All those figurines on Paul's shelf staring out at me. The birds and angels and globes of glass. The memory of those gnomes, scarves wrapped around their thick necks, lying strangely on our lounge chairs.

"Well, um . . ." I said, groping for words, "I'm about to publish something, actually."

I've never been a good liar, but this one came out easily.

"Oh, good Lord!" he said, clasping his hands. "That's great news! Really great." Paul looked genuinely relieved. For a moment, his expression softened, and there was a heaviness in his eyes. I knew what was coming before he said it. He looked uncomfortable. "I know this hasn't been easy on you," he said. He didn't say Phaedra's name, but I could feel her specter haunting our conversation.

"I'm fine, Paul." My throat clenched. "Really. I'm good."

He nodded, like he had more to say, then thought better of it.

"Well, I'm glad to hear it." He picked up a small wooden tree, hand-carved in some German town or other, and mindlessly rolled it between his fingers. "When is it coming out?" he asked.

"What?"

"Your article?"

"Oh, soon." I stood to leave before he could dig for more details. "Really soon." As I hoisted my bag onto my shoulder, something on Paul's desk caught my attention.

A neat stack of papers in the corner. "Oh, goodness," he said, looking down. "Have you seen this? Awful, just awful." He pulled a page off the top and handed it to me. "I offered to distribute them around campus."

In the center was a photograph of a girl's face. She was staring at the camera, lips parted, hair long and dark, a dimple in one cheek. *Have you seen me?* was written across the top. Below the photograph was her name: Lucia Vanotti. She was 20 years old.

"Oh, and Neil," Paul said, "please do let me know when the article comes out."

***

Jack Sheridan was in the dining hall when I arrived, the remnants of a ham sandwich on his tray.

"How'd it go?" he asked.

I sank into the chair across from him and dropped my head into my hands. "I told him I was about to publish something."

Jack winced.

"Well, it could be worse," he said. "You could be grading papers about Martin Heidegger fucking Hannah Arendt. While being a Nazi. And married."

"No!"

"Yes!" he flashed me a student paper. Jack pretended to be exasperated, but I knew better. He loved those kids, and they loved him right back. I remember when teaching felt that way to me. When I'd step into a classroom, and all the chaos inside of me would go quiet. When a two-hour lecture was a bulwark against my own disappearance.

Still, Jack had something I never had. He was handsome. Outlandishly so. With his shirt sleeves rolled up and his suede boots worn in. Jack's classes had waiting lists. His waiting lists had waiting lists.

I swiped a potato chip off his tray and glanced around the dining hall. That's when I saw her. I wasn't intentionally looking. I swear, I wasn't.

Jack swiveled in his seat to follow my gaze.

"Oh, for fuck's sake," he said.

"What?"

"Stop."

"I'm not doing anything. I'm just looking around."

"Well, stop looking. It's pathetic."

I didn't respond, but I shifted in my seat so that I could no longer see her. Phaedra, my wife. My ex-wife. Her head bent low, talking to Tim Janek, her new husband. Also in our department.

"Hey," Jack said, "want to grab a drink tonight?" Solid friend. I appreciated the effort.

"I don't know." The meeting with Paul had soured my mood. And now, Phaedra. Even though we taught in the same department, I could go weeks without seeing her. Things were easier when our paths didn't cross.

"Come on," Jack pushed. "One drink."

"I should write."

"Ah, okay. Good for you." He meant it. Jack was concerned about my dim prospects for tenure.

Across the dining hall, a student was making his way through the tables collecting signatures for one cause or another. Before Phaedra left, I used to sign each one. Ban plastic bags. Save endangered wolves. Support elections somewhere. *Show me the dotted line.* It's not that I cared so much about changing the world. Change is illusory and unreliable. It's that I wanted my students to believe in change. To believe that their voices mattered. These days, I found it excruciating to look them in the eye when they sidled up with their hopes and their good intentions.

"Let's go," I said.

"Relax," Jack said, slurping his Diet Coke. "I'm not done."

Too late. The boy with the petition was standing at our table.

"Hi," he said, setting a piece of paper down in front of us. Only, it wasn't a petition. It was the same flyer that Paul had given me. The dark-haired girl. The one who was missing.

The boy pointed a fluorescent green nail at the flyer. "Anyone with any information should call this number," he said.

I studied the page as he moved onto the next table.

The girl's name was Lucia, which I pronounced "Lu-see-ah."

Jack corrected me. "Luchia. With a *ch*." His eyes were glued to the page, and when he looked up, I was staring. "What?" he said defensively. "It's Italian. Lu-chia, not Lu-see-ah."

He finished his Diet Coke, and we headed outside. It was late March, and the sun burned high in the sky. All around us, campus was abuzz. There were students in the quad, a couple of frat boys playing hacky sack. Jack was quiet, distracted.

"You all right?" I asked him.

"You bet," he said, patting my shoulder. "Get some writing done, professor. I'll catch you tomorrow."

We parted ways, and I lit a cigarette. Smoked it down to the filter. Disgusting habit. I was planning to quit. Outside the parking lot, there was another student handing out flyers. The missing girl again.

"Already got one, thanks," I said, tapping my bag.

Later, I would look back and marvel at the day. When Lucia was just the name of some girl I did not know. Soon, of course, she would be everywhere. On the news, in the papers, whispered about in the hallways, and I would struggle to remember a time when Lucia Vanotti did not consume my every waking moment.

CHAPTER 2

LUCIA

Then

(A year and a half earlier)

People do things for all sorts of reasons. Because it's hot. Because they're bored. Because what's the worst that can happen when the worst has already happened? That night, I did it because he had a nice smile.

His name was Eric, and I saw him while I was waiting in line for the bathroom.

"Where do I know you from?" he asked.

We were at a frat party. People moved in eddies around the furniture and congregated in the halls. Music drifted upward, Kendrick Lamar pumping through the house. Downstairs, the line for the bathroom was monstrous, so I came upstairs looking for another. Now the boy with the smile was squinting, trying to place me.

"Macroeconomics," I said. "Last year."

Be humble. Sit down, said Kendrick Lamar.

"Oh, yeah, yeah, yeah," Eric said. Full lips, straight teeth. "You're that pretty girl who sat in the back."

Other people's flirtation is cringeworthy. Less so when it's yours.

"Your hair's longer," I noted.

"Yeah, I'm growing it out." He ran a hand through it. I could picture his bedroom, down to the didgeridoo in the corner. It would be one of those expensive ones, aboriginal, first-class from Australia.

I stood with my back against the wall. Eric moved closer so we didn't have to shout over the music. When the bathroom door opened, I smiled and pushed past him. He was waiting there when I came out.

"You want to see my room?" he asked.

I took a sip of my beer, let the bitterness sting my tongue and run down my throat.

"Yeah, sure."

As we passed the stairs, I glanced down at the crush of people. A boy was pumping the keg. There were beer cans everywhere and a three-foot bong on the table. I followed Eric into his room. No didgeridoo, but a djembe drum, hand-carved with little elephants along the bottom. I watched him rifle through a drawer and pull out a bag of pills.

"You down?" he asked.

I shrugged then opened my hand.

"Don't you want to know what they are?"

"Not really."

He laughed. "You're crazy." He placed two pills in my palm, and we clinked our beers and swallowed them.

My favorite moments are the ones leading up. Not the act itself, but the prelude. The moment when you know something is going to happen but hasn't yet.

I could feel Eric's eyes on my body. The way they came to stop at my belly button, where my shirt didn't quite cover. He stood there, studying the curve of my hips. It's easier to love yourself in these moments when you can see yourself through someone else's eyes. Tandem-riding their desire. It's fleeting, of course. Easy come, easy go. But if you can catch it, it's the best drug there is.

Eric smelled like clean laundry. He lifted his hand and brushed his thumb against my breast.

"You cold?"

I looked down. My nipple was erect. Boys are so stupid.

Then his mouth was on mine. His hands moved across my body, under my shirt. He fumbled with the button on my jeans, and I tried to let my mind go. To be present. But already, I could feel it slipping. Feverish anticipation sputtering out in the technical details of reality.

In my mind, I could hear Michelle: *Scoundrel*, she would say. She would be talking about me, not him. Afterward, I climbed off the bed, got dressed, and opened the door. From downstairs, the music came surging upward.

"It's Vicodin, by the way," Eric called out, but I'd already shut the door.

I could see the top of Naseem's head from the stairs. There were bodies all around him. High or drunk, in various stages of disrobing. He craned his neck and looked up at me. I knew, right then. He was furious. He turned and pushed his way through the crowd and out into the night. I stumbled after him.

Outside, the street was wet from the rain, and the asphalt reflected the street-lights in slick halos of yellow.

"Naseem," I shouted. "Wait up." He walked quickly, and I hurried to keep up. I was feeling the Vicodin now, a groggy warmth spreading across my limbs. "Slow down!" I jogged up behind him.

He stopped abruptly. Stood there in the middle of the street, his feet planted in a pool of light. A few months earlier, I'd asked him about his relationship with God. "Do you believe?" I had asked. God had abandoned me when I was nine years old. I was fascinated by those who still managed to believe.

Naseem had thought about it. That was how he was. Not impulsive, like me. Deliberate, slow. When he answered, it wasn't what I thought he'd say. He said God came to him as a patch of blue light on a navy carpet. The sun passing through a stained-glass window, gold lettering at the base of the dome. For Naseem, it wasn't about the rules. Not about pressing his head to the floor, shoes by the door. It was standing in that patch of light that moved according to Earth's rotation.

Naseem was the best thing that had ever come into my life. Now we stood in the middle of the street. I looked at him and felt my body gripped with fear. I reached out, but he pulled away.

"You drag me to this fucking party, then you ditch me the entire time."

"I didn't ditch you the entire time. I had to go to the bathroom."

"For an hour?!"

I wasn't sure what Naseem knew. But here's the cruelty of suspicion: it imprisons the doubter.

"It wasn't an hour," I insisted. "It was only, like, fifteen minutes." I had no idea how long it had been, but I preferred to fight on this level. Over logistics, details. Minutes on a clock.

Naseem exhaled, and I could see the shape of his breath in the cold air. He was shaking his head. His eyes were wet. Not crying. Not *not* crying.

"I don't know, Lu. I don't know," he kept repeating. *I don't know.* It hung around us, terrible and heavy.

"Don't say that," I begged. "Don't say, 'I don't know.' Please."

"What do you want me to say?! You give me no choice. You take away all my words. You make everything impossible."

Naseem's friends didn't like me. They didn't think me worthy of him. I wasn't. No one was. Even Michelle had said as much after I introduced them. Or rather, she'd said: "He's lovely. I feel sorry for him."

I tried to hold his gaze, but he kept shaking his head.

"I love you, Lucia. But you pull this shit, and—I don't know. I don't know."

My chest was so tight, it was hard to breathe.

In a way, I suppose that's what I was chasing. That moment when my own emptiness disappeared behind something terrifying. The fear of Naseem leaving—the look on his face, the hurt, the vulnerability. Only then did I feel frightened; only then did I feel alive.

"Look at me. Please," I said. We stood there a long time like that.

I stepped close to his body. I wanted no space between us. I tucked my head against his chest, and finally, reluctantly, he enclosed me in his arms.

That night, we lay in his bed. I could hear the voices of his roommates down the hall, their words muffled and their laughter far away. I turned on my side and looked at him. His eyes were closed, his profile illuminated in the blue light of his electronics. I lifted my finger and traced the hills and valleys of his face.

"Don't ever leave me," I whispered.

In his sleep, Naseem inched toward me and draped an arm across my body.

CHAPTER 3

NEIL

Now

In the fridge was a package of ground beef about to expire. Once upon a time, I would've scoured the internet for recipes. Spicy larb, stuffed peppers, empanadas. Phaedra and I, bent over the stove, an open bottle of red wine on the counter. What was the point now? I tossed the beef in a pan, watched it gray, then brown.

After Phae and I had received our job offers, we'd come down for a weekend. I remember walking the campus and feeling how different it was from grad school in New England, where you were always aware of your smallness in the great pantheon of ideas. Here, the buildings were a mashup. Pink marble against polished steel, Beaux-arts next to cool modern. The very architecture seemed to insist that everything could be remade. And by extension, you could be relevant to the history of thought.

I remember feeling like the whole thing was a coup Phaedra and I had somehow pulled off. We rented a car and drove around, bypassing all those Southern suburban enclaves for a loft in the industrial part of town. No neighbors to complain when Phaedra cranked the music. When she stepped out of the shower naked, towel twisted up on her head, singing at the top of her lungs. Sleater-Kinney, Souxsie and the Banshees, The Slits, and Ari Up.

I know that it hurts, but my love died, quickly, she sang into the open space of our bedroom.

Now Phaedra had a new life, and I had a shitty apartment. I tried to picture her leaping onto the bed naked, dripping wet on the duvet, all-girl punk bands blaring, Tim standing dumbstruck in his wire-rimmed glasses and tailored slacks.

I ate the ground beef. It tasted like despair.

When I finished, I left the dish in the sink. Add it to the pile. Tonight, I needed to write. Because of tenure. Because I'd lied to Paul. Because, if I could produce just one solid piece of writing, maybe I could find my way back.

But as I pulled a book from my bag, the flyer for the missing girl went sailing to the floor. I picked it up. For a split second, I felt a pinprick of recognition. Like I'd seen her before. Some fragment of a memory, too hazy to recall. Just the edges in focus, but none of the details were clear.

I stared at her. Lucia Vanotti. She was pretty.

She looked nothing like Phaedra, who had short, blonde hair and heavy eyelids and a more severe jawline. And yet, looking down at Lucia's picture, I suddenly had a memory of Phaedra, standing in the doorway of our loft as I moved the last of my boxes out.

"I love you, Neil," she'd said. "But I can't be with someone who isn't an agent in his own life."

"What does that even mean?" I'd asked at the time.

"It means you're not someone who *does* things. You're the person to whom things are done."

I don't remember what I said in response, and it doesn't much matter. What matters is how those words have floated up to the surface of my consciousness time and again. I think of that beach in California. This is what Phaedra was saying: *You are not a man who saves. You are a man who stands on the shore. You will always stand on the shore, watching the woman drown.*

I stared at that picture of Lucia Vanotti, that strange feeling of recognition tugging at the corners of my mind. Instead of balling it up and throwing it out, I smoothed the flyer against my wall and taped it in place.

***

In class the next morning, we were discussing the Zimbardo experiment from the 1970s. A group of Stanford students were divided into prisoners and guards before the whole thing went off the rails. The guards became sadistic; the prisoners, submissive.

Adam Steadman raised his hand but didn't wait to be called on.

"Wasn't this whole thing, like, debunked or something?" he said. "I mean, didn't it turn out that the prisoners were faking it or something?"

A few weeks earlier, Adam had asked me to sign a piece of paper. His frat house was being suspended for some ungodly reason or another. I signed without reading it. Honestly, I didn't want to know.

"Well, yes and no," I responded to the Zimbardo question. I still taught Zimbardo—like I still taught Kitty Genovese—mostly because of inertia.

"So, we're just wasting our time reading it?" he asked.

"Depends," I said. "Is Newton a waste just because Einstein came along?"

Adam seemed to consider this.

"I mean, kind of. Yeah."

The analogy was terrible. This wasn't Newton and Einstein. It was simply bad research. I taught it because I had taught it a thousand times before. Because to scrap it would mean re-engaging with the material and preparing something new. I glanced at the clock. Forty-seven fucking minutes to go.

After class, I took my time gathering my things. A few students lingered, and I eavesdropped half-heartedly.

"They should call it *Just the tip*-line," Adam said. He pretended to pick up an imaginary phone. "Hello, you've reached *Just the tip*-line. Do you have *just the tip* to share?"

"Ohmygod, you're the worst!" Cora said. "That's actually not funny," though she was laughing.

It occurred to me right then that they were talking about the missing girl.

"Mr. Steadman," I said, "may I have a word?"

Cora grabbed her bag and ducked out of the room as Adam trudged to my desk.

"What?" he said. "I was just playing. I don't care if we read the Zimbardo thing." He had the kind of translucent blue eyes that make you feel uncomfortable.

"Very gracious of you," I said. "Was the young woman you were just talking about Lucia Vanotti?"

"I was just messing around. I didn't mean it."

"It's fine. You're not in trouble. It just occurred to me that you might have some information—for *Just the Tip*-line."

He rolled his eyes. Then his expression changed.

"Wait, me? I don't have anything. Why would I have anything?" There was something refreshing in Adam's absolute disregard for my authority.

"I'm only asking," I said, "because the provost asked each of us—the faculty, I mean—to be the eyes and ears on campus. To pass along anything that might be useful in locating her." The ease with which I was able to lie these days was concerning. The provost had asked no such thing. I didn't even know whether a provost would have jurisdiction over something like this. Yet, the very act of saying it sent a tiny jolt of excitement through me.

Adam looked put-out.

"What do you want to know?"

"What is there *to* know?" I asked, trying to mute my enthusiasm, though my body was thrumming.

"Nothing." He shrugged. "I mean, nothing really. Honestly, she's probably not even missing or whatever." Adam watched me with his disquieting blue eyes.

"Why do you say that?"

"I don't know. I mean, it's not like I knew her well. And I never did anything with her. I swear to God! I wouldn't touch that girl with a ten-foot pole." He held my gaze. "But a lot of other guys would. All I'm saying is, she seemed like the kind of girl who did what she wanted."

"What does that mean?"

"She got around, okay? Some of the guys in my house, they knew her. Like, *knew her*, knew her. They called her Doxy behind her back."

I furrowed my brow in confusion.

"I didn't make it up!" he insisted. "That's just what they called her."

"Why?"

"You know, like a doxy. You know what a doxy is?"

I didn't. But the last thing I wanted was for Adam Steadman to educate me.

"All right, yeah, I get the point."

It suddenly felt wildly inappropriate for me to know this fact about Lucia.

***

After school, I didn't meet Jack in the dining hall. Instead, I drove home, opened my computer, and searched for Lucia online. The first thing that came up was the missing person flyer that I already had taped to my wall. Beyond that, there were her social media accounts. All set to private. There was a short article with no more information than the flyer—with one small exception. One word. So insignificant, I almost didn't notice. "Local Girl, Missing Since Friday."

There it was. That small rush of satisfaction. Like solving the first word in a crossword puzzle. An invitation. A step forward.

Local.

Unlike the rest of us, who seemed to only be passing through this college town, Lucia Vanotti was from here. A local girl.

CHAPTER 4

LUCIA

Then

In the passenger seat of Naseem's car, I practiced the pick-up line he taught me in Urdu.

"Oh, my God," he said, busting out laughing. "Your accent is terrible. It's not Italian, you know."

We'd been trading them. I'd given him the cringiest one I knew in Italian: *"Se vuoi salire ti mostro la mia collezione di farfalle."* If you come upstairs, I'll show you my butterfly collection.

"People do not actually say that!" he'd exclaimed.

"Works like a charm," I said, though I had no idea if it actually did. No one had ever used it on me.

In exchange, Naseem taught me a sweet one: "Your smile is so charming." But I couldn't get the accent right, apparently.

Naseem had told me countless stories about his family. Parties when he was a kid, where his aunts would chase after him, embarrassing him, trying to get him to blush. "What a charming smile," they teased, as he cowered behind his mother's legs.

Now we drove through town and pulled into the parking lot. Naseem got out and tossed me the keys.

"Chocolate chip or coffee?" he asked.

"Or!?"

He rolled his eyes and left me sitting in the passenger seat while he went inside to order.

These Sunday rides had become our ritual. Naseem had taken me here on our first date. Picked me up in his beat-up, old Honda. We drove west until we found the ice cream place he had in mind—Lynette's Old Town Creamery. We ate it on the rusted roof of his car and talked about tennis and books, poets, and the classes we were taking.

He was from a town called King of Prussia, Pennsylvania.

"That is not a real place," I said.

"Swear," he said. Little lines formed around his eyes when he smiled. "Actually, we're kind of famous."

"For what?"

"Biggest mall in the world."

I laughed out loud. It felt easy to laugh with him.

"Well, it used to be, anyway," he said. "I think there are bigger ones now."

"Bet you bag a lot of babes with that one. *Hey girl, not sure if you've heard, we have the fourth largest mall in the world.*"

"It's a chick magnet. You have no idea."

From that first date, our conversation flowed, even without alcohol. Silences were comfortable. I knew I liked him because the small details of his life were endlessly fascinating to me. I loved listening to stories about his family, the ski trips to Seven Springs, the Eagles games, the parties. The way a night would break into music.

"At some point, my uncle will just bust out his drums." Naseem described what those parties felt like when he was a child. The music. The women dancing. The older girls chasing him until he clung to his mother or pretended to play with his baby sister, Zaima, just to avoid them. The aunties, cupping their hands beneath his chin. "What a charming smile you have." To be fair, he did.

I had no family in the states besides my parents and my sister. So, yeah, maybe I was romanticizing his life a little bit. The fullness of it. The texture.

Unlike Naseem's, my memories of family were broken and strange. Hiking in the woods with my father as a little girl. We would park the car and duck through the trees. One of the patrons at my father's restaurant had told him about a lake hidden in the woods. On that first afternoon we set out to find it, we left my mom at home with Elena, who was barely old enough to walk.

Those woods still lived inside of me. Rich and earthen, smelling of summer. Dogwoods, redbuds, sweetgum trees, and river birches. They were part of a large parcel of land. Southern and dense. Dappled light cut through the trees. When we finally found the lake, my dad was ecstatic. He kicked off his shoes, pulled off his shirt, and dove into the water in his underwear while I stood guard. Another time, a huge electrical storm moved in. Through the dark clouds up over the hills, the sky lit up with lightning. We hunkered beneath a boulder while the storm crashed overhead.

Now those details felt far away. My father and I stopped going to the lake when I was nine years old. Right after Giancarlo came to visit that summer. The summer that everything changed.

I didn't tell Naseem about that.

Instead, I told him about my parents growing up in Brindisi on the Adriatic Sea. *Castello Rosso*, the red stone castle in the distance. Boats coming in and out of the harbor. The smell of fish. My father, running along the docks at night, sneaking into buildings, "borrowing" bikes from the city center and leaving them wherever he liked. Memories that didn't even belong to me.

"He didn't know a word of English when he got here," I said about my dad. "Neither of them did." I could feel the cool metal of Naseem's car beneath me. The sticky drippings of ice cream on my fingers. "I can't imagine doing that. Just picking up and leaving. Going somewhere you don't even speak the language, somewhere you've never even visited, and just plunking down. Starting a family and a restaurant. It's crazy. I've never been anywhere. Not even Italy."

Naseem sat there watching me. Listening.

"You know how old they were?" I asked. "Like, two years older than we are right now."

"Sounds brave," he said.

"Or stupid."

After we ate ice cream at Lynette's on that first date, Naseem drove me home. Not to my parents' house across town, but to an apartment I was renting near campus, where five girls shared a single bathroom, and the drain was always clogged with hair. He walked me to the door and hugged me goodbye.

Hugged me goodbye. *What the fuck!*

My dates usually ended in someone's bedroom, groping for my underwear in the pre-dawn light. Naseem hadn't even tried to kiss me. I swiped my room-mate's Cutty Sark on the way to my room and had already downed two glasses when Naseem texted.

"You're a lightning storm in the woods," he wrote. Pause, then his next text: "Holy shit, that was bad."

I pressed the phone to my chest. The feeling was everywhere all at once. Warmth, spreading out to every limb. Not just from the Cutty Sark. It was him, his gaze. The way he listened with his mouth closed, unhurried, not waiting for his turn to speak.

"Free verse," I texted back. A heart emoji.

That was September. Now it was late December, and we ate ice cream every Sunday on the roof of his car, our church.

Naseem walked out with two cones. A single scoop of mint for him, a double chocolate chip and coffee for me. I climbed onto the roof and tried to feel that newness again, the giddiness of that first date. Its electricity. All the things we said to each other that night, and all the things we've said since. There were late-night whispers, dining hall jokes, shared stories, new memories we created together. But for everything said, there were also the unsaid things. And sitting on the roof of his car, I felt those, too. Their enormous weight.

There were the pills in my mother's bathroom. Ativan and OxyContin. Xanax and Percocet. Sometimes I would pilfer them when I needed to block out the world or slow it down. There was the cheating, those shameful moments that felt branched off from the regular passage of time. There was, of course, the scar on my arm. Naseem had run his fingers over it a thousand times, but never asked. Not directly.

But mostly, mostly there was the summer of my ninth year. The summer that language died. Or when it was reborn into words I still cannot speak.

The summer that Giancarlo came.

CHAPTER 5

NEIL

Now

Every spurned lover is an amateur sleuth.

Tim Janek turned me into one two years before I'd ever heard of Lucia Vanotti.

The first time I met him, Tim was not Phaedra's new husband. He was just a professor the school was trying to court. Paul Rutger had called Phaedra and me in a panic. Could we take this prospective hire out for dinner? Someone had bailed last minute. This guy was supposedly someone special.

Phaedra and I didn't even shower. Just peeled off our jeans and dressed ourselves up. We picked up Tim Janek at the conference center where he was staying. Phaedra sat in front and swiveled around to talk to him. The school had made Tim a sweet offer: a joint position in philosophy and neurobiology. He hadn't given them an answer yet.

That night at dinner, Phaedra leaned forward, elbows on the table, as we downed Chenin Blanc and two bottles of Châteauneuf-du-Pape. She asked him questions about his work, philosophy of mind and AI. Tim had collaborated with big names. David Chalmers on the "hard problem" of consciousness, Daniel Dennett, Andy Clark.

A few months earlier, Phaedra herself had become a minor celebrity. She'd published an op-ed in the *New York Times* lambasting the latest attempt to suicide-proof the Golden Gate Bridge in San Francisco. People had the right to take their own lives, she argued.

Tim listened with his whole face as she spoke.

Midway through the conversation, I interjected. "Supposedly, though, most of the jumpers who survive say they regretted it the moment they did it. Don't you think it would be better just to suicide-proof the whole thing since they change their minds halfway down?" I don't know why I said it. They both turned and stared like I'd suggested we sacrifice a goat right there at the table.

Phaedra leaned in. "They may regret it," she said, her eyes blazing. "But the good thing about human beings is that we have the right to make regrettable decisions."

When dinner ended, I offered to drive Tim back to his hotel, but Phaedra wasn't ready.

"One more drink," she said, looping her arm through his.

It was close to 2 a.m. when we finally dropped Tim off. For all Phaedra's chattiness throughout dinner, she was somber and withdrawn on the car ride home.

"You all right?" I asked.

"Mm-hmm."

When we got home, she disappeared into the bathroom. She came out five minutes later wearing pajamas, brushing her hair.

"You barely said anything tonight," she said. "It was weird. You were being weird."

"I was not. I was letting you talk. You seemed to have a lot to say." I kicked off my shoes.

"Oh, you were *letting* me talk. You were letting me. How kind of you."

She yanked down the covers and climbed into bed. I stomped out to our roof deck barefoot. I needed a smoke. When I finally crawled into bed, she was asleep, or pretending to be. I curled up next to her and put my arm around her waist. But Phaedra has always been a fitful sleeper, and soon, she rolled out from underneath it.

***

It was Tim Janek who truly taught me to research. Not like the research I'd done for my dissertation. Sure, I had been invested in it, but it never left me feverish. It never sent me running to the toilet, clutching my stomach. It never made me want to die. My research on Tim was all consuming. In those early months, I whizzed past the obvious stuff. The published papers, the books.

I found an old black-and-white photo that someone had uploaded. Tim, gangly as a teenager in Nashville, a book in his lap, looking startled at the camera. I found a precocious essay about transience he'd published in high school. "Postcards from Nashville. From Memphis. Gallatin. Smyrna. Mount Juliet," he'd titled it. Apparently, he'd grown up in the foster care system, and this was his homage to the experience. Besides that, there was a short piece on golf. Tim had a four handicap.

Good for him.

Tonight, I needed to channel some of that old research passion. Where had that initial spark gone, the one that had ignited my own work for so many years? That memory of the drowning woman. Kitty Genovese. Phaedra.

I put my fingers on the keyboard and closed my eyes. Nothing came. I must have sat like that for an hour. Eventually, I put my head down and fell asleep sitting right there.

I dreamed of my wedding day. Phaedra in a short white dress. Me in slacks, no tie. We stood before a Justice of the Peace. In my dream, the officiant asked, "Do you, Neil Weber, take Phaedra Anne Lewis to be your lawfully wedded wife . . ." *Yes*, I said. But he seemed not to hear me. *Yes, yes!* I screamed. I grabbed the officiant by the collar. *Yes! You idiot, I said, yes!*

I woke up with a stiff neck and a deep sense of self-loathing. Outside it was dark. I flicked my computer back to life. The page was open to Lucia Vanotti's face, the online flyer I'd found. Again, that tugging feeling that I knew her.

And then, there it was. A memory taking shape in my mind. I was sitting on a bench outside the Philosophy Department, smoking a cigarette when a girl—Lucia, it must have been—flung open the glass doors of the building and raged out into the afternoon. Even from a distance, you could see the energy coming off her. She was angry. Or hurt. Upset about a grade. Or a fight with a boyfriend. It didn't strike me as unusual at the time. These kids wear their emotions so entirely on their sleeves.

Lucia stormed toward the bench where I sat and threw her bag down on the far end. This must have been six months ago, maybe eight, sometime in the fall after everyone had returned to school. Abruptly, she turned to me, and I did something I would normally never do. I held out my pack of cigarettes to her. Even at the time, it felt wrong. To offer an undergraduate a smoke, particularly unprompted. But there it was. She took one and slipped it between her lips.

"Thanks," she said. I lit it for her.

"You a professor?" she asked, exhaling a line of smoke. I told her I was. "What subject?"

"Ethics," I said. By then, my own work felt so alien to me, I found it hard to muster enthusiasm.

"What about ethics?"

"The discrepancy between how we think we'd behave and how we actually behave," I said. "Turns out they're quite different sometimes."

She stared at me for a long moment, then laughed. A genuine laugh.

"Maybe I should take your class," she said. "Maybe ethics is exactly what I need." She was smiling, but I could see pain behind it.

I could have said anything right then. I could have said: *yeah, you should*. Or: *these kinds of questions are important*. Or even asked: *what's your interest in it?* Instead, I said none of these things. Instead, I summoned all my bitterness and apathy and loneliness, and I shrugged.

"Honestly, don't bother," I said. "It's all just a waste of time."

And I swear, that girl's face fell. Lucia shook her head and stubbed out her cigarette. "You're all so fucked, you know that?" she said, which seemed like the truest thing anyone had said in a long time. She got up from that bench and walked away.

Now the memory returned with force. Maybe the exchange had been meaningless—just two people shooting the shit over a cigarette. Yet I couldn't help but imbue it with meaning now that she was missing. And somehow, it seemed to stand in for all the other ways I'd failed over the years. All my shortcomings, contained in that one exchange. So, why did I feel a sudden rush of adrenaline recalling it now? A slight twinge in my fingers—that once-familiar sensation, that hunger to write that expressed itself in my body. Something was coalescing inside of me, and it took the shape of a question: *what can one person ever really offer another?*

That's how it always used to begin for me. A single question would form and it could propel me into a breathless night of work. By morning, I'd get up from my desk, bleary-eyed from staring at my computer screen, fingers sore from typing all night, body ravenous from work, but something miraculous would have transpired.

How badly I wanted it now. I cracked my knuckles and placed my fingers on the keyboard, willing them to do what they used to do so easily. If I could just harness that feeling, grab hold of that question, maybe things could go back to the way they were.

But there on my computer screen was the missing persons flyer for Lucia. It was the same one that was taped to my wall. Only, online, some of the details were clearer. One detail in particular: the faint smudge of a sign behind Lucia. A storefront. I leaned in closer. No, not a storefront. A restaurant. A family restaurant.

Vanotti's Italian Cuisine.

I pulled my hands off the keyboard and sat staring.

In my mind, I could feel two versions of the night spiraling out from this moment. In one version, I would write. I would sit here until morning, channeling everything I was feeling into my work.

In the other version, I would turn off my computer, walk outside, and drive across town to Lucia's family's restaurant. In that version, instead of writing about bystander apathy, I would simply choose *not* to be a bystander.

***

Lucia's family's restaurant was clear across town, in the suburbs forty minutes from campus. Solid, working-class area. No gleaming athletic centers. No state-of-the-art concert halls. Nothing designed to entice students and their out-of-state tuitions.

Instead, there were strip malls and liquor marts. Chain stores and Dollar Trees. A Piggly Wiggly, its parking lot crowded even on a Saturday night. Vanotti's restaurant was a white stucco building with a green awning. Inside, it looked generic. Pasta and red sauce. On the walls were framed posters of old Italian movies.

Notably absent was any police presence. I'm not sure what I'd expected, but whatever it was, it wasn't there. Instead, there was a bald man loading drinks onto a tray who waved for me to sit wherever I wanted. I grabbed a menu and took a seat near the window. Outside, the parking lot was dark. The trees beyond it, nearly black.

A waitress came up to my table.

"Can I get you something to drink?" she asked. When I looked up, I felt my blood go cold. The waitress was slender and dark-haired with wide-set eyes and a dimple in one cheek. Lucia. Or as near to Lucia as anyone could be. The girl asked again if I wanted something to drink.

"Um—" I glanced at the menu and ordered a Peroni. She brought it to my table with a basket of bread. I devoured a large piece and watched Lucia's double float through the restaurant.

Eventually, she came back to take my order.

"What's good here?" I asked.

"Depends," she said. Her voice was very quiet. I found myself leaning in to hear her. "There's steak. Pasta. Pizza." She had long fingers, a smudge of yellow paint on one of her nails. "The lasagna's good. Lots of people order it."

"Then I'll have that."

As I ate my lasagna, I let the reality of what I was doing sink in. What had seemed perfectly reasonable in the quiet of my apartment now seemed insane. To be sitting here in Lucia's family restaurant, practically stalking a girl who had to be her sister—a cousin at the very farthest.

And yet, when the girl came to take my plate away, I found myself saying, "I'm sorry, I don't mean to pry," she looked at me with confusion, "but I work over at the university across town." I saw her tense up. I wasn't sure where to go from here. "It's just—there are posters all over the school." This was mortifying. A huge mistake, yet I felt powerless to stop myself.

The girl stood perfectly still for a solid moment, then said: "My sister, Lucia. She's, um—We're looking for her."

"I am so sorry," I said. "Everyone on campus is devastated. I can't imagine what you and your family must be going through." I told her I was surprised there wasn't more police presence around.

She made a small movement with her head.

"Yeah. I mean, they've talked to us." She glanced down. "My parents haven't left the house. Just in case she calls or comes back. They say that's what happens most of the time. A person runs away, with a friend or boyfriend or something. They said, in most cases, they come back on their own. When they're ready. They're looking, but—" She hesitated.

"For what it's worth, I know that all of us on campus want to help in any way we can. I'm talking to my students, people who knew her, her boyfriend—"

The girl looked up.

"Naseem?" she said.

I made a mental note. She must have noticed because she wrinkled her brow.

"Did you say you were a professor?"

"Yes. In the Philosophy Department. Neil Weber." I offered her my hand. She looked at it, then shook it.

"Elena," she said. Her fingers were strong—stronger than they looked. "It's funny, Lucia hated philosophy actually."

I smiled. "I can't say I blame her," I said. "Do you know if she ever took any philosophy classes?" The image of Lucia on the bench came flooding back.

Elena scrutinized my face.

"I'm sorry, did you say you knew her?"

"No. I didn't."

She nodded, eyeing me.

"Well, I should probably be getting back." She motioned toward the kitchen. The bald man who worked there was now staring at us. When I looked at him, he looked away.

Elena collected the last of the objects on my table. My empty beer bottle, the breadbasket. She was just turning away when I stopped her.

"One last thing," I said. "Um, Naseem? Do you know his last name? Just in case I run across him."

Elena paused, like she couldn't decide how much to reveal. Then, having made up her mind, said: "Bashir. Naseem Bashir."

CHAPTER 6

LUCIA

Then

Naseem wanted to meet my family. That's what he said. He wanted to see where I grew up, meet the people who brought me into this world.

Fine, I said. *Keep your expectations low.*

I invited him to dinner on New Year's Day. It had seemed like a good idea at the time, but it didn't feel that way now. At the table, my father stole glances at his watch like he had somewhere to be. My mother looked uncomfortable in her flower-patterned dress that pulled too tight across her chest. My younger sister, Elena, sat across from me, elbows and razor-sharp wrists, hands folded in her lap.

"Lucia, is getting cold," my mother said in her broken English. No one has ever practiced English so diligently yet spoken it with such shame. She kept her eyes on the spaghetti. "*Servi tu,*" she said, defaulting to Italian.

Serve him.

You have no idea, I could've said.

I watched Naseem eat. His fork circling the pasta, lifting it to his mouth. Bolognese sauce splattered on his chin. "Thank you, Mrs. Vanotti. It's delicious." He said it after the salad, after the spaghetti, again after the dessert.

Naseem and I had met at a house party. Half-full Solo cups abandoned on the countertops. Lights low, music high. We'd been circling each other all night. I'd look up, and he'd be across the room, talking to someone. I'd look away and feel his eyes follow me. By the time he made his way to me, I felt like we'd been having this private conversation all night long.

"Hey," he said when our paths finally crossed, "I saw you earlier. It's Lucia, right?" "You been following me?" I teased. "What? No, I just—"

"I'm joking, Naseem," I said. "I've been waiting for you to come up and talk to me for, like, five hours."

From that moment on, it just felt easy. He wasn't like the other boys. Yeah, he was hot and a good athlete and all that. But it wasn't about that. What drew me to Naseem was the way he took up space. The way he could stand at the center of a group, everyone talking, laughing, trying to get his attention. He always seemed to be there, in the middle of things, but also separate somehow. Sturdier than everyone else. He had a younger sister and also a brother who passed away from a congenital heart problem before Naseem was born. He didn't like to talk about it.

When I'd pressed him on it once, he said, "I never knew him."

"Yeah, but he must have been present. I mean, even after he was gone. The memory of him. With your parents, at least."

Naseem thought about it.

"Of course," he said, "But mostly, we didn't talk about him. Sometimes, I would hear my mom crying in bed at night. Just this muffled sound. My dad talking to her real low. But in the morning, at breakfast, everything was always okay."

I tried to imagine the world that Naseem was born into—what a gift he must have been when he arrived. Maybe that's why he seemed older, more solid than the rest of us. Sometimes, when I was with him, I would become aware of my own pettiness. The shit-talking and gossip. Naseem wasn't like that. He just wouldn't go in for that kind of thing. It made you realize how desperate you were to be liked.

Now he sat at our dinner table, napkin in his lap. I saw my family through his eyes. The strange cadence of our dinner. My mother fumbling with her words. My father's restlessness. My sister's silence. Sometimes, when I looked at them, I felt like I saw everything as it truly was. Like we were just playing at being a family. One flick of the finger and the whole house of cards would come toppling down.

Our dinner that night felt stifling. I just wanted to speed it up, feel myself against the edge of something. I reached for Naseem's hand under the table. Long, delicate fingers with calluses along the inside of his palm where his tennis grip had toughened the skin. I pressed his hand against my thigh. He stiffened his arm but didn't pull it away. I slid his hand higher, under my skirt, worked his fingertips beneath the elastic of my underwear.

***

Later that night, we sat in my childhood bedroom, pink comforter beneath us. "That was messed up," he said. Posters of Radiohead and David Bowie were still taped to the walls. I straddled him and kissed his ear.

"I was *actually* trying to make a good impression," he said, lifting me off.

"Has anyone ever told you that you have a *very* charming smile?"

"You shouldn't have done that," he insisted. "Not with them sitting right there."

"Maybe if you'd told them the food was delicious—"

Naseem pretended to punch me in the shoulder, then flipped me on my back. He pressed his lips to my stomach. In a million years, he would never sleep with me in my parents' home. Instead, we lay on my pink bedspread, looking up at a handful of glow-in-the-dark stars that still clung to the ceiling.

"Hey," I said, grabbing for his hand, "You never told me your New Year's resolution."

The night before, we had gotten drunk off his roommate's bathtub gin. People streamed in and out of the house as sirens blazed up and down the boulevards. Naseem and I made out at midnight and slept in late.

Now he rolled over onto his elbows. He ran one finger along the length of my arm, stopping when he came to the marbled pink scar on the inside of my bicep. He put his lips to it.

"To know everything about you," he said.

"That's not a resolution," I said and pulled my arm away.

"Oh, I'm sorry," he said. "I didn't realize I was talking to the gestapo of New Year's resolutions."

"Well, now you do," I teased. "Pick a new one."

He bit his lower lip like he always did when he was thinking.

"Hmm, I don't know. To practice more?"

"No! No way. No tennis."

"To skydive."

"Better, but bullshit."

"To make love to you in your parents' house."

"You wouldn't."

He laughed. And right there, I saw it. The way he looked at me: open and honest and unguarded. Sometimes I wondered what he saw in me. I asked him once, and he answered without a second thought. "Because you make me feel alive." It was the nicest thing anyone had ever said to me. Then he added, "Just kidding. It's cause you're hot." But it was too late; I had seen the look in his eyes and I knew. He was real. No one has ever looked at me the way Naseem Bashir did.

"I don't know," he said. "I don't have a good resolution. What's yours?"

I glanced up at the ceiling. Orion wielded a lopsided shield. I closed my eyes. In my mind, I could hear my sister, Elena. Not what she said, but the way she held back her words. The way she'd hold her breath at the dinner table. Worried, always, about what I might say. What I might do.

"Well, I'll tell you what it won't be," I said. "It's not going to be something stupid like practicing tennis."

"Good! Because you're the worst tennis player I've ever seen."

In truth, if I had a resolution, it wasn't something I could share with Naseem. Or with anyone. I've heard that some people block entire segments of their memory that are too painful or too horrible to recall. I often wonder what lives there instead. Just a blank space where pain used to be? Sometimes I wish it were that way for me. But in my nineteen years, I have found the opposite to be true: I can will myself to remember, but not to forget.

"I know," I said. "To learn to make . . . what's that weird mountainy dessert you love with all that ice cream inside?"

"Baked Alaska?" Naseem said.

"To make Baked Alaska better than anyone, so you'll never be able to taste it without thinking of me."

Naseem's eyes searched my face, pausing on my mouth. For a moment, I felt like he wanted to say something—or ask something. But instead, he kissed me.

When he leaned back, he said, "You know you can tell me anything, right?"

I felt my chest tighten.

"Yeah. Of course," I said, but it was a lie. Some things can't be said. Even to the ones you love most.

CHAPTER 7

NEIL

Now

I spent Sunday avoiding my own work and, instead, researched Naseem. Like Lucia, his social media accounts were private. But his profile picture was of a boy with his arms wrapped around a bright-eyed, smiling girl. Lucia.

I found an article from the previous year in the student paper. An interview he'd done after a tennis match. It was clear Naseem was the MVP. The student journalist pressed him on his decision to attend this school when he clearly could have gone to a Division 1 tennis program.

His answers were polished and considered.

"Education has always been important to my parents," she quoted him as saying. He gave credit to the school, the tennis program, his teammates, the pre-med major.

In all my years of teaching, I'd never gone to the tennis courts before that Monday. Nets waving dully in the breeze, tennis shoes squeaking on the green asphalt.

The team was finishing practice, and Naseem was easy to spot. He was smashing the ball with deep, powerful strokes. Along with his obvious raw power, there was something elegant to his movements.

After practice, the coach blew a whistle, and everyone huddled together before breaking off for the athletic building. For a moment, I felt a surge of panic, a clear sense of the absurdity of the situation. Me, standing there at the gate, hunting the people closest to Lucia. Yet I doggedly plowed on.

When I called out to Naseem, he was standing in a group of friends. He stopped and turned. His friends stopped, too. From a distance, I could see him squinting, probably trying to figure out who I was. Around him, his friends exchanged wary glances. I waved him over.

There was no way to be delicate about this. I didn't know how long he'd be willing to talk—or if he'd be willing to talk at all.

"Hi, Naseem," I said as he approached the fence where I stood. "I was hoping to have a word with you. It won't take long."

"Okay," he said. The front of his shirt was drenched with sweat. The strap of a tennis bag was slung over his shoulder, and he wore one of those terry cloth wristbands.

"It's about—" I began. "It's about Lucia."

"Are you another detective?"

"You've spoken to one already?"

"Detective Waters," he said. He tilted his head. "I'm sorry, who did you say you were?"

I cleared my throat.

"Actually, I'm a professor. Here at school." I decided against the provost angle. Too risky. "I'm here because I talked to Lucia's sister—"

"Elena?"

"She's the one who gave me your name."

He looked at me sharply.

"Elena wanted you to talk to me? Why?"

I shrugged.

"Because she's worried. Apparently, the police think Lucia will come back on her own, but Elena—"

"Yo, Nas!" someone shouted from the tennis court. Naseem turned. The guy threw a hand in the air, like *you want us to wait?* Naseem shook his head, then turned back to me.

"Yeah, well I don't know what I can tell you that I haven't already told the police." Naseem's eyes were brown with flecks of yellow. "What do you want to know?"

"I don't have any specific questions. I guess, I'm just trying to do my part to pay attention on campus." I bit my lip. "It's just, you know, there's some talk around school that maybe—Lucia left on her own."

He narrowed his eyes. "Who said that?"

"No one in particular. Just talk."

Naseem shook his head. There were streaky, gray clouds in the sky above. They didn't look like much, but you can't trust the clouds in the South. At any minute, they can open up and unleash a torrent of rain on you.

"I don't know," he said, not looking at me. "It doesn't—I don't know."

I tried to get my tone just right.

"You knew her better than anyone."

He let out a small laugh.

"Lucia—" he began. "She's—I mean, I could see how someone would think that, that she'd take off. But—" He sighed. "I, honestly, I don't know. I have no idea where she is. I left her a thousand messages, then found her phone at my place. Plugged into the wall right where she left it. I'm no detective, but it doesn't sound like someone who was planning on running away. Why would she just leave her phone behind?" He looked up at me. His face was worn and tired. Dark circles around the eyes. "But who knows. All I know is, if Lucia left on her own—I mean, if she doesn't want to be found—there's not a person in this world who's going to find her."

Naseem adjusted the strap of his tennis bag. I could feel the conversation winding to a close, and I was desperate to keep it going.

"You been playing long?" I asked.

"Since I was a kid," he said with a shrug.

I already knew this, along with many other things about him from the article I'd read. Little details, like who introduced him to the sport: his uncle. What racquet he favored: Babolat Pure Aero Plus. How he mentally prepared before a match: "No Worries" by Lil Wayne.

"You play?" he asked.

"No." The closest I'd ever come to playing tennis was one night with Phaedra in grad school. We went to the courts, stoned out of our minds, and whacked balls back-and-forth until they went sailing over the fences.

Naseem stood there for an extra minute.

"Anyway—" he said, "I gotta go."

"Yeah, of course," I said. I thanked him for his time and watched him lope off toward the building. His shoulders rounded, his head bent. He looked back at me once, briefly, before disappearing inside.

***

Someone had defaced one of the Lucia posters. The word "WHORE" was written in red ink. The posters had been up on campus for a week, but Lucia had been missing for longer than that. Twelve days since anyone had seen her. It seemed a long time to vanish without a trace.

I glanced around at the red brick buildings and beyond them, the white colonnades of the Theater Arts Department. No one was around. I reached up and tore the defaced poster from the wall, then slipped it into my bag.

***

I was sitting in the dining hall when Jack walked up holding a tray with a roast beef sandwich and a carton of milk.

"Is that oat milk?" I asked.

"Yeah," Jack said. "I'm done with cow milk. Humans aren't supposed to drink that shit."

"Just eat their flesh."

"Correct."

He sat down. I hadn't caught up with him since the previous week.

"How's the writing going?" he asked.

Sadly, that momentary flash of inspiration I'd felt the other night had not returned. So, instead of writing something new to submit for publication, I'd pulled out an old essay that never went anywhere. I was trying to breathe new life into it. It was not going well.

"I'm submitting something soon," I told Jack. "Just doing some last-minute edits."

"Praise the lord," Jack said, unwrapping the sandwich. "I didn't want to say it, but about fucking time!"

"Actually, I've been busy—with something on the side."

"Oh, really?" he said, lifting an eyebrow. "Does she have a name?"

Lately, I'd been doing that—phrasing things oddly with Jack, appealing to his baser instincts. Maybe I wanted to convince him that I was fine. For Jack, fine meant getting laid. After Phaedra and I split, he told me I needed to sleep with twelve girls. That's how many it would take to stop thinking about her every night. For Jack, twelve was the magic number.

"Her name is Elena," I said. "But it's not like that."

"Elena," he repeated, chewing a bit of his sandwich. "I like it."

"Yeah, well, she's about twenty-five years too young." My own food was getting cold on my tray. I wasn't hungry. "Seriously though, it's not about that."

"Whatever you say, boss," he said, licking mustard off his finger.

"She's Lucia's sister." I dropped it like a bomb, and Jack went still.

"The missing girl?"

I nodded. For a moment, I thought about telling him that I'd actually met Lucia once. Or, at least, I was 99% sure it was her. And she'd asked about my ethics class that day, and I'd fucked up. But I wasn't sure I could explain it—the significance that the encounter now had in my imagination—so I kept my mouth shut.

Instead, I said, "They have this restaurant—"

"Jesus, Neil." He leaned back in his chair.

"It's a restaurant. It's not like I was sneaking in her window."

"What are you thinking?"

"I don't know. I just—I haven't been able to concentrate, and it was something to do."

"*Something to do*! Do you hear yourself?"

Ever since Phaedra and I split, Jack had been my biggest champion. I didn't know him well at the time, mostly because Phaedra had been my everything, had filled every role. But a few weeks after I moved out, Jack sent a text: *Burger and a beer?* That's all he wrote. I remember looking at those words like they weren't English. It was unfathomable to me that other people were going on with their lives. I didn't text back. Jack reached out three more times before

I finally agreed to meet up. Later, when I asked him why he'd pursued our friendship so doggedly, he acted genuinely surprised.

"You texted every week for a month," I told him.

"I did no such thing!"

"You did! I wouldn't call it infatuation, but close."

"Agree to disagree," he said, laughing. Neither of us bothered to check our official text record. Whatever our true origin, Jack was my closest friend. And now, he was looking at me with concern.

"I don't know what's going on with you lately," he said. "With your work, or tenure, or whatever. But *this*, with the girl and her sister—I'm not going to lie, Neil, it sounds really strange."

Jack was right. It did sound strange, but only when you considered it in its totality. Each discrete step—finding the restaurant, talking to Elena, talking to Naseem—had felt reasonable, necessary even. A natural progression. But I didn't know how to explain it, so I changed the subject.

"You doing Nietzsche today?" I asked.

He nodded.

"Maybe I'll tag along."

Occasionally, I used to sit in on Jack's classes. I liked to watch him teach. It reminded me of the old days when I still gave a shit about things.

In class that day, they were reading *Zarathustra*.

"'Mankind is a rope fastened between animal and overman . . .'" Jack read aloud. His students sat listening with wide, unblinking eyes. "'. . . a bridge and not a purpose.'"

Jack looked up when he was done. He didn't ask any questions, just lowered the book and waited. I tried to imagine what would happen if I did that in my class now. My students would shift in their seats. The awkward silence would destroy us all.

One girl with a nose ring and bright green eyes raised her hand. "I think Nietzsche means that mankind is not a *thing*." The seats were arranged in a circle so everyone could see everyone else. "Like, it's not *being*. It's *becoming*."

"But what does that *mean*?" Jack pressed.

"That we're always overcoming. We're always on the way."

"Good," Jack said. "On the way to what?"

"It's like, there's danger in becoming something else," another girl said. "Nietzsche keeps using that word: *dangerous*. He likes danger. This creative, destructive power. There's risk to it."

Jack nodded, smiled at the girl. I caught her blush.

I had heard Jack teach Nietzsche many times before. For some reason, these discussions always made me think of my father. Not that he was a reader of Nietzsche. Farthest thing from it. I doubt he'd ever heard of Nietzsche. It was something about creative destruction that seemed to perfectly capture him.

When I was eleven, a neighbor, Clark Soskin, kicked me out of his treehouse, which was basically a shitty platform with a rickety ladder. When I got home, my father was there.

"Well, how big is he?" my father wanted to know.

"Bigger than me."

Two weeks later, I came home to find my father sitting on the front porch, a cigarette hanging out his mouth, an Old Milwaukee next to him. He was lean and ropy and reminded me of a starved fox.

"C'mon," he said, standing and picking up his beer.

"Where?"

"Quit asking questions and c'mon."

The woods behind our house were dense. My father and I tromped through the overgrowth, and when he came to a stop, I looked up. My jaw dropped. There, in that thicket of trees, my father had built a treehouse. Not just any treehouse. The mother of all treehouses. It had windows and a steepled roof. It had a balcony. It had eaves! He had rigged up some intricate pulley system, and there was a tire leaning against the trunk.

"I'm gonna haul that up, make a tire swing," he said, crushing the butt of his cigarette underfoot. "Just didn't have time yet."

We both stood there, gazing at it. My father looked as astounded as I did. Almost like he couldn't believe he'd done it. It was so outlandish. It was so *him*. One minute, raging, the next, lavishing something on us that we were all afraid to touch.

"You let Ethan up there, you hear me," he said, referring to my brother. I nodded, dumbstruck. He turned to me. "You're the boss, Neil, you understand? You say who, you say when." Now his face got stern, his eyes hard. "But if I ever hear that Soskin bastard gets up into that house, I will tear the whole goddamn thing down, board by board. You got it?"

As it turned out, my father didn't get around to making the tire swing. And I didn't have to keep Clark Soskin from entering because we moved less than a month later. I have no doubt, the minute we were gone, Clark Soskin claimed that castle for himself.

Human beings are a bridge and not a purpose.

A boy was in the middle of speaking when I turned my attention back to the *Zarathustra* conversation. They were talking about pity and why Nietzsche disdains it.

"Because it's condescending," the boy said. He looked like a football player.

"No, he hates it because it robs people of their suffering, and suffering is essential for living," the girl with the nose piercing chimed in.

"You're both wrong," another boy said. I looked up to see a student dressed all in black, dark hair, dark eyes. "Nietzsche hates pity, because pity—like gossiping and everything else superficial—belongs to women."

Everyone went silent.

The dark-haired boy continued: "Overcoming is for men."

"You're an idiot, Luke," said the girl with the nose-piercing.

"The word is Over*man*, Shayna!" Luke snapped back. "It's right there in the word. Over-*man*."

Shayna rolled her eyes. "Yeah, like I am so *over* man," she said. "It's time we all get over man and his egotistical destruction of everything."

Jack cleared his throat to interrupt.

"Technically, in German, the word is *Mensch*," he said. "Overman is *Übermensch*. It means human being, not man *per se*. Superhuman."

"Regardless of the German word," Luke said, "everyone knows Nietzsche hated women."

There was a new tension in the room, one that I wasn't used to experiencing with Jack. And he seemed agitated—uncharacteristically so.

"I think, if we take a radical approach to overcoming," Jack said, "it would include all boundaries, categories, anything that locks us down. Even gender categories."

Luke was loudly flipping pages in a spiral notebook. I could see the notebook from where I sat. There was writing all over it, and Luke began to read: "Nietzsche says, and I quote, 'What is truth to a woman!' The corner of his mouth twisted up into a smile. "... her great art is the lie.'" He looked up, self-satisfied. "It's right here. *Beyond Good and Evil*."

I looked down at Luke's backpack. An iron cross was stitched onto the fabric. Next to it, a skull and crossbones.

Jack tried to salvage the conversation, to pry Nietzsche from the grips of misogyny. He explained that, for Nietzsche, "woman" was also the animating force of metaphor, creativity, overflowing, and art. The opposite of positivistic science and its stifling impact. But for all the nuance of Jack's argument, Luke's had the benefit of succinctness. It was quotable. Jack's meandered, seemed complicated.

***

When class was over, the students filtered out, and I wandered up to his desk.

"Who's the kid?" I asked.

"Luke-fucking-Lariat." Jack said. He was shoving books into his bag. "He's trouble." I'd never heard Jack use that language about a student before. Well, not in a serious way. "He takes every single one of my classes, and we get into it every single time. It's useless to argue with him. I should know better, but you just get sucked in, you know?"

We walked out of the classroom and into the quad. A tired sun shone down through the thinning branches of a white oak tree. Students crisscrossed the lawn. All around us, Lucia's face stared out from posters. I thought about the one I'd seen that morning. The word WHORE in all capital letters. It was tucked into my bag now. The image of it collided with so many other things in my mind. Lucia, Nietzsche, my father. Before we reached the Philosophy Department, I turned to Jack.

"Hey, out of curiosity, did you know that girl, Lucia?"

At the time, I said it because her face was everywhere. Her posters on every wall.

But Jack looked at me blankly.

"The missing girl? Again?" He shrugged. "How would I know her?"

"I don't know. Class? Maybe you taught her? It's weird. When I was talking to her sister, she said that Lucia hated philosophy. It's a strange thing to say, right?"

"No," Jack said, dismissively. "I didn't know her."

***

At home that evening, I pulled out the defaced poster from my bag. The word WHORE so insistent. I thought of my father, erecting a treehouse in retaliation. Some slight that he felt the need to redress, even though it had nothing to do with him. All the ways in which life throws down the gauntlet, challenges you to step up and take a stand. I taped the defaced poster to my wall, right next to the first poster of Lucia. Two identical images staring out at me.

***

On Mondays, I had judiciary committee where we met in the basement of a brick building to hear cases on plagiarism, cheating, stolen computers, pilfered headphones, fake IDs, drug sales on campus, and the like. Outside of our building was a statue of a Jesuit priest from the early days of the university, a regal high-mindedness in his expression, his cassock flying loose around him. Maybe if the judiciary committee had windows that looked out onto that Jesuit priest, it would have felt like a hallowed space. But we didn't. We were in the basement. Low-ceilinged and claustrophobic.

Abby Preacher was our presiding student officer. I liked Abby. She had auburn hair and an RBG sticker on her notebook and a moral fortitude that, frankly, sometimes scared me. That Monday afternoon, Abby called the meeting to attention and announced the case. The first to enter was the accusing party. A girl with violet hair and a Chinese character tattooed on her wrist. She was followed by the respondent. He wore combat boots and an army jacket and dropped his backpack on the table.

It was his backpack that I recognized first: the iron cross, skull and crossbones. The kid from Jack's class. Luke Lariat. He pulled out a spiral notebook and slapped it on the table. I could see his handwriting across the front.

Abby shifted in her seat and straightened her blouse. She read the school's honor statement then passed it around so we could all sign.

"Code 6.3, Section A: Stalking," Abby read, her eyes flicking up at Luke then back down. "And Code 6.5 Section C: Online publication of lewd, offensive, or detrimental material without the permission of the subject."

For the next fifteen minutes, we listened to the case against him.

The accusing party, whose name was Samantha, leaned forward as she spoke. "He waits in the parking lot next to my car. Or across from my dorm, looking up in my window, like a bona fide freak."

"Language, please," Abby said.

"When I come out of my classes, who is waiting there? This creep."

"I didn't realize you owned the school," Luke retorted. "Do I need your permission to use the bathroom?!"

Abby shot him a look. "Please wait until the charges have been presented in full; then you'll have your chance to respond."

Luke folded his arms. Both students had waived their rights to legal aid. *Idiots.*

I was only half paying attention when Samantha pulled a photograph from a folder of "evidence" in front of her. She slid it across the table. Abby looked down at it and flushed red. Then she passed it around the table.

It was a picture, taken from behind, of a woman on all fours, as a man entered her. It was graphic, shocking in its detail. The man's face was outside the frame, but the woman was looking back over her shoulder at the camera. Samantha's face. You could tell it was Photoshopped. At the neck, the lines didn't match up, and the skin tone was off. Someone had typed the words, "Squeal like a pig," across the top.

I felt Luke's eyes on me as I glanced at the image. Maybe because I was the only faculty member in the room. Or maybe because he recognized me from Jack's class.

When it was his turn to present his side, Luke stood up.

"You don't have to stand," Abby said, her voice frostier than she probably would have liked. Luke ignored her and went right on standing.

"'The Rape of the Sabine Women,' by Nicolas Poussin," Luke began. "'Young Virgin Auto-Sodomized by the Horns of Her Own Chastity,' by Salvador Dalí." He looked at each one of us. "Some people explore taboo subjects, and their work ends up in the Louvre. Others are forced to sit in front of a judiciary hearing at their biased universities."

"Oh, my God, you can't be serious!" Samantha interrupted. She picked up the Photoshopped image. "You're comparing yourself to Dalí?!"

"I would please ask all parties to wait their turn," Abby insisted.

Luke turned to his notebook and began rifling pages until he found what he wanted. I was sitting close to him—close enough to see the words "SchopArmy" written at the top of the page.

"At this school, we study Schopenhauer in my philosophy classes," he said. "Here is what Schopenhauer says, and I'm quoting, 'Women are the second sex, inferior in every respect...'" The room felt airless as he explained how Schopenhauer thought that women relied not on strength, but purely on manipulation. "Which is why Schopenhauer so clearly says, '...hence their instinctive capacity for cunning.'"

"How is this relevant to your case?" Abby asked, managing to keep her tone level.

"I didn't write this," Luke insisted. "Schopenhauer did. And at *this* school, we pay thousands, *hundreds of thousands*, of dollars to read it." I could sense his oratorical excitement. I imagined him rehearsing in his bedroom in front of a mirror. "It is *exactly* the kind of double standard that I would expect from a school like this. If I were Dalí or Schopenhauer, you would be *framing* this picture. But because I'm not, it's considered an offense."

Luke's argument ambled over art, free speech, women and their countless unkindnesses. By the time he finished, everyone looked glassy-eyed. Abby seemed to be struggling between the need to let the respondent defend himself and the vileness of his defense.

It took us no time to find Luke responsible for the offenses against Samantha. The more difficult question was how to sanction him. Warning, probation, suspension, expulsion.

Both parties left the room, and our deliberations began.

"I think we should consider aggravating circumstances," Terrance said, flipping through some of the papers in front of him, stopping at a photocopied document from Luke's file. "Mr. Lariat has a history of disturbing behavior." Apparently, in high school, someone had filed a restraining order against him. A female student claimed he'd tried to assault her. "The guy is straight up dangerous," Terrance said.

"Or he's just talk," Yume said. She was a thoughtful girl who chose her words carefully, so when she spoke, you listened.

"Yeah, sure," Terrance said. "Just talk—only, with a restraining order."

"The charges were dropped."

"Are you on his side?"

"Not at all," Yume said. "I find him personally reprehensible. I'm just trying to be fair."

Abby lifted her hand to quiet them. They debated the details of Luke's case and decided on probation and five sessions with the campus psychologist. All the while, I found my own mind wandering. It had become fixated on one small detail I couldn't shake: Luke's handwriting. On the cover of his notebook, and again on the page with his Schopenhauer notes, were neat capital letters—similar to the penmanship on the Lucia poster, the word WHORE in bold, red ink.

***

That night, I didn't work on my piece-of-shit article. Instead, I started clicking around online and stumbled into a vortex of strangeness called the "manosphere." I had never seen anything like it. Women-hating men, vocal in their outrage. There were websites and online forums. Blogs and media outlets.

Incels, they called themselves. "Involuntarily celibates" who depicted women as cruel and shallow. Women were the oppressors, and men needed to arm themselves with whatever means necessary. Acid attacks, gang rapes, shootings, intentional car accidents, all justified by the gender war foisted upon them.

There was an entire vernacular. *Blackpills, Chads, Normies, Stacys, #yesallwomen*. Everything recast in the language of slight. Every romantic rebuff was an affront. Every rejection, a call to arms. The flip of a girl's hair was evidence of superficiality. Her smile, pure artifice.

I read with a combination of horror and amusement, not because it was funny, but because it was utterly insane. I scanned subreddits, forums, anywhere users could comment.

At 4 a.m. I stumbled upon it.

An avatar who went by the name of "SchopArmy." He had seven posts. Three dedicated to Elliot Rodger, an incel who had killed students in Santa Barbara. Three posts complaining about his own physical attributes: his height, his jawline, and his limp (respectively) as the main reasons he wasn't "getting girls." He decried his virginity and the stupid *femoids* that prevented him from losing it. The final post was a meandering exploration of Nietzsche and Schopenhauer on the subject of women.

***

The next morning after class, I walked across campus to the registrar.

In the months after Phaedra and I split, a history professor had set me up on a date. The woman's name was Janet, and she worked in the registrar's office. I liked Janet. There was something refreshing in her frankness, the way she let her gray roots grow out because, "What's the use of pretending?"

On that date, we drank radlers with lemon. Lots of them. The drunker I got, the more I talked about Phaedra. At one point, Janet reached across the table.

"Honey, you are *not* ready," she said, patting my hand. "Not even close." She slid out of the booth to use the restroom. As I watched her pear-shaped form cross the bar, I felt a sudden urge to make love to her.

I never did.

Sometimes we would meet for lunch, and I'd talk about Phaedra unabashedly. Unlike Jack, Janet indulged it.

Now, when I entered her office, she looked up and waved. We headed to the cafe in the back of the building for lunch and grabbed a table under one of the umbrellas. I didn't waste any time. With Janet, you didn't beat around the bush.

"I need a student's records," I said between bites of my burger.

Janet set her fork down and swallowed a mouthful of romaine. She dabbed at the corner of her lips with her napkin.

"What kind of records?"

"Nothing weird. A list of classes, that's all."

She nodded, but her eyes were narrow and questioning.

"And this is because—?"

"It's for the judiciary committee," I said.

"Uh-oh. Is it bad?"

"Pretty bad. I can't get into it—obviously."

"Of course."

"But yeah, there's some concern about this kid's behavior toward women. I just want to take a look at his classes." It was a strange request, but Janet didn't rule it out immediately. She took a long drink of her iced tea, then said okay.

There was no one in her office after lunch, and she printed out a list of Luke's classes. Jack was right. Over the years, Luke had taken three with him. The Nietzsche one. A class on Schopenhauer and Kierkegaard, and a special topics course in 20th-century philosophy.

I was about to walk outside when I had a thought. I turned and went back to the desk.

"Sorry, one last thing."

Janet looked up at me, a hint of annoyance in her eyes.

"It's just, this kid has written some legitimately concerning stuff about women. I need to see a printout for the other students in these two classes. Right here," I tapped. "Professor Jack Sheridan. Schopenhauer and 20th-century philosophy."

"Neil, I—"

"Please, I promise. This is it."

Janet was quiet as she printed them out.

When she handed them to me, she said: "You should go. Before everyone gets back from lunch."

Fair enough. I had worn out my welcome. I tucked the papers into my bag and headed toward my office. But instead of going inside, I sat at the bench across from the Philosophy Department. There were birds in the trees overhead, and their calls filled the air.

I honestly don't know what I was hoping to find. I was moving on instinct. I scanned the Schopenhauer list first. Nothing of note. I flipped to the other class on Modern European philosophers. Jack taught it every few years. I'd sat in it before. It was a good course: fast-paced, dense, and demanding.

The year Luke took it, there were only eleven students in class.

Luke-fucking-Lariat was one.

Lucia Vanotti was another.

CHAPTER 8

LUCIA

Then

Professor Sheridan encouraged us to keep journals to jot down little things we noticed over the course of a day. "Become attuned to the world," he said. "The equipment you use, the things you pick up because they're there, ready-to-hand. Notice what happens when they break? Your computer. Your car. How they suddenly assert themselves in different ways."

I liked to watch his mouth as he spoke.

It was Michelle who convinced me to take his class in the first place.

"Why?" I had asked her. I was an econ student and had already fulfilled my general ed.

"So . . . we can finally take a class together?"

"Not a good enough reason."

I had met Michelle Alvarez freshman year. She had olive skin, hawk eyes, and a static level of impatience. The day we met, she was standing in the dining hall, staring at a piece of chicken.

"Does that look gray to you?" she asked. I wasn't sure if she was talking to me. I looked at the chicken.

"It doesn't look gray, but it doesn't look good."

She turned to me, buffet tongs in hand.

"There's a box out back with the words, 'Fit for human consumption,' on it.
How disgusting is that?"

We'd been friends ever since.

"I don't care if you take the class or not," she said, "but the teacher's supposed
to be hot."

***

I remember when Professor Sheridan walked in that first day. Every one of us
gaped. Even Michelle, who exclusively sleeps with girls.

"What are the most dangerous words ever written?" he asked.

We offered all sorts of examples.

Heil Hitler.

How dangerous could it be to split an atom?

Let's call it "Facebook."

Professor Sheridan stopped us after a while and looked at the class.

"Descartes, 1637. *Cogito ergo sum,*" he said. "I think, therefore I am."

The class laughed, as he probably intended. Then he went on to tell us why.
Descartes, in the moment of the *cogito,* separates the mind from the body and
the body from the world outside—other people, the environment. Each piece
becomes cordoned off, separated from everything else. "How much destruction
can we trace back to that single utterance?" he asked.

One day, he went around and asked each of us why we had signed up for the
class. If he'd asked it on the first day, it would have seemed like a gimmick, an
annoying get-to-know-you exercise. But it wasn't the first day, which made it
feel important.

When it was Michelle's turn, she turned up her New Jersey accent.

"Why am I taking the class? I'm taking it because the 20th century was messed-up. Nazis, fascists, genocide, civil wars." Michelle was a Marxist. Not like all those other Marxists who drive Range Rovers and upgrade their Mac-Books every three years. Michelle's father had been a dockworker who operated a pallet jack and carried 85 lbs. on his back for half his life. When his joints gave out, the only thing that became clear to Michelle was how expendable he was. His company needed a body—one that could lift, heave, and break with circadian rhythms to work a 4 a.m. to 2 p.m. shift. Michelle was the first person in her family to go to college. Her older sister, Jasmin, worked at Best Buy. Her brother, Manny, was stationed overseas. She was here on a merit-based scholarship. She was going to be a lawyer, fighting for all those expendable bodies everywhere.

"So, yeah," she said. "I want to know what these famous philosophers have to say about the real world. Like, does your philosophizing matter at all? Does it *actually* affect anything in the world, or are you just up in your ivory tower, jacking off with words?"

Professor Sheridan didn't flinch, but the class got very still. The only sound was an air conditioner clicking on and off in the background.

"All valid questions," Professor Sheridan said. "I hope we can answer them." Then he turned to me. "Lucia, what about you? Why are you taking this class?"

I looked at him. His perfect face, his cool professor vibe.

"Because it fit in my schedule," I said.

He cracked a smile.

"Radical honesty. I like it."

***

For our mid-term papers, we were allowed to write on whatever we wanted, provided it tied back to the themes of the class. Michelle chose national socialism. I chose the poet Rilke. And death.

In his only novel, *The Notebooks of Malte Laurids Brigge*, Rilke writes about death as something that belongs to us. "One had one's death within one, as a fruit its kernel," he writes. Rilke says that death gives us "a singular dignity" and "a quiet pride." What did that mean? I wanted to know.

My paper was not a philosophical argument. It did not progress through points and counterpoints. It ambled. It was a paper about death. Not, like Heidegger, for whom death is always outstanding, shaping time and space, a death I will never experience because, the moment it arrives, I am no longer.

For Rilke, death was different.

Everyone has their own death growing inside them. Something we carry around. We don't die just any old death. We die the death that is ours. The death that belongs to us. I liked the idea that one had to become *worthy* of one's death. You only get one, after all. You'd better make it spectacular.

I asked Michelle to read it before I handed it in.

When she gave it back to me, she said: "I don't even know what this is."

***

On the day Professor Sheridan returned our papers, I avoided eye contact. I suddenly felt mortified for having written it. It wasn't philosophical. It wasn't smart. It was strange, full of starts and stops, groping around, celebrating death. I wanted to leap from my chair and bolt from the room, but I was frozen in place.

Professor Sheridan walked around the room, handing them back. "Once you get your paper, you're free to go," he said. But no one did. Instead, everyone sat in their seats, reading his comments, flipping the pages to find their grades. Michelle grinned as she scanned his feedback.

Mine was the last paper in the stack. He set it on my desk, face down. Held his finger on it for an extra second until I looked up and met his eyes. Then he lifted his hand and walked back to his desk.

I ran from the room with embarrassment, didn't even wait for Michelle. I wanted to read his comments in private.

Only, when I scanned the pages, there were no comments. Not a single mark in the margins. Nothing at all.

On the last page was my grade. "A."

Two words scribbled beneath it in a hasty hand: "See me."

CHAPTER 9

NEIL

Now

Unlike the humanities buildings, Treyton Hall was a shiny, metallic structure that housed engineering and computer science departments. Geodesic architecture, gun-metal walls, and windows of mirrored glass. I smoked my cigarette down to the filter, stubbed it out, and wandered the halls.

I found Luke Lariat's classroom on the first floor. From the schedule that Janet had printed, I knew that he was taking a computer science course called, "Hackers, Disrupters, and Renegades." I imagined a room full of wannabe Mark Zuckerburgs and Elon Musks, primed to disrupt the system. Any system. Every system. You could almost hear their little innovations barking inside their brains.

I arrived early and tried to get clear on what I wanted to know. Of course, the most important question was not one that Luke could answer: why Jack had lied. Perhaps if Lucia had been some nameless face in a large lecture hall of a hundred students ten years ago, fine, I could understand. But she was one of *eleven* students in a small seminar. And now she was missing. There was no way Jack didn't remember her. I knew that Luke couldn't tell me why Jack had lied, but maybe he could provide a glimpse into the dynamics of that classroom a year ago.

When the lecture hall door finally opened, students streamed into the hallway. Their sneakers squeaked on the vinyl floor; their voices bounced off the walls. I waited for Luke. Then waited some more. For a long time, I didn't see him. When I finally did, he was halfway down the hallway, having exited a separate door. I watched him for a moment, the way the skull and crossbones on his backpack swayed from side to side. It struck me then that Luke Lariat walked with a limp.

When I caught up to him, I said his name, and he whipped around, startled.

"Professor Weber," I introduced myself, "from judiciary committee. Remember, I was at your hearing the other day?"

"Oh," Luke said, looking confused. There was a spray of acne around his hairline. High up on his cheeks, tiny indentations where scars had left their mark.

We stood for a moment, staring at each other. I had spent so much time tracking him down, I wasn't sure how to begin.

"Is this about my case?" he asked.

"Oh. No. Sorry," I said. "You should be receiving a letter about that soon. This is about—something else. Could we maybe go somewhere and talk?"

Luke looked skeptical but followed me outside into the overcast April day. The sun was half-heartedly trying to pierce through the clouds. In the courtyard in front of Treyton Hall were a handful of picnic tables. Modular chairs affixed to the ground. We sat down, and Luke drummed his fingers on the table impatiently.

"How'd you hurt your leg?" I asked, just to fill the silence.

"Bone dysplasia," he said flatly. "I have a lift in my shoe."

Oh, God. Off to a terrible start. I'd forgotten about the limp from his online rantings. I decided to take a different tact.

"Look, Luke, you don't seem like a bullshitter, so I'm not going to bullshit you."

"Okay."

"Lucia Vanotti," I said. "The missing girl. I'm sure you've seen the posters around campus."

He folded his arms across his chest and looked suddenly less comfortable. If you looked at Luke from a distance, the prevailing sense of him was darkness. Dark hair, dark clothes. A dark scowl on his face. But, sitting this close to him, I could see little pockets of light. His skin was pale, almost translucent. Highways of blue veins crisscrossed just beneath the surface. When you considered the particulars, rather than the general, Luke seemed younger, frailer. I was gripped with a sudden urge to grasp him by the shoulders, shake him, and say: *Look, kid, don't screw up your life.* But I didn't.

"I wanted to ask you about Lucia because I happened to see a list of your classes. The ones you have currently, but also the ones you took in the past. I noticed that you took a class with her last year."

"Yeah, so?"

"So, I was wondering how well you knew her."

Luke snorted, shook his head.

"Not well." He looked at me. "Or, at least, not as well as half the guys at this school."

"Were you friends with her?"

I already knew he wasn't. In no world was a guy like Luke friends with a girl like Lucia.

"Uh, yeah, *no.* I would not say that we were friends."

"But you did have a class with her. Would you say the class was close?"

"What do you mean, *close*?"

"Like, you know, did you all get along pretty well?" This line of questioning was worthless. I knew it even as I asked. But I wasn't sure how to get at the thing I wanted.

Luke shifted in his chair.

"Why are you asking me this?"

I could feel him retreating. I needed to reel him back in.

"Well," I said, groping for a reason. "One of her missing person's posters was defaced." I cleared my throat. "I'm going to level with you, Luke. The other day, I happened to notice your handwriting on the front of your notebook."

"Okay."

"And it looked like the same writing on the Lucia poster that was defaced. Any chance you wrote it?"

"Wrote what?"

"The word 'whore'?"

Luke laughed. He had a high-pitched laugh, like a young boy's. When he stopped, he didn't look amused.

"No, I didn't write it." He was staring at me intensely. "But she was one. That's not me saying it, and it can't be used against me."

"I'm not interested in using anything against you. I'm interested in helping to find a missing girl. I'm just trying to talk to people who knew her. People who might have some idea where she might be."

He scoffed. "How would I know where she is?"

I shrugged, but my expression must have landed poorly, because he became suddenly agitated.

"What do you think? I have her chained up in my basement? That I'm holding her captive? That what? I raped her?"

My expression must have been one of horror because he said, "You're the one who implied it!" and slumped back against the chair. Behind him, I could see the trees wavering in the reflection of the building's windows.

"I didn't rape anybody, okay?! I've never had sex with anyone. I've never even kissed anyone. Which is not going to change at this stupid school. So, your theory is debunked."

"I didn't mean to imply—"

"She probably got the hell out of here and went somewhere better than this shit school." Luke reached for his backpack. Then he stood up, somewhat laboriously. "I don't know where Lucia is. Or what she's doing." He looked out across the courtyard. A shuttle was approaching. With his limp, there was no way that Luke could catch it. "If you want to find her so bad, why don't you start with that stupid party they go to?"

"Party? What party?"

A breeze stirred the air.

"Don't look at me. It's not like they invited me." He paused. "You know they're prostitutes, right? Like, real prostitutes."

An image of Lucia—not the one from her posters, but the hazy memory of her sitting next to me on the bench—flashed through my mind. The way her face looked when I told her not to waste her time on ethics. I tried to imagine her as someone who got paid for sex. My image of a prostitute was so cliché, so simplistic, it was hard to reconcile it with the girl I'd met.

"I honestly don't know what you're talking about."

Luke huffed as if this only proved how inept the entire school was.

"Like I said, they never invited me, so I have nothing to tell you." He readjusted his backpack. "All I know is it's called the Dionysus. And the only reason I remember *that* is from Nietzsche. Some wannabe intellectuals throwing a sex party, thinking they're better than everyone else just because they know the name of a stupid Greek god."

However abhorrent Luke's views were, at least on this point, he was correct. In *The Birth of Tragedy*, Nietzsche writes about Apollo and Dionysus. Form and excess. Constraint and overflowing. Two opposing gods who hold each other together. It made me wonder if he was correct about anything else.

***

My head was spinning on the walk back to the Philosophy Department, which was why I didn't notice Phaedra until I was practically on top of her.

She was stubbing out a cigarette. Her blonde hair, loose around her face. Heavy eyelids over smoke-colored eyes. At times, Phaedra looked so young she could pass for a student. Others, she looked as wizened and weary as a tenured professor—which she was, even though we'd started at the same time.

I cleared my throat, and she startled.

"Holy shit, Neil!" She held her hand to her chest. "You scared me."

"Hiding out in the Economics Department?" I asked. Then, nodding to the cigarette she'd just extinguished, I added, "Thought you'd quit."

"I did." She eyed me conspiratorially. "You saw nothing."

I zipped my lips, and she flashed me that classic Phaedra smile. It made my heart lurch.

For months after our breakup, I tried to coordinate our comings and goings, hoping to bump into her without Tim. It never worked. Not once. And now, here she was, alone.

"How've you been?" she asked, her eyes scanning my face.

"You know," I shrugged, "Same. Trying to write. Get something published."

"That's great, Neil. Really."

Before we split, I shared every piece of writing with Phaedra. She was my first reader, practically my co-author. But even then, Phaedra was secretive. She didn't share her work with others, not before it was published. She used to say that she had no use for other people's unsolicited advice. Only once did she let me read something beforehand, and she was so guarded about it, I half-jokingly offered to sign a nondisclosure agreement.

"Well, hey," she said, tucking a strand of hair behind her ear, "let me know if you want to bounce some ideas around."

I looked at her with suspicion.

"What?" she said, defensively. "You know I've always admired your work." For a brief second, she reached out and put her hand on my arm. Then, perhaps thinking better of it, pulled it away.

"I'd like that," I said.

But I think we both knew that those days were long gone.

***

On the second floor of the library was a bathroom with a window that looked out on the quad and the philosophy building across the way. Ivy crept up one wall. A handful of oak trees dotted the grass. The quad itself was the beating heart of the school. It was where students gathered, studied, and sunbathed. In the springtime, it was all exposed skin, cut-off jean shorts, tanned shoulders, and naked toes. A game of frisbee or hacky sack. Peals of laughter. These kids had no idea that they would be chasing these moments for the rest of their lives.

But not today. Today the quad was quiet. A dull gray sky overhead. I stood at the urinal and stared outside. There, near the largest oak tree, I caught sight of two people talking. It took me a moment to register that one was Jack. His hair was pushed back, his arms folded across his chest. The other was a student. A girl, her backpack dangling from one shoulder, her dark hair swept off her face. I could only see her profile, but I could tell they were arguing. It was something in her stance, the way she leaned forward, her neck taut, her lips moving quickly. Jack's body in retreat.

Then, out of nowhere, Jack shot out his hand and gripped the girl by her arm. My jaw dropped. I zipped up my fly and glanced around. There was no one else in the quad. The girl tried to pull away, but Jack held tight. Even in that fading light, I could see the intimacy of their argument. Like lovers. After a moment, she yanked her arm back. I could see she was crying. As she turned to leave, I got a perfect look at her face.

***

The next day, Jack sent me a flurry of texts. He wanted to get drinks.

"And no bullshit about writing," he texted. "I know you haven't typed a word."

We agreed to meet at a gastropub across town where they played Drive-By Truckers, served bison burgers, and featured beers that no one's heard of. I found Jack at a communal table in the middle of the room, looking like he'd already had a few.

"This good man needs a drink!" he bellowed when he saw me.

The waitress had blonde, wavy hair and bright eyes. Jeans and a tank top, an apron cinched around her waist. She took our orders, and when she left, Jack turned to me.

"Did she just wink at you?"

"No."

"She did." He was leaning back in his chair, looking amused. "She's cute."

"She is."

"You should get her number."

"I should."

"But you won't."

I didn't answer because the waitress was back, setting a pale ale in front of me. An IPA in front of Jack.

"What's your name?" Jack asked her.

She smiled, like she'd been down this road before.

"Tara."

"Well, Tara, this is my good friend, Neil."

She glanced at me.

"Ignore him," I said and felt my face flush.

"Nice to meet you, Neil."

After she left, I didn't even bother to give Jack shit. He took a swig of his beer and leaned forward.

"Where you been?" he asked. "I haven't seen you for days."

"Just busy," I said with a shrug. "Oh, by the way, I saw that student of yours, Luke Lariat. In judiciary committee."

"Uh-oh. What'd he do?"

"He's a weird one." I filled Jack in on Luke's Photoshop skills and the SchopArmy postings.

"Fuuuck," Jack said.

"Also, he's a virgin. In case you were wondering."

"Jesus. These kids."

He finished his beer and told me about a conference he would be attending back home in New Jersey. He planned to rent a car, drive out to visit his folks. I knew he didn't get out there often.

My own memories of home always felt like excerpts, segments cut from a whole that I could never fully piece back together. Sometimes, I would catch a flash of one.

A windy October afternoon when I was sixteen, sitting in the basement of Sam Kitcheson's house, blasting 2 Live Crew. "*I know he'll be disgusted when he sees your pussy busted.*" The two of us singing along like we had any idea what a pussy even looked like outside of a magazine or his dad's VHS porn collection. I remember walking home for dinner, my Chuck Taylors on the sidewalk, momentarily forgetting how fucked up everything was at my house. My brother, Ethan, stood out front on the dried-up lawn. Fourteen years old. His huge brown eyes always downcast. His voice rarely louder than a whisper.

"It's bad, Neil," he said when I walked up, like he expected me to do something about it.

After Phaedra and I got married, she wanted to meet my mom and Ethan. I agreed, but the moment we pulled up to my mother's house, my body went cold. For reasons that once felt clear to me, I had chosen not to see my mother or Ethan for almost a decade. When my mom opened the front door, she had lines around her eyes and streaks of gray in her hair. I didn't realize I was clenching my jaw until Phaedra took my hand.

That afternoon, Ethan came by for lunch. He had married his high school girlfriend, and they had a kid I'd never met. I watched my mom and Ethan move around her kitchen, the way he reached around her to open a drawer, the way she lifted a tray from his hands mid-sentence—all these little movements, choreographed by time and repetition, a dance I did not know.

If either one of them had come out and asked me point blank why I'd stayed away all those years, I don't know how I would have answered. Probably, I would have made up an excuse. Grad school. My students. Papers to write and publish. What else could I say? How could I explain it? The way it felt to be around them.

The way it made me hate myself. But they didn't ask. So, we did what we were best at doing—pretended everything was fine.

After lunch that day, my mom looped her arm through Phaedra's. She wanted to show her the garden. They wandered off and left Ethan and me sitting at the table outside, struggling at small talk. At one point, Phaedra looked up at me from across the yard. Her eyes suddenly sharp. I couldn't hear what they were saying, but it lodged a pit in my stomach. Later, when I asked her about it, she brushed it off. "It was nothing," Phaedra said. "Just stories about you as a kid."

After Phaedra and I split, I got a voicemail from my mother. How sorry she was to hear the news. How much she had liked Phaedra that one time. I deleted the message before it was finished.

***

At the gastropub, Jack and I ate dinner, then I slipped outside to smoke. Through the glass, I could see him chatting up two women in their mid-thirties who had joined our communal table. By the time I got back, the three of them had ordered a round of tequila shots.

One of the girls was round-faced; the other was tall and skinny. I found neither appealing. Jack would have gone home with either, but he seemed to be leaning toward the round-faced one. I could picture an entire evening play out, a sloppy trajectory that ended with their clothes in a heap on the floor.

It was that image—combined with all the things I had seen and heard over the last few days—that set the rest of the night spinning. The clearest thought I remember having was: *Fine. Fuck it.*

The four of us clinked glasses, threw our heads back, and took down our tequila like medicine. Eyes squinted, lime smiles. When the waitress passed, I called her out by name.

"Tara, c'mere." *Yeah, I could be that asshole. I could do that.*

I motioned her over, draped an arm around her shoulder. Jack grinned. "How many shots come in a bottle?" I asked.

Bless her heart, she let my arm rest there.

"I don't know. Sixteen? Seventeen, maybe?" I knew that another drink would be one too many. I'd been down this road before. Too many times to count. But in that moment, I didn't care. What I wanted was the erasure that alcohol promised. I'd deal with the consequences later.

"Perfect!" I smiled. "We'll take the bottle."

The girls clapped. Jack whooped.

"Yes," he said. "*Hell* yes!"

For the next hour, I committed myself to obliteration. I could tell I was slurring my words. The drunker I became, the less enthused Jack seemed, but it didn't bother me one iota.

In the end, the round-faced girl did not go home with Jack. Instead, the girls paid their tab, said goodbye, and left. I tried to wave, but I was having trouble staying upright on my chair.

"Okay, buddy," Jack said, clapping me on the back. "That's probably enough."

"No way! We're just getting started." I was shaking my head, which felt only loosely connected to my body. A Cartesian brain in a vat. I felt like I might vomit. "There's so much—there's all this other stuff—I need to tell you about," I mumbled.

"Okay," he said, humoring me.

"I'm serious."

"All right," impatiently. "What?"

I forgot what I wanted to say. Then remembered. It was taking a tremendous effort to keep my eyes open.

"Oh, yeah!" I said. "*Ohyeah, Ohyeah, Ohyeah.*" I hiccupped. "It was—*oh yeah.* It was about that girl. Lucia.*" Her name came out as a slur, but Jack heard me, and his face went dark. "Cause see, here's the thing—" I was pointing at him with one wavering finger. "I know you knew her. I do." I was nodding. "*I do, I do.* You wanna know how I know?" I caught a whiff of tequila on my own breath and winced. "I saw her name on your schedule."

Jack stayed quiet, his attention laser-like on my face.

"You're drunk."

"Give this man an A!" I shouted. Then, looking at him: "But I'm not wrong."

Somewhere in there, the atmosphere changed. Time slowed.

"You checking up on me, Neil?"

Everything was tilting. Or I was tilting. Same difference. I shook my head, and the room was spinning. I shrugged. I didn't care if I fell off my seat. Let them scrape me off the floor.

"You tell me," I said. The reek of the bar, the grease of fried food, nearly bowled me over. Jack stood up. He was shaking his head.

"What are you thinking? That you're going to solve this mystery and—what? You're going to win Phaedra back? You're going to get tenure? Your life is suddenly going to mean something?"

I laughed drunkenly. It came out as a snort. "And what if I am? What's so wrong with that?"

Jack exhaled. Then he pulled $200 from his wallet.

"Look at the rich guy," I guffawed.

He leveled his gaze at me. "You're drunk. I'm going to chalk it up to that." Jack's face was close to mine, and I could see his teeth. Ha! They weren't perfect! They were crooked. Right there on the bottom. The man did have a flaw. I thought about pointing it out, but he looked displeased. "I'm not getting

into it with you. Not here. But you have no idea what you're talking about."
It came out like a whisper, which proved the exact opposite in my humble
opinion—that I knew *exactly* what I was talking about.

I watched him walk to the door and disappear outside. Then I fumbled for
my own wallet. My credit card fell to the floor. I made a big show of picking it
up. I put everything on my card, then tipped Tara lavishly. On top of it, I left
Jack's $200 for her as well.

Just as I was tucking my wallet back into my pocket, Tara appeared next to
me.

"Hey there," she said.

I turned to her. She was so pretty. Nothing like Round-Face or
Tall-and-Skinny.

"You have such a sweet voice," I said. "Like an angel. You should sing. I'm not
even joking! You should."

She smiled. "I do. And play guitar." She flashed her left hand. Callouses along
her fingertips.

"I knew it!" I shouted.

"How you getting home, honey?"

Her voice was like syrup. I smiled at her. I wanted to touch her hair.

"I have a car coming," I lied.

She nodded. Seemed to consider something, then said: "This is definitely a
terrible idea, but I'm off in half an hour. If you wanna wait, I could probably
give you a lift home."

"You're so pretty," I said. I touched her shoulder awkwardly, then stumbled
to the door. On some gut level, I knew I wasn't up to the task of managing a
night with this girl. Pretty as she was, she wasn't Phaedra. I heard the bartender
call out. Tara muttered something in response about a car coming.

I found my car outside. It took me three tries to buckle my seatbelt. I knew I shouldn't do it. Just like I'd known I shouldn't do it all those other times. But fuck it. I did it anyway. Somehow, I managed to drive four blocks before plowing into an embankment. I kicked the door open and dragged myself out. My car looked so sad, front wheels down in the ditch, back ones up on the slope. I apologized to my car for abandoning it. Then I began the long walk home.

In that part of town, a thicket of woods runs along the edge of the road. It was 14.4 miles to my house. I confirmed the mileage later. It took me six hours in that condition. I remember only fragments of the walk. The black, curving asphalt cutting through the woods. Tree limbs draped with vines. I didn't spend one moment thinking about Jack. Instead, I thought of Phaedra. I hallucinated her around every bend, pretending she was there with me. Phaedra always loved the woods.

I smoked every last cigarette, flicking the butts into the trees. It was not a road meant for pedestrians. No sidewalk, only a thin stretch of shoulder. Occasional cars passed, their headlights blasting my eyes.

It was nearly sunrise when I walked in my front door. I fell asleep, and my dreams were monstrous. My mother's arms, black and blue. A laceration down the side of her face. Stitches above her eyebrow. I still remember the strange parabola of a landline hurled through the air. The *thud* of a telephone against soft flesh, the silence that followed.

CHAPTER 10

LUCIA

Then

Professor Sheridan's door was ajar, but I knocked anyway. He looked up and smiled.

"Lucia," he said. "Come in."

There were books everywhere, disorganized in a way that meant he was brilliant rather than just messy. He motioned to a chair across from his desk and I took a seat.

I'll always remember what he looked like that first day we were alone. A blue button-down. His eyes the same color as his shirt. He asked if I brought my Rilke paper, and I handed it to him. There was silence as he scanned through what I had written. When he was done, he set it flat on his desk.

"So, you're an economics major?" he asked.

I nodded.

"How come?"

"I don't know." I'd never considered anything else. "My family has a restaurant," I said. "I run inventory." I felt his eyes on me. I could have worked that gaze. Adjusted in my seat to ensure that he saw my body in the way I wanted.

But I wasn't interested in that kind of seduction. I wanted to hear what he had to say.

"So, you're an econ major for practical reasons?"

"I guess. But also, for other ones." He waited for me to elaborate. "I don't know. Because it's transactional. I like that. It's grounded in the world." I shrugged. "Because I'm good at it."

"Fair enough."

He was tracing his fingertip along the edge of my paper.

"I'm asking because your paper is very good," he said, tapping it. "I could see you doing this."

"Doing what?"

"Philosophy. Poetry."

I shook my head.

"No?" he asked.

"Sorry," I said. "It's just—I like to read it and write about it. But—"

He waited.

"But it's not real," I said. "It's just people talking about ideas. It doesn't really—change anything. No offense."

"None taken." He smiled, then looked back down at my paper. "Still, this is well-written. I'm not sure if you know, but there's a student journal here on campus. By students, for students. It's called *No Vacancy*. Really smart writing. You've got to be nominated to even be considered, and each piece is evaluated by a panel of readers. It's a huge honor to be accepted. Anyway, I was thinking about nominating you. Your Rilke paper, I mean."

"To be published?"

"I can't guarantee it would be selected, of course. But, yeah, to be considered." He nodded. "I think your writing is that good. There's something about

it. Not just the stuff about Rilke. There's something—almost sorrowful. I hope
you don't mind my saying."

I could feel my leg shaking, my throat dry. "I don't mind you saying it. But I
don't want it to be published."

Professor Sheridan looked surprised. "Oh, I just assumed—" he began.
"Most students are honored—" He looked uncomfortable.

"No. I am honored. I just—it's private."

He nodded, but I felt as if I'd somehow disappointed him.

"Well, then," he said, looking down at my paper as if suddenly seeing it in
a new light. "I guess I should thank you for trusting me with it. It was truly a
pleasure to read."

"You inspired it, so—"

For a moment, his face flushed red. It faded almost immediately, but I had
seen it. He handed me back my paper. As I reached across the desk for it, I
accidentally exposed the scar on the inside of my bicep. That patch of skin that
had once been smooth and soft. I saw his eyes flick to it. And something shifted
in the energy of his office.

"Lucia—" he began but trailed off. What did Professor Sheridan see as he
looked across his desk?

They say that some people experience phantom pains in a limb that has been
removed. My problem was the opposite. The limb remained, but the pain had
become a phantom. I could still feel the memory of that summer residing there
on my arm. It's why I had needed to burn it and, years later, cut it with a straight
razor. So that I could excise the pain.

I remembered that day so clearly. My father, scooping me off the bathroom
floor, covered in my own blood. My mother screaming over and over: *Lucia,
what have you done?* On the car ride to the hospital, my father's mouth moved
in prayer. The irony was, when my arm finally healed, the phantom pain did

not. Instead, it became trapped there in the scar tissue of my arm. A reminder that I could never excise it. That summer would live with me, on my body, along my skin, until my dying day.

***

Michelle started referring to him as my "secret lover."

We were lying in the quad, our backs on the dewy grass, her head resting against my stomach. When I laughed, her head bobbed up and down.

"I'm listening to your food," Michelle said.

"What's it saying?"

"It's not good," she said.

One time, shortly after I'd met her, I kissed Michelle at a party. She had been sitting with her legs tucked underneath her on a couch. She let me do it. When I stopped, she cocked her head, ran her tongue along her upper lip.

"No," she said, shaking her head.

"No what?"

"You're hot, but you don't do it for me."

That was then. Now, on the quad, she wore big, round sunglasses that made her look famous as she stared up into the wide-open sky.

She said: "If you had to explain why you like him, what would you say? I mean, besides the fact that he's hot."

I never felt judged by Michelle. Even when she gave me grief, I never felt judged. I had a boyfriend *and* a crush on my teacher. To Michelle, these were not mutually exclusive. They were simply facts.

"You wouldn't understand," I said. "You're a lesbian."

"Wow. Thank you for that insight. You should be a private investigator." She was barefoot and spread her toes in the grass.

"I don't know why."

By then, I'd been going to Professor Sheridan's office hours regularly. Sometimes he would give me books to read. Poetry. Paul Celan's *Atemwende*. Billy Collins's *Art of Drowning*. Sometimes, when we were standing at his bookshelf, he would suddenly turn to me, and all the air would leave the room.

Michelle sat up. "So, what? You want him just *because*?"

"Maybe." I sat up, too. "I don't know."

She was plucking up shoots of grass by their roots and tossing them in front of her.

"All I'm saying is, if you want him so bad, why don't you do something about it?"

I laughed.

"I'm serious," she said.

"Okay, like what?"

She cocked her head, flashed a smile.

Michelle had a friend, someone from New Jersey.

"Well, not really my friend. Jas's friend." Her older sister, Jasmin, had this friend, Lotus.

"That's not her real name," Michelle clarified. "That's just what she calls herself."

Lotus had apparently been living here for a while, since before Michelle came out for school. I didn't understand all of it, and Michelle only had rough details, but the gist of it was this: this Lotus girl was somehow involved in these parties on the outskirts of town. "A fetish club," Michelle called it. The Dionysus.

"I mean, it sounds like a straight up sex party," Michelle said, lifting her sunglasses. "And guess who shows up to this place?"

"Who?"

"Professors."

"Bullshit!" I said. "She told you that?"

"Not in so many words. But yes. Then she freaked out. Lotus was like, 'No, no. I have it all wrong. Forget it, blah, blah, blah.' Honestly, she sounded super sketchy about it, like she'd made this big mistake in telling me. Wanted me to forget all about it. Though, I swear to God, one second earlier, she was basically trying to recruit me. Anyway, I put two and two together, and I'm fairly certain *your* secret lover is one of them."

"No way! I don't believe you."

"There is a way to find out—" Abruptly, her expression changed; she was glaring at someone behind me on the quad. I turned. A boy from our philosophy class was sitting there. Luke something or other.

"What are you staring at?" Michelle said to him. "You got a problem?"

"I'm not bothering you," he said, scowling back at her.

"You are when you're listening to my fucking conversation."

"Fuck you," he said and struggled to get up off the grass. There was something wrong with his leg. "Bitch," he muttered as he walked away.

"That was rude," I said when he was gone.

"He was staring!"

"Who cares? Let him stare."

CHAPTER 11

NEIL

Now

The second girl went missing three weeks after the first.

On Monday morning, after I forked over an outlandish sum of money to get my car repaired, I drove my rental to campus and saw the poster.

It hung beneath the one of Lucia. Two missing girls. This second one had black hair, pulled up in a bun. Her skin was caramel, her eyes, blue-black. A small crowd had gathered to stare at the poster.

"My parents are seriously about to pull me out of school," one girl was saying to her friend.

I glanced at the poster, and a wave of nausea passed over me. I recognized the girl's face. I had seen her before. Once. When she had been arguing with Jack in the quad.

Michelle Alvarez, the poster read, *missing since Friday*.

There is no playbook for teaching class when two students have vanished into thin air. How do you lecture on Kant and the notion of duty or Aristotle on virtue when people are disappearing around you? That morning, I did something I hadn't done in so long: I went off-script. I closed my book, walked to the front of my desk, and perched on the edge.

"Why don't we put our discussion on hold for a minute," I began, "and talk about what's happening on campus."

For a moment, I felt that old feeling. Standing in front of the classroom. Like something was possible. Like our discussion might go somewhere unexpected if we let it.

"I don't have answers for you," I said, "but whatever you're experiencing—fear, outrage, sadness—you're not alone."

For a beat, my students stared at me, seemingly unsure what was required of them. Then, Adam Steadman raised his hand. He shifted in his chair, then started talking.

"I guess, like, when Lucia first disappeared, it kind of seemed like—I don't know. Like a joke," he said.

In front of him, Zeta whipped around. "Dude, are you serious?" She usually sat right in front of me and doodled small anime characters on her notebook all through class.

"Can you let me finish?" Adam insisted. "I'm trying to tell you that when Lucia left—or whatever happened—I kind of imagined that it was—I don't know—like a prank. Or that she had just bailed, you know? But now—" He looked around. "I mean, I wouldn't want my sister going to this school. And I just think that all the girls should be really careful."

"That's sexist," Zeta said.

"Stop looking for messed up ways to interpret what I'm saying," Adam said. "I'm only trying to say that, if someone needs me—or, I mean, I can't speak for the other guys in this class, but I imagine they would agree—if someone needs us, we're here."

"Thank you, Adam," I interrupted before Zeta could pounce. "I think what you're trying to say is that we need to support each other right now. We need to keep our eyes open and offer kindness where we can."

***

When class ended, I took my time repacking my bag. I was in no rush. I had nowhere to be. I wanted a minute to think, to figure out what I was going to say to Jack when I finally saw him again.

But I heard a rap on the door and looked up to find a tall Black man standing in the doorway.

"Professor Weber?" he said in a deep, unhurried voice.

"Can I help you?"

He stepped into the empty classroom.

"Not sure if you can or can't." His smile might have been warm, except that it set me on edge. "I'm Detective Waters; I'm looking into the disappearances on campus. I was hoping we could talk."

He pulled a small notebook from the inside pocket of his jacket. And in that simple gesture, you could feel his authority. Not loud and clamorous, but quiet and self-contained. The kind of authority that does not have to prove its point.

"Oh. Um. Okay. Not sure I'll be of much help, but I'm happy to talk."

His eyes, which sloped down ever-so-slightly at the corners, settled on me.

"Good," he said. "Is there somewhere we could go? In private?"

"Yeah, sure. Of course. We could, uh, we could go to my office."

He smiled again, and I understood on a visceral level how real power is measured: not in words, but in gestures. How power can take the form of magnanimity, politeness rather than brusqueness, calm rather than fury. Whatever authority I had been faking these last few weeks—with Elena, Naseem, Luke—Detective Waters actually had it.

We walked toward my office.

Small buds had begun to appear on the trees. Pinks, magentas, purples. Spring had sprung overnight—and beautifully. Nature's incredible indifference to human tragedy.

"It's just over here," I said, pointing. I wondered if anyone was watching me walk with Detective Waters. He didn't look like a police officer. Not in any obvious way. He wasn't wearing a uniform, just a clean suit, simple and utilitarian. But if you watched him walk for even a second, you knew.

I unlocked my office. Unlike every other office in our department, mine was sparse. No photographs. Nothing to stake any claim, intellectual or otherwise.

I offered him a seat, but he ignored it. Instead, he walked to the bookshelf where the only object of any meaning stood.

It was a brightly colored, miniature statue of an armadillo standing on its hind legs. It was the only thing I'd brought back from the one international trip I'd taken with Phaedra. We had driven along the coast of the Riviera Maya in Mexico, long sandy beaches that stretched across the eastern side of the Yucatán. Moody clouds over an agitated sea. We had already been hired, so our jobs were secure, and we splurged on the trip. What I remembered most were the insignificant details. The sweat-drenched sheets, my wife's small body gripping me in those pre-dawn hours when the rest of the world slept. The two of us, lying on a beach. The sun beating down. The drunken belief that, wherever we were headed, we had already arrived.

"*Alebrije?*" Detective Waters said, pointing at the small statue.

"Impressive," I said. It was an alebrije sculpture, Mexican folkloric art from Oaxaca. I had bought it at the airport on the way home.

"What is it that you teach, Professor Weber?"

"Moral psychology."

He knitted his eyebrows.

"It's a branch of ethics," I said. "I guess you could say I'm interested in how people behave. Not how they think they'll behave, but what they actually do when it comes right down to it." It struck me that those were almost the exact words I'd used with Lucia on the bench that day. It sent a wave of panic through me.

Detective Waters cocked his head, and I wondered if he could read my thoughts.

"Maybe our jobs aren't all that different," he said. "And this girl, Lucia Vanotti"—he was still glancing around my office—"was she in one of your classes?"

It was easy enough for Detective Waters to get a list of Lucia's classes, without flattering Janet from the registrar's. For all I knew, he already had one in his suit pocket.

"No, sir."

"Did you know her—outside of class?"

Again, I shook my head. There was absolutely no point in telling him about that meeting on the bench. I couldn't even be 100% sure it was her. And even if it was, it didn't mean anything—surely, not in any way that mattered.

He took a deep breath, then let it out slowly.

"So, help me figure this out, Professor. You didn't know her. Didn't have any classes with her. Presumably had no relationship with her. And yet, whenever I talk to someone about this case, they say, 'It's like I told that philosophy professor . . .' So, I'm standing here, trying to figure out why every line of questioning leads back to you."

I thought about Lucia's sister, Elena, about Naseem. I thought about Jack.

"So, I'm going to ask you," he said. "Real simple, real straightforward. What is your interest in this case?"

It was a reasonable question. But that didn't mean it had a simple answer. How could I explain the way apathy had seeped into my life, the way it informed all kinds of decisions? How could I explain Phaedra and tenure and my shitty article that would never see the light of day? How could I explain a drowning woman on a beach in California or all the years of silence that had slipped between me and my family or the yawning emptiness that gripped me when I was alone in my apartment? The way days and nights can become indistinguishable when there's no reason to get out of bed? How could I explain that one brief, otherwise unremarkable encounter with Lucia had now become a stand-in for everything that had gone wrong in my life. For every missed call, every missed opportunity. That Lucia felt like an opportunity for redemption, a way back to myself.

None of this could be said out loud. So, I took a different approach.

"I teach ethics, sir. It is my job to reflect on how we live our lives. Whether we embrace our moral selves or shrink from them."

I could feel him studying me. I imagine detectives listen with a different set of ears than the rest of us. One trained on the words we use; the other on the words we don't.

"All I can say is, I saw the poster of Lucia and felt morally compelled to do something. Talk to my students, at the very least. Talk to anyone who was willing to talk."

Detective Waters thrust out his lower lip and nodded. I knew that this paltry explanation would not be enough to cross me off anyone's list of suspicious characters.

"Let me be clear," he said, his warm smile gone. "I don't want to hear from another person that some philosophy professor is going around asking questions. You may mean well, but your presence disrupts things. You scare people. You accidentally tamper with evidence. You end up with information you don't know how to read, and I end up with nothing useful. We got two girls missing. This is no game."

"I understand," I said, duly chastened.

"One last thing," he said.

"Sure."

"You wouldn't be opposed to giving a buccal swab, would you? Just to collect some DNA. It's real simple, painless. A quick swab of the inside of your cheek." He cocked his head. I felt like he was peering into my soul. "You know, just to dot our i's and cross our t's."

"Oh. Of course."

After Detective Waters collected my sample, he moved toward the door. As he opened it, muffled sounds from the hallway spilled in. He looked up at me, a sharpness to his gaze. "Just so we're straight, I won't go trying to do your job, Professor—I'm sure you do it perfectly fine all by yourself. Don't try doing mine."

I nodded. Once he was gone, I picked up the business card he had left on my desk. "Jerome Waters." His phone number underneath.

I don't know where he went after he left my office. If he walked down the hallway, turned right, and knocked on Jack Sheridan's door. Or if he walked back outside into a world full of potential suspects. Maybe he was on the trail; maybe he was chasing shadows. He'd made it clear that it was none of my business.

There was so much I still didn't understand. So much that would later come to light. As it turned out, Lucia's was not a case that Detective Waters could solve.

Only I could.

I just didn't know it yet.

***

I stayed so late in my office that it was evening when I finally opened my door. The hallway was empty, Detective Waters long gone. The only sound, a pair of voices arguing.

A man spoke. A woman replied in terse, one-word answers. I couldn't make out their words, but I recognized the scene. I knew it intimately. The specific tenor of Phaedra's withdrawal. That monstrous way she would fight by going silent. When we were together, I told myself it was the only inheritance she ever took from her mother.

The little information Phaedra revealed about her childhood was dark. The rules she lived under, draconian and arbitrary. She was not allowed to play music because it gave her mother a migraine. The blinds were always drawn because light hurt her mother's eyes.

On Phaedra's back, stretching from scapula to mid-spine, was a patchwork of discolored skin. The first time I saw it, I gasped. Phaedra told me the story in the most hauntingly flat voice I'd ever heard.

Her mother had been carrying a pot of scalding oil when she tripped and spilled it down Phaedra's back. Phaedra was eight years old. Questions ripped through my mind: *Why was she carrying oil? Where was she going with it? Why did she trip?* But Phaedra remembered very little of the event itself, only what came after. Waking up in the hospital, the surgeries and skin grafts. The cream she had to rub onto her flesh for months to minimize the scarring and keep the skin from getting tight.

"Does it hurt?" I asked that first time.

"I don't feel anything," she said.

Now, listening to her fight with Tim, I knew that he had not learned to navigate her moods.

"I'm going home," he huffed. "You let me know when you're ready to talk."

Phaedra said nothing in response, and I listened to his footsteps retreat. I waited another beat before coming around the corner.

When Phaedra saw me, she smiled. Even she could appreciate the cosmic comeuppance of overhearing your ex-wife fight with her new husband.

"How lucky am I?" she said. "To run into you twice in one week."

"Technically, Friday was last week. So, twice in two weeks."

"Best to be precise," she said, nodding.

For a long moment, there was a quietness between us. I like to imagine it was the comfort of an old friend, someone who knows you to your core.

"You headed to the parking lot?" she asked.

"I can if you want me to be."

She slipped her arm through mine, and we walked out into the evening exactly as we were supposed to: arm-in-arm. The sky was a dusky blue, that time of night when objects turn into silhouettes of themselves, when you can't trust your own eyes. The only sound was our shoes on the pavement. When we reached the place where the posters of the two missing girls hung, Phaedra paused.

"It's shocking," she said. "Truly. I cannot think of another word for it."

I knew what she meant. The feeling that we were living in a dream, or a nightmare, where girls disappeared into thin air.

"You know," she said, "Paul Rutger was telling Tim some weird stuff."

"What?"

"I can't really imagine it's true, but apparently, we're on some sex-trafficking route between here and Florida. I don't know. Honestly, it sounded far-fetched."

I immediately thought of the club that Luke Lariat had mentioned.

"Where did Paul hear that?"

"Who knows with Paul," she said. "Could have been from the police or, just as likely, some conspiracy Subreddit. You know how it is with him."

We turned toward the parking garage and started walking again. All this time, her arm still linked in mine. When I glanced down, I noticed she wasn't wearing her wedding ring.

If someone had taken a snapshot of the two of us in that moment and showed it to me on the day I met Phaedra in grad school—if they had said, *See, look here, this is what your future will look like!*—I would have signed on the dotted line so fast, the ink wouldn't have time to dry. Of course, it would have been a misrepresentation. I could walk Phaedra to her car, but not crawl into her bed. I could talk to her about Paul's conspiracy theories, but not curl up on the couch with her.

When we arrived on the second floor of the parking garage, I saw her old, beat-up Mitsubishi and laughed.

"She's still running!" I exclaimed. Phaedra could have upgraded long ago, but she hadn't, and that said something.

"Barely. But yeah. Mine 'til the bitter end."

Her face was lit up under the halide lamp, and I wondered what she would do if I kissed her.

"Can I tell you something?" I asked.

Maybe it was habit. Maybe it was simply to keep her standing there, but I opened my mouth, and all the things I wanted to say came out in a jumble. I told her about Jack and his lie about not knowing Lucia. I told her about the quad, where I saw him grab Michelle Alvarez's arm on the same day she disappeared. I told her about Detective Waters, his admonition to stay away. Phaedra listened without any reaction. It's how she listened when something was important, her stony expression absorbing it all, so you never really knew how she felt. It was only when I told her about the Dionysus that I saw her eyes narrow.

When I finished, she took a long breath.

"I don't know what to say, Neil. That's . . . a lot."

"I know."

She was watching me, unblinking. It dawned on me only after the fact that she might not read things exactly as I had.

"You think I'm crazy," I said.

"No," she said, shaking her head. "I know you're not crazy."

"I'm not making this up, Phae!"

"I don't think you are. But there's a difference between having these—I don't know what to call them—*fragments* of information and making a pretty serious accusation of one of your best friends. It may not add up to anything at all."

"I'm not accusing anyone of anything. All I'm saying is that Jack kept a pretty enormous secret. I mean, shit, Phaedra. He *knew* her."

"Maybe he forgot."

If the tables were turned, Jack would never be so generous with Phaedra.

"There were eleven people in his class. *Eleven*. Would you forget?"

"No," she said. "Of course not. I'm not saying you're making it up, okay? It's just—sometimes you're—"

"—What?"

She looked out at the darkness beyond the parking garage.

"Tell me," I insisted. "Sometimes I'm what?"

"You can get a bit *fixated*, is all." I was glad I hadn't mentioned my encounter with Lucia on the bench.

"Yeah, okay," I said, stepping away from her. "Forget I mentioned it."

"Wait!" She reached out for me. "Hold on. You're taking this the wrong way. I'm sorry. I'm just—I'm tired and this is . . . a lot." She looked me in the eye. "You're a good man, Neil. And I believe you. I do. I just want you to be careful. This is some serious shit here."

When she finally hugged me goodbye, I could smell the sandalwood scent of her perfume. I closed my eyes and breathed it in.

It wasn't until I crawled into bed that night that it struck me. The thing that had been nagging at my brain. It wasn't anything Phaedra had said. It wasn't the doubtful expression she wore when I told her everything. It was that quick, stunned look on her face when I'd mentioned the Dionysus.

CHAPTER 12

LUCIA

Then

More than anything else, Professor Sheridan taught me to think the impossible. In his office, with Kierkegaard open on my lap, he taught me to hold two conflicting beliefs at once. Abraham and Isaac. Abraham believes that Isaac will die, that Isaac *must* die. That he will be sacrificed by Abraham's own hand. And at the same time, Abraham believes that Isaac will be spared. Both simultaneously.

"It is not about understanding," Professor Sheridan said. "Kierkegaard does not try to understand Abraham. He does not attempt to make Abraham intelligible. Only to allow the unintelligibility of Abraham to shine through."

In *Fear and Trembling* Kierkegaard writes: "I cannot understand Abraham, I can only admire him."

I told Professor Sheridan that I had this recurring dream. My parents standing at my gravesite.

"It's not morbid or anything," I said. "It's like that contradictory thing that Kierkegaard says. Like I'm alive and I'm dead, all at the same time."

"Death belongs to life," he said, surveying me with his eyes. "I can tell you're interested in it."

"Isn't everyone?"

He smiled. Then, out of nowhere, said, "When I was in high school three of my best friends died. All at once." He cleared his throat. "So, I know what you mean by recurring dreams." That was all he said about that. He changed the subject right after.

It was through Professor Sheridan that I became attuned to my life in a different way. The small details, the daily tasks I did without thinking. Pouring a glass of orange juice in the morning, filling up Naseem's car with gas, a breeze on my face when I fell asleep on the quad. Fleeting affirmations of existence that were powerful precisely because they demanded nothing of me. Because they were forgettable.

One week, I missed our office hours. My dad needed help at the restaurant. Also, I wanted to see if Professor Sheridan would notice. After our next class, I waited until everyone else had gone, then approached his desk.

I wore a cropped shirt, my midriff at his eye level where he sat. I could feel him intentionally not looking at my body. His wanting combined with his restraint. He looked up and met my eye.

"Missed you in office hours," he said. I saw his Adam's apple bob up and down as he swallowed. Every word felt charged.

On the last day of school, I went to his office to return some of the books he'd lent me. We stood at the bookshelf, and time seemed to stop. I could see his chest rising and falling. I knew if I reached out and touched him, his heart would be racing. My presence seemed both pleasing and frightening.

"Lucia, I—"

But before he could say another word, there was a knock on his door. Another student had come to say goodbye before the summer. Jack stepped away from me like we'd been caught doing something, though we'd done nothing at all.

"Just a minute," he called back. Whatever had transpired a moment earlier seemed to vanish. His voice was professorial and distant. "I meant what I said, Lucia. About you and philosophy. I think you should consider it."

All I wanted was to go back to that moment at the bookshelf because I knew that it would not come again. That the summer would wedge itself between us. Sure, I'd return in the fall, but the momentum would be gone. We'd have to start all over again, sifting our way back through Paul Celan and Kierkegaard and Rilke and everything else.

Professor Sheridan leaned down and gave me a hug. A simple embrace, nothing more. Afterward, I walked out. In the quad, people were lying on the grass. School was over; summer was here. Everyone was celebrating. To me, the sunshine felt like a punch in the gut.

***

A month later, I was at Michelle's house. She'd decided not to go home for the summer and instead had found a job in town with a community organizer. Nothing major, just answering phones and making photocopies. It wasn't a full-blown takedown of the system, but it was a start. It was obvious she was excited. Things were falling into place for her.

That night, we had finished half a bottle of wine. Some cop show was on in the background.

"It's always a girl's body," Michelle said. "You ever notice that?"

"What?" I looked at her. My mind had been wandering.

"I'm just saying, the dead body is always a girl. It's like, people get off on seeing dead girls."

"I want to go to the Dionysus," I said.

"Okay, *non sequitur*."

"I'm serious."

"All right!" she said. "Wait, like, right now?"

***

By 9 p.m., we'd emptied the contents of her closet onto the floor. Michelle and I were big and small in the opposite places. She had boobs, but her ass was a "pancake," as her sister would tease. I was flat-chested but had hips and a butt. None of her clothes fit me right. I settled on a pink dress.

"I look like cotton candy," I said.

"You look hot. Anyway, it doesn't matter what you wear. No one's going to know it's you."

That was one thing Lotus had revealed to Michelle. Masks were mandatory at the Dionysus.

By the time we climbed into the Uber, we had cat-eyes and fake lashes and glitter trails on our cheeks. In the backseat, she opened her hand. In her palm were little tablets.

"Hello, Miss Molly!" she said.

I opened my mouth, and she placed one on my tongue.

The Dionysus, it turned out, was about a million miles away from campus. From the highway, the city disappeared behind us, and an industrial landscape sprouted up. Large, windowless buildings. Warehouses storing God knows what. The kind of place you passed on the way to somewhere else.

From the outside, the Dionysus looked like any other warehouse building. Metal sheeting along the walls, dead shrubs outside. The only difference was, outside this run-down warehouse a line snaked the perimeter.

"Oh, hell no," Michelle said.

The clientele waiting in that line were a mishmash of styles. Louboutins next to Vans. Gold lamé next to ripped jeans. One man wore a dress entirely of black lace, fluorescent green platform shoes, and a matching thong that peeked out underneath. A halo of peacock feathers fanned out above him like a Byzantine crown. The guy next to him wore Adidas and a White Stripes T-shirt. The only thing everyone had in common was anonymity. Every face was disguised by a mask.

A bouncer stood at the door. Behind him was a sign that read: "Come as you were."

My own mask itched. It was part of an old costume Michelle had worn to some party freshman year. It smelled like sweat and beer. The drugs kicked in right when we got to the bouncer.

"IDs, ladies," he said. He was a large man with a bald head and a simple black Zorro mask.

"What's the point of masks if we have to show IDs?" Michelle asked.

The bouncer did not look amused. We handed him our fake IDs. Beyond the entrance, I could hear music. Dim yellow light poured out when someone opened the door. My body was tingling. I wanted to dance and to find Professor Sheridan. The bouncer squinted at our IDs. He rubbed them between his thick fingers, then handed them back to us.

"Sorry, girls, not tonight. Next."

But Michelle didn't budge. "Is this a joke?"

The bouncer didn't even look at her when he said, "Step aside, miss."

"I know Lotus," Michelle said.

No one cared.

All I wanted to do was go home and crawl into bed with Naseem. He was only here for a few more weeks before going home for a month to be with his parents and Zaima. But Michelle was feeling the drugs—she kept running my hand along the spandex of her pants.

"Do you feel that?" she kept saying.

So, we didn't go home; we found another club closer to school. They didn't bat an eyelid when we handed them our fake IDs, which made me apathetic and bored. We still had our masks on.

The club was three stories of dance floors. All around us were jocks, sorority sisters, and other nobodies. People shouted drink orders at bartenders and groped each other on the dance floor.

At one point, a tall girl started dancing with Michelle. In the flashing lights, I could see her long flamingo limbs and plump lips. She looked like a model with coconut skin and dark, short hair. Michelle turned to face her, and the girl wrapped an arm around Michelle's waist, whispered something in her ear.

Then Michelle grabbed my hand and all three of us went to the bathroom.

"Nurit," the girl said, introducing herself.

In the bathroom, I could see how truly stunning she was. She pulled a vile of coke from her bra and offered us each a bump.

Nurit, it turned out, wasn't a student. She was twenty-four years old and worked in a "*financial institution.*"

"What's that supposed to mean?" I asked Michelle later. "Like, if you work in a bank, just say, 'I work in a bank.'"

Michelle said I was just being jealous.

By 3 a.m., we had danced and sweated and snorted so much coke, I could feel my muscles jittering. My mask was long gone. The last I'd seen, some beefy guy was wearing it and spraying champagne into the air.

That night, Nurit came home with us. I crumpled onto the couch, while they tumbled into Michelle's bedroom. I fell asleep to the sound of Michelle's orgasms.

***

The next morning, I felt like death. Every limb ached and my head throbbed something violent. When I looked up, Nurit was sitting cross-legged on the floor. She wore a towel and no underwear. When she saw me steal a glance, she smiled.

I watched her use the edge of a credit card to cut straight lines of powder. "Couldn't find any coffee," she said. "Want some?"

I rubbed my eyes. A fake eyelash came away at the corner and I ripped it off.

"What time is it?" I asked.

Nurit looked around, shrugged.

"No idea. Seven maybe? My phone's dead."

It took a Herculean effort to pull myself up. I was still wearing the pink dress from the night before.

"I'm good," I said. I thought I might vomit.

"Suit yourself."

She bent over and snorted, then rubbed her nostril.

I splurged and called an Uber rather than take the bus back to Naseem's. I let myself in and crept down the hall. When I got to his bedroom, I peeled off my dress and crawled into bed. Naseem opened his eyes lazily and looked at my face and hair.

"Thought you guys were watching *Law and Order* last night," he whispered.

I curled myself into the hollow of his body and fell asleep. He didn't ask me about it again.

CHAPTER 13

NEIL

Now

The same night I walked Phaedra to her car, I fell asleep dreaming of her. I awoke drenched in sweat in the middle of the night and smoked an entire cigarette in six drags. Then, I did what I had been putting off: submitted my shitty article. The essay itself was neither rigorous nor interesting. It was neither vital nor original. But I could feel tenure closing in, and if I didn't submit it soon, it would be too late.

Before going back to bed, I did a quick search for the Dionysus. The results were mostly about fertility and wine, Bacchus, and Ancient Greek tragedy. It took a while before I found anything relevant. When I did, it was a short article from a few months before Lucia disappeared.

A fire had burned the Dionysus to the ground.

The author described the place as a fetish club, nestled alongside storage facilities and distribution centers full of industrial carpet, ceramic tile, and laminate flooring. The club, the author wrote, drew in the city's bored billionaires, disaffected hipsters, and intellectual wannabes. "They went in looking for *Eyes Wide Shut*," he wrote, "but instead, found a fetish club as lackadaisical as the

DMV." The cause of the fire was unknown, but there was an ongoing investigation into arson. One of the club's owners, Leon Schultz, had apparently disappeared with the smoke. There had been no deaths, but a nearby warehouse worker had been admitted to the hospital with third-degree burns.

I closed my eyes and tried to picture the Dionysus burning. But the only image that came up was one from my childhood, back before my dad left. All of us, standing in the backyard around the grill. My father wore an apron that said "Kiss the Cook" across the front.

As usual, my father was talking about one of his conspiracy theories: the Helderberg flying red mercury to South Africa to build a nuclear bomb, Area 51, cattle mutilations.

"I'll tell you what, though," my father said, pointing the spatula at our neighbor, Stu Mills. In his other hand, he held a cigarette, from which ash floated to the grass. "Those cows didn't cut out their own body parts."

"So what?" Stu asked. "You figure UFOs?" I never knew whether Stu Mills believed what my dad said or thought he was a joke.

"Government experiments," my father said matter-of-factly. "That or goddamn aliens."

He flipped a burger. Some of the older kids started tossing a football, and I left to join the game. My aunt tried to push Ethan in from the sidelines when my dad suddenly looked up.

"Don't bother," he shouted from clear across the backyard. "Lost cause." He was referring to Ethan.

Later that night, it was Ethan who shook me awake. The curtains had gone up in flames, then the walls. My mom was already working her shift at the hospital, so she missed the whole thing. No one dared come right out and blame my dad, but everyone assumed he'd been responsible. A cigarette left unattended. A rogue ember from the day. In reality, he probably had nothing to do with the fire, but blame stuck to him like a bad habit. We were only renting the place and didn't stick around for repairs.

The only thing the Dionysus fire could possibly have in common with my own memory was this: the feeling that something important was lost and could never be recovered. Secrets gone up in smoke.

***

On Wednesday, our department hosted its monthly lecture series. The speaker this time was the venerable Tim Janek, Professor of Philosophy; director of the Institute on Cognition, Memory, and Consciousness; joint lecturer in the Department of Neuroscience and the Department of Computer Science; founding member of Quantum Philosophers and the Qualia of Atomic Physics; and most recently, author of "You're Sitting On My Materialism" (*Noûs*, 2017) and "While My Radiator Gently Weeps: The Ethics of Universal Consciousness" (*Journal of Cognitive Science*, 2018).

Also, and most notably, the man who currently shared a bed with my ex-wife.

The lecture hall they had chosen was not the usual small conference room in the philosophy building, but a special one that could seat one hundred twenty-five. By the time I arrived, it was nearly full. Attendees spilled into the aisles and sat on the carpeted stairs, notebooks balanced on their knees. I spotted Phaedra near the front. Paul Rutger sat next to her; a visiting professor from Switzerland sat next to him. Jack Sheridan was nowhere to be found.

Tim Janek stood at the podium, talking to someone in the front row.

I would have preferred a seat with a clear view of Phaedra's face. Their fight still loomed large in my brain, but I was stuck in the back, squished between two grad students who took notes even before Tim started speaking.

A hush fell over the crowd as Tim looked out at the audience and adjusted the microphone. He cleared his throat and began to speak.

"For those of you who are used to hearing me drone on"—a small wave of sycophantic laughter—"you know that no matter what topic I'm discussing, I am, fundamentally, always talking about consciousness. The relationship between this thing we call mind and everything else. Our brains, our bodies, the external world."

I'd already tuned him out. I wasn't interested in hearing Tim Janek talk about consciousness. What I wanted was to watch him, unabashedly. Just to stare in a way I couldn't in regular life. The small things, the minute gestures. The way he moved his hands, which were oddly delicate, almost dainty. *Never trust a man with soft hands*, my father used to say. *He's never worked an honest day in his life*.

Then, unexpectedly, Tim Janek, ever the orator, looked uncomfortable. He took off his glasses, which made his face strange and vulnerable.

"But today," he said, "I want to do something different." A stunned excitement rippled through the audience. You could feel the entire room collectively holding its breath.

"So, let me start with a scene."

I glanced at Phaedra. I couldn't see her face, but I could tell from the position of her head, cocked at an angle, that she had no idea what was coming.

Tim took a breath and continued.

"This scene takes place in a motel. The kind where people stay for extended periods. Everyone coming and going at all hours." Tim waved one delicate hand in the air to demonstrate.

"Inside this motel room was an eight-year-old boy and his two younger siblings. Half-siblings," he corrected himself. "Barricaded in the bathroom was a woman, raging mad. Outside the hotel room, police officers gathered. They banged on the door, rattled the hinges. Later, the boy would wonder why they didn't just ask the motel operator to open it.

"Through a split in the curtains," Tim continued, "the boy could see the policemen. 'Go on and open it, son,' one policeman said. From the bathroom, the woman—the mother—screamed, 'Don't you dare open it, Timothy, or I swear to God, I will kill you.'" Tim shifted at the podium. Not an audience member stirred.

"Of course, the mother would not have killed the boy. That's just how she spoke. But the policeman had a gun at his hip, and the mother only had her screams. So, the boy unlocked the door.

"When the policemen entered, the boy assumed that the children were in trouble because their mother let them stay up all night. Because she let them watch *Dr. Who* until their eyeballs stung. She never made them brush their teeth. She let them skip school if they didn't feel like going or if she didn't feel like driving them.

"That night, they all left the motel—but separately. The mother, paranoid and high, had to go someplace special. The two half-siblings had a father in Chattanooga. He didn't want them, but their grandmother did. So, they were taken away. The boy was the only one who had nowhere to go. No relatives. No father. So, he went somewhere alone.

"First to a lady's house where nothing smelled familiar. Mothballs or mildew, something thick that clogged his nostrils. The sheets on the bed were too stiff, the bedroom too quiet without the television on. He couldn't sleep in that quiet.

"It was the first of eight foster homes the boy would live in over the course of the following ten years." Tim was gripping the corners of the podium. "And I tell you this to give you context. When you move from foster home to foster home, one after another, over and over, the thing you start to feel like, above all, is an *object*. Something handed off. Passed from one place to the next. After a while, you find yourself asking: *What is it, in fact, to be me? To be a body, a mind? To be more than an object?*"

Tim looked out across the room. For once, no pens were moving. No one was taking notes. But every eye was riveted to him. I saw his head turn in Phaedra's direction. He was staring at his wife. Waiting, perhaps, for a look, a nod, a sign of support before he began his formal lecture on consciousness.

In his searching glance, I understood that this opening monologue was an offering. A secret, expressed in a private language for Phaedra and Phaedra alone. The rest of us had simply been witnesses.

Rather than return his gaze, Phaedra looked down. And for the first and only time in my life, I felt sorry for Tim Janek.

***

After the lecture, we all migrated into the hallway, where a table had been set up with a cheap plastic tablecloth and disposable glasses of wine. There was a charcuterie tray from the grocery store with cubed cheese and deli meat, the price tag still on the plastic top next to it.

I downed a glass of red wine in two sips, then picked up another. Across the room, I could see Tim, swarmed by his groupies.

His lecture had been the strangest talk I'd ever attended. Yet the energy in that room had been undeniably raw and charged. *What had transpired exactly?* It was a rare moment, watching a thinker unpack his origin story, rooted not in the tidy realm of reason, but in the messy dealings of life.

Out of the corner of my eye, I glimpsed Phaedra, moving like a shadow. She was not standing with Tim. He was talking to a group of grad students. A pretty brunette stood to his right.

As Phaedra disappeared around the corner toward the bathrooms, I watched Tim watch her go, then lean down, his ear close to the brunette's mouth, as if he were having trouble hearing her. His thin lips broke into a smile, then a laugh. He put his hand on the small of the brunette's back and held it there for a moment before pulling it away. When Phaedra returned, he left the brunette and stood by his wife.

At the time, there were things I didn't understand, things I would eventually learn—like the fact that Phaedra had accused Tim, beforehand, of being separate from his work. "It doesn't keep you up," she had said. "It's just a logic game to you." To Phaedra, there was no greater insult. Tim's lecture had been an answer of sorts—proof of just how personal it was.

Of course, I didn't know that then, as I stood there, downing my third glass of wine, watching them circle each other like sharks.

At the time, there was only one thing I felt with any certainty at all: Tim Janek was having an affair.

CHAPTER 14

LUCIA

Then

In July, Naseem left to visit his parents and sister. He invited me to come. "They'll love you," he said. I tried to picture myself standing by his side at those family parties with the aunties who chased him around when he was a little boy.

"I'll be waiting for you at the airport the second you get back," I said. "I promise."

Naseem left me his car for the month, which should have made me happy, except I felt my world shrinking even before he boarded the plane. Naseem was gone, and Michelle had relocated to the world of Nurit. We would make dinner plans; then she'd call, claiming that she and Nurit had just woken up. Could we reschedule? Or that they had decided, last minute, to drive down the coast for the weekend where they would blow a bunch of Nurit's money—which turned out to be Nurit's dad's money.

Michelle talked about her as if she were a minor celebrity. Nurit had been reared on the club scene in Miami. She was into guys and girls, so long as no one tried to pin her down. She had traveled to San Francisco and to Paris. Once, in high school, a forty-year-old man picked her up in his Aston Martin and she marched across the lawn as her classmates watched.

"You're acting like a jealous lover," Michelle told me one evening when we finally met for dinner. They had been on a three-day bender, and Michelle showed up with a puffy face and dark circles under her eyes.

"I thought you were the proletariat," I said. "She's the fucking bourgeoisie."

Michelle rolled her eyes.

"Don't be so literal." She pushed a french fry around her plate. Her hamburger sat untouched. "Marxism isn't about specific people. It's about structures of power."

"How convenient."

"You know what your problem is, Lucia?"

"What's my problem?"

"You want everyone to be there for you, right when you need them. Me, Naseem, your sister."

"Ohmygod, please—"

"No, let me finish." Her eyes had a cagey, restless look to them. "You know what I think? Honestly? You don't want me to be happy."

"Oh, really. Is that what I want?"

"Yes," she said. "Because it means I might not be there for you right when you snap your fingers." She dragged the fry through a pool of ketchup but didn't eat it. "I'm happy right now."

"Are you? Your face doesn't look happy."

Michelle touched the dark circle under one of her eyes. "I think it's hard for you because, for once, it's got nothing to do with you."

For a long moment we were silent.

"Okay," I finally said. "If you're happy, I'm happy."

"Thank you," she said, but the remainder of dinner felt performative, and I was glad when it ended.

***

The following Saturday night, I went to my closet and slipped on a black dress, sheer nylons, and heels. I brushed my hair, wore it long and straight, parted down the middle. Red lipstick and a plain black mask. No frills, no glitter, no gimmicks.

This time, I went to the Dionysus alone. I cleared the bouncer in ten seconds flat. He barely glanced at my ID, just nodded his large, bald head, and pulled open the door to let me in.

No one in the entire world knew I was there.

Inside, the Dionysus was not what I expected.

When you entered, you walked into a large room with tired yellow walls and faded damask curtains. There were cocktail tables where people sat in groups of two, three, four. At the far end of the bar was a small stage with a single dancer on it. She must have been seventy years old, dressed in a black bra and underwear, her spindly legs moving robotically and arms waving above her head. The expression on her face was boredom. There was a David Lynch vibe to the whole thing. It was impossible to imagine that this was the Dionysus—it was unlike any sex club, rave, or party I'd ever been to.

I took a seat at the bar and ordered a vodka soda. There was a recklessness to it, sitting alone in that room, unsure what would be required of me. For me, recklessness had always felt like power.

I drank my vodka soda and waited.

Every ten minutes, a man wearing a tuxedo, a mask, and an earpiece would emerge from a side door, scan the room, and approach one of the tables. He would extend his hand to one of the guests—sometimes a man, sometimes a woman—who would accept and be led away. The chosen guest always looked giddy, nervous, or downright afraid. Then they would disappear behind that same door through which the man had entered. Meanwhile, new arrivals were let in one-by-one or in pairs. This way, the number of people in the room never changed.

Finally, close to 11 p.m., the man approached me and extended his hand. It was intoxicating to be chosen. I wondered if everyone in the room would be so lucky, or if some would go home having never entered the inner sanctum of the Dionysus. The thought was insane because, while women got in free, men paid an entry fee. The guy in front of me had paid $300, and I could still see him sitting at a table sipping his drink, waiting. As I crossed the room, I felt those familiar stirrings—the way that sex and power and control chased each other until they became indistinguishable. The man with the earpiece opened a door, and we entered a small, dark space.

"Everyone goes alone," he said.

In the darkness, his features were indistinct. But he gave me a small nod of encouragement, and I stepped inside.

It was a tunnel of sorts, and it was pitch black. I groped my way forward, arms extended in front of me. The walls, if you could call them walls, were made of drapey fabric that brushed against my skin.

At the end was a large, dim room, where I was greeted by a woman in lace lingerie, a mask, and an earpiece.

"Welcome to the Dionysus," she said in a silky voice. Then she explained the rules. And there were a lot of them. Phones were off limits, though mine had no signal anyway. Cameras were strictly forbidden. There were towels and sanitizer stations and wipes everywhere. You couldn't touch anyone unless you asked permission. You could masturbate only in designated areas, which seemed to be geared more toward the men.

She showed me an area where I could stow my clothes in exchange for a little coiled bracelet with a key dangling from the end. It looked like a gym locker room, except men and women used the same one. Most were naked, and the lighting was designed to be flattering. They even had flip flops if you didn't want to go barefoot.

Then the woman left me, and I felt this incredible mix of panic and excitement. I didn't disrobe, but made my way to the bar, ordered my obscenely expensive drink, then set out to explore.

The space was huge. It had been sectioned off into different rooms. Some were unremarkable. In one, people were shooting pool and playing foosball, only with their genitalia hanging out. Their bodies were far from perfect. There were all shapes and sizes, some with soft, doughy flesh; others with hard, toned muscles. After a while, the shock of so much nudity wore off. I turned to find a woman standing behind me.

"I love your hair," she said. "Can I touch it?"

Behind her was a man, her husband or boyfriend or whatever. He watched her touch my hair.

"Can I kiss you?" she asked.

She could have been twice my age, or even older. I had no idea. But she seemed like a safe way to enter this space. When she kissed me, the man behind her got aroused.

"Do you want to watch us?" she asked me.

"Watch you?"

She laughed and took my hand. She led me through the Dionysus until we reached a room that had the word "Play" written above the entry. "Sit," she said, and pressed me down onto a settee, while she and the man climbed onto a giant bed, already full of people. For the next few minutes, they fooled around, but she kept her eyes on me the entire time.

After a while, she beckoned me to join them. It was terrifying and exhilarating climbing onto that bed. I joined their lovemaking, feeling both a part of it and an outsider. Hands, bodies, mouths. I could feel the slow, confident movement of the woman's tongue between my legs, the hard press of her hands on my hips. At some point, she moved away, and the man took her place. I watched him slide a condom on as he asked for my consent. When I said it was okay, he lowered himself down, and we began our own rhythmic dance. The whole thing was so strange, so public, it felt like a performance. Like it was me, but not me at the same time. I don't know how long we were there. You lose track of time in the Dionysus. But I do know that when it was all over, we stood and exchanged niceties—*thank you* and *that was fun*—like we'd been doing nothing more than shooting a game of pool or playing darts.

Afterward, we went our separate ways. They headed to the bar, and I set out to continue exploring. Many of the rooms were exactly as I expected. Cages and swings. Restraints and whips. Everywhere, people were watching and being watched. In one room, there was a woman lying on what looked like an examination table, her feet in stirrups.

I continued to wander, moving from room to room, letting myself drift on the current of other people's limbs, touches, smells. Kink and leather, feathers and fetish, lace and latex. Each room seemed to have its own identity based on whatever constellation of bodies happened to be there. Other rooms were shocking. In one, there was a life-sized cross on the wall with restraints for the arms and legs. It looked barbaric, and no one was on it. In another was a swimming pool—an actual swimming pool—with black, bottomless water. I could see shapes floating in it, naked bodies, except for their masks. The room smelled of chlorine, and Dionysus workers scurried about, laying out towels and wiping down lounge chairs.

Amid the grunts and moans, I caught snippets of regular, boring conversation. People talking about the summer, the humidity, vacations they were planning or places they had just visited. I suddenly wished more than anything that Michelle were there. She would've cracked the perfect joke, reduced the whole absurd scene to a single, hilarious punchline. But she wasn't, and I wandered the rooms alone.

I was looking for one person only: Professor Sheridan. But I knew that I would never find him among all those naked bodies. Not there. Not like that. To find Jack Sheridan, I needed to find the girl named Lotus.

And then I saw my chance.

There was a man standing with his back to a door wearing the uniform of the Dionysus. A suit, a mask, and an earpiece. I walked toward him.

"Excuse me," I shouted over the music. I could feel the base drum in the soles of my feet. The man kept his eyes forward, paying no attention to me.

"Excuse me," I repeated, louder this time. "I'm looking for Lotus. Do you know her?" That changed things.

The man broke his faraway gaze and looked down at me.

"You the new girl?" he asked gruffly.

I nodded.

"You're not supposed to come in this way. There's a door for you in back." He glanced at his watch, then shook his head. "C'mon." He pressed his back against the door, and it opened onto a long hallway lit by mauve lights.

I followed the man down a corridor that was lined with doors. Sconces hung on the walls between them. There was a softness to the light, everything cast in red.

"Lotus," the man called out. "Got your new girl here. You gotta tell them to stop coming through the front."

A girl not much taller than me turned.

"I didn't tell her anything," the girl snapped. "She's Gina's contact."

"Well, here she is," he said, pushing me forward.

The man walked away, and I was left standing face-to-face with Lotus. My first real look at her. Later, I would study her face like a map. But that first day, in the dim light, I could see only pale skin, dyed red hair framing dark, distrustful eyes.

"You were supposed to be here an hour ago," she said curtly. "Let's go."

I followed her down the hall. But all I kept thinking was: *Has Jack Sheridan been inside of you?*

"Did Gina fill you in already?" she asked.

I shook my head. I had no idea who Gina was, though it seemed important to pretend I did.

"Of course not!" Lotus said, as if that were exactly what one could expect from Gina. She huffed. "Ground rules: No real names. Not yours, not theirs. Not ever. We collect payment, you don't." She was ticking off each rule on her fingers. "There's a panic button on the wall. Don't use it. Not unless you're unconscious in a pool of your own blood—"

"If I'm unconscious, how do I press it?"

"Exactly. You don't." She looked at me, seemed to consider me for a moment. We were standing in front of a door. "They don't always know what they want. It's your job to figure it out."

Then, without warning, she opened the door, pushed me inside, and closed it behind me.

The lights were on, and the sudden brightness was piercing. I looked around. There was a chair, a shower, a bed with restraints, and an overweight man dressed in a button-down and khakis. His mask barely covered his round face.

I immediately dimmed the lights. It seemed easier that way.

"I'm Randy," the man said, which seemed an odd name to choose, if you could choose any name for yourself.

"Salomé," I said. It was the first one that popped in my head.

"You foreign?" he asked.

"Yeah. Greek." Close enough to Italy.

I wondered why someone would pay extra to come back here, when there was a full-fledged sex club on the other side of the door. There must have been something erotic about paying for it. The exchange of money that turns sex into a transaction.

Yet it quickly became clear that Randy was not interested in sex. His request was specific. He wanted me to watch him strip. Then, he wanted to sit himself on the edge of the bed with his hands behind his back, palms facing upwards. My job was to climb up there and stand on his open palms.

"With my shoes?"

He nodded, then began to undress. I kept my eyes on him. It felt important not to flinch when he bared his round, hard belly; when he slid off his pants and stepped out of his briefs. He sat on the bed, palms open, and I climbed on. I eased my shoes onto his upturned hands.

"Dig them in," he said.

"My heels?"

"Yeah. Harder." I ground my foot into his flesh. In the half light, I saw wiry hairs jutting out of his shoulders. The doughy meat of his back. Under my shoe, I could feel all the little bones in his hand. He cried out in pain, and I pressed harder.

For the next forty minutes, we worked through different variations of my feet on his hands. First with shoes. Then in my stockings.

His breath came fast when he felt the slip of my nylons along his palms.

"Would you mind taking them off?" he asked. "The stockings?"

I slid them down. Then I placed one naked foot in each of his hands, his fat fingers curling up around the edges of my feet. As I opened my toes and mashed them into his fingers, he bent forward and started sobbing. I jumped off.

"You all right, Randy?"

He stopped crying, and in a perfectly flat voice said, "Can you get back on?"

There was a certain camaraderie in the scene we were creating.

"Smell them," I said, and lifted one foot to the middle of his back. I pressed it against his shoulder blades, a row of small pimples beneath the ball of my foot. I lifted it higher until it rested on his shoulder.

He turned his head, so his nose was directly against my skin.

"They're dirty," I said.

"Please, no."

"They're disgusting. You don't even want to know where they've been. Lick them." I had no plan. I was improvising. He licked my foot and got hard.

Over the course of our time together, Randy told me he was a customer service representative. He hated his job. Every second of it. He complained that everyone walked all over him, which struck me as odd given what he was literally paying me to do. When our time was up, I pulled on my stockings and slipped on my shoes. He was my one and only date of the night.

It earned me $250.

***

The following Saturday, I entered through the back door right into that converted hallway with all the bedrooms. The moment I stepped inside, I looked up to see Lotus storming toward me.

"You lying bitch," she growled. "You sure as shit don't know Gina. So, who do you know?" I thought she might actually strike me.

"Michelle," I said, as if her name might protect me.

"Michelle? Who's Michelle?"

"Alvarez. Jasmin's sister."

I watched her register this.

"Oh, hell no." she said. "No, no, no, no, no. No way." She looked at me. "How old are you? No, don't tell me. I don't want to know."

"Old enough to be here," I said. Though I wasn't sure that was technically true. I was over eighteen, yet not old enough to enter a bar. But prostitution was illegal anyway, so what did it matter?

"You need to leave. Now. If Leon finds out, I swear to God—"

Despite her mask, I could tell that Lotus was exceptionally pretty.

"All I want is one night with Jack Sheridan, then I'm gone."

Lotus flew at me, slamming me back against the wall, her finger shoved in my face.

"Don't you ever say that name or any name. No real names! You understand?"

I nodded.

"Not ever."

There was no one else in the hallway.

"Just one session and I'll leave."

"You'll leave now."

"One session, or I'll tell Leon."

The words came out of my mouth before I had a chance to fully consider them. I had no idea who Leon was, but it was obvious that he exercised power over her.

"Are you threatening me?" she said.

"I'm not trying to get anyone in trouble."

"Trouble?" Lotus laughed. "You don't know trouble. That guy, Leon, the one you're going to tell—yeah, I watched him beat a man half to death with his bare hands. You know why? The guy spat on the sidewalk, and it landed near his shoe. Not *on* his shoe, *near* his shoe."

"I just want one session. Then I'll disappear."

She shook her head. Then said, "Anyway, the person you want—he's not even here. He doesn't come on weekends."

"When does he come?"

A door opened at the far end of the hallway and a man came walking toward us. A customer. Lotus straightened and smiled. The man nodded at her, then ducked into a room. In his wake, something changed. Maybe it was resignation, or weariness, or just a deeper sense of futility. Whatever it was, Lotus's tone changed.

"Wednesdays," she said. "If he comes at all, he comes on Wednesdays. But I haven't seen him in a long—"

"Okay, Wednesday."

"Not for months," she said.

I had no idea how the logistics of the Dionysus operated. How clients communicated with Lotus. How they booked their sessions. How they paid. All I knew was that she was the gatekeeper.

"All right," I said, moving toward the door. "I'll see you on Wednesday."

"No chance."

"One session," I said, hoping to exude confidence. "If the *person* I'm looking for is here, I get one session." She started to say something, but I cut her off. "If he's not here, I go home, and you never see me again."

"No."

"Then I'll go to the cops. I'll tell them your name and Leon's name. I'll tell them about this back hallway. What you do back here. That you sold an underage girl to a paying customer."

I watched her nostrils flare, and I braced for the attack. But it didn't come. Instead, Lotus shook her head.

"Fine," she said, a weariness to her voice. "It's your funeral."

CHAPTER 15

NEIL

Now

On the day they found Lucia's body, the temperature spiked thirteen degrees. The night before, it had been pouring rain. The morning brought with it a sweltering heat, like summer had come early and vengeful.

Twenty-six days.

That's how long Lucia had been missing. Twenty-six days, lying there in those woods. Not a mile from the road. It seemed impossible to me that she had been out there all that time, so close and yet unreachable. No one knew anything for certain, but rumor was, she'd been found strangled and partially clothed.

When the news of her death reached me, I ran to the bathroom and vomited.

The mood on campus that Thursday was somber. Paul Rutger told me there had been discussion among administrators about canceling classes, but ultimately, it was decided that routine was better than free fall. Students needed a place to go. In class, we mostly just sat in stunned silence.

Afterward, I went in search of Jack. He wasn't in his office or the dining hall. I tried his cell, but there was no answer. I thought about calling Phaedra but didn't.

Paul sent out an email to the department. In light of everything, there was to be a meeting at the Red Baron. Tenured professors, associates, adjuncts, lecturers, administrative assistants, and grad students were asked to attend.

***

The Red Baron was a colonial-style building with white columns. Christmas lights hung from the eaves, though it was long past Christmas. A wide porch held rocking chairs and side tables. Back in the 1800s, the building was a servants' quarters. Now it hosted most of our department's events. Annual Christmas parties, awards ceremonies, conference dinners. The walls needed painting, and the carpet was threadbare, but it wore its shabbiness like an antebellum badge of pride.

By 5 p.m., the faculty of the department had filtered in. Chairs had been placed in rows, and a podium stood lonely at the front. Everyone looked ragged and shell shocked as Paul made his way forward.

"I'm not sure how to begin," he said into a microphone, which seemed unnecessary. "Can y'all hear me?" Heads nodded. Then he pushed the mic aside and took off his glasses. He looked small and unprepared.

"What we've learned today chills me to the bone," he began. "Not just the death of a student, which is always painful, but a death so gruesome and terrifying, it destroys language." He put his glasses back on. "In the coming days and weeks, your students may find themselves distracted. Or frightened. *You* may find yourself distracted or frightened. There is no handbook for this."

Phaedra sat two rows in front of me. Tim Janek sat beside her. I could see him staring out the window. I spotted Jack standing in the back near the door, his face ashen.

"As someone with children—and grandchildren," Paul continued, "I feel particularly shaken by the events of the last few weeks. One young girl is deceased; another is still missing." These were facts we all knew, yet to hear Paul say them out loud made them solid. "I expect to see a heavy police presence on campus. I *hope* there is, for the girls' sake—and for ours.

"Should the police try to speak with you, please do your best to comply. Should you need to take personal days, I encourage you to do so." He steadied himself. "I also hope you'll think of your students, who may need you in ways you do not fully realize. For many of them, you are their primary connection to the adult world. Their parents are not here. There are counselors on hand, of course, but students may not avail themselves. Instead, they will turn to each other—and to you."

Paul said that there would be a candlelight vigil for Lucia later that evening. He would be in attendance with his wife, and he hoped we would be there, too.

When he finished speaking, we stood. Unsure what to do with ourselves, we lingered around the seats, whispering questions no one was able to answer. *Who had found her? Was she . . . ?* No one said the word "raped," but it was implied by its omission.

I was exhausted by the chatter and felt an irrational sense of ownership over my investigation of Lucia. To mute the noise, I stepped outside to smoke.

Three wooden benches formed a semi-circle on the back patio. Usually at the Red Baron, there were at least four or five of us smoking out there. Me and a handful of grad students. Today, there was only me.

I sat down, pulled a cigarette from the pack, and let it rest between my lips for a long time before lighting it. I couldn't stop thinking of Lucia's face on those posters. How alive she looked.

"Mind if I bum one?"

I looked up.

Tim Janek was standing in front of me. I extended him the pack, and he sat down.

"The other day, I came across this magazine article," he said, gazing off into the woods beyond the Red Baron. "Some piece on urban agriculture, and it talked about all this kudzu out here." Tim gestured toward the trees. "Apparently, it was all planted by the Civilian Conservation Corps during those terrible droughts in the 30s. No water for miles." He took another drag, a pinprick of orange in the waning light. "And you had all these Southern farmers worried about soil erosion. So, what'd they do? Plant a bunch of kudzu as ground cover." In the sky, a neon sunset was taking hold. Tim leaned back, resting his elbow on the arm of the bench. "It just goes to show, you think you know a thing. All that James Dickey stuff. Kudzu, 'the vine that swallowed the South.' When, in fact, they planted it themselves. Right here."

I looked at him with bewilderment. I wondered if he had been thinking about kudzu the entire time Paul talked about Lucia.

"I don't know about all that," I said, stubbing out my cigarette. "However it began, it seems pretty invasive now."

He nodded and tapped ash on the ground.

Behind us was a large window, and inside, I could see my colleagues moving around the bright room. If you didn't know better, you might mistake it for a festive occasion. Jack was nowhere to be found. At the far end, near the bar, I spotted Phaedra. She was the only person not engaged in conversation. She was standing by herself, staring at me.

Tim stubbed out his cigarette after only a few drags, then slapped his hands on his thighs and pushed himself up. "Thanks for the smoke, Neil," he said and ducked back inside. I watched him cross the room to his wife, wrap an arm around her shoulder, and guide her toward the door. But for just one moment before they stepped out into the night, Phaedra turned back and caught my eye.

***

That evening, a crowd gathered outside the Economics Department. How many of them were Lucia's friends? How many, like me, knew her only as an idea? How many had come simply because tragedy exerts its own seduction?

Near the center of the group, I saw Naseem Bashir. Next to him, looking more like Lucia than ever, was her sister, Elena. If her parents were there, I didn't see them. I tried not to think about what that house must feel like right now. Their worst fears realized.

Soon, candles were passed around and lit. The group made its slow procession across campus toward the main quad. When it came time for speeches, there were only two I cared to hear: Naseem's and Elena's. But neither of them spoke. Instead, they stood silently, their faces made strange by the flickering candle flame.

CHAPTER 16

LUCIA

Then

On Wednesday, I went back to the Dionysus.

"Forget it. I changed my mind," Lotus said when she saw me.

"That's not fair," I said.

"Fuck fair. You're in the wrong profession for fair."

"I'll go to the cops."

"No, you won't."

Honestly, if she'd pushed just a little harder, I would have left right then. But in that split second, she looked back over her shoulder, and I knew.

"He's here, isn't he?" I meant Professor Sheridan, but she leaned in close.

"You want to know who's here?" she whispered. "Leon is here. You're so tough, why don't you go talk to him? Let's see how that goes."

She was daring me, calling my bluff. It's true, the fact that I'd slipped in through the cracks showed weaknesses in the system. She would likely be punished for that. But she seemed willing to take the risk.

"You need to go. Now—" she said. But before she finished, Leon appeared in the hall. I could tell it was him by the way her entire body went rigid.

Leon was a heavy-set man in a suit who reminded me of the men that sometimes came into my father's restaurant. When they were there, my father shooed Elena and me into the back. He waited on the men himself, all smiles and nods.

It took less than a moment for Leon to reach us.

"This the new girl?" he asked, nodding at me. His voice was gravelly. He was the only person there not wearing a mask. He reached out and took my chin in his hand, moved it this way and that.

"What's your name, doll face?"

"Salomé." I tried to hold his gaze.

"Turn around, Salomé."

I turned, slowly. I could feel him surveying me. He ran a hand along my spine, from my shoulders to my waist, left it perched at the small of my back.

"You have scoliosis," he said. I looked back at him over my shoulder. "You'll see my chiropractor. He's the best." Leon sucked in his breath and turned to Lotus. "Who's our little Salomé with tonight?"

"Well—I wasn't sure. I was thinking about waiting another night before I put her on the floor. Just until she's ready."

"She's ready." He was talking to Lotus but looking at me.

"Most of the girls are already assigned." She was making things worse.

Leon ran a fat hand across his mouth.

"How about Rob Terrell?" he asked.

Lotus shook her head. "I don't think she's ready. I was going to put Gina in with him."

"I can wait," I interjected. I didn't want to go with Rob Terrell. I wanted to go with Jack Sheridan.

Leon eyed us both.

"What is going on here? Are we running a daycare? Put her the fuck in with Rob Terrell."

Lotus nodded obediently, then seized me by the arm and pulled me down the hallway.

We stopped outside a door, and she turned to me, eyes blazing.

"All right, you little bitch. You wanted it, you got it," she hissed.

It took me a moment to understand what she meant.

"Rob Terrell. It's him," I whispered.

"If you fuck this up—if he recognizes a single hair on your head—I will kill you myself."

"I won't. I promise."

Lotus's face suddenly broke into a smile. An actress, transforming into character. She smoothed my hair. "Let's make someone happy, shall we?" And I stepped inside.

***

Later, I would think about the words that hung over the entrance of the Dionysus. *Come as you were.* The Dionysus, with its dark tunnels and tight passages, was like moving through a birth canal. Only backward. A return to something warm and immersive. The club was designed to satisfy your private desires, your strangeness. I tried to imagine what a *return* would mean for me. To go back to the time before cheating on Naseem. Before I began cutting myself. Before my father's friend Giancarlo ever set foot in our house. Only, right at that moment, sitting on that bed waiting for Jack Sheridan to arrive, I had no desire to go back. There was nowhere else I wanted to be.

I knew I would do whatever he wanted. Nothing would be off limits. The only aspect of the experience I needed to control were the lights. I shut them off and waited.

When the door finally opened, I could see a figure backlit by the red hallway. More than anything, I wanted to turn the lights back on and see his face. Let him see me. But I didn't. I rose and went to him. I took his hand and led him away from the door toward the bed.

"It's dark," he said.

"Do you mind it?"

There were, of course, countless details to worry over—that he might recognize my voice, my hair, the scar on my arm. But all those particulars seemed incidental compared to the enormity of this moment. We sat on the edge of the bed.

"I want to see you." He reached for my hair. "I want to look at you."

But I didn't get up to turn on the lights. Instead, I guided his hands across my face and neck. The topography of my breasts, the smooth plank of my waist, then lower. I brought his hand to the inside of my thigh.

"What do you want?" I whispered.

He didn't answer, just held himself very still.

Jack let me push him back onto the bed, and I began to undress him. I wanted time to stretch out. I wanted every moment to last an eternity. But I was moving so fast, afraid that it would all be taken away at any moment.

Jack's skin tasted of salt. His mouth, like the memory of something long forgotten. I felt the muscles of his stomach tense as I ran my hands across them. Everything unfolded as if it were a dream. An event I had been waiting for my entire life, so when it happened, it felt inevitable, as if every moment had always only been leading here, to this, to Jack Sheridan lying beneath me.

Afterward, we lay on that bed, breathing hard and trembling.

He traced the outline of my breasts with his finger.

"Salomé, the dancer," he said languidly. "Is that why you chose it?"

"Are we breaking the fourth wall?" I asked.

I couldn't see his face, but I could sense him smiling.

"You don't have to answer," he said.

"I will if you will. Why'd you choose Rob Terrell?" But Jack became silent, and I sensed I'd overstepped. "Sorry," I said, hoping to backpedal. "I shouldn't have asked you that."

"No, it's fine," he said. "I'm the one who brought it up."

In the dark, Jack's voice sounded different. Physically closer, but also more distant. For a long time, we lay there, engulfed in that quiet.

Then he began to speak:

"Robert Terrell was a friend of mine. A long time ago." Jack paused, and I could feel a heaviness in his voice. "I remember, he, uh, he had all these comic books. Not the popular ones that everyone had. Obscure stuff. Japanese comics, Ultraman, stuff like that. His brother was living in Kyoto, always sending him things. Rob took those damn comic books everywhere."

I reached out and let my hand rest on his arm, but I didn't say a word.

"We were in high school," Jack continued. "It was spring break. I remember because it was freezing and raining, and we were pissed off about it, 'cause, you know, it was our vacation." It was clear right then that Jack was not talking to me. He was speaking to the darkness. To himself. It felt important to stay quiet.

"We'd all piled into Jimmy Chaplain's car—an old '75 Buick Skyhawk." He turned to face me. "I don't know how old you are. You probably don't remember those, but it was a beauty of a car. Cherry red. Two doors. Only suckers sit in back." He cleared his throat. "That's what I used to say. *Only suckers sit in back.* Nate and Rob, they were the suckers. Me and Jimmy up front. Me in the driver's seat, even though it was Jimmy's car." I moved my hand to his chest and left it there. "It was raining hard. I was driving, and uh, you know . . . Well, anyway, I don't remember much of it. Of the actual event, I mean. They said we hit a puddle and started hydroplaning. Next thing I know, we're flipped upside down. Our shit tossed all over the road. Those comic books, scattered across the highway, just flapping in the rain."

Jack took a ragged breath.

"You don't have to talk about this if you don't want," I said.

"They said, uh—" He swallowed hard. "They said Jimmy and Nate died instantly." For a full minute, he said nothing. "It took a long time for Rob. I was tangled in my seat belt. I couldn't get it open, you know? But I could see him, flung out of the car. I don't even know how. He was just lying there in the rain. Not that I could have done anything. My leg was shattered. You can still feel the scars." He grabbed my hand, ran it along his leg. I couldn't feel anything, but I didn't tell him that.

"Even now, thirty years later or whatever, I just hear it, you know? Like it's still in my mind. The sound of Rob, struggling to get air. His lungs filling with blood. But it's just—this sound, like sucking through a straw, just trying to get a breath."

Jack must have become aware of himself, of what he was divulging to a stranger. "I'm sorry. I can't believe I'm telling you this. I don't even know how we got on this subject."

I wanted to tell him it was okay. That he could say anything he wanted. That nothing was off limits. But instead of using my words, I climbed back on top of him.

This time, the experience was different.

Jack took control. He flipped me on my back, his weight pressing down on me. He leaned forward and brought his hands to my throat. For a second, I felt a flash of terror as he closed his fingers around my neck and began to squeeze.

Harder and harder he pressed, tightening his grip until my eyes hurt from the pressure. I flinched and clawed at his hands.

Instantly, he released me.

"Am I scaring you?" he asked. "Oh, God, I'm so sorry. I just—I assumed that you knew. I thought Lotus told you—"

So that was it.

That was what Jack came to the Dionysus to do. Some men wanted you to stand on their hands, dig your feet into the flesh of their palms. Others wanted to reenact their most painful memories by gripping your throat.

"It's okay. It's fine," I said, still clutching my neck. "I just—I didn't know. No one told me."

I had killed the mood.

"I'm sorry," Jack repeated, as he climbed off me.

"No, Rob," I said, which felt strange, now that I knew the story. "I want you to do it. I do."

I took a breath and guided his hand back to my neck. In a way, I suppose, I did want it. For his sake. I wanted to be exactly what he wanted. What he needed. If this would help him drown out the memory of a boy dying on the side of the road, then I could do this.

"Please," I said.

Finally, he let me guide his fingers back to my neck. I pressed them down tight until he took over, clamping down hard. This time, the pain was slow, building until I could feel him crushing my esophagus. I imagined my windpipe, all the small bones in my neck, my spine where it ran upward into my skull. My life in Jack's grip. My neck: the place where Jack's pain got written onto me, where he deposited his memories, where they became one with my own. And that's what I wanted. For his hurt to become mine. For his story to be written on my body. And maybe, in exchange, he could hold mine. What one man took from me, perhaps Jack could restore. Not physically, but in a way that made living possible.

Only, the body's struggle for breath is so acute, so automatic, it resists. How do you willingly court death? Jack thrust himself inside of me as his fingers squeezed out my life-force.

He released his fingers the moment he came, and all the blood came rushing back. Jack collapsed on top of me. Then, he slid to the side and let his fingertips amble along my skin. Across my collarbone, to my shoulder, and down my arm until he was touching my scar. He had found the wound that I had branded into my skin. The place where my own pain lived. It was there that his fingers stopped.

In that instant, it all became clear. Jack knew it was me. He had to. His fingers rested on my arm and didn't move.

"You didn't tell me why," he whispered.

"Why what?"

"Why Salomé. Are you a dancer?"

This was it. He was asking. More than asking, he was stating, in no uncertain terms, that he knew. *I see you, Lucia*, he said without saying. *I see you.*

"I'm not a dancer," I said. "It's for Lou Salomé." Rilke's lover, Nietzsche's obsession, Freud's intellectual heir. I let her name sink in.

Next to me, Jack went still. So still, he seemed not to breathe. He said nothing, and the room became suddenly cold.

"You all right?" I asked, reaching out a hand. "Jack?" I said, accidentally using his real name. "Are you okay?" And there it was. This irrevocable thing that couldn't be taken back.

CHAPTER 17

NEIL

Now

Detective Waters was a figure in beige lumbering up my driveway.

It was Saturday, over a week since Lucia's body had been found, and I was leaning out the window, smoking a cigarette. When I saw him, I ducked inside.

A quick glance around my apartment told me I needed to get out before he got in. Two posters of Lucia still hung on the wall, one with the word WHORE written on it. I grabbed my keys.

I was nearly at my car when the detective approached.

"Professor Weber," he called. "I was just coming to see you."

I feigned surprise.

"I was just leaving."

"So, I see. Where to?"

"The office," I lied. "I have tenure coming up." As if that explained everything.

He surveyed me.

"No books? No bag?"

"I keep everything there."

He'd been in my office. He'd seen those barren shelves.

"I was actually hoping to have a word with you."

"Here?"

He looked around. I could see the general decrepitude through his eyes. The splintered asphalt, the peeling paint, the ramshackle look of the place. Only the dogwood trees with their bright white blossoms lent it any beauty. And they'd lose their flowers soon.

"I was thinking, my office might be more conducive," he said.

"The police station?"

He raised his eyebrows. "It's where I work. Unless you've got a problem with coming down there."

Sure as fuck I had a problem with going down there.

"Not at all." I was suddenly very aware of my hands, which felt awkward and cumbersome. "It's just that I've got all this work—"

"It won't take long. But it'll be easier if we talk there."

"Well, I—"

"I'll tell you what. Why don't I give you a lift, then I can drop you back off here." He cocked his head.

"I can drive," I said. I had just gotten my car back from the repair shop and felt a wave of relief that Detective Waters didn't see it after I'd run it into the ditch.

"Suit yourself," he said, shrugging. "But I find it's sometimes easier to talk in the car. Keep it casual, you know?" He flashed a smile. He had the straightest teeth I'd ever seen. Million-dollar smile.

***

We drove through the city in his car. Above us, heavy clouds threatened rain but didn't break. The farther we got from my apartment, the more acute my sense of dread became.

Out the window, you could see the colors on the trees. Eastern redbuds with their electric pinks, azaleas, and Japanese maples. The world, regenerating itself.

Detective Waters caught me looking.

"Pretty, aren't they?" he said. "I don't care what anybody says, nothing like springtime in the South."

I nodded noncommittally.

"Where you from, Professor?" he asked.

"Midwest," I said. "Indiana."

"Yeah? What kind of trees you got out there?"

It suddenly seemed very difficult to picture my hometown. Certainly, there had been trees. Loads of them, but they all blurred in my memory. The landscaping of every house and apartment we'd lived in during those years.

"I don't remember," I said. "But in New Jersey, where I went to grad school, I remember we had this jacaranda tree outside our apartment. It would drop purple flowers all over the ground in the early summer." In my mind, I could see Phaedra standing on a carpet of violet.

"Who's *we*?"

"Oh. Me and my wife. My ex-wife," I corrected myself.

He nodded.

"What about you?" I asked. "Where you from?"

"Houston," he said. I nodded. But he wasn't done. "Then Augusta. Shreveport. New Orleans for a stint. Up to Joliet, then back down south." He glanced at me. "And that was before high school."

"Wow. Sounds like lots of trees."

Detective Waters laughed. A big, bellowing laugh.

"How long you been here?" he asked.

The city *whooshed* by as we got onto the highway.

"Six years this summer."

"You remarried?" he asked.

I looked at him sharply.

"I'm not interrogating you, Professor. Just making conversation."

I looked out the window again.

"No," I said. "I'm not remarried."

***

The police department was a stout brick building with various flags outside. Detective Waters led me through a back door and up to the second floor, where his office was. He got us both a cup of coffee, then showed me into a room. It was bare except for a table and some chairs.

After a moment, the door opened, and another man walked in.

"Professor Neil Weber, this is Detective Liu." The other detective had a stack of papers under one arm. He dropped them on the table before sitting down. Suddenly, everything felt very formal.

"Before we begin," Detective Waters said, "I just want to make it clear that you're not under arrest. You're free to leave at any time. The door is unlocked. We're just having a simple conversation that you can choose to end at any point."

It felt alarming to hear him say it because I hadn't for one second considered that I might be under arrest.

"So, let's just take this real slow," Detective Waters said.

"Take what real slow?" I didn't like the direction this was going, and we hadn't even started.

"Did you know Lucia Vanotti?"

Gone was his friendly laughter, his sparkling teeth.

I shook my head. "I told you, I didn't know her. What's this about? You asked me not to talk to anyone else about the case, and I haven't. Why am I here? I haven't done anything wrong."

"Not saying you did," he said calmly. "You worried about that?"

"I'm not worried about anything. Except the fact that I'm sitting in a police station being asked about a dead—about a deceased girl."

"We're just trying to cover our bases," Detective Liu said. He was clearly the backup. The number two. Detective Waters was running this show.

"Listen, Mr. Weber. Neil. You're not the first person we've brought in here and you won't be the last. Our job is to talk to everyone. Cast as wide a net as possible. So, let me ask you again, how did you know Lucia Vanotti?"

"I didn't know her." It seemed more important than ever not to mention our exchange on the bench.

He nodded, flipped through the papers that Detective Liu had brought in.

"All right," he said. "What were you doing on the night of Friday, March 15?"

I gave them a look of confusion.

"How should I know? That was over a month ago. Am I a suspect?"

"Should you be?"

"No, of course not!" This was a mind fuck of the first degree, and I felt poorly prepared to handle it.

"And you have no idea where you were?"

I reached for my coffee and saw my own hand shaking. I pulled it back.

"Um . . . I don't know. I was probably home. Cooking dinner."

He made a note in a small pad. Nodded, smiled.

"Any idea what you made?"

I scoffed. "Do you remember what you made for dinner a month ago, Detective?" He was clearly not amused. "No idea," I said, throwing my hands in the air. "Cereal? Toast?"

"Not much of a dinner man, eh? Me, personally, I can't go without a proper dinner. Meat, starch, vegetables. Gotta have all three."

"Honestly, I don't know. It was an unremarkable day."

"Fair enough. So, you're home." He lifted his eyes: "Alone, I presume—?"

"Yes, alone."

Detective Liu watched me, like his presence was meant to be a quiet reminder of how serious shit was.

"I don't even remember the night. Every night is the same for me." I exhaled. "Just because I eat cereal for dinner and don't have someone sleeping over doesn't make me a suspect."

"No," he said. "It doesn't. I'm just trying to understand why a professor who's never even met the victim is running his own investigation."

"I told you last time. It didn't seem like anyone else was doing anything. I just wanted to help."

"Right!" he said. "The ethicist."

Coming out of his mouth, it sounded lecherous. Then he paused for a long time, like he was thinking things over.

"You're a smoker, aren't you, Professor Weber?"

"Yeah. Why?" There was no sense in denying it. Every article of clothing I owned reeked of it. My fingers, my breath, my teeth, all of it gave me away.

"See, there's this one piece that I can't quite figure out. Even if everything you say is true."

He looked at me studiously.

"What I still can't understand is what your cigarette was doing next to the victim's body?"

The utterance was so unexpected, so colossal, that I slumped back in my chair, unable to speak. He let me sit like that for a long time, then out of nowhere, he produced a plastic bag. There was a large white evidence label on the front. I couldn't see what was inside. It could have been filled with anything. It could have been filled with nothing. But the implication was clear. It was a cigarette butt, and it belonged to me. He set it on the table between us.

I stared at it, as if it might detonate and kill us all.

"What's that?"

"Your cigarette."

"That could be anyone's," I said.

"True." Detective Waters nodded. "But in this case, it's yours."

"How can you know that?"

I was no detective, but I knew that you needed fingerprints to make a match. I'd never been arrested. Never so much as received a speeding ticket, despite the numerous times I'd driven drunk clear across town. I looked down at the coffee cup that Detective Waters had given me. True, my prints were all over it. But unless they were able to run forensic tests while I sat there in front of them, there was no way this coffee cup could implicate me.

Detective Waters seemed to read my mind.

"Your buccal swab," he said. "The one I collected in your office." He let that percolate for a moment. "After the deceased was found, we went back to comb the area to pick up anything we'd missed. And we find this cigarette butt lying right there next to the place where the body had been. So, we ran it through CODIS. Lo and behold, we got a hit." He was leaning forward. I felt my stomach turn. "It matched the DNA profile of this professor . . . who works at the very same university that the victim attended. Imagine that. A professor, who I'd actually had the pleasure of meeting because he was running his own investigation into her disappearance." I had to hand it to him: the man's delivery was impeccable. Damning and terrifying. "So, let me ask you *one last time*. How did you know Lucia Vanotti?"

I was too stunned to talk. I could feel my heart running riot in my chest. He waited. He was prepared to draw this out.

I raised my hands, as if their emptiness proved something. I racked my brain. Then, slowly, a night came back into focus. The bar with Jack. The waitress, Tara. Ordering a bottle of tequila. The girls next to us. My attempt at driving home. The car crashing into the embankment, then me walking along the shoulder of the woods—the same woods where Lucia had been found. Flicking cigarettes into the trees. It was ludicrous as far as explanations went. It was more than improbable; it was downright impossible, but I explained it anyway.

Detective Waters listened to me with his mouth in a tight line. When I finished, he said, "So, let me see if I have this straight. You flick a cigarette from the road—"

"More like the shoulder—"

"You flick a cigarette from the shoulder of the road into the trees." I was nodding. "And that cigarette migrates, what, a good mile? From the edge of those woods to where her body was recovered."

"There were lots of cigarettes. I probably smoked ten or fifteen along the way."

He narrowed his eyes, cocked his head to the side, like I was crazy.

"Look, I'm not saying this makes sense," I stammered. "I don't think it makes sense either. But I swear to God, I swear, I did not know her."

For one dark and terrible moment, I thought about Jack. About all the things I did know. All the things I could say right then. I could offer up an equally plausible—*more* plausible—suspect. I'd like to say that it was a deeper sense of loyalty that held me back. But it wasn't. Not one bit. I kept quiet only out of fear that naming another suspect made me look *more* guilty, not less.

In that moment, one thought became crystal clear.

"Can I make a phone call?" I asked.

It was the first time all day that Detective Waters looked caught off guard.

"You're not under arrest, Mr. Weber," he said. "We're just chatting here."

"So, can I?"

"No one's stopping you," he said. "But you should know that no one else we've brought in has asked to make a phone call. Can it wait ten minutes? We're almost done."

I knew this request didn't make me look better. On the contrary, it made me appear even more suspicious. But I was ten seconds away from a full-blown panic attack.

"No, it can't wait."

Detective Waters exhaled. I saw the muscle in his jaw clench.

"Go ahead." He didn't hide his irritation. "We'll be outside."

The two detectives got up and left me in the interrogation room to make my phone call. Not for one second did I hesitate about whom to call. It felt like the simplest, smartest choice I'd made in a lifetime. I dialed her number from memory.

Phaedra answered on the third ring.

"Neil?" she said. "Is that you?"

I can't imagine what it must have been like to be on the receiving end of that call. Everything spilled out, but not in chronological order. In broken sentences and fragments. Phaedra absorbed it all.

"Listen to me," she said, when I finished. "Don't say another word, do you hear me?"

"They're asking me all these questions, Phae. I can't just ignore them."

"You tell them you want a lawyer. Tell them you won't answer another question until your lawyer is sitting there. You got it? You there, Neil?"

"I'm here."

"They can't question you without a lawyer. Not if you've asked for one. So, they're either going to hold you until one arrives, book you, or they'll let you go." I could feel the gears of her brain turning. This was Phaedra in her element. Transforming chaos into order. "I doubt they have enough on you, or they would've arrested you already."

"Arrest me!" I dropped my head into my hand. "I don't even have a lawyer. Who would I even call?"

"We'll find you one. We'll figure this out, okay?"

I thanked her and was about to hang up when she said: "You want me to come get you?"

***

Within half an hour, Phaedra picked me up at the police station and drove me back to my apartment. She pulled up the driveway and parked behind my car. She had never been to my place before.

For a moment, we sat there in silence.

"You want to come in for a minute?" I asked. I knew it was probably a bad idea, but I wasn't ready for her to leave.

She dropped her eyes. "I should really be going."

"Yeah, yeah, of course. Sorry, I just—"

"Are you going to be all right?"

"I'll be okay. Thank you. For the lift. For everything."

I smiled at her, and out of nowhere, she reached out and placed her hand gently on my cheek. It didn't feel romantic. It didn't feel seductive. It felt familiar.

I got out of her car and tried to hold onto that feeling, the touch of her fingertips against my skin. A connection between two people who know each other that well.

But already, the feeling was slipping. By the time I got inside, it was gone.

***

For the rest of the weekend, I alternated between restlessness, anger, and fear. My mind returned obsessively to the cigarette, crushed in Detective Waters' little bag. My DNA on it. It made no sense, and yet, there it was.

When Phaedra had dropped me off, she'd said the police would most likely be surveilling me. In a way, I could feel them. Their ghostly presence. It's not that I caught glimpses of suspicious cars in my rearview mirror or parked down the block; it was just a general sense of being watched.

***

The person I suddenly wanted to see more than anyone was Jack. So, on Monday evening, when I went to the parking garage, I headed up to the floor above where I parked to see if his car was there. It was. His blue Mazda in its usual spot. I was prepared to wait all evening. But I didn't have to.

After twenty minutes, he came walking up, but paused when he saw me.

"Hey," he said. His tone was even, but I could still feel the tension from our last drunken exchange.

"You're hard to find these days," I said. One of the sodium lights in the garage had blown out, and long shadows crept up the wall. "Can we talk?"

"Yeah, okay," he said after a moment. "You want to get something to eat?"

This was not a conversation I intended to have in public.

"Can we just sit in your car?"

He looked at me askance but unlocked the door. Inside were a handful of parking tickets smashed into the cup holder. It made me smile.

"Starting a collection?" I said, nodding to them.

"Just doing my part to keep the city funded."

Despite our best efforts, conversation was strained. I realized there was no point in pretending things were fine. Things were way past fine. I told him about the police, about Detective Waters and my cigarette near Lucia's body.

"Jesus," he said when I finished. "I don't understand."

"I don't either, but there it is." I'd come to the part that couldn't be avoided. The thing that needed to be said. "Listen, Jack, I'm not trying to make your life difficult. Believe me, I'm not. But you can understand how I might have some questions."

He looked down. His hands were pale on the steering wheel. A nearby car pulled out from a parking spot and drove away.

"What do you want to know?" He didn't look at me when he said it. And for a moment, I despised him for making me say it out loud.

"I want to know about Lucia. And about Michelle Alvarez."

I was watching his face. The muscle in his eye twitched.

"I didn't hurt her, if that's what you think."

"I don't think anything. I don't know what to think."

He leaned back against his seat and closed his eyes. He kept them closed.

"Lucia was my student. Last spring." I'd already deciphered as much from the list of classes. He opened his eyes. "Lucia was a smart girl, whip-smart. And—strange. She liked poetry and words. I don't know. She just had this way of looking at things. She was different. But I swear, that was it." His voice had a pleading tinge to it. "Yes, I'll admit, I was drawn to her. But we never crossed any boundaries. I wouldn't have done that. Ever." He stared out the windshield into the darkness.

"But then, one night, I went to this—this kind of *club*, I guess you would call it."

"The Dionysus," I said.

Jack turned to me, surprised.

"I read about it," I offered. "Some kind of fetish club. The article said it burned down a few months ago."

He nodded.

"By the time it burned down, I hadn't been back in six months. Maybe longer. Not since that night."

Jack ran his hand across his mouth, left it on his lips, as if he wanted to physically hold back the words.

"The Dionysus," he said, "is hard to explain. It was this place where you could act out these—*ideas*. However bizarre or experimental. And it wasn't always about sex. I mean, I could go and find someone to sleep with at a bar right now if I wanted to."

I laughed. Humility had never been his strong suit.

"I'm just saying, it wasn't about sex. It was about uncovering some-thing—deeper."

"And that's where you saw her? Lucia?"

"No!" he insisted. "I didn't *see* her. I booked a session."

"How?"

"You would set it up through a point person. A girl named Lotus. I don't know. She managed it. Anyway, I got into this room and there was this girl. But it was dark, pitch black. And you wear these masks. They're supposed to provide anonymity. Give you permission to—I don't know—be whatever or whoever you need to be. But I'm telling you, it was *pitch* black in there."

He grew quiet again. Ran a hand through his hair.

"What I'm saying is, I didn't know it was Lucia. I would have run for the hills if I had known." He took a breath and seemed to retreat into his memory of the night. "But if I'm being perfectly honest, right up until the moment I found out, it was fucking amazing. Like I could talk to her. It wasn't even anything she said. I can't believe I'm even saying this out loud." He seemed to pendulum between catharsis and revulsion. "It sounds crazy, I know. *I* sound crazy."

The headlights of a car driving down from the level above swept over us. Our faces lit up for a moment until it passed.

"Not a day goes by that I don't regret it. I wake up in a cold sweat every single night. And now! *Ohmygod*, now that she's gone. I am terrified and sick."

On the one hand, I felt the desire to comfort him; on the other, I felt such an acute—and wildly selfish—sense of betrayal. All this time, and I'd had no idea it was happening.

"But you know what?" Jack said, looking suddenly changed. "You know what? I'm glad it's coming out now. I am. Because I've been living with it every day, and it's been eating away at me like a cancer. And now," he laughed, humorlessly, "now there's no more hiding. Now, it's out. And you can take it to the police or whatever you want to do with it. But I swear—*I swear*—I did not kill her. I would never hurt her. Never."

"I'm not going to the cops," I said after a long silence. "I believe you."

"Why?" he asked, narrowing his eyes.

I didn't know why. I had no objective reason to believe him; I just did.

"Police work on hunches all the time," I said.

He let out a small laugh. "You know how many innocent people have been arrested or put to death on hunches?"

"Did you ever see her again? Afterward, I mean?"

Jack furrowed his brow.

"I tried to avoid her. Whenever I saw her around campus, I would run the other way. Literally. Once, I saw her in the hallway outside one of my classes and bailed on the entire class. Didn't even show up. Sometimes I imagined I was seeing her. Near my office. Outside my apartment. But then it would turn out not to be her. My mind was playing tricks on me." He shook his head. I wondered if that was why I had bumped into Lucia on the bench that day. Had she been looking for Jack? "Finally, it got to be too much. So, I went to the bank. I pulled out a thousand dollars and I went to her."

I widened my eyes.

"She took it?" I asked.

He nodded.

"So, she wanted money?"

"I have no idea what she wanted. But I didn't see her after that. Not really. One other time, but it was nothing."

He spoke with a sense of unburdening. I wanted to believe him. I *did* believe him, but there were other pieces, too.

"What about the other girl? Michelle?"

"Alvarez," he said. He ran his hand down his face. "Yeah, she was in my class—with Lucia. I have no idea what happened to her."

I hesitated. I knew that whatever needed to be said needed to be said now.

"I saw you with her, Jack. On campus. Right before she disappeared."

Now he turned to me, narrowed his eyes.

"She was a drug addict," he said. "That's the truth. Maybe not at the beginning, not when she was in my class. But by the end. That day she came up to me, howling about Lucia, going on about this and that, asking what I knew about her friend. She needed money. She wanted money for something. She threatened me. Said if I didn't give it to her, she was going to go to the police."

"So, she knew about you and Lucia?"

He seemed to equivocate on this.

"Actually, I don't think she did. Or not all of it. Just by the way she was talking, I sensed she knew something. But none of the details. Not what had happened."

Sitting there, looking at him, I realized Jack had aged. I didn't know when, but he seemed older, more world-weary.

"I have no idea where she is," he said. "I can only imagine the two of them got caught up in something bad. Something they shouldn't have. And whatever happened to Lucia, Michelle got tangled up with it too."

By the time I climbed out of Jack's car, a thick fog had crept onto campus. It made the streetlights glow an eerie blue.

That night, I took a circuitous route home. I went out of my way to drive by the woods whose perimeter I had walked that night after the bar. Somewhere in those woods Lucia's body had been found. I knew it was foolish—downright stupid—to drive that route if there were police following me. What would they think of my detour? Maybe, in a strange way, I wanted to pay my respects.

Afterward, I was going to head home. But at the last minute, I changed my mind. I drove back to the bar where Jack and I had been that night. Wilco blared from the jukebox. I found a seat at a high-top table and scanned the room. A blonde waitress appeared. Not the one I wanted.

"Is Tara working tonight?" I asked when she came to take my order.

"Sorry," the girl said. "Tara's off until Wednesday. Can I get you something to drink?"

I shook my head.

"You're welcome to leave your name," she said. "I'll make sure she gets it."

"That's okay," I said. Then, on second thought, I ordered a beer and a burger and wolfed it down. I hadn't eaten all day.

It was 10:15 p.m. by the time I got home. I went to the kitchen window and pulled out a cigarette. Outside, dark trees stood against a dark sky. Beyond them, I imagined two figures in an unmarked car.

CHAPTER 18

LUCIA

Then

In August, Naseem returned from visiting his family. He'd been gone only a month, but it felt like a stranger who came back.

Or maybe I was the stranger.

"You all right?" Naseem asked. I had picked him up from the airport, and we were back at his apartment. I tried to put on a pleasant face.

"I'm fine, babe," I said, resting my head against his shoulder. "I'm just happy you're home."

And I was.

I hadn't slept soundly while he was gone. My dreams were filled with Jack. With the expression on his face when he realized who I was that night at the Dionysus. The way he said *NoNoNoNoNo!* without taking a breath in between. He flipped the light on; we looked garish in its brightness.

I thought you knew, I said. *When you touched my arm, I thought you knew.* And the look of genuine terror on his face as he pulled on his clothes, tripping on the leg of his pants, stumbling into his shoes, socks left on the floor. And me, sitting in bed, the sheet pulled up tight. Our masks, discarded like dirty laundry.

Jack left before I did. I didn't stop to collect my payment. I'm not sure how I managed to escape without seeing Lotus or Leon. But I managed to call a car and ride through the sticky summer night, collapsing into Naseem's empty bed. I slept for two days. When I woke, I wasn't me anymore.

***

Naseem and I slept together the first night he returned. His voice in my ear, his breath against my neck, and I understood that Naseem could not save me. Of course, he couldn't. He never could. But the force of his will—his boundless desire to do so—had once seemed enough.

In the morning, he knelt over his suitcase wearing only boxer shorts. His slim body bent as he rifled through his belongings. When he found what he was looking for, he climbed back into bed.

"Brought you something." He placed a small brown bag on the covers in front of me. "I didn't have time to wrap it." I sat up in bed and opened the bag. It was a book. "Seemed like something you'd like," he said.

It was Virginia Woolf, *Moments of Being*. I started to cry.

"Lucia!" Naseem said, wrapping his arms around me. "What is going on?" I clung to him wordlessly.

***

Before Naseem came home—back in July, after my night with Jack—I had reached out to Michelle. On the phone, her voice sounded like sandpaper. We decided to meet at a coffee shop, and she was already there when I arrived, slumped in a velvet green armchair, dark sunglasses covering her eyes. In her hands was a steaming Americano, which she cupped like she needed the warmth.

She had lost her job with the community organizer for failing to show up too many days in a row. Sitting there in her big sunglasses, she looked like a rock star after a bender. Despite everything, the sight of Michelle lifted my spirits.

"Good time last night?" I asked, bending down to kiss her cheek.

"The parts of it I can remember." She took a squirrelish little sip. I still hadn't told her about Jack.

The night before, she and Nurit had *gone out*, which meant coke in a crowded bathroom or vodka shots until she couldn't stand anymore. A few days earlier, Michelle had told me that she'd tried fentanyl.

"Are you fucking kidding me?" I had said. I remember feeling heartened that I could muster any emotional intensity at all after Jack. But fentanyl? That was not just a fun night of blow or a party on molly.

Fentanyl was all the ways Michelle and I no longer knew each other.

Now she sat, slumped in an armchair, looking two steps from dead. She was still beautiful, but it had faded. She wore a jacket despite the heat, like a celebrity in disguise.

"Nurit wants to move to California," she said, then coughed.

I felt a stir of relief. *Good riddance.*

"Why California?"

"Her aunt has a place in San Francisco. Like an extra apartment or something."

San Francisco was as foreign to me as Madagascar.

"Are you bummed?" I asked.

She looked at me for a moment with confusion.

"Why would I be bummed? I'd be going with her."

My eyes widened.

"Wait, you'd just drop out of school?"

She shrugged.

"I don't know. It sounds fun."

"Are you serious?"

"I don't know, Lucia." She sounded tired, put-upon. "It's just an idea; you don't have to get ferocious about it."

I suppose some friendships run like wildfires, burning everything up all at once until there's nothing left to consume. Maybe that was Michelle and me. Maybe the kindling was gone. She shifted in her armchair, pulled her knees up to her chest, her coffee cooling on the side table.

"Anyway," she said, "where have *you* been?"

Here was my chance to tell her everything. About Jack, our night together, that it had finally happened—that it was perfect until it was the exact opposite of perfect. And that, somehow, the whole thing had annihilated me until I didn't even know who I was.

I hesitated, and Michelle emerged from her stupor.

"What are you not telling me?" she said, and for just a moment, the old Michelle flared up. Michelle before Nurit—when it was I who filled up the whole of her vision.

In the end, I did not tell her about Jack.

"No, nothing," I said. "I've just been working at the restaurant. Staying with my parents a bit. Nothing exciting."

She eyed me suspiciously.

"Mm-hmm, sure."

A week later, she texted.

"Talked to Lotus. Wtf happened?!? U DO IT??"

I didn't respond.

"Scoundrel," she wrote. "Tell me!"

"Nothing to tell," I wrote back.

"Damn, girl. Got excited for a sec. Thought we had something to celebrate."

I sent back hungry-faced emojis with hearts for eyes.

"Still pining," I wrote.

***

School started up again at the end of August. I'd convinced myself that, if I could just see Jack, explain things, then we could go back to normal.

But I didn't see him, though I searched for him everywhere. I found his teaching schedule online, tried to bump into him. I caught a glimpse of him by the History Department, but he turned a corner and disappeared. Once, I saw him outside a classroom, but then he was gone. Another time, I sat outside the Philosophy Department, talking to some asshole about ethics. Turned out he was a professor, which just goes to show you what a bunch of bullshit everything truly is.

Then one afternoon—a Friday in early September—I was sitting on a bench near the library. The light had this soft brightness to it.

And suddenly, there he was. Jack Sheridan, walking straight toward me. He pushed back his hair with one hand. I sat stone-cold, as he approached.

"Hey," he said.

"Hi, Professor Sheridan," I replied. "I've been looking for you."

"I know," he said. "I see you waiting outside my classes. Outside the department."

"I just wanted to talk."

He was nodding his head over and over, like a nervous tic.

"Lucia, there's nothing for us to talk about," he said. "I . . ." He trailed off, then, unexpectedly, sat down on the bench next to me.

For a minute, I thought he might put an arm around me. But he didn't. Instead, he pulled his messenger bag around to the front and slid his hand beneath the flap. He removed an envelope. *A letter?* My heart stirred.

"Take it," he said, putting it on my lap. I didn't move. "Please. Just take it."

I picked it up, but I was afraid to look inside.

"What is it?" I asked.

When I looked back at him, his eyes seemed sad and tired.

"I'm not saying you took advantage," he said. He seemed to be carefully plotting his words. "But here we are, and I don't know what you want."

"I don't want anything! I just want to be near you."

"No!" he said firmly. Then again, whispered: "No."

At our feet, small weeds poked out between cracks in the walkway. What tenacity to be a weed.

"I'm sorry," he said, "but I can't have you saying things like that." His chest was moving up and down. I reached out to touch him, but he pulled back. "There is nothing between us, Lucia. You were my student. I was your teacher. Nothing more."

I watched him without blinking. He nodded at the envelope in my hand.

"There's a thousand dollars in there. It's all I could scrape together."

I imagined the bills, crisp and stacked. Not the wrinkled kind you get from the ATM. The kind you need to go into a bank to retrieve. Jack seemed pleased by the fact that I was holding it.

"I realize that you can do whatever you want with the information you have," he said. "You can go to the dean. You can get me fired. You could even go to the police." He looked down at his shoes. They were a dull brown suede. "You have all the power here, Lucia. I am asking you, please."

But he didn't say what he was asking for.

I sat there on that bench for a long time after he left. People moved around me, but I didn't see them. I didn't see anything. The money stayed there in my hand. It felt treacherous. Not a gift, but a punishment. Services rendered; services paid. When the light started to fade, I closed my fingers around the envelope and put it in my bag. All around me, it seemed, campus exhaled as if it had been holding its breath.

CHAPTER 19

NEIL

Now

On Thursday evening, there was a knock on my door. I opened it and found Phaedra standing there, wearing jeans and a T-shirt, her hair loose on her shoulders.

I must have looked shocked because the first thing she said was: "Sorry, I should have called."

"No, it's—I'm just—come in."

I stepped aside, and my ex-wife walked into my apartment. Looking around, I realized this place was a true testament to how far I'd fallen. There were only a few tired pieces of furniture in the living room. Nothing on the walls—except two posters of Lucia, one with the word WHORE written across it. Empty cupboards in the kitchen. A handful of books on the shelf. My life as I'd known it was still packed in cardboard boxes in my storage unit.

"I have news," she said, assiduously avoiding the Lucia posters. "And a bottle of Burgundy." She pulled the wine from her backpack and surveyed it. "2015. Possibly shit."

I smiled. Phaedra Lewis. *Be still my heart.*

We went into the kitchen. I got us a couple of glasses and handed her the bottle opener. We stood there, shoulder-to-shoulder, like we'd done a thousand times. Food and drink were always her domain. Phaedra used to go to the grocery store and, each time, come home with an ingredient she'd never heard of or didn't know what to do with. Rambutans and mangosteens. Shichimi Togarashi. Yellow-eye beans with birthmarks of gold. We would try new recipes. Some worked. Many did not.

Now, in my kitchen, she extracted the cork in one smooth pull, no debris floating in the bottle. Her movements swift and self-assured. She poured us each a glass. We clinked.

"Tim got you a lawyer," she said. That was her news. That's what she had come to say.

"Oh," I said, setting the glass down.

She frowned.

"I thought you'd be relieved." Somewhere outside, a dog barked.

"Sorry. I am relieved. Of course, I am."

"Then why do you look like you just got punched in the gut?"

"I guess—I don't know."

"What?"

"I guess I would've just preferred if it hadn't come through Tim."

"Ahhhh," she said. "Well, a lifeguard doesn't ask a drowning man if he likes the color of the life-preserver."

I laughed. "I wouldn't say I'm a drowning man."

"No?" I saw her eyes flick to the poster of Lucia. "Then what are you?"

She reached into the back pocket of her jeans and pulled out a card. *Simon Prichard, Attorney at Law.*

"Tim met with him yesterday," she said. "You're lucky. Simon's the best at what he does."

"The *best*," I said, taking the card. I studied it. It was thick card stock, creamy and embossed. "Sounds expensive."

"Insanely expensive! Fortunately for you, he owes Tim a favor."

I raised an eyebrow.

"Nothing crazy. Tim helped get his kid into Yale. The boy's an idiot. But the father's a genius."

"I always knew Tim was corrupt."

Phaedra laughed.

"Call Simon," she insisted. "He's expecting to hear from you. Best case scenario, you won't even need him. But you should call."

I lifted the card and thanked her. Then I set it on the counter.

"I wish I had known you were coming. I could offer you something to eat," I said. "I wasn't expecting—"

"No, no," she said, waving me off. "I can't stay long."

I nodded. "Of course. You have to go. I understand."

She smiled. "Well, don't kick me out yet."

Then she refilled both our glasses and we went into the living room and sat down on the tattered brown couch. Between us, there was that familiar electricity. A thrumming that came from her body and mine. Maybe it was only muscle memory, but I liked to imagine it was more.

"You know what I just thought of?" she asked, turning to me. "Remember that time we locked ourselves in your apartment and drank so much, we literally had to take turns vomiting in the toilet?" Her eyes were shining. "It was right before oral exams, you remember that?" She leaned back on the couch and took another sip. "I don't even know what made me think of it."

I did remember. Perfectly.

We had driven to the liquor store and come home with eight bottles. Phaedra had wanted eight. Obscure labels. Different colored liquids. It was shortly after she lost the baby, which was a night that was seared in my memory. The two of us, driving through Lawrenceville in the sleeting rain. Phaedra in the passenger seat, clutching her abdomen. I remember wanting her to make a sound, *any sound*. But she said nothing. She was so quiet I could hear the ringing in my ears.

When it was all over, when we left the hospital, I felt a closeness with her. But also, something else. No name for it, except maybe—fear. Fear over the way that Phaedra managed pain. The way she disappeared into herself. I imagined what it must have felt like for her to lose the baby, something she herself had created, not with words, but with her body—and mine. Her greatest creation. The anguish, so large she could not see the edges of it. How it took her to the very limits of her control. A reminder that, despite herself, she could not determine the outcome of every situation. It devastated and frightened her, which is why she pulled away, why she started to lash out at me so violently—to mask her sadness, powerlessness, and anger. Not that she ever explained it like that in so many words. She didn't need to. I understood her perfectly.

After the miscarriage, she underwent that procedure, the vacuum thing, and I drove her home. I tried to keep pace while she poured the contents of those liquor bottles down her throat. Determination in the hard set of her jaw. With the same intensity she brought to her work, she shifted to the project of losing consciousness. In the aftermath, there were empty bottles scattered across my floor, a shrine to some inner darkness that Phaedra kept private.

"Yeah, I remember it," I said. "You puked all over my gray sweater."

We both laughed.

At 9:30 p.m., Phaedra stood up. I expected her to go, but instead, she asked where the bathroom was, and I pointed her down the hall.

While she was gone, I picked up our glasses and put them in the sink. I dropped the empty bottle into the trash. When she came out a few minutes later, she was holding a framed photograph. She turned it around so I could see it.

"Christmas," she said. "Eight? Nine years ago?"

I groaned, feeling humiliated.

"I'm surprised you still have it," she said.

In the photograph, Phaedra's hair was long and whipping around her face in the wind. I had taken the picture of us, the camera held at arm's length, so it was too close, my head partially cropped. But I loved it. It seemed to capture those days when everything was hopeful, when nothing had gone stale.

"I put all the other ones away, I swear," I said defensively. "It's just—it's only that one."

She set the picture frame on the coffee table.

"Does it bother you?" I asked. "That I still have it out?"

She shook her head. "It doesn't bother me."

What happened next happened so quickly, so naturally, it's hard to follow cause and effect. What led to what. All I know is Phaedra was suddenly coming toward me, and I was standing to receive her. She on tiptoes, pressing herself into me, as I folded my arms around her. Motions so familiar, they felt automatic.

Then her lips were on mine. The gentle pressure of her. Our bodies, responding to each other, remembering each other. We fell back on the couch as she fumbled with her shirt, trying to pull it over her head. I lifted it off and threw it on the floor. Tiny goosebumps lit up her arms, and everything felt like home. The taper of her torso, the outline of her ribs. That pale pink blemish in the shape of Florida just above her right breast. A bra I didn't recognize. Small flowers embroidered in lace. Soft padding inside, creating extra cleavage. I unclasped it, let her breasts fall forward.

I carried her to my bedroom and unbuttoned her jeans. I just wanted to look at her, this body sprawled on my bed. The impossible, unimaginable event of it, so outlandish I would never have allowed myself to fantasize. I was afraid to speak, for fear of breaking the spell. I wanted to take my time, mostly because I could already feel her departure: the end of our lovemaking inscribed in its beginning. Once it was over, I knew she would be gone.

So, I ran my lips along the inside of her thigh, memorizing her all over again. Her underwear, a silky thong. I wondered if she put them on earlier knowing precisely how they would come off. Phaedra always saw into the future, the eventual undressing that belonged somehow to the selection of each garment. I pulled them down and felt her body shudder.

I didn't use a condom. I didn't even have one, which she was shocked to hear. Three times I thought I might finish, and three times I coaxed myself down. I wanted to feel her, hear her. She clamped her legs around me, squeezed tight, and I felt her release.

Afterward, we lay on the bed, staring up at the popcorn stucco of my ceiling.

"I can't remember what our old ceiling looked like," I said. It seemed impossible that I would forget a detail like that.

"I think it had that"—her thin arm shot up, tracing the memory of our forgotten ceiling in the air above us— "you know, it had that painted white concrete thing going on." Her wrists were narrow like a ten-year-old girl's. She dropped her arm back down on the bed and it made a *poof* sound against the comforter.

Under the covers, I slid my hand onto her leg, so that she would feel me. This light pressure. But I felt her stir, and I saw the whole series of events play out in my mind: her getting dressed, heading for the door, driving away, even before she was out of bed. I wanted to keep her there, hold her attention.

The first thing that popped into my mind was the Dionysus.

"Can I ask you something?" I said. "When we were talking last week about Jack and Lucia, when I walked you to your car,"—already it felt like a lifetime ago—"I mentioned a club. The Dionysus."

She lay there a moment in silence.

"What's your question?" she asked. This was classic Phaedra. Making you spell things out.

"Had you ever heard of it?"

A pause. She flipped onto her side to face me. Her cheek, resting on her open palm.

"Tim told me about it," she said.

"Tim? Did he—go there?" *What the actual fuck? Was our entire department frequenting this sex club?* I wondered if she knew what kind of club the Dionysus was. If she did, I doubted she'd be sharing this.

"I think Jack told him about it."

"No way," I said.

Jack would not have told Tim about something like that. Jack hated Tim. The kind of hatred that belongs to academia. For Jack, Tim was a charlatan, pedaling ideas that rightfully belonged to others. *It's just Heidegger with AI thrown in*, is how Jack described it when he was feeling particularly cruel. And the fact that Tim Janek had multiple departments kissing his ass made him all the more deplorable.

"Believe it or don't," Phaedra said, "but it's true." She fell onto her back. "It was a few years ago if I'm not mistaken. At the department Christmas party. Too much wine. Everyone trashed. Enemies were friends for a night. You know how it goes. Some grad student's girlfriend leaning against my arm, like we were best friends." Phaedra readjusted on the pillows. I suddenly couldn't recall when I had last washed the sheets. "I remember it on the car ride home, because Tim said he'd told Jack about experimenting with ayahuasca, and Jack—"

"Tim does ayahuasca?"

She brushed her hand through the air, like I was missing the point.

"Sometimes. Anyway, it was some stupid pissing contest. Tim had done ayahuasca. Jack had gone to some weird club. Trading war stories like they're the only two assholes who've ever dared to live."

I searched my memory for the night Phaedra described but came up empty. Two years ago would have been the year that Phaedra and I had split. If I had been at that Christmas party, my attention would have been razor focused on her, not Jack. Maybe it had happened, but it seemed doubtful.

"Why are you asking anyway?" she said.

I shrugged, and she looked at me slyly.

"You think it's tied to Lucia."

"I don't know." I shook my head. "I don't know what to think."

She rolled over and kissed my shoulder.

"You should call Simon Prichard," she said. "Let the lawyer do the thinking for you."

Right then, I could have told her about Jack, shared every detail about his night with Lucia in the back rooms of the Dionysus. It might have kept her there longer. But I didn't. Instead, I lifted her hand. Those perfect half-moons of white on her nails. I kissed her fingers.

"What happened to us, Phae?"

It was stupid to ask. I knew it instantly, and I felt her stiffen.

"Can we not do this?" she asked, pulling her hand back.

"Not do what? We've never talked about it," I said. "That's why I'm stuck on this loop of you. Maybe if we did—talk about it, I mean—then maybe I could let go of you."

"What if I don't want that?"

"Want what?"

"For you to let go of me."

"Seems a little unfair," I said. And now that I had said it, the need felt urgent. "So, why did you leave?" It was the most direct question I had ever asked about us.

She waited for a long time before responding.

"What do you want me to say, Neil? There was so much going on at the time."

"I'm asking because, this—what we're doing right now—*this* feels right to me."

She didn't answer, just sat up and let the covers pool around her waist.

"What do you want to hear? That I still love you? That I made a mistake? What would that change?"

I put my hand on her back, could feel the sharp points of her spine. When she looked back at me, her face was agitated.

"Everything," I said. "It would change everything."

"Can't we just—be in the moment."

No, I could have told her. *We can't*. But I didn't say it. Just sat up, kissed her shoulder, and got out of bed. We dressed mechanically. Then I walked her to the front door. But before she left, she crossed the room to the Lucia posters and stood there, staring. In one swift move, she ripped the first one from the wall. Then the next.

"No! What are you—"

Her expression was hard and uncompromising.

"You have a dead girl's poster on your wall. Two of them. Your cigarette was next to her body. You are not thinking."

I opened my mouth, then closed it.

"You need to get smart," she said. "Smarter than you're acting." She folded each of the posters—imperfectly, since they were large and made of stiff paper. I could still see one of Lucia's eyes staring out from below the fold. Phaedra shoved them both into her leather backpack. "You can't even throw them out in your own garbage. You've got cops going through your trash. You see what I'm talking about? Get smart, Neil." She walked over to me again and squeezed my hand.

With the posters gone, the room felt even more barren. If Phaedra hadn't done it, I never would have. I would have left Lucia staring out from my wall for all eternity.

"Thank you," I said. "For the lawyer and the wine. And for coming over."

"You'll call him?"

I nodded, and we hugged goodbye.

From my smoking perch at the window, I watched Phaedra walk down the driveway and disappear behind a tangle of trees. I wondered if the stakeout cops were parked down my street. And if so, what they would write in their notepads.

Ex-wife entered at 8 p.m.

Exited at midnight.

Relationship unclear.

***

That night, after Phaedra left, I dreamed of my mother and Ethan. We were at Ollie's Bargain Outlet back-to-school shopping. I wanted a pair of Wrangler jeans. My mother tried to caution restraint as I loaded things in our cart. The checkout girl rung them up, and I could tell by my mother's expression that the jeans were too expensive.

"I thought they were on sale," my mother said to the girl.

There was a line of people behind us, waiting, listening. The checkout girl looked bored and slightly annoyed.

"I can put them back, ma'am," she said. "But they aren't on sale."

My mother glanced down at me.

"No, no," she said. I watched her pull a sweater from the pile—the one item she had chosen for herself—and hand it to the girl. "I'll put this back instead."

The girl tossed it aside, as if it were garbage.

I awoke that morning unsure whether the dream was a memory or if I'd made it up. The impression of Phaedra's body was still fresh on my sheets, her smell on my pillow.

***

By now, teaching was a joke. I still went through the motions, but I wasn't there. In class, we were discussing moral relativism. I was posing large, open-ended questions that allowed me to participate peripherally. *Are there absolute moral principles that transcend cultural differences? What right do we have to judge practices that differ from ours? What about caste systems, polygamy, stoning, prohibiting women from driving?*

Invariably, when I posed these questions, someone would shout out "incest" as proof of a fundamental ethics. This time, it was Adam Steadman.

He didn't bother to raise his hand, just called out.

"No one thinks incest is okay," he said.

"Maybe," I said. I could do this dance in my sleep. "But is that for moral reasons? Or because it's evolutionarily advantageous to diversify the gene pool? What about the fact that some cultures are repulsed by the idea of marrying your second cousin, but other cultures embrace it?"

I lobbed these questions like chum to sharks. I needed time to parse my own ethical questions. The ones circling around my mind. *Is infidelity always wrong? What if it's with your ex-wife?*

"You all right, Professor Weber?" Adam Steadman was looking at me. The entire class was looking at me.

"Fine," I said. "I'm fine."

Adam shrugged.

"You just look—I don't know. Kinda pale."

At the end of class, my students grabbed their things and bolted. I had the sensation that our class was a sinking ship. They were leaping overboard, but I was the captain; I would have to go down with it.

Adam Steadman lingered, loading his backpack, waiting for me to look up and acknowledge him.

"Did you have a question, Adam?"

"Yeah. Well, no." He fidgeted with his backpack. "Not exactly."

I felt exhausted.

"What is it?"

Adam was wearing a maroon hoodie, blue shorts, and Nike Airs. He had this easy way about him, an overconfidence that would probably take him far in life.

"It's just that—well, I was thinking about something you asked me. A while ago," he said. "About that girl, Lucia."

I felt myself go rigid. In the tsunami of Phaedra, Lucia had disappeared entirely. My singular focus for the last month, forgotten in an instant.

"Okay?"

Adam kicked the toe of his shoe absently against the metal leg of the desk.

"I guess, I've been thinking about what happened to her. Some of the details, I mean."

He looked unsure.

"You know, like the fact that she was—" He didn't say the word "strangled," but brought both hands to his neck and pretended to choke himself. It was astonishing to watch it. The brutality of the gesture.

"What about it?"

"I'm only mentioning this because you asked me about her that one time."

"I understand." I nodded. "Go on."

"I just know that—man, this is awkward. I mean, you're a professor."

"Pretend I'm not." It hardly seemed difficult, considering the way I'd been acting. He nodded, kept his eyes cast downward.

"It's just—" He bit his lip. "I know she was into some weird shit."

"Weird shit? Like what?" For a moment, I thought he, too, might know about the Dionysus. My God! The whole world knows. But it didn't turn out to be that.

"Like, I don't know." He looked up at me. Startling blue eyes. "Like, choking and stuff."

That was not what I was expecting.

"What do you mean, 'choking and stuff'?"

He exhaled, as if it cost him something to have to spell it out like this. He rubbed his eyebrows.

"Argh. Okay, I'm just going to say it. But only because you're asking."

"Yeah." I waved him on impatiently.

"So, anyway, like—one of my fraternity brothers hooked up with her. Just a one-night thing. I mean, everyone knew about it, not just me." Adam shoved his hands in his pockets, looked at the ground. "And I guess, while they were—you know, doing whatever they were doing—she grabbed his hand and . . ." He gestured by bringing his hand to his throat again. "I guess, she wanted him to, like, choke her or something."

My face flushed.

"And did he do it? Your fraternity brother?"

Adam shrugged.

"I think he tried it, for like a minute. But it kinda killed the vibe. He wasn't into it. He said it was weird, so they stopped." He looked at me, and I wondered for a moment if Adam himself were the fraternity brother in question. "Anyway, I just thought that maybe, who knows? It might be useful." He didn't turn away, just stood there. "I mean, what if this whole thing was just some sex fantasy gone wrong? Like maybe she wasn't murdered. Maybe she was just doing her weird choking thing and it ended bad."

I fought the urge to say *badly*. It ended *badly*.

I was studying his face. I could see his whole life play out in the straight line of his jaw. The doors that would open for him, not just because of his good looks, but because of his honest-to-God belief that he deserved opened doors.

"Why are you looking at me like that?" he asked. "I didn't have anything to do with that girl." He took a step back, as if I'd scalded him. "Don't get me wrong. She was hot. Maybe if you didn't know about everything she was into—" He shook his head, his mouth turned down in disgust. "But then you find out all this other stuff. I don't care how pretty she is." He lifted a hand. "I'm not hating; I'm just saying, it's not my thing. But a lot of guys don't care about that. They had no problem hooking up with her." He looked frustrated, like his good deed had not landed the way he'd expected. "Anyway, I didn't have to tell you any of this. Forget it," he said, hefting his backpack onto his shoulder. "Forget I even mentioned it."

He began to move to the door.

"Wait, Adam," I called. "I do appreciate this. I don't know if it will be useful, but it could be. I'm happy to pass it along."

His expression hardened.

"I don't want to talk to any cops," he said. "I don't need any more shit with the police." He looked down again at his shoes. "But maybe, I don't know—you could tell the provost." *Ah yes, my lie.* That the provost had recruited me to help with the investigation.

"Definitely. I'll talk to the provost."

"Cool," he said. He walked to the door, waved one hand in the air without turning around. I felt a sudden surge of gratitude. Adam was dragging me back into the beating heart of Lucia's story. Making it relevant again. Making me relevant.

***

It was late afternoon when I climbed into my car. A light rain had begun to fall, though the air was still warm. The birch trees that lined the streets waved in the wind. When I came to my turnoff, I didn't make a right, just kept on going.

I drove the winding streets for another two miles, then turned down a road I'd never allowed myself to visit. The afternoon sun was fading. You could feel the velvet darkness of evening on its way.

Up ahead, I saw what I was looking for. In my imagination, the house was more suburban, more despicable. In reality, it was a quaint two-story with beveled diamond windows, a brick chimney, and timber framing. I slowed my car and killed the lights.

As if on cue, suddenly there was Phaedra, a figure in beige slacks and jacket running across the lawn, holding her bag over her head to shield herself from the rain. She looked so alive, so assertively herself, it seemed fitting that she should materialize like this, just when I wanted her to. I watched her duck under the eaves.

For a moment, I thought about calling out to her. I could tell her about Adam Steadman, the new information he'd shared. But I knew Phaedra would fold her arms across her chest and warn me not to get involved. I could hear her telling me, once again, to be smart. That if it *was* some sex thing gone wrong—if Lucia had wanted to be choked—the least I could do was leave her that bit of agency.

In front of the house, there was a small hill of grass that followed the walkway to the front door. A bird came swooping down to scoop something up from the lawn. A worm or an insect. And Phaedra, key in the door, turned back to stare at the flurry of wings. I caught her expression, and for just a moment, it filled me with the deepest sense of dread.

CHAPTER 20

LUCIA

Then

As it turned out, Michelle did not move to San Francisco with Nurit. They continued to perform their riotous love affair right here, where all could watch. One day, they'd be cuddled on the couch or out at the clubs, and the next, Michelle was puffy-eyed and needy, calling me at all hours until I went over and comforted her.

In the meantime, I was disappearing. I felt like I was crawling out of my skin. I couldn't breathe. Sometimes I'd wake in the night to find myself mid-scream. Naseem would dart up in bed and grab for me.

On a Wednesday afternoon, I let myself into my parents' house. My father was at the restaurant, and Elena was working her shift. My mother would be down the block playing *Scopa*, three Camparis deep. Sometimes, when I was alone in the house, I would catch an eerie quiet along the hallways and in the empty rooms. An agitated quiet that belonged to restless nights and invasions of privacy. I went into my mother's medicine cabinet, then climbed into bed with all my clothes on, pulling the covers over my head, and swallowed enough Temazepam to silence the voices.

I fell asleep thinking about Jack's money, still in its envelope in the nightstand next to my bed. One thousand dollars was more money than I'd ever had all at once. I could spend it on anything. Books, clothes, drugs. But I didn't. It felt poisoned.

I slept the sleep of the almost-dead and woke to the glare of morning forcing its light through the window. I padded downstairs and went into the kitchen where I bumped into my mother.

"*Ma, che succede*?!" she shouted when she saw me. She didn't know I was home. Her chest was heaving, her nightgown rising and falling, her hand pressed to heart.

"You scared me!" I said.

"*Io? Cosa fai qui*? What are you doing here?!" Her nightgown had small yellow flowers on it. Her hair was pulled back, but half of it hung free around her shoulders.

"Nothing," I said. "I slept here." I slumped toward the coffee maker, but my mother shooed me out of the way.

"Does Elena know you are here?"

I shook my head no and perched on the stool as she set a cup of coffee in front of me, then poured one for herself. I could feel her watchful eyes as I took a sip. Her gaze narrow, her lips pressed together.

I know my mother was once beautiful. I have seen their wedding photos, her slim figure, her bright smile. But when I look at her now, I find it nearly impossible to see the younger version tucked inside. The layers of padding that had softened her waist, her hips. Thick wrists and heavy breasts. The once-sharp angles of her beauty had gone slack. At the top of her nightgown, a single thread had come loose.

"I'll make you breakfast," she said.

"I'm good," I said. "Just coffee."

"Psh," my mother waved off the idea. For her, love was counted in calories. She was already pulling out a pan, opening the fridge, unloading its contents. Eggs, cheese, pancetta.

"I'm fine, Mamma. *Non ho fame.*"

She watched me with those suspicious eyes. Once, when I was thirteen years old, standing right in this very kitchen, I doubled over in pain, clutching my stomach.

"You see?" she cried at the time. "Is because you don't eat. You waste away."

She called my father home from the restaurant in a panic. As it turned out, I had appendicitis. I spent three days in a room with another girl who wailed when the nurses came by. When I came home from the hospital, my mother was furious. "Now I must watch you always, to make sure you eat."

"It was appendicitis, Mom. It had nothing to do with food."

But she wasn't interested in science; she was interested in her own assessments of the world.

Every once in a while, when it was just me and her in a room, I would feel something weighty and sorrowful. The totality of everything unsaid, all the ways we avoided honesty. In those moments, I would catch her stealing glances at me from across the room, and my brain turned to the question it always returned to in the end: *Did she know?* A mother's intuition and all that. When I imagined that she knew about Giancarlo, I hated her with bitter violence. When I imagined she didn't, I felt disgust for her obliviousness, hard and compact as a tumor.

In the kitchen, my mother seemed unsure about whether to put the food back into the fridge or just go ahead and make the omelet.

"When your father gets up, he can drive you back," she said, cracking an egg into a bowl. "So, you don't have to take the bus."

I hopped off my stool and picked up my coffee mug.

"Thanks," I said, walking out of the kitchen and into the hallway, "but I'm not going back."

She hustled after me and stood at the base of the stairs as I climbed. "Lucia," she called. I kept walking, not even turning around. "Lucia. *Ascoltami*!" She shouted. "*Scusa, eh*!" I trudged back into my bedroom and slammed the door.

***

When I woke again, I wasn't sure what day or time it was. I heard voices in the hallway.

"Let her be," Elena was saying. "She's okay."

"No, she is not okay," said my mother's anxious voice. "Don't tell me she is 'okay.' She is sleeping the whole day. She is not okay." I could picture her entire body shaking with anger and some other emotion she couldn't quite place.

"She's fine. Let her rest," Elena said. My sister, always courting stillness. That deliberate, careful way of hers, at odds with the storms that raged inside of me. My mother's friends would reach for Elena's face, cupping her chin, smoothing her long, black hair. *Why don't you have a boyfriend, eh? Sei così bella!* they would say to her. And she would shrug, shoulders always hunched slightly forward, gangly arms and legs. Tall like a model, but tentative in her movements. With one exception: when she was painting. When she was painting, she became fully alive.

"And so what?" My mother was building to a crescendo. "She gets kicked out of school?"

"They aren't going to kick her out of school because she sleeps here for a night," Elena responded.

"You know what they will say? They will say, *Lucia, you don't go to class. You don't do your work. You don't eat. You don't eat!*" My mother had worked herself into a frenzy. "They will say, *Lucia, you are trouble. You have always been trouble!* And they will be right!"

I knew that, soon, Elena would come into my room and perch at the end of my bed. She would take up my mother's bidding because that was her job; she could slip across enemy lines and broker a truce in a way the rest of us couldn't. But when she did finally come in, she didn't talk about my mother.

"Naseem has been calling," she said. "I think he's worried."

I turned to her. She was sitting on my bed, her back pressed up against the wall.

"Naseem said he'd come get you if you want. Bring you home." At the beginning of the summer, I had let my apartment go.

I have no home, I could have said.

Sometime in the last year, Elena had become beautiful. Or maybe she always was, and I hadn't noticed because she flitted around in my shadow. When we were younger, other people's compliments landed on me because they didn't see her.

"Did you have a fight?" she asked.

I shook my head.

"So, what then?"

"I'm just tired," I said. I inched closer to her and put my head in her lap. She ran her long fingers through my hair.

***

That night, I dreamed of the summer my family went to Tybee Island off the coast of Savannah. I must have been eleven years old. Maybe twelve. The lighthouse jutting up into the pale blue sky, a long stretch of sand, gray in the early morning. My skin was covered in brine, making it sticky and salty.

Laid over the memory-dream was the sound of a piano, wafting out from an open window somewhere. A piano at the beach, mingling with the sounds of seagulls and waves along the shore. I remember feeling overwhelmed—the shocked good fortune of being here at all, in this world, listening to this piano, which was part of the waves and the seagulls, part of time itself. But I was also aware of the eventual end. That I was on borrowed time. And mostly, that I was alone.

When I thought about Jack, that loneliness seemed to wither. A glimpse into some higher truth: that the boundaries that separate us are permeable and illusory. That the piano belonged to the waves in some primordial way. But now, there was $1,000 in my bedside table, and the loneliness revealed itself as absolute.

I woke to my empty room and the footfalls of my father along the stairs, moving down the hallway. He opened my door gently.

"Lucia," he whispered, but softly, like he didn't actually want to be heard. My back was to the door, and I didn't turn around. "*Luci.*"

I squeezed my eyes shut. I heard him sigh. My father slunk backward and pulled the door closed behind him. The room fell back into darkness.

CHAPTER 21

NEIL

Now

The text from Phaedra came early Saturday morning.

"Remember that tiny town up north we wanted to visit?" she wrote.

I rubbed the sleep from my eyes and tried to remember. There had been countless tiny towns we wanted to visit when we'd first arrived. Old antebellum towns with gabled roofs and dark histories.

Before I had a chance to write back, she texted again.

"I'm here. Come find me. I got us a room."

This was Phaedra, distilled to her essence. Perhaps her most singular gift was to take the everyday and transform it into something exceptional.

Once, when we were visiting New York City, she had an idea to walk the length of Manhattan, end-to-end. Only, not together. She would start in Battery Park; I would start at the Broadway Bridge near the Harlem River. Her idea was for each of us to follow a designated path. She figured we would pass each other at some point near East 72nd Street. She wanted the encounter to be very specific. At the moment of passing, we were allowed to make eye contact but nothing more. No kiss "hello." No slapping five. The point was for each of us to be perfectly inside our own individual walk, yet also together. No one would know. No passerby would suspect. It would be ours. Our secret.

When the day came, I remember thinking it took much longer to walk that city than I imagined. Nearly seven hours. I was alone, but the whole time, I felt as if I were with her. Not physically, but that we were creating something together. In the entire city, only the two of us knew. Yes, it was inconsequential. It changed nothing for anybody else. But for us, it was art. We were shaping the city with our footsteps. For Phaedra, life at its best was performance.

"Can I get a clue?" I texted back, but I knew it was pointless to ask.

I found a map of the state online and scoured the north. Names of small towns leaped out at me, but it could have been any one of them. I had two options if I wanted to meet her: continue to stare at my computer screen or get in my car and just go.

I drove north for two hours, pulling off at unfamiliar exits, stopping for coffee or gas, asking every barista and gas station worker if there were any good towns to visit in the area. They looked at me like I was strange.

Close to noon, I started to send her texts, photos of highway signs followed by question marks. She didn't respond to any of them. In the far distance, I could see the Blue Ridge Mountains and felt something stir inside me. Some memory of Phaedra, lying on her belly, a travel magazine spread open before her. Her reading glasses perched on her small, upturned nose. "Let's go here," she said, flashing me the page.

What was that town called?

On the highway was a large billboard. Wineries and gold in the hills. That felt familiar. But the novelty of the adventure was beginning to wane, and I decided that if I didn't find her soon, I would have no choice but to turn around and go back. I pulled off at the winery exit and made my way to the main square.

The town was quaint, colorful, and touristy without being flashy. There were a few hotels in the area, and I picked one at random.

"I'm here to meet Phaedra Lewis," I said to the woman who worked reception. No Phaedra Lewis. Not at the first hotel, not at the second, nor at the third. At the fourth, I was feeling particularly despondent. I gave the man her name and watched him click at his computer. He looked up at me.

"Your name, sir?"

My heart ticked up a beat.

I gave him my name, and *praise the Lord*, the man handed me an envelope.

"Neil Weber," written across the front. I thanked him and went up to the room.

The hotel itself had old-world, country charm. Gilded paintings of men in Civil War regalia. A carpet runner on the wooden floor that creaked when you walked on it. An elevator that belonged to the dawn of elevators. It clanked and jangled as it carried me up.

I found the room and let myself in without knocking.

When I opened the door, Phaedra was sitting at the small table, her open laptop in front of her. She looked genuinely shocked.

"I'll be damned," she said, closing her laptop.

"Oh, ye of little faith."

I had left in such a rush that morning, I hadn't even packed a bag. I had nothing to set down, nothing to unload. Just me, standing in that narrow doorway.

Phaedra rose and walked toward me. Her hair was pulled back in a ponytail. I could see the freckles across the bridge of her nose.

"I'll tell you one thing, Neil Weber," she said. "No one can accuse you of being a quitter."

We made love that afternoon with a passion that does not belong to regular life. It belongs to illicit rendezvous and secret hotel encounters, moments stolen from our daily routines. Afterward, we lay in the twisted sheets, looking up at the crown molding, and I tried to keep my mind on the here and now, Phaedra in my arms. I picked up her hand, felt the delicate bones of her fingers.

"Actually, I was surprised to get your text this morning," I said. I looked at her and could instantly feel the ghost of Tim Janek, that presence that haunted our every interaction, whether we acknowledged it or not. "Did he ask where you were going?"

"No," she said matter-of-factly. "He's at a conference in Chapel Hill."

In my mind, I recalled the pretty brunette standing by Tim's side, his hand on the small of her back. I wondered how much Phaedra knew. How much she was hiding even now. *Is that why she needed me?* I tried to push the thought away. Love is a complicated thing. Looked at from a particular angle, one might mistakenly believe I was her lackey. But weren't power relations more complicated than that? Didn't Hegel teach us about masters and slaves and the reversal of roles? In the life-and-death struggle for self-consciousness, isn't it the master who needs the slave in order to be seen?

"I forgot to tell you," I said. "I learned something new about Lucia."

I felt her body go still beneath the covers.

"Did you call Simon?" she asked.

"Simon?"

"Prichard. The lawyer."

"Oh. Shit. No. But listen—"

"Neil—"

"I told you I would, and I will. But no, this is something else. It's from one of my students."

We lay in bed on our sides, facing each other. I proceeded to tell her every-thing Adam had told me. Lucia's promiscuity, the choking. I knew Phaedra would be intrigued, even if she thought I was foolish for pursuing it. Phaedra was attracted to the extremes of existence. Chris Burden, nailing his palms to the hood of a VW Beetle. Marina Abramović, carved up with knives as performance art. Self-harm as self-expression.

After I told Phaedra everything I'd learned from Adam, she took a deep breath.

"Auto-erotic asphyxiation," she said. I looked at her with surprise. "You know, like people who get off on being choked," she said, staring up at the ceiling as she seemed to consider it. After a moment, she said skeptically, "I don't know, Neil. It's usually men. Not to say a woman couldn't be into it. It's just, you hear about it more with men." I had no desire to ask her how she knew this. "Anyway, seems like a strange thing for your student to tell you, don't you think?"

"Not really, no."

"Why would he tell you this?" I could feel her radar turning on. For a mo-ment, I felt an urge to defend Adam Steadman.

"Because I'm his teacher," I said. "Because he trusts me."

Phaedra rolled her eyes. Her pedagogy maintained firmer boundaries than mine. *You're not there to play shrink*, I could imagine her saying. *You're there to teach them a thing.*

"Are you going to mention it?" she asked. "To that detective?"

By Phaedra's tone, it was clear she thought I should.

"I don't know," I said. I braced myself to hear to a lecture about why I needed to, but that's not what I got.

Instead, she said, "I don't think you should." It caught me off guard, and I was about to say something, when she changed the subject. "Tell me about California."

"California?"

"Yeah, California." She pushed herself up on an elbow to look at me. The curve of her shoulder was white and smooth. "You know, when you were little."

"The drowning, you mean?"

She nodded.

I rubbed my eyes. Little transparent floaters danced in the dark.

"You already know that story." She must have heard it a hundred times before.

"Tell me again."

"What else is there to say? We were sitting there on the beach when I saw people running—"

"No, not that part." Her hair was tousled from lying in bed. "I know all that—everything in the foreground. I want to know about the background."

"Like what?"

"Like—what were you doing on the beach?"

I scrunched up my eyes. "I don't know. Building a sandcastle."

"I thought you said you were digging a trench."

I laughed. "Okay, digging a trench. I was six. I don't remember it perfectly."

"What were you wearing?"

I looked at her.

"What?" she said defensively. "I just want to picture you."

"A bathing suit." This was becoming slightly irritating.

"What was your father doing?"

My father?

"I don't know." I hadn't thought about my father. In my memory, there was only my mother, Ethan, and me. "Maybe swimming."

"Swimming in the riptide?"

"Maybe getting a drink. I don't know. Why are you asking me this?"

She put her hand on my thigh. It was thin and cold.

"I'm not trying to upset you," she said. "I'm just—I'm trying to know you again. You're the one who always said it was the most important thing that happened to you. The *reason* you are who you are. The reason you do what you do. I just think it's weird that you don't remember it."

"Of course, I remember it."

So, in that hotel bed, I told her about California again. What I had seen that day, and what it had meant.

***

That afternoon, we drove out to a winery. She sat in the passenger seat and fiddled with the radio until she found a song she knew. The window was down, and her hair blew wildly around her head. So blonde in the sunlight, it looked white.

Echo and the Bunnymen came on the radio, and Phaedra sang along with the music, utterly unselfconscious.

Under a blue moon I saw you.

Outside the window, fields of grapes flew by in a tapestry of vines.

Sitting in that car next to her, the world blowing past outside, I felt alive. Entirely inside my body and the moment. Just the two of us, cutting across open country. We were separate and together. We were walking the length of Broadway across Manhattan. We were forging a path. We belonged to time, to each other.

Echo and the Bunnymen sang:

The killing moon

Will come too soon.

***

Over the course of the next two weeks, I saw Phaedra four more times. On Tuesdays when Tim had his standing golf game and on Thursday nights when he taught his graduate class. She would arrive. We would talk, then fuck, then lie there in the orange glow of the streetlamp. Conversation wafted like cigarette smoke, never lingering too long in one place. So many topics tacitly off-limits: Tim, our marriage, our divorce, her miscarriage.

Lucia, it turned out, was our safest terrain.

Whenever conversation steered around to Lucia—her death or my arrest—I felt Phaedra come alive. It's not that she was aroused by the macabre, though she was. It's that, for all of Phaedra's vitality, Lucia had something Phaedra did not. Lucia had death. And on the continuum of metaphysical allure, death wins out.

It could also be that Phaedra was just jealous of Lucia's pull on me, but I'm probably deluding myself.

On one of those evenings, we lay in bed. Her body, a warm object next to me.

"I want to know you again," I said. I hadn't planned to say it, the words just came.

She laughed. "What do you mean? You do know me."

"No, I mean, *really* know you."

"Like what?"

"I don't know—like, what are you working on these days?"

I could see the glint of her teeth between her open lips.

"I'm serious," I said. "I want to know."

She went quiet, then said, finally: "A book."

"Okay. About what?"

She seemed to consider it.

"Mourning. And melancholia."

Phaedra had always been drawn to the place where philosophy and psycho-analysis intersect. Her first book had been about shame. Her second, about kleptomania, the breakdown of impulse control as a fundamental condition of human existence. She had also written a scathing piece on the American use of music as a device of torture to "break" prisoners, quoting Jacques Lacan: "in the field of the unconscious, the ears are the only orifice that cannot be closed." But whatever Phaedra was writing about—libidinal investments, the economics of loss, or sidewalk sales—in the end, I believe she was always writing about one thing: her mother.

I had met the woman once. Phaedra had agreed to take me to Jacksonville after she'd met my mom and Ethan. *An eye for an eye*, I'd said. So, we loaded our things into the car and drove south. We passed her elementary school, crab grass piercing through the concrete. There was a swing set with one of the seats missing. A basketball court with no net. Everywhere, a sense of the forlorn, something forgotten or left behind. I found it impossible to believe that Phaedra had been raised there.

During that trip to Florida, we stayed in a hotel.

"No way I'm sleeping at that woman's house," Phaedra had said about her mother. In any case, her mother hadn't invited us to stay, but we met her for dinner at an unremarkable restaurant where the food was smothered in gravy, and the carpet smelled like decay. The woman who arrived that night was nothing like I expected. She was small, like Phaedra, and appeared younger than her years, also like Phaedra. There was something contained about her movements, tight, birdlike gestures that didn't square with the monster in my mind. In a way, it was anticlimactic to meet her, lips pressed together, hands folded in her lap. She brought fork to mouth with such deliberateness, as if no expenditure of energy could be wasted.

Between mother and daughter, there was no warmth. At least, none that I could see.

"She seems all right," I said when we got back into the car—which was tantamount to treason.

"Yeah, totally. She's great. For someone who pours scalding oil down your back."

"Phae, I didn't mean—"

"I know," she said. She was staring out the windshield, looking at the white lines of the tarmac. "You don't expect the devil to be so short."

When we got back to our hotel, Phaedra went into the bathroom and turned on the water. For the first time, perhaps ever, I wondered if she were crying. But when she came out, she had her hair pulled back in a headband, her face bright pink from washing.

"Are you happy, now?" she asked, accusatory. "Can we leave?"

It was frustrating to find myself in this position. She had agreed to this. She had invited me, and somehow, I was now to blame. Phaedra had this way of always needing to be right—of twisting things around so you became guilty by default. But now wasn't the time to bring any of this up. It was never the time.

"Whenever you want," I said, moving toward her. We had planned to stay two more days, but I would follow her lead. I wrapped my arms around her waist. Her body was rigid and unyielding.

"I want to leave now."

"All right. We'll go first thing in the morning." It was already after 11 p.m.

"*Right* now."

Looking back, it was possibly the most vulnerable I had ever seen her.

Now, all these years later, I lay next to her in bed. It seemed fitting that she was writing on mourning and melancholia.

For Freud, mourning is "successful" when one gets over the lost object. It is the sign of good health, the ability to replace the object of libidinal cathexis: you lose someone, you eventually find a substitute. Melancholia is the aberrant form that mourning takes when someone is unable to accept the loss. Instead, they remain fixated on the lost object, internalizing it until it produces terrible self-loathing.

"Melancholia is the pathology that haunts every instance of mourning," Phaedra said.

But all I could think about was whether Tim had met her mother.

"Can I read it?" I asked.

It was getting late, and I knew she'd have to leave soon. I could see her profile, all those familiar angles of her face.

"You know I can't do that," she said somberly. "Please don't ask me."

I wanted to leave it alone. *I truly did.*

"Has Tim?"

"Has Tim what?"

"Read it?"

She huffed. "Can we please not talk about Tim while I'm lying here, with you, in *your* bed?"

"Fine," I said. "But has he?"

"He's my husband, Neil."

I didn't respond, but let my silence be an enormous, dead weight in the room with us.

"No," she said finally. "He hasn't. Are you happy?"

I'll admit, it did make me happy.

"So, no one's read it?"

"I didn't say that."

"Then who?"

She shook her head, gave a small laugh.

"You're relentless," she said. "Only one person has read it, okay? And they're no threat to you. So, stop pestering me."

I thought about it.

"Christina!" I exclaimed.

Christina Clayton was her editor. The only person Phaedra trusted with her work. A mousy girl who spoke without moving her lips, but who edited Phaedra's writing with just the right scalpel blade, excising the fat while leaving the beating heart. She was the only true reader of Phaedra's unpolished words.

"As soon as I'm ready to share, you'll be the first to know."

***

That night, I dreamed of my mother again. It was my birthday. She had taken the day off work to bring cupcakes to my school. They were store-bought and tasted like powder. KellyAnne Dolan's mom had brought in handmade chocolate cake for hers. My mother sat next to me in a chair meant for a child as everyone sang "Happy Birthday."

My dad didn't come home that night. His presence was unreliable anyway. He'd be gone for weeks, then home for months. Then gone again without warning. It always felt safer when he was away. We could breathe, and I was momentarily free from that suffocating feeling that it was my responsibility to do something to protect my mother. Mom couldn't take any more time off work, but she left a present on the table with money for pizza. It was just me and Ethan with the TV in the background.

We didn't sing happy birthday because it would have been weird. Just Ethan singing to me. I tore open the present she had left. A Takara G1 Sunstreaker, bright yellow and new.

In the past handful of weeks, I had begun to dream of my mother almost every night.

***

The last time Phaedra and I slept together was a Thursday, only a few weeks after we began. The sex was good. *It was fine.* It's shocking how quickly even the forbidden becomes routine.

That night, I watched her dress, as I always did. Putting on her jeans, pulling on her T-shirt. I tried not to picture her taking those same clothes off again, in a different house, a different man lying in bed. I wondered if she showered before she climbed in with him. Could Tim smell me on his wife?

Phaedra came back over to me, leaned down to kiss my face.

"I'll let myself out," she said.

"I'll just be here, fantasizing about you."

I watched her move toward the bedroom door. Before she opened it, I called out to her.

"Hey, Phae." She turned. "I noticed they were playing *The Cremaster Cycle* on Saturday. Number three, I think." Those terrible Matthew Barney films that I couldn't stand, but Phaedra loved. "I thought—I don't know—maybe you'd want to go."

Her expression was inscrutable. Looking back, it's hard not to wonder how things would have transpired if I hadn't said it. It wasn't anything about the film in particular; it was simply the asking. The failure on my part to understand what this was and what this was not. What it was not, *apparently*, was the kind of relationship where you went out on dates and pretended that time could be rewound.

"What?" I asked, my panic coalescing into something hard.

"Nothing," she said.

"Doesn't look like nothing," I shot back.

She took a breath and walked back to the bed. I could see it written on her face, right there on the flat line of her lips. She didn't even have to say it out loud.

"I think we have to stop," she said.

"Why?!" I exclaimed. "It was just a suggestion. Forget the fucking *Cremaster*. I don't even like Matthew Barney."

She shook her head, put her hand on the covers where my leg was.

"It's not that. You know it's not that."

"I don't know anything." I shifted, and she pulled her hand away. I didn't care if I sounded petulant. "We're just—we're just getting started. I thought you were happy. Doing this." I motioned between us. "Whatever this is."

"I *am* happy."

"Then why?"

"Because."

"Because is not a reason."

She shot me a look.

"Because maybe we don't deserve to be happy."

"Screw that!" I said. "I perfectly well deserve to be happy. And so do you."

"Maybe I don't."

Always this strangeness. This performance. I was sick and tired of it.

"Why?" I insisted. "Tell me! Why in the world don't you deserve to be happy?"

"Because I've hurt people. I hurt you."

"You did, yeah. And now you're not. You're changing that."

"It's not that easy."

"I don't understand. Honestly, it makes no sense. It—"

"Tim knows."

She detonated it. Just like that. Two words. *Tim. Knows.* The finality that belonged to those two words felt massive. I let them sink in.

"Are you sure?"

She nodded. "I mean, he didn't come right out and say it, but yeah, I'm pretty sure."

"Well, so what?"

Right then, I wanted more than anything to tell her what I had seen, how convinced I was that Tim was a lecherous piece of shit who was having his own affair, but I didn't say anything. I slumped back against the pillows.

Suddenly, I was back there, in our old apartment. Phaedra standing in the living room saying, "I think we both know that this isn't working." There was a lamp in the corner of the room, and for one second, I swear to God, I thought she was referring to the lamp.

Now, as she stood at my bedroom door, prepared to leave, I was sullen and distant.

"Please don't be like that," she said.

"Turn out the porch light when you go," I said sullenly.

I saw the small movement of her head.

"All right, Neil," she said finally.

I heard her move through my apartment, collect her bag and her keys. Before she let herself out, she came back to the bedroom where I still lay in bed. She stood in the darkened space of the doorframe. I couldn't make out her expression, but her voice was quiet.

"*The Crypt at Last Light,*" she said.

"What's that supposed to mean?"

"The title of my book."

I didn't respond. I knew that, for Phaedra, this disclosure was an act of love. But her love was a barbed object that I didn't know how to hold.

CHAPTER 22

LUCIA

Then

I stayed with my parents for a week and a half, trudging up and down the stairs, pushing food around a plate under my mother's watchful eye. The more I didn't eat, the more elaborate the meals became—ravioli with sage and butter, branzino and lemon, involtini with veal. It allowed her to perform her grievances more wretchedly.

Mostly, I slept. Sometimes, I fielded calls from Naseem. Lying in bed, the phone pressed to my cheek.

"Are you ever coming back?" he asked.

"Yes."

"When?"

"Soon."

"At some point, they're going to drop you from your classes, Lucia."

"So, let them drop me."

I could feel his frustration.

"Will you just stay on the phone with me until I fall asleep?" I asked.

When we weren't on the phone, I would read the book he gave me. Virginia Woolf, writing about her half-brother, Gerald Duckworth, as he propped her up on a countertop and explored her body with his fingers. How she hoped he would stop, but he did not.

She writes: ". . . how I stiffened and wriggled as his hand approached my private parts. But it did not stop."

I felt my own body stiffen at the reading of it. George Duckworth touching her. My own private parts tingling. And how her feeling of aversion was so strong, it seemed to issue from deep within her—but also from beyond her. From something ancient and protective. It was as if Virginia Woolf's instincts had been shaped over millennia, an inheritance passed down through generations. The injunction, inscribed on her body, across time, handed down from woman to woman like an heirloom. She writes, "from the very first encounter instincts already acquired by thousands of ancestresses in the past."

And yet, even with that company of ancestresses behind her, Virginia Woolf still filled her pockets with stones and marched into the River Ouse.

***

One morning, I dragged myself downstairs. The kitchen was empty. My father was already at work, my mother in bed. I walked through the hallway toward the garage. The door to the basement was ajar, and I could hear Elena moving around down there.

A few years earlier, she had fashioned a painting studio out of a corner of the basement. It was dark and musty, totally unsuited to painting. But it was quiet, and no one bothered her, which, I suppose, is what Elena wanted most of all.

I crept downstairs.

The basement was cold and smelled of oil and turpentine. On the easel was a painting Elena had been working on. In the center was a coral-colored smear. It was abstract, just color and texture, but my first thought was that it looked like a wound. A gash in the skin, grotesque yet somehow beautiful.

I stood on that bottom stair looking at it.

"Too bright?" Elena asked.

I hadn't seen her. She was standing at the other end of the basement, considering the painting. Now she nodded toward the canvas.

"Do you think it's too bright? Right in the center like that?" She cocked her head to the side, contemplating her work. In her hand was a paintbrush with the same red-orange pigment as the wound.

I entered the room and stood next to her to examine it. From this remove, the canvas took on a different aspect. The blue-black of the background. The coral hue in the middle. There was something violent about it. Bruised skin. Flesh curling. Pain captured in color.

"I like it," I said.

She smiled.

"Are you feeling better?" she asked.

"I don't know what's wrong with me. It's just this feeling of—it's like, when I'm awake, I just want to get back in bed. When I'm in bed, I'm crawling out of my skin."

She nodded. Then asked, "Did something happen to you?"

There it was. The question. So simple, and yet, I wondered for a moment if anyone had ever really asked it before. *Did something happen to me?* No. And yes. Something happened. Something always happened. Giancarlo happened. Michelle happened. I cheated on my boyfriend. I slept with my professor. I lost my friend. I accepted $1,000 for sex. All of it felt inevitable, unavoidable. Like each of these events were indistinguishable from who I was, from who I was becoming, and in that sense, didn't constitute anything remarkable at all.

"I don't know," I said. "What I'm feeling, it doesn't feel specific. It's just this haze over everything."

Elena nodded, but I wasn't sure she understood. She and I were close, but there was a distance, too. I always felt as if her purity made me dirtier in juxtaposition. When I looked at her, I saw everything that might have been, had Giancarlo not come that summer.

"I don't know," I repeated. "I think I'm just tired." I nodded at her canvas, "I do like your painting. It's kind of strange—and beautiful."

I turned to go back upstairs, and my sister stood, watching me go.

"Hey, Lu," she called after me. "Have you ever thought about going to a meeting?"

I stopped and turned to her.

"Like, what kind of meeting?"

"I don't know." She shrugged. "There are all kinds, I think. Just people, getting together. To talk about stuff in their lives."

"You mean like AA?" I felt my body get tense. "It's not like I'm an alcoholic or something."

"I didn't think you were."

***

On Saturday, I woke up drenched in sweat. It was 5 a.m. I kicked off the covers and reached for my laptop. After an hour of searching online, I found what I was looking for—a meeting, like Elena had suggested. This one was scheduled for today.

I tiptoed down the hall to my parents' bedroom. It smelled of stale breath overlaid by some vanilla plug-in scent that made the air sickly sweet. I glanced at them, my parents, their bodies a mile apart in bed. My mother's mouth was slightly open.

"Can I borrow your car?" I whispered in her ear, hoping not to wake her.

"Mmm," she muttered in her sleep, which I took as a "yes." I lifted the keys from a silver dish on her dresser and left before she woke.

The streets were empty that Saturday morning as I pulled onto the highway. I drove for an hour and fifteen minutes with the radio turned off and the windows down. A sharp chill in the October air.

***

The meeting I had chosen—far enough from my house and from campus that I wouldn't run into someone I knew—billed itself as a place where women could come and share. I pulled into the parking lot. Beyond it, there was a browning lawn where chairs had been set up outside.

I wore an oversized sweatshirt and a dirty ponytail. I couldn't even remember the last time I'd showered. When I caught my reflection in the rearview mirror, I looked ten years older.

From the car, I watched the other women arrive and waited until the last minute to force myself out. One woman seemed to be in charge, greeting each person who approached. She had long gray hair and a pair of beaded earrings, a wool skirt with teal blue tights.

"I'm Caitlin," she said, extending her hand.

Right then, I panicked. I didn't want to give my own name. So, instead, I gave another.

"Elena," I told her. I could be my sister for a day.

"Welcome, Elena," Caitlin said. "We're so glad you made it."

"I don't have to talk right away, do I?"

Caitlin smiled warmly. "No one *has* to talk. We invite you to share." She looked at me, craft-fair earrings dangling. "But you should think of this as a safe space. I hope you'll find a good community here."

I found an empty seat, and so began the first of my group meetings.

There was Maricela, who struggled with binging and purging. There was Lynn, the elderly woman whose twin brother had died when she was young, and she still hadn't made peace with her own survival. There was Dmitria with the stash of pills and Monica with the razor blades. There was Caren (not to be confused with Karen), who was trying to work on her "promiscuity," and Karen, who couldn't hold a relationship.

The woman directly across from me had a name I didn't catch. She was blonde, slightly overweight, and painfully insecure. To Caitlin's gentle questions—*How was your week? What's one thing that went well? What did you struggle with?* —the woman seemed to wither. Her husband was verbally abusive. At night, when they slept together, he would call her a beast. He said that no man in his right mind would want to fuck her. That she was lucky she had him.

To each one of these women, Caitlin brought a conspicuous listening.

Last to speak, besides me, was a girl called Anne. I scanned her face. She was pretty. It was hard to tell how old she was. She could've been a few years older than me. Or in a different light—in different clothes, or a different space—she could have had me by a decade. She sat with one leg folded beneath her in an oversized cardigan with a T-shirt underneath. I tried to read the words printed on it but couldn't make them out.

When Caitlin asked how her week was going, Anne shrugged. Her expression was something between bored and skeptical.

"Not much to report since last time," Anne said.

Caitlin nodded patiently.

"And are you still feeling the same way as last week?"

"Yes," she responded.

"Still, it might be helpful to put it into words. To name it so that it has shape and life outside of you."

Anne squinted her eyes and shifted in her seat. *Bikini Kill*. Those were the words on her shirt. She caught me looking and cocked her head. She held my gaze as she said, "There's nothing to say. That's the problem. I don't feel anything at all."

"Well," Caitlin said. "You felt enough to get up this morning, to get yourself here, to listen to all of us share our challenges."

But I could see it in Anne's eyes. She was thinking: *I don't give a shit about any one of you.*

Caitlin now turned to me. I felt startled by her sudden attention. She had told me I didn't need to speak, yet here she was, boring into me with her eyes.

"Elena, welcome. I know you're feeling reluctant to speak, but I'm hoping you feel a bit more comfortable after listening to others."

I looked around at all the blinking eyes. Their attention razor-focused on me.

"What brings you here today?" she asked. I didn't answer, so she tried a different angle. "Maybe, try to describe what you're feeling?"

I let my gaze drift to the empty space between Dmitria and Monica. To the cypress tree behind them. I took a deep breath.

"There's this feeling—" I said. "It's in my chest. It doesn't have a name. It isn't even a thing, really. It's just this feeling of—I don't know—loss, maybe. But a loss that isn't specific. More like, it's part of me, on the inside. Like it belongs to me." I looked around. "Does that make sense?"

Caitlin opened her mouth, but it was Anne who answered.

"Yeah, it makes sense," she said.

I don't remember anyone saying anything particular after that. The conversation just seemed to move on.

From the entire experience, one moment stands out in my memory.

It was when the girl called Anne looked up, and our eyes met. It was just for a second, but I saw it. The transformation. The moment you go from being a nobody to a somebody. I saw myself become a somebody right then and there.

CHAPTER 23

NEIL

Now

In the absence of Phaedra, Lucia returned like a specter. For nights, I tossed and turned. When I had dreams, they were strange and violent. In one, I saw Lucia. She was running. A man was chasing her with a knife. As he plunged it into her body, she screamed. Kitty Genovese all over again. Lights went on in the apartment windows overhead, but no one did anything. When I woke up, I felt like I had been the man wielding the knife.

***

I arrived on campus and taught my Monday morning class while Adam Steadman watched me with narrow eyes. I'd come to think of him as a barometer of my own degradation. His expression told me all I needed to know.

When I got back to my office, I opened my computer to find an email from the *Southern Journal of Philosophy*. They were very sorry, but my article was not going to be published. I read the email three times, though it consisted of no more than four sentences.

On my desk sat a pile of essays. I'd been ignoring them for two weeks, hoping they would just go away. My students had started sending emails inquiring. They wrote things like, "Dear Professor, I need to know my grade before finals!" Forget the niceties. There was something refreshing about their candor. The calculations that went into how much they should study based on their current standings. Their essays could wait a little longer.

I took out a piece of paper and started to make a list.

1. Lucia disappeared on or around March 15.

2. Her missing person posters went up on March 20.

2. Her body had been found on or around April 11.

3. A cigarette butt with my DNA on it had been discovered in the woods near her body (when?).

4. A year earlier, she had taken classes with Michelle Alvarez (currently missing) and Luke Lariat (incel).

5. She had studied with J. (I intentionally didn't write Jack's full name.)

6. At some point (?), Lucia "worked" at the Dionysus.

7. Last summer, she had sexual relations with J.

8. Afterward, she had blackmailed him (maybe?).

9. According to Adam Steadman, she slept around (possibly into choking).

10. She had a sister, Elena.

11. She had a boyfriend, Naseem.

12. The Dionysus burned down a few months before she went missing.

13. The owner (?) of the club, Leon Schultz, disappeared.

The act of writing the list was soothing. It didn't fall into the category of work, but it was something I could approach with logic and good intention—I could say this about nothing else in my life.

***

It was close to 9 p.m. by the time I finished grading and left the office. Outside, the temperature was warm. Not the sticky summer heat that would soon settle across the South. Campus was quiet. Only a thin shaving of moon in the sky above.

Dotting the walkways to the parking garage were streetlamps, wrought iron with a stylized flourish. As I passed under one, I heard a sound up ahead just beyond the reach of the light. I stopped. At first, I thought it might be an animal, but after a moment, I knew it was a person. Two people. There was a whisper, a laugh. I stepped off the path and into the shadow of a nearby building.

A man and a woman suddenly came into view. They weren't doing anything indecent, but even from this distance, I could see that there was an intimacy between them. Under the next streetlamp, they parted ways. The brunette walked in one direction, the man—Tim Janek—went in the other.

For just a moment, I felt a sudden, outrageous urge to laugh out loud. As if this were the punchline to a joke, and my entire life up until this moment was the set up. Tim Janek bedding a graduate student, while I lose my wife all over again.

From a distance, I followed Tim across campus. At the parking garage, he took the stairs two at a time, and I lost him on the level below mine.

I drove home, replaying everything I had seen.

Away from campus, the trees had a startled, gaunt look to them, like they had been caught unawares, branches lifted against a heavy sky. The streetlights thinned as the road twisted alongside the woods.

In my rearview mirror, I saw headlights. Someone had turned on their high beams. The road had only one lane in each direction, and I wanted to pull over to let the car pass, but there was no good turnoff.

Finally, I slowed at a shoulder; the car behind me slowed as well. I stepped on the accelerator; the car behind me did, too. My heart pounded as we took those winding turns at high speed.

When I glanced back up at the rearview mirror, the headlights were coming fast. I gripped the steering wheel with both hands at the very moment of impact. My car lurched forward. Then, I felt it again. A second impact, only this one clipped my back bumper and spun me out. I tried to get a glimpse of the driver as they flew by, but it was dark, and the car disappeared around the next bend.

For the rest of the ride home, my body vibrated with fear and adrenaline. I had just been hit. Actually hit. It was taking my brain a solid moment to process this information because the sequence of events felt slippery and ungraspable. What exactly had happened?

The second the question took shape, so too did the answer. Not as one possibility among many, but as *the* possibility. Tim Janek, the only logical one. He has seen me on campus. He knew that I knew. He'd followed me home. Of course, he had. It made perfect sense to me in that terrified state.

When I reached my apartment, I didn't even turn on the lights. I popped the cork on a half-empty bottle of burgundy, downed it as if it were water, and smoked every remaining cigarette until they were nothing but ash.

I reached into my pocket and pulled out the list I'd made about Lucia earlier that afternoon. All those little facts, lined up straight. I pendulum swung between the delusion that I could crack this case open and the delusion that I was a hunted man. Was either true? I couldn't say. They felt true, but I had no firm grasp on reality anymore.

As I looked over my list, a single word pulled itself into focus. I had no idea what it meant or why I remembered it just then. When Jack had said it in the car that evening, it felt irrelevant. Entirely beside the point. But now it imposed itself on me with sudden urgency, and I jotted it down so that I wouldn't forget it.

Lotus.

***

The first thing I did Tuesday morning was call the lawyer, Simon Prichard. I fought the urge to tell him about the car accident the night before. I had no proof that it was Tim, but I would have bet my life on it.

As it turned out, Simon Prichard knew Detective Waters. He said he'd make a few calls and get back to me.

When I thanked him, he said, "Don't thank me. Thank Tim Janek." Like hell I would!

The next call was less cordial.

I phoned Phaedra and told her I was 99% certain her husband had tried to run me off the road. She was silent on the other end of the line.

"You don't believe me?" I asked.

"I believe you believe it," she said.

"Don't be patronizing."

"What do you want me to say, Neil?"

"I don't want you to say anything. I just want you to know that your husband is a psychopath."

She didn't respond.

I was sitting in front of my computer, fiddling with a pen, when I glanced down at the list I'd made the day before. At the bottom was the word *Lotus*, scribbled in a shaky hand.

"Hey, listen," I said, changing my tone. "Remember a while back, when we were talking about that club, the Dionysus, and you said that Tim said that Jack had told him about it? I'm just wondering, did Tim ever go there?"

She sighed. "You already asked me that."

"Yeah, but you never answered."

"This needs to stop, Neil."

"I just need to know if he went there."

"No!" she shouted. "No! He did not go there. Whatever you're looking for, it's got nothing to do with Tim." In the background, I heard her close something, a drawer or a closet. A small click shut.

The thought of her, bustling around her little manicured house, defending her lying, cheating husband, fielding my calls like I was the crazy one, set me off.

"He's seeing someone, Phaedra," I blurted out. "One of his graduate students. I saw it."

For a long time, there was nothing on the other end. When she spoke again, her voice was frighteningly calm.

"Go on your silly goose chase if you want," she said. "But leave us out of it."

***

That afternoon, I climbed into my car and started driving. I didn't know exactly what I hoped to find, but I felt pulled by a deep internal need.

I found the address of the Dionysus in the article about the fire. It took me almost an hour to get there, and it wasn't until I got off on that industrial stretch of nothingness that I questioned the sanity of this decision.

Someone had put up graffiti on one of the corrugated warehouse walls. A cartoonish picture of a bird with stick legs. "Suck my balls" was written underneath it. Where the Dionysus had once stood, there was now a razed lot. On the site next to it, men were loading pallets onto a truck.

I parked on the gravel and stepped out of the car. There was no signage, no half-burned bar. Whatever the Dionysus had been, there was no trace of it now. I wandered around, trying to conjure Lucia in this place.

"Can I help you?" someone asked. I turned to see a man in a bright yellow vest and a hard hat. He looked to be in his mid-fifties.

"I don't know," I said. "Neil Weber." I introduced myself and extended my hand. But the man didn't move toward it or even acknowledge it. Just stood there staring at me. "I'm doing a little bit of research. On that club that was here. The one that burned. I was hoping to find someone who knew about it."

The man looked around and shrugged.

"Can't speak for these guys," he said, nodding at the men behind him, who were shouldering heavy objects onto the raised platform of a big rig. "Some are new." He looked at me. "Others don't like to get involved."

"I understand," I said.

"I've worked here for the last twenty-three years. So, if anyone knows anything, that'd be me. Carl Vargas, warehouse supervisor." Now he offered his hand. "What're you looking for exactly?"

The problem was, I didn't know.

"Anything, really," I said. "Any information you can share. Did you know much about it?"

"The club?" He studied me with his small blue eyes. "Didn't frequent it, if that's what you mean."

"What was your impression of it? Did it seem—" I searched for the right word, "—legitimate?"

He snorted. Then said, "You a cop?"

"No, sir."

I was prepared to lie and claim I was a journalist, but Carl Vargas didn't seem interested. He shoved his hands in the front pockets of his jeans.

"Cops came by here after it burned. Asking all sorts of questions about who's coming and going around here. No one had any answers, of course. Like I said, no one wants to get involved. But I will tell you, one of our guys got burned. Real bad. Third degree all over his body." He made a gesture across his chest and arms. "And man, let me tell you, until you seen it up close, you can't imagine what a burn can do to the skin." He was shaking his head. "I went to see him over in the hospital. Poor bastard. He was on so much morphine, couldn't barely keep his eyes open." He shook his head. "I'll tell you what, though, that's the damn shame right there. When a man can't work. Sure, there's workers' comp and insurance and all that, but that man's life is not gonna be the same. Not ever."

I nodded. "What about the club itself? What'd you make of it?"

He whistled.

"Oh, I don't know much about that." He looked back over his shoulder at the men loading pallets. "Brought in a bunch of lowlifes, if you ask me."

"Like who?"

"Not like the kind who come in guns-blazing. Nothing like that. Rich folks with nothing better to spend their money on."

"Ever see anyone coming in or out?"

He squinted into the sunlight. A smattering of clouds drifted across the sky.

"Sometimes. We'd be opening up when that club was closing down in the early morning. You'd see these young girls. Skinny, all bones and knock-knees. Looked like no more than children, if you ask me." He gave me a look so I'd catch his drift. "Those girls were young. I'm talking *real* young. You can't have young girls working a job like that. It's not right." He was shaking his head.

"You think they were trafficked?"

"Trafficked?" he repeated, recoiling. "What the hell should I know about *trafficked*? Do I look like a federal agent? I got no idea about what's trafficked." He leaned in. "But I'll tell you what. If I ever caught my daughter coming to a place like that—" He was shaking his head, nostrils flared. "I tell you what right now, I would lock her in my house so fast. Throw away the key." Behind him, someone rolled shut the back door of a big rig, and Carl leaned closer. "Between you and me," he said, "it's a damn good thing that place burned. Raze it to the ground." He dragged his boot through the gravel. "Sorry can't help you more than that. I should be getting back."

"Of course. Thank you." As Carl turned to leave, I said, "Oh, just one more question. The guy that owned the place, you ever see him?"

He thought for a minute. Shook his head.

"Naw. But don't need seeing to believe. They say he killed a man once. 'Course, could be all talk. People like ugly stories."

"What about the girl who ran it?"

"You said *one* question."

I raised my hands in defense. "Last one, I promise. There was a girl who ran it, I guess. Lotus something or other. You ever see her?"

He crinkled his face.

"Don't think so, no." Then he smiled. "Pretty flower though. Lotus."

A flower. I hadn't thought of it.

"Yeah, I guess it is," I said. "Don't know much about flowers myself."

"That's a sacred flower, right there. Grows in water. Wife's a botanist. Amateur, but you know." He hooked his thumbs on the front of his neon yellow vest. "Got these plants all over my house. Verbena. Ever heard of verbena? No, course not. Ivy and snake plants—mother-in-law's tongue. Ah, got all kinds of flowers. Lotus flower. Pretty little thing. It's rare. But uh, yeah," he said, as if remembering my question, "a girl named Lotus? Can't help you with that."

I thanked Carl for his time. He nodded, turned, and walked away, muttering something about sunlight and soil density.

When I got home, I went online to pull up a picture. The lotus flower anchors its roots in the mud. Each night, it sinks into the water; each day, it blossoms anew. Death and rebirth, over and over. Time circling back on itself, endlessly.

CHAPTER 24

LUCIA

Then

The following Saturday, I borrowed Naseem's car and drove an hour and a half to the meeting. It was ludicrous to go that far. For what? Some shred of anonymity? I could have switched, found a meeting closer to campus. But I didn't.

When I arrived, Caitlin was there, just like last time, welcoming everyone. She wore a knee-length corduroy skirt and feather earrings. Next to her was a table with coffee and store-bought pastries.

"Welcome, Elena," she said when she saw me. It was startling to hear my sister's name. I'd forgotten I'd lied.

When we were all seated, one of the girls, Maricela, began talking about what she'd eaten that week. How she'd resisted the urge to vomit on Thursday, then made up for it on Friday with a vengeance. Anne arrived while Maricela was speaking. Jeans and a pale blue sweater over a T-shirt. Bright red lipstick this time, a smudge of it on her front tooth. It made her look oddly older. Maricela stopped talking, and Anne gave a small nod, then sat down next to me. Her presence shifted things, electrified the air.

Others took their turns before Caitlin turned to me.

"How was your week, Elena?"

"It was okay, I guess."

"Any feelings come up for you this week that you'd like to share?"

I shrugged. "Nothing much happened this week."

"Did you think of hurting yourself?" Caitlin asked.

I must have looked startled because Caitlin gave a knowing nod toward my arm. My hand shot up to my bicep. I hadn't realized that everyone could see my scar. I pulled at the sleeve of my shirt.

"I was wondering if you feel comfortable sharing with us how it happened?" Caitlin asked. The way she framed questions made it hard to say "no." Everything gentle, extended like an invitation. I kept my fingers curled around my arm.

"I did it to myself," I said.

Caitlin nodded, as if this much was assumed.

"I burned myself." I could feel the group's silence. Their listening. I could feel Anne's eyes on me, her face in my peripheral vision. "Then I cut myself."

"You burned yourself, then cut yourself." Caitlin's voice was unhurried. "Always in that same spot?"

"Other places, too. But yes, mostly here."

"Why there?"

I took a breath. And in an instant, I was back there. Not the day I'd mangled my arm, but the summer that had forced me to do it.

"I, um, I think I was trying to dig something out."

Caitlin sat silent, as if waiting for me to elaborate. She seemed to know when to push and when to let up. But I didn't say more.

"And did you? Dig it out?" I could feel Anne eyeing me from the side. Her red lipstick, a pop of color.

I shook my head. "No."

***

Over the years, there were things I'd wanted to share with others. With Naseem. Michelle. Elena. There was this feeling that words might shift the balance of things. But I'd spent half my life silencing them, and now they refused to come. I never ended up sharing in the meeting, but if I had, this is what I would have said:

I was nine years old when Giancarlo arrived. My father's oldest friend from Brindisi had come to spend the summer with us. Even before he arrived, his presence loomed large. Stories of the two of them skipping school, smoking cigarettes by the sea, running along the docks at night, chasing girls. *Porca miseria*, Giancarlo said that first night sitting at the dinner table. *How many girls!*

In our imaginations, he was part legend, part God.

When Giancarlo spoke, we listened. He nodded toward my father.

"With Pietro, it was always perfect," he said.

Giancarlo had learned "business English" in Naples, where he said the American tourists were fat and shoveled pizza into their mouths like they'd never seen one before. Giancarlo had a dark mustache above his upper lip that moved up and down when he spoke.

"The two of us were everywhere. I would tell your father, let's go, and—" Giancarlo whistled between his two front teeth "—we were gone, doing all kinds of tricks!"

"Don't listen to him," my father said, flapping his hand. "Giancarlo is a storyteller. You can't trust him." My father had taken the day off work. In all my life, I had never seen him take a day off work. That night, my father laughed with his mouth open.

Giancarlo said, "And then this big shot moves to the U.S. of A.," slapping my father on the back, "leaves me behind with the fish."

"And the girls."

"Who are not half so beautiful as Annalisa," he said, gesturing toward my mother, who blushed. The whole night, my father and Giancarlo finished each other's sentences. I wondered if my mother was jealous.

"And now look at him! The life he makes, eh! With his beautiful wife and his beautiful children. You are already family to me," he said.

He told us to call him "Uncle Gianni."

In the daytime, he came downstairs in shorts, loafers, and an unbuttoned linen shirt that butterflied open when he walked. In the afternoons, he took Elena and me for ice cream in my father's car, driving like a maniac. Two scoops each, chocolate syrup, sprinkles on top.

Uncle Gianni blew into our lives in a rush of slurred Italian and hairpin turns. The first night he came into my room, he kneeled down next me, his face level with my pillow. His breath warm and smelling of something strong and spicy, the grappa that my father drank sometimes after dinner.

"*Stai dormendo*?" he asked, first in Italian, then in English. "You sleeping, Lucia?"

I kept my eyes shut tight, and he left.

The next time he came in, he lay down on top of the covers. I could feel him shivering, like he was cold, though it must have been eighty degrees in there.

He didn't check to see if I was sleeping, he just began talking, like we were in the middle of a conversation.

"All day my attention is split," he said. "Your mamma, Elena, Pietro, you." I could feel the expansion of his chest as he breathed. "But is important you know, Lucia, you are very special to me. My oldest friend's oldest daughter." He turned and touched my face. "You understand what I am saying?"

Soon he was coming regularly. On those nights, I was afraid to move. Afraid to encourage him, but also, afraid that he would get mad. My father looked up to him, loved him like a brother. What would it mean if Giancarlo hated me? If he told my father that I was no good, not the kind of daughter he'd hoped for his best friend? He'd whisper to me, "You're a very special girl," and the word *special* hung in the air, sanctifying everything. My dolls, my books, the wire mobile I had made in school that year and hung in the corner above my desk.

The first time he took my hand and brought it to his body, I could feel something hard. I tried to pull my hand back, but he whispered. "*Stai calma, tesoro.* Just relax. It's natural. It's just our bodies." He held my hand against him. After a minute, he leapt from the bed and fled the room.

But the next night, he was back. I never knew when he would come and when he would not. That summer, I stopped sleeping. I've never been a good sleeper since.

"Do you like this?" he asked me once. "How close we are?" I didn't answer. By that point, he had begun to put my hand down his pants, not just over his pajamas.

One night, he said: "I want you to feel good, Luci."

He inched down to the foot of the bed and lifted my nightgown. Everything in me wanted to scream. The fine hairs on my legs stood up straight, my body exposed in that moonlit darkness. He pulled my underwear down, and I could feel his mustache brush against the skin of my inner thigh. "I want you to know how much you mean to me. You're not like anyone else. Don't ever forget that."

What did I experience in that moment? I don't know. I can't even tell you because I wasn't even there. Physically, yes. I lay frozen. A corpse. But inside of me, another girl had arrived. She had my name, my face, my hair, my night clothes. My body belonged to her. But I was elsewhere. Descartes says there is mind and there is body, and I understand this separation as intimately as anything in the world. I let Giancarlo have my body. I was glad to be rid of it.

On the last night he stayed with us, he came to my room, as I knew he would. I was happy he was leaving in the morning, but already, I understood that what he had done could not be reversed. *There was damage.* Or *I was damage.* I never could decide on the accurate subject of that sentence, but I knew that the answer mattered. That it held some deeper truth—whether there was hope for me, or not.

When Giancarlo climbed on top of me that last night, I let my mind go, hoping for something to distract from the searing pain between my legs. On the far wall was a Mickey Mouse clock. I could hear the second-hand ticking. Orion shone in glow-in-the-dark stars above me. *Cucciola*, he whispered. He had been gripping my arm so hard that his fingers left marks around my bicep.

Of all the places on my body that Giancarlo violated, my upper arm seems the least significant. So, I'm not sure why it became the locus of all my pain. My fixation. If I could cut away the feeling of his fingers around my arm, then maybe I could be free of him. I could stop smelling his breath when I slept, his cologne on my pillow. I burned my skin; I dug a razor into my arm, yet he remained. The pain didn't go away, only wedged down deeper, until it spread to every organ, every limb, every cell.

The morning after, there was blood on my sheets. My mother congratulated me on getting my period for the first time. My real period wouldn't come for three more years. As for my father, he never broached the subject. But between us, there grew a distance. For me, it became tied to the feeling that I had done something wrong. That I had disappointed him. That he knew, or sensed, what had happened. And that I was to blame.

***

I said none of this to the group, and Caitlin moved on to someone else. Only Anne seemed to keep her eyes fixated on me.

Another girl from the group was speaking when, somewhere up in the trees, a crow cawed. Another crow responded. I glanced up into the canopy and tried to spot them. People say crows are smart animals. I've seen them drop walnuts onto the road and wait for passing cars to crack them open, so they can eat the insides. Someone once told me that crows have culture. They teach each other things; they learn from one another. That's what culture is. I once saw a crow standing guard over another whose wing was broken. It just stood there, shrieking at anyone who dared to get close.

Right then, Anne leaned in next to me. "Murder," she said under her breath.

I turned to her. Her eyes were on the girl who was speaking, but she nodded toward the trees.

"That's what they're called," she whispered. "A murder of crows."

I looked up. The birds had gone silent.

After the meeting ended, I waited for her.

"How'd you know that?" I asked. "About the crows."

She smiled. A few strands of her hair had come loose from her ponytail and flew in thin wisps around her face. She didn't answer, just asked a new question.

"You know what a bunch of apes is called?"

I shook my head.

"A shrewdness."

"Really?"

"A bunch of rats?"

"A posse?" I ventured.

"A mischief," she said.

I laughed out loud. Some of the women were standing around the pastries, and they turned to look.

"My mother was a zoologist," Anne said. "Before she got married." She glanced up at the trees, but the birds had flown off.

"That's cool," I said. I imagined having a zoologist for a mother, and it made my life feel small and colorless in comparison.

Anne shrugged.

"It's good for trivia," she said. "See you next week. Elena."

I watched her walk to the parking lot and drive away.

CHAPTER 25

NEIL

Now

The lawyer, Simon Prichard, left a message on my voicemail.

"I have news," he said. "Call me back."

When I reached him, he said that the news was good, mostly.

"Looks like they're pursuing other leads."

"Other leads. What does that mean exactly?"

I heard the crinkle of leather, as if he'd just shifted his weight on a plush and probably expensive chair.

"It means, stay vigilant. But also, you can take a deep breath."

"So, am I in the clear?"

"No one's in the clear," he said. "But it doesn't sound like you're their prime suspect."

"Who is?"

He laughed. "Are you running your own investigation?"

I wondered if Phaedra had told him.

"No, I'm just—"

"How about you let me worry about your case. You worry about avoiding trouble. Just steer clear of this whole thing, okay?"

After we got off, I phoned Jack.

It was the first time we'd spoken since that evening in his car weeks earlier—the longest silence since our friendship began.

"Professor," I said.

"Professor," he responded.

We chatted for a moment, then he got quiet.

"What is it, Neil? I can feel you not asking me something."

I hadn't planned on coming right out and asking, but now there was no point in pretending. I told him that I'd been thinking about the girl, Lotus, from the Dionysus. I wanted to know how I could get in touch with her.

"I don't know what to tell you." He sounded annoyed. "I don't even know her real name."

"Didn't you used to call her? Or text her or whatever? I mean, when you wanted to—set something up." There was no delicate way to put it.

Jack gave me her number.

"But you won't find her," he said. He was right; her phone was disconnected.

***

It was, thus, out of desperation that I found myself parked in front of Vanotti's Italian Cuisine again.

I took a seat at an empty table near the window. The place looked different to me now. Not in a physical way. It's just that, last time I was there, Lucia was a missing person. Now, she was a murder victim.

A waiter stood at my table, and it took me a second to realize it was Lucia's father. He had her same dark hair. The same dimple in his cheek. He looked exhausted, barely there.

It had been over a month since they found Lucia's body, but still, I was gripped by the unbearable demands that life makes of survivors. This man's daughter had been murdered, left in the woods, half-clothed. And here he stood, carrying on with the daily business of living.

More than anything, I wanted to talk to Elena. So, when he greeted me, I said, "Last time I was here, there was a waitress who recommended something. I can't remember if it was eggplant parmesan? Or lasagna?"

He turned toward the back of the restaurant. "*Ele*," he said, calling to his daughter. "*Vieni qui*!" Elena came out of the kitchen. When she saw me, her expression changed. Her father didn't seem to notice. "*Quest'uomo qui . . . ,*" he began and then slipped into a long monologue in Italian.

"*Faccio io,*" she responded. And just like that, she took his place.

I hadn't seen Elena since the evening vigil on campus, though she hadn't spotted me. Now, sitting this close to her, I could see the delicate way she held herself. Like a bird with its wings folded.

"What can I get you?" she asked.

"Whatever you brought me last time," I said.

She nodded. For the rest of the evening, she left me to myself. Deposited my food and didn't come back until I asked for the check. In the interim, I had decided it was foolish to be there. I wasn't even sure what I wanted to talk to her about. Except that, as I paid, I found myself saying, "I wanted to ask you something."

She quickly glanced around the dining room and, to my surprise, sat down at the table across from me.

"I'm sorry to bring all this up again," I began. "It's just—I overheard some kids on campus talking about this place called the Dionysus. I was wondering if you'd ever heard of it."

She seemed to consider it, then shook her head.

"Should I have?"

"How about someone named Leon? Leon Schultz?"

Again, she shook her head. I saw her glance toward the kitchen.

"How about someone named Lotus?"

At Lotus's name, Elena looked at me hard. Her eyes flashed, and I saw something change in her expression. Then she shook her head and stood up.

"I should probably be going. I have to check on my other tables."

"Of course," I said. She took a small step away, and I felt this urgent need to keep her there. "Listen, I realize you don't know me. I'm just some professor who works at her school. But I really am trying to help."

She looked around again and folded her arms across her chest. Not defiantly; protectively.

"I can't talk here," she said in a low voice. "Can you meet me somewhere? Tomorrow? There's a park near here. Just around the corner. At noon?"

***

The next day, I arrived at the park early and found a bench under an elm tree. The park was small with a grassy field and a playground. Two children were on the swings. A third flung sand in the air. Summer wouldn't be here for a few weeks, but I could feel it. A shift in the air.

Just after noon, I saw Elena coming toward me. She wore a flower-patterned dress and sandals with bare legs. I stood to greet her.

"Thank you for meeting me," I said.

"I wasn't sure I would," she admitted. She bit the corner of her lip, then looked at me sharply. "Do the police know you're doing this?" she asked.

I thought about lying but decided against it. "No," I said.

"They've taken in Lucia's boyfriend," she said. "For questioning, I guess."

"Naseem?"

She nodded.

"What do you think of it?" I asked.

"I don't know what to think anymore. I mean, I'm not an idiot. I know people are capable of horrific things. But Naseem—no, it doesn't sit right."

"I met him only briefly," I said, "but I know what you mean—about it not sitting right."

One of the children had leaped off the swing and ran in circles around the playground, shouting, disturbing the quiet.

Elena turned toward me.

"Last night, you asked about Lotus," she said. "I should have been clearer: I don't know anyone named Lotus." I tried to mask my disappointment. "I apologize if I gave you the wrong impression," she said.

"No, it's fine," I said. "It was a long shot anyway."

She was staring out across the park. A man had arrived and was juggling a soccer ball on his knees.

"But I did find something," she said. "In Lucia's nightstand. At the time, it didn't seem important. It's not like I was trying to keep it from anyone. I honestly hadn't thought of it until you asked me last night."

Elena reached into her bag and pulled out a book. *The Odyssey*. She handed it to me, Homer's epic poem.

"Was Lucia—reading it for school?" I asked. I didn't see the connection.

"I don't know," Elena said. "It was inside a drawer in her nightstand. I went in there, right after she—when she didn't come home. The cops hadn't even shown up yet. Anyway, I found this book. Inside of it, there was a thousand dollars. All cash."

Jack's money. Lucia had taken it after all.

"I told the cops about the money, told them where I found it. I didn't mention the book because it didn't seem relevant. Just a place to stash it, you know?" Elena pushed a lock of dark hair behind her ear. "The police are looking into the money, whatever that means." She stared at me. "But that's not what I came to tell you. Last night, you asked if I knew Lotus, which, as I've said, I don't. But—" she opened *The Odyssey* to a page that was folded down. "This is where I found the money. Right here on this page."

Someone—presumably Lucia—had circled a passage in the book.

It read: "...we set foot on the land of the Lotus-eaters, who eat a flowery food."

I looked up at Elena. In the margin of the book, someone—presumably Lucia—had written, "Reinhardt."

Elena was staring at me.

"Lucia never wrote in her books," she said. "Never. She was really protective of them. She wouldn't even lend them out. No writing. No markings at all. Except this." She tapped the page. "Reinhardt. Right here next to the word Lotus."

Light came down through the branches of the elm and made her eyes shine.

"What does it mean?" I asked.

"I don't know," she said. "I thought—when you asked about Lotus—maybe you had some idea."

The expression on her face was terrible to look at. Disappointment and sadness. She closed the book and put it back into her bag. I wanted desperately to offer her something, some hypothesis, some explanation. But I had none.

"Anyway, it's probably nothing," she said. "It was a stupid idea."

"No! It wasn't. I don't know what it means, but right now, anything could be relevant."

She nodded as I spoke, but I sensed that my words slid off her. She folded her hands in her lap. Long fingers that lay perfectly still.

"Were you close with her? Your sister?" I asked.

Elena took a breath.

"I was." She paused. "I mean, as close as you could be to Lucia."

"Was she hard to get close to?"

Elena shrugged. Her thin shoulders looked frail, breakable.

"Yeah. Well, no. Not exactly. She was easy to get close to. But there was this distance. This part of her that she always kept hidden."

In that moment, I thought of Phaedra. Easy to get close to, but always hidden away.

"I loved my sister," Elena said. She was watching the man juggle the soccer ball across the park. "The last time we saw each other, we had a fight. I mean, it wasn't a *real* fight. Nothing big. Just sister stuff, you know? But I keep replaying it in my mind. Not that it matters now." She fingered the hem of her dress. "It's just, I can't seem to let it go. That it was my last conversation with her."

We sat on that bench for a good while in silence. The weather was hot and the breeze insufficient. I desperately wanted a cigarette but didn't reach for one.

"I should probably be going," Elena said after a while. I watched her stand and smooth her dress.

"I'll let you know if I find out anything," I said. "About Lotus, or Reinhardt, or anything at all."

She said she'd appreciate that.

As I watched her cross the park, I knew I would not see her again.

CHAPTER 26

LUCIA

Then

The first and only time I brought Naseem's hands to my neck, I regretted it instantly. I was on top of him. I reached down and took his hands, slid them up to my neck.

"What are you doing?" He pulled them away.

"Can we try this?" I asked, but I found it hard to look at him.

"Yeah, okay." But I could hear the hesitation in his voice.

Between his reluctance and my micromanagement, everything felt wrong. He didn't press hard enough. I placed my hands on top of his, tightening his grip against his will.

Finally, he pulled back.

"This is weird," he said. "It's not—it's not working. I don't know what you want me to do."

We finished in missionary. Normal, safe. Afterward, we lay there in silence, increasingly our most common language.

***

On Saturday when I arrived at the meeting, Anne was already there. I sat across the circle from her. You could never tell whether she was looking at you or something just behind you, whether she was smiling or tearing you apart in her mind.

She had one leg folded underneath her, an elbow bent on her knee. This time, her T-shirt read *Nouvelle Vague*.

For the next hour, I listened to the women in our group talk about all sorts of things. Caitlin gently coaxed their stories out of them. But I realized, there were never any resolutions. Not for Maricela and her purging; not for Lynn and her survivor's guilt; not for Dmitria and her pills nor Monica and her razor blades. Not for Caren or Karen and their compulsive one-night stands. There was only listening. How far could listening go?

What did I want, Caitlin asked me.

"To stop feeling like this," I said.

"Like what, Elena? Try to put it into words."

I looked at their faces.

"Like I can't fucking breathe."

***

At the coffee break, I made my way toward Anne.

"What's that, French?" I asked, nodding at her T-shirt. She had poured herself a cup of coffee and glanced down.

"It's a band." Then, "Want to hear them?"

She pulled out her phone and scrolled through her music. She held it in the space between us. Both our heads tilted toward the phone as the drum brushes came in. Then a guitar, slow and rhythmic. I could smell her perfume, something musky. A whiskey-throated girl began to sing.

When they kick at your front door,

How you gonna come?

Anne raised her eyes at me and smiled. She wore an olive-colored cardigan over her T-shirt. It made her eyes look bright. I could feel Caitlin watching us. The next moment, she was calling the group back together, but I didn't want to move. I wanted to stand there, listening to the raspy sound of Anne's voice singing along with the lyrics, catching the scent of her perfume.

"It's originally by The Clash," she said, clicking off her phone. "Nouvelle Vague just covers it."

For the rest of the meeting, I heard her voice in my head. Afterward, we walked to the parking lot together.

"How long you been coming here?" I asked.

Anne squinted her eyes.

"Oh, I don't know. Not long. A few weeks, maybe." Then she turned to me. "But this is my last session."

I felt a sudden, irrational stab of panic.

"Why?"

"I don't know. Just wanted to try it out."

"So, you're done?" I wasn't ready for her to leave just yet. I searched for a way to hold her there just a bit longer. "What do you do?" I asked.

She seemed to think about it. "Office job."

I started firing questions. How old was she? *Thirty-four*. Woah. That was older than I expected. Where did she live? *Not far*.

I lied and told her I was twenty-six. Lied again and told her I lived nearby.

"Well," she said, once we'd exhausted the questions, "it was good to meet you, Elena." She was about to climb into her car.

"Hey," I blurted out, "do you maybe want to go for a hike next week? I mean, instead of coming here?" I didn't care if it sounded desperate or pathetic.

"You should keep coming," she said. "You seem like you're getting something out of it." I couldn't tell if she meant it as a slight.

"I wasn't going to come back either."

"Oh, really?" She raised her eyebrows in a skeptical way.

"I know a good place to hike."

She laughed. A nice, unrestrained laugh.

"Yeah, all right," she said, squinting into the sunlight.

I told her where to meet me. It was just a stretch of road. There wasn't even a parking lot. I'd look for her there.

She nodded, and I watched her drive away. It wasn't until I got into Naseem's car that I realized I'd forgotten to get her number. I had no way of contacting her. If I wanted to see her again, all I could do was drive to the meeting spot the following week and hope she showed.

On the ride home, I played Nouvelle Vague as loud as Naseem's speakers would go. I imagined Anne's voice, singing along.

CHAPTER 27

NEIL

Now

I checked out *The Odyssey* from the library after class on Friday. I owned a copy, but like the rest of my life, it was tucked away in some forgotten box.

I reread the passage that Lucia had flagged. There wasn't much there, barely more than a paragraph. Odysseus and his men are on their journey home and are blown off course by strong winds to the land of the Lotus-eaters, who offer them food, the "honey-sweet fruit of the lotus." The men who eat it suddenly have no desire to go anywhere at all. They're happy to plunk down right there, "feeding on the lotus, and forgetful of their homeward way."

So, Odysseus drags the men kicking and screaming back to the ships, and "bound them fast." As it turns out, the danger of the Lotus-eaters, those little drug peddlers in disguise, is not sleepiness or drowsiness. The danger is the risk of losing one's path. Of forgetting Ithaca. Forgetting home.

Next to that passage, Lucia had written, "Reinhardt."

***

Let me be clear: I am not a believer in fate. There is no divine hand. No omnipotent driver guiding things toward one another. But if there were a single moment in my life where fate seemed to intervene, it was on that Saturday when I discovered Reinhardt's.

I was driving—not headed anywhere in particular, just trying to avoid the stifling loneliness of my apartment. Twenty minutes from campus was a Target, and I drove in that general direction, a route I'd taken hundreds of times. On all those other drives, I'd never once noticed the small cafe wedged between the Ace Hardware and the Tae Kwon Do studio.

But like a newly learned word you suddenly see everywhere, Reinhardt's seemed intent on being noticed.

I slammed on my brakes.

Outside was a blue sign. Reinhardt's Konditorei in large type. I swerved my car into the first parking spot I found, nearly getting rear-ended in the process, and went inside. Reinhardt's, it turned out, was a bakery. Austrian pastries. Topfenstrudel, Linzer torte, milk-cream cakes behind the glass. I ordered a coffee and a donut-like pastry and scanned the room.

I had no idea what I was looking for. Maybe Lucia had written the word down in her book because she was meeting someone here. Maybe she had written it down for no reason at all.

All I knew was that I wanted to find Lotus, the woman Jack had mentioned. Maybe this Lotus person had answers, maybe she didn't. But with nothing else to divert my attention, the project of finding her felt paramount.

So, when my coffee was ready, I leaned over the counter and straight up asked the barista if he knew anyone by that name.

He looked no older than a teenager, with deep acne scars in the hollows of his cheeks. He seemed to consider the question, then said: "Nope, don't think so. But I've only been here a few weeks. My manager's in back if you want me to ask."

He disappeared, came back shaking his head.

"Sorry. She's never heard of anyone named Lotus."

Of course, she hadn't. It was absurd to have imagined otherwise.

I thanked him, picked up my donut and coffee, and headed for the door. Outside, the sun was shining. I walked out into it and closed my eyes. For a second, I could pretend I was anywhere. I was far away from here. The door to Reinhardt's was propped open to let the spring air in, and just before I turned to walk back to my car, I heard the barista call out.

"You could always try the other location," he shouted.

I turned and flew back inside.

As it turned out, this Reinhardt's was a sister-location to the original on the other side of town. I drove like there was a ticking time bomb that only I could diffuse.

Unlike the sister-location, the other Reinhardt's Konditorei was a wide-open space full of indoor plants with tables scattered throughout. There were large windows where light poured in and patrons lounged around, reading the newspaper or punching away on their laptops.

I made my way to the counter, ordered another coffee and a turkey sandwich. I made a big show of dropping a $5 tip into the jar, where *Show us your tips* was written in a sloppy hand.

I asked the boy who worked the counter if anyone named Lotus worked there. He barely glanced at me when he said, "Nope."

"Any chance you could check? 'Cause she told me she worked here."

The boy looked annoyed. He stared at me, then, without turning around, called out at the top of his voice: "Anyone here know a Lotus?"

No one responded.

"Lotus," he called again. "Going once. Going twice." He flashed a patronizing smile. "Sorry, no Lotus."

I wanted to reach into the tip jar and pull out my $5 tip.

Yet I noticed that, when he said it, the girl who worked the espresso machine
went very still.

I stepped off to the side to wait for my sandwich, and the girl stole a glance at
me. When she caught me staring, she averted her eyes.

The girl had red hair with blonde roots peeking through. There was something about her—about her movements or just the way she seemed intent on
avoiding eye-contact—that made me want to stay. I sat down at a table where I
could see her and pretended to read the local weekly magazine.

After forty minutes, she heaved a large black trash bag from the garbage can
and carried it to the hallway that led out back. I leaped from my chair and
followed her. I was waiting in the hallway when she made her way back.

"Lotus?" I inquired. No greeting. No formality. If this was Lotus, I wanted
to know.

"Excuse me," she said and tried to push past me.

But I raised my hands in a gesture of surrender and said, "Please. Are you
Lotus?"

She narrowed her eyes. "Who are you?" she asked. Up close, I could see she
was very pretty. Her eyes were catlike, eyebrows plucked thin. Upturned nose
and a strong chin.

"Nobody," I said.

"What do you want?"

"Just to talk."

She looked far too young to be the woman I was looking for. Nothing at all
like I'd imagined. I'd pictured a jaded older woman, someone who had been in

the business for a long time and had seen it all. This girl couldn't be more than twenty-five.

She shook her head and started to move past me.

"Wait," I implored again.

"Get out of my way."

"It's about Lucia," I blurted out. She paused and stared at me. "Please," I said again. "I just want to talk. It won't take long."

"Are you a cop?"

I shook my head. "A professor," I said.

The girl's expression was hard to read, but she took a breath and exhaled like the world had dumped a tremendous burden on her shoulders and there was nothing else to do but bear it.

"I get off at six," she said. "Now, please leave."

***

I was waiting outside when she got off work. Before she was willing to go anywhere with me, she had her own set of questions. She asked them under her breath, like someone might leap out from behind any bush.

Did I know Leon? *No.* Was I working for him? *No.* Had I ever met him or done business with him? *No.* Did I know where he was? *No.*

She knew a bar down the street called The Slingshot. We could go there to talk. But she was only going to answer the questions she felt comfortable answering. Was that clear? Yes, I told her. It was.

The Slingshot was a dive bar, dim and dank, a few old men sitting on barstools—they had probably been perched there all day. Lotus nodded to the bartender, and we headed to a small table in the back.

"So, your name's obviously not Lotus," I said, once we'd settled in with our drinks. Whiskies for both of us.

She eyed me then said, "Sara." Under no circumstances was I allowed to call her Lotus. Not in front of anyone. Not ever. There were other words, too, I wasn't allowed to say out loud in her presence: "Dionysus" and "Leon" foremost among them. I didn't bother pointing out that she had just used his name when interrogating me.

"Does he know you're here?" I asked, intentionally not using his name.

Sara laughed. "If he knew I was here, I wouldn't be here," she said. "I'd be in a ditch somewhere and no one would find me for a thousand years."

I leaned back, looked at her face.

"How old are you?" I asked.

"I'm fucking eighty years old," she said, cocking her head to the side. "Do you have a cigarette?"

I was grateful to her for asking. We smoked sitting right there in the bar. On her ring finger, there was a tattoo of a chess piece. The queen. She saw me looking and moved her hand.

"Did you leave because of the fire?" I asked her.

She eyed me, blew out a line of smoke.

"Before the fire," she said and took another drag. "I hadn't planned it. It was just—" she looked out across the bar. Her gaze had a faraway look to it. She got quiet, and I waited. I was willing to wait the entire night if that's how long it took to hear her story.

"It was just a regular night," she said finally. "I walked outside, and there was this guy, waiting for a car. I hadn't even intended to go. But there he was. He asked if I wanted a ride, and I climbed in. That was it."

I watched her face as she spoke, feeling like she wasn't really speaking to me, and that whatever access I had been granted could be revoked at any time.

"That night, I didn't have anything with me," she continued. "No money, no clothes. I obviously couldn't go back. He would have killed me. And I'm not talking metaphorically. The guy—the one who offered me the ride—he let me sleep on the couch. In the morning, I stole $60 from his wallet and just started walking. I was looking over my shoulder the entire time. I still haven't stopped." She studied my face. "So, yeah, if you want to go to the cops, go. I don't even care anymore. I'm so tired of running."

"I don't want to go to the cops. I'm just trying to understand what happened to one of the girls who worked there."

She turned her head sharply, narrowed her eyes.

"Don't say her name," she said. "Anyway, I didn't know her by that name. At the club, she had a different name. She was Salomé. But I didn't know her. Not really. She came by once. Twice maybe. That's it."

"I'm not accusing you of anything, Sara. Honestly. I'm having a hard enough time understanding how someone ends up working in a place like that."

She laughed. "The same way everyone does. By chance. Because one thing leads to another. Because you don't have other options—or you feel like you don't. Because you've alienated every single person who gives a shit about you. For a million reasons that don't matter in the end, because there you are. And you just keep moving forward."

"Did you—I don't know what to call it—*recruit* her? Or did Leon?"

She slammed her hand on the table. "Don't say his name! And no, I didn't *recruit* her. It was dumb luck that she showed up when she did. She knew this kid I grew up with, Michelle." *Michelle Alvarez.* The pieces were beginning to come together. "That's how she found out about it. Through Michelle. But *she* came to *us*. We were waiting for someone else. Our girl didn't show up. Salomé did. She took advantage. But let me be clear, she found her own way in."

"Is there any chance that he—" I raised my eyebrows to indicate Leon without saying his name "—did something to her?"

One of the old men at the bar stumbled off his stool. We both looked up as he tottered toward us and then to the bathroom.

Sara took a long sip of her drink, then said: "When I found out about it—about what happened—I kept asking myself that same question." She shook her head. "But no, I don't think so. It's not his style. Anyway, he's been gone since the fire. I don't see him popping up just to punish some girl who came to the club twice."

She polished off her drink.

"You want another?" she asked. I finished off mine. I knew I shouldn't, but I told myself I needed to keep pace with her. So, I nodded and she went to the bar to get us two more.

When she sat down again, I asked, "Did you ever see her again? After you left?"

For a long moment, Sara was quiet. Then she said, "Yeah. A few times. At Reinhardt's. She found me."

I thought of Lucia's book. *The Odyssey*, the writing in the margin. She had been looking for Lotus. *Why?*

"What'd she want?"

"An Americano," Sara said sarcastically. "I don't know. She was a weird girl. Who knows what she wanted? She would come in and just sit there, staring at me. Like she wanted me to see her. Wanted me to know she was there."

Right then, the old man stumbled out of the bathroom, a piece of toilet paper stuck to his shoe.

"Was she alone when she came in?"

"Mostly, yeah. Except one time. She brought a friend with her. They sat at a table, drank their drinks. They didn't talk to me or anything. But your girl,

Salomé, she would glance up every so often, like she wanted to get my attention. Then they left. They didn't say anything to me and that was it. That was the last time I saw her."

I listened to Sara speak, all the while, my own thoughts were racing. I don't think I'd fully come around to my theory until I was sitting right there with her. And even then, the whole thing felt so tenuous, so wrapped up with my own feelings of jealousy and vengeance and, let's be honest, liquor. In truth, when I scrolled through my phone to find a photograph of Tim Janek, I didn't really believe it would amount to anything. I knew he knew about the Dionysus, possibly—though doubtfully—from Jack. I knew he was a cheater and a liar, but it was a pretty big leap from that to killing Lucia.

Still, I found his picture online and showed my phone to Sara.

"You ever seen this guy? When you worked there, I mean."

Sara didn't look down at my phone, just said, "I don't talk about clients. Anyway, they wear masks."

"Ah, okay. Well, it's a long shot. But maybe if you could just—"

But I didn't need to say it. I saw her glance down at the image of Tim. His author photo, barely smiling at the camera, one fist propped under his chin in that most unnatural of poses. She didn't need to say anything. I saw it written on her face. She knew him.

"I need another cigarette," she said. She smoked this one with a shaking hand. I didn't rush her. When she was ready, she stubbed it out on a plate we were using as an ashtray and looked at me. Her eyes were hard and angry.

"Yeah, I know him," she said. "He violated one of the girls."

"What do you mean, *violated*?"

"What exactly do you not understand? He violated her." She sounded out each word as if I were a child.

"But I thought it was a brothel." It was a stupid thing to say, and I regretted it the second it left my mouth. Sara looked at me as if I were the stupidest person she'd ever encountered.

"What the fuck do you mean? You don't think sex workers get attacked? I thought you were smart. Aren't you a professor?"

"No, it's just—I'm just trying to understand."

"Let me make it real simple for you: that man," she stabbed her finger at my phone, "is a predator."

Sara explained that the rooms at the club had these panic buttons in them, but the girls were dissuaded from using them. In this case, the girl had hit the panic button. A hundred times. Only, it never went off.

"People come in with all kinds of fantasies. Weird fucked up shit," she said. "You'd be surprised how many of them involve breaking a woman like she's a wild horse."

My mind was spinning. I found it hard to concentrate. I was thinking of Tim, but also of Phaedra. How well did she really know her husband?

"Did the girl press charges?"

Sara gave me a look. "We have other ways of handling things," she said. "Or normally we do. Only, I fucked up. I didn't know how to find him. I paid for that mistake with three broken ribs."

"Jesus." It dawned on me only then why Sara was going to such lengths to hide her identity from Leon. "Any chance this guy—this predator—is the one who did something to Salomé?"

She finished her second drink.

"How should I know? I don't think he ever met her. At least not while I was there. Your girl was long gone before he ever showed up."

We sat at the table for a little while longer. I couldn't focus on our conversation. I was thinking about Tim. About what he may or may not have done, assuming Sara had identified him correctly—which was not at all clear.

When Sara finally stood to leave, she looked at me, a hard expression to her face that aged her ten years.

"One thing you learn pretty quickly in my line of work," she said, "is that most people have the devil inside them, just waiting to come out."

***

I should have gone home. Right then, I should have called it a night. I'd already had too much to drink and I needed sleep. But I blew past my turnoff and headed for a stretch of bars near campus. All the while, I replayed my conversation with Sara.

Of course, she could have been wrong about Tim. The farther I got from her, the less likely it seemed that Tim was the guy. She'd only taken a quick glance at his photo. And what were the odds that the man I despised more than any other had also violated a woman at the Dionysus? Plus, Sara herself had admitted that the clients wore masks. Yet, I couldn't shake that sinking feeling. Because even if Sara was wrong, she'd nailed the essence of Tim. And that's what mattered in the end. That he was a first-rate piece of shit.

I called Phaedra. It rang three times and went to voicemail.

"Call me," I said, leaving her a message. "It's important."

I found a bar in the middle of the block, grabbed a seat, and ordered an old fashioned. This was ill-advised. Even more so when I ordered another. I called Phaedra again. This time, she picked up.

"Stop calling me, Neil," was all she said, then hung up.

"Fuck!" I yelled to no one on the other end of the line.

A woman at the far end of the bar looked over, smiled.

"Lady trouble?" she asked. The woman had long brown hair and a gap between her two front teeth. She got up and scooted down to the empty seat next to me. "Victoria," she said, extending a hand.

I shook it and realized I was much drunker than I'd thought.

Victoria was a practitioner of reiki.

"Not only does it reduce pain," she explained, holding her open palm an inch above my arm, "it helps with depression by redirecting energy and releasing it." I nodded because I liked the sound of her voice and the gap in her teeth. I ordered another drink. The bartender hesitated.

"He's good, Kenny," Victoria said, the little angel.

"Yeah, Kenny," I said. "I'm good."

Kenny ignored me, lifted his eyes at Victoria.

"You're responsible," he said and set a clean cocktail napkin in front of me.

I leaned over and patted Victoria's knee.

She said, "Reiki is about being present." I had no idea what she was talking about. At some point, I leaned over and kissed her, mostly because I wanted to press my lips against the gap in her teeth.

Afterward, I dug in my pocket and dropped a wad of cash on the bar. I didn't bother to count it. Just got up and left. It was close to midnight.

***

Outside, a homeless man shouted at a parking meter, as another man tried to wrangle his dog while picking up its mess from the sidewalk. Everything felt untethered. I slumped into my car and turned the ignition. The back bumper was still dented from where Tim had hit me. As I drove, I gripped the wheel like I was in middle school playing Hard Drivin' at the 9th Street Arcade, my friend, Sam Kitcheson, goading me on. It was difficult to stay within the white lines because they kept swerving. When I came to a stop sign, I counted one-one-thousand, two-one-thousand, three-one-thousand out loud.

It was in that sub-optimal state that I drove to Phaedra and Tim's. Half my brain was functioning normally. That half knew with perfect clarity that this was truly demented. But the other half was hell-bent on carrying it through to the end.

The windows in the house were dark, and as I darted across the grass, I could feel the damp seeping into the ankles of my socks. On the back porch was a bird feeder.

"A fucking bird feeder," I said out loud, as if it confirmed something essential about Phaedra and Tim. To punish them, I tromped through their flowers.

The back door was locked. Through the window, I could see the kitchen sink and a refrigerator. The window was also locked. Every window was locked. Except one.

A small, rectangular pane, cracked open just slightly. It was high and narrow, but I was drunk and irrational. It took three tries to shimmy through. When I landed on the dining room rug, I actually chuckled to myself. I stood up and the house spun wildly. I held my head in my hands to stop the tilting. It didn't work.

At the end of the hall was an African mask perched on a metal stand, and on the wall, an expressionist painting. Next to it was a photograph of a young Tim Janek shaking someone's hand. It looked like Gandhi, but I was too drunk to be sure.

I crept toward the stairs. "You trying to die?" I asked myself. Then stifled a laugh. Truly, I was out of my mind. But it didn't matter. What mattered was the rage inside me, finally making its way out. It felt incredible.

Along the staircase were framed pictures of dead jazz musicians—Sam Coltrane, Thelonius Monk, Charlie Parker. They were playing for me, cheering for me, prodding me on.

I gently opened a door at the top of the landing. A bedroom with no one in it. Next to it was a bathroom. I was taking a tour of the house. I resisted the urge to pee.

I discovered the master bedroom down the hall and opened the door, silent as the ninja warrior I was. The lights were off. Good. Bring on the darkness. I crept forward on stealthy feet.

In the middle of the room was a large bed and a figure lying there asleep. I moved closer. Phaedra's blonde hair was splayed out on the pillow. Sleeping beauty. Sleeping bitch. *How many times had I looked down on her like this?* The gentle rise and fall of her shoulder with each breath. I knelt beside her. All I wanted was to look at her. The shape of her face.

"Phaedra," I whispered. My mouth, inches from her ear. "Phae—"

Everything in me was directed toward her. Love, protection, need. There was nothing outside of Phaedra. That is what I had come to realize. Phaedra was the beginning and end. Birth and death. Dusk and daybreak. She was everything—which is why I didn't notice, didn't care, that Tim's side of the bed was empty. Because there was no Tim. For me, right then, there was no one. There was no Sara, no Dionysus, no Jack, no tenure, no Lucia. There was only Phaedra.

When the door creaked, I was slow to turn. Slow to leave behind the world I had created and re-enter the world as it was.

It took me a long time to realize that Tim Janek stood in front of me, golf club in hand. His face caught in an arc of moonlight through the window.

"Hello, Neil," he said, then wound up and swung his golf club full throttle at my head. Phaedra's scream lit up the room with sound. The last thought I had before I blacked out was an image of my brother from a local newspaper when we were kids. We were at the aquarium. A seal was planting a kiss on Ethan's cheek. On his face was a huge smile. When the newspaper came out, I remember looking at it and thinking that I had never seen my brother smile before.

That thought. Then the world went dark.

CHAPTER 28

LUCIA

Then

I was in the library when I met Micah. He was a graduate student with floppy hair. His hips were narrower than mine, but he was willing to grip my neck in the right way.

"You like being close to death," he said that Thursday night when we hooked up for the first time. He was an anthropology student and thought he'd figured me out. "Edgeplay," he said.

"What's that?"

"You know, BDSM?"

"Why does everything have to have a name?" I asked.

He ignored my question.

"We need a safe word." I could feel his enthusiasm building. "You're supposed to have one."

I walked naked across his bare bedroom, collecting my clothes.

When I got back to Naseem's house, I looked up "edgeplay" online. It didn't sound like what I was doing. I wasn't trying to intensify sexual pleasure. I wasn't indulging in a fetish. I was trying to feel alive.

***

On Saturday morning, I drove Naseem's car to meet Anne. I had no idea if she'd show, and this uncertainty had its own allure.

It had been over a decade since I'd been to those woods, but the moment I pulled off, the memory of them came rushing back. The dogwoods and river birches, the fractured light slanting down through the leaves. The last time I'd been here was with my father. I wondered if I could find the lake on my own.

On the shoulder of the road, there was only one other car, and it wasn't Anne's. I waited twenty minutes. Just when I'd convinced myself she wasn't going to show, there she was.

She wore the same red lipstick as last time. Her hair in a ponytail. Leggings and a T-shirt. Anne was not beautiful in a traditional sense, but she was the kind of person you couldn't look away from.

"Hey," she said as she got out of her car.

"Hey," I said in response. It was the first time all week that I felt calm.

Even though the lake was only a mile or so from the road as the crow flies, there wasn't a straight path. You had to hike for miles through those woods to get to it. But the second we set out I knew I'd find it. My body had its own memory. We didn't encounter anyone else on the way since it wasn't an official hiking spot. It was just the two of us—Anne and me—trekking through those woods.

"How do you know this place?" she asked, after we'd been walking for a while. The ground was soft with fallen leaves and the air was cool, summer turning to fall.

"I used to come here with my dad."

Even now, I could picture him, jumping into the freezing water, me standing guard.

Soon, the woods gave way to a small rise, and my lungs began to work harder. It felt good, for once, to be in my body. To engage my legs. To climb higher into the trees, away from the city below.

At the top of the rise was a jagged path. Down below was the lake. It was smaller than I'd remembered. The shore was only a thin band of rock and water weeds. Anne was standing next to me, looking down on it. For some reason, I felt the need to apologize—for its size, for its failure to match my memory. But when I looked at her, she looked thrilled. And I was suddenly back there, with my father, braving a thunderstorm beneath a rock.

I told Anne about it.

"The storm came up over those hills," I said and pointed. Anne looked off in the distance. They weren't real mountains. Nothing dramatic like the ones they have out west. But that's where the lightning had come from.

"We were the only ones out here when the storm came in," I told her. Anne was watching me. I could feel her eyes on my face, studying me. "The lightning was—so intense. It hit a tree. Right over there." In the place where the tree had been, a new copse had taken root. "The tree just exploded into flames. But it was more like the fire hollowed it out. Like, the outside of the tree was still there, but inside, it was burning. Like the tree was holding the fire."

For a long time, Anne was quiet, and I felt suddenly self-conscious, like I was talking too much.

Then, out of nowhere, she said: "You ever read *Frankenstein*?"

"Like, the book?"

She laughed. "Yeah, like the book. There's this part, before Victor creates his monster, and the same thing happens. Exactly. Lightning hits a tree. 'Nothing remained but a blasted stump . . . I never beheld anything so utterly destroyed.'"

I looked at her.

"What?" she asked.

"Nothing," I responded. But it wasn't nothing. It was everything. It was her. With Anne, there were no transitions, just slippage.

A raven flew past us. Anne looked up and said, "Corvus." I looked at her with confusion. "You know, the god, Apollo? His sister, Artemis, kills his lover after he catches her with a human. It was corvus, the bird—the raven—who ratted her out. Later, Apollo felt guilty as shit, blamed the raven, and in a fit of rage, turned its white feathers black."

There was no one like her. That was my takeaway, even on that first hike in the woods.

We found a spot to picnic. I had brought bread and cheese. She had wine with a screw top, which we passed back and forth straight from the bottle.

I was holding a piece of cheese, not eating it, when Anne looked at me and asked, "Do you starve yourself?"

The question caught me off guard. No one had ever asked me that directly before. Not even my mother, who hovered over me and wrung her hands. Anne's candor was exhilarating.

"No," I said. "Not exactly. It's just, I like the feeling of emptiness."

"Yeah, that's called an eating disorder, Elena," she said. Her gray blue eyes picked up the light.

"Actually," I began, "my name isn't Elena, it's—"

"I don't want to know," Anne said, cutting me off.

"But, I—"

"Seriously. I don't want to know."

"Why?"

She seemed to think about it. Then shrugged.

"You chose it," she said. Her clavicle was a sharp angle against her skin. "You must've had a reason."

For a long time, we sat by the lake, looking up at the clouds. The lake itself was no more than a large pond, but soon the rains would come, and it would get bigger. I thought of Caitlin, right this very moment, leading the group therapy session, looking around, perhaps wondering if we'd show. I knew already that I'd never go back.

On the hike back to the cars, I asked Anne why she went to the group meetings.

"Just to listen," she said.

"To what?"

"Other people's pain, I guess."

She was walking behind me, and I turned back to look at her, her face tilted down, looking at the trail.

"That's kind of messed up," I said.

"I know," she said.

It was late afternoon when we got back to our cars, and I felt that familiar wave of anxiety. The sense that I would never see her again. But before she got in her car, she turned to me and said: "Next week? Same time, same place?"

CHAPTER 29

NEIL

Now

In the memory, I was in the back seat of my father's yellow Oldsmobile Cutlass, my brother sitting next to me, staring out the window at the brown fields that *whooshed* past. Tan leather seats, the BeeGees on the radio.

Then I get night fever, night fever.

We know how to do it.

My father turned up the volume. The tarmac beneath us had its own rhythm.

Now, I opened my eyes to a muted yellow wall, a single window framing a rhombus of sky. Tubes snaked down from machines above my head into my body. My brain felt like it was on fire, a crushing pain behind my eyes.

A nurse came. She reached up, and I saw the soft flesh of her upper arm, pink and loose, wavering with each movement. She pressed a series of buttons on the machine overhead, and I disappeared. When I awoke again, the patch of sky had changed colors. It was dark now, purple-black and ominous.

Instantly, I knew that I was not alone. I struggled to lift my head, and it sent a wave of pain through me. I groaned and squeezed my eyes shut. When I opened them, a face came into focus, a face I knew but was so out of place, it took me a long moment to identify it.

"Trouble seems intent on finding you, Professor Weber." Detective Waters was standing by my bedside. "How you feeling?"

I tried to speak, but my voice didn't sound familiar. It was scratchy and rough and startling.

"Settle down," Detective Waters said. There was a cup of water on the bedside table, and he lifted it to me to drink. It was strangely intimate.

"Know where you are?" he asked.

I nodded.

"Sounds like you gave everyone quite the scare."

I resisted the urge to ask whom. I closed my eyes. The room had a metallic smell layered with Pine Sol and bleach. I could hear the soft whirring of machines, rubber shoes squeaking down the hall. The beeping and chirping of instruments. Somewhere, someone was watching television, its hum traveling through the walls.

"Know how long you've been here?"

I shook my head.

"Two days," he informed me. He pulled a chair toward my bed and sat. "From what I hear, sounds like you were pretty lucky. Could've been much worse."

I didn't feel lucky.

Detective Waters pulled out a notepad and reached out a hand to press the button for the light that was on the side of my hospital bed. "Mind if I turn this on?" he asked. He didn't wait for an answer, and the blinding light made me wince.

"Sorry 'bout that," he said. "This'll just take a bit." He looked at me appraisingly. I wondered what I looked like in the light. "You remember anything that happened on Saturday night?"

The detective wore a gray jacket, flecked with small threads of blue. I forgot his question. He repeated it. I closed my eyes and tried to remember Saturday night. So many images blurred, it was hard to separate them.

"So, you're telling me, you don't remember anything?" He raised his eyebrows like he didn't believe me. "No recollection of breaking into your ex-wife's house?"

Everything was moving in slow motion. When I closed my eyes, all I saw was Lotus. Or Sara, whatever her name was. Her dyed-red hair, the shape of her lips.

"I don't know."

The detective leaned forward, elbows on his knees, and rubbed his mouth with his hand. I heard the chafing of fingers against stubble and saw a flash of the woman at the bar, my hand on her knee. Reiki. Something about Reiki. She moved energy around the body.

"All right, Professor," he said. "Let's just take this slow."

But I was no longer in this hospital room. Suddenly, I was in a different one, standing next to my father, a bouquet of dead flowers on a nightstand. My brother, still as a statue by my side. "Look at him," my father was saying while he gestured to the bed in front of us. His own father lay there dying. I remember the crepe-like skin on the backs of my grandfather's hands, blackened in places. So thin, it looked like it might tear. His eyelids closed but fluttering. "Sonofabitch," my father said under his breath, and I didn't know if he was talking to himself or to Ethan and me.

"Am I under arrest?" I asked Detective Waters.

He leaned in.

"Should you be?"

There was a ringing in my ears. So loud, I wondered if he could hear it. I shook my head no.

"I don't plan on arresting anyone just yet," he said. "We're just having a conversation right now. That's all." It was something about his face that brought Saturday night surging back into my consciousness. A flash of Tim, his golf club wound up behind him.

"Do homicide detectives usually investigate assaults?" I didn't want to sound insolent, but I suddenly felt very afraid.

Detective Waters raised his eyebrows.

"Assault? Who said anything about an assault?"

"I was hit in the head with a golf club. Isn't that assault?"

Detective Waters let out a breath, then cocked his head.

"I don't know how things are back in Indiana," he said. "But in this state, you break into someone's house, son, and you're hard pressed to call whatever happens to you an assault."

I opened my mouth to say something, but Detective Waters didn't let me.

"The man who hit you," he glanced at his notepad—"Tim Janek"—he looked back at me. "He's entitled to defend his person and property. You're lucky—he's not interested in pressing charges. Though, to be frank, there's not much anyone can do once it gets to the DA."

"The DA?" I repeated. "But he's the one who hit me—with a golf club!" The night was coming back in bits and pieces.

Detective Waters shook his head.

"If Mr. Janek had gone right ahead and killed you, he would've been within his rights. We got stand-your-ground laws here."

The headache was back, in full force this time.

"And that's why you're here?" I asked. "To tell me that Tim Janek could've killed me, and it would've been fine?"

"I'm here," Detective Waters said slowly, like he was talking to someone who had a hard time understanding, "because, when a person of interest in a case I'm working suddenly ends up in the hospital after breaking and entering, it's exactly my job to be here."

"I thought I wasn't a person of interest anymore."

He squinted, like he was trying to decide how he wanted to field this. He steepled his hands.

"You aren't. Or you weren't. Now I'm not so sure."

"Because of my cigarette?"

He eyed me, then seemed to decide on his approach.

"Your cigarette was dry," he said abruptly.

"What does that mean?"

"It doesn't mean shit, except that everything else was soaking wet."

Detective Waters explained his predicament in slow, careful words so I could understand. It had rained around the time they'd found Lucia's body. I remembered it—those rains. Her body had been wet. Everything had been wet, except my cigarette. As far as he could tell, it meant that my cigarette ended up there *after* the fact. He stared at me, unblinking. "So, I'm sitting here, asking myself, how to put two and two together," he said. "And then, here you are, coming back into the equation."

I felt a ragged tiredness combined with a new sense of emergency.

"What about Tim Janek?" I asked.

"What about him?"

"Well, have you looked into him?"

Detective Waters looked at me askance.

"You got some reason to think Tim Janek is involved in this case?" I thought of what Sara had said about him assaulting a girl at the Dionysus. I had no idea what Tim Janek was or was not capable of, but after getting hit in the head by his golf club, I felt certain it was greater than anything I'd imagined.

"Maybe," I said.

"Tim Janek is married to your ex-wife, isn't that right?" Detective Waters asked.

He didn't have to spell out the next part; it was clear enough. A man accusing his ex-wife's new husband of a treacherous crime is not exactly a firm lead.

"But you'll be relieved to know that we did look into Tim Janek," Detective Waters said. "After you went and got your face all smashed up."

"You did?"

"Let me be perfectly clear," he said. "The only reason I'm telling you this is so you'll leave this thing alone. Tim Janek was at a conference in New Orleans when she disappeared." I started to interrupt, "—*which* has been confirmed by multiple witnesses. So, unless you have some very legitimate reason to believe that he was involved, I suggest you leave Tim Janek and your ex-wife alone."

There were bags under the detective's eyes that I hadn't noticed before. Or maybe it was just the angle of the light. A general exhaustion laid over everything in my world. The detective rose from his seat and made his way to the door.

"He knew," I said.

Detective Waters stopped and looked back at me.

"Who knew what?"

"Tim. He knew it was me before he hit me."

Detective Waters pulled a face.

"That's not how he tells it. He says it was dark. He couldn't see anything at all."

"He's lying," I said. "He knew."

Detective Waters took a long breath. Maybe he believed me, maybe he didn't. It wasn't his job to settle personal disputes.

"Take care of yourself, Mr. Weber. I sincerely hope we do not meet again."

***

In my dreams, I could hear low voices in the hall. Nurses speaking in medical terms. *Subdural hematoma, intracranial pressure.* Words that had broken free from their context and slipped inside my brain. When I woke again, it was day, untouched food on the bed stand, a cup of applesauce, a package of crackers. A man, sitting in a chair.

"Hello, Neil." I startled. It was Tim Janek, sitting there, smiling.

I froze, unable to blink.

"Not looking so good," he said. "I apologize for that. I had no idea it was you." He clicked his tongue. "Phae's sorry she couldn't make it. You know how she gets with finals. She sends her regards."

"Finals?"

"Oh, don't you worry about that," he said, waving a hand. "Jack offered to teach your last few classes. He's a good friend to you." I imagined my students staring at Jack as he walked in. I imagined their astonishment when they realized how different their class might have been. It was almost laughable.

Tim got up and walked to the window.

"Wow," he said, drawing it out. "You can see all the way to campus from here. Great view! Not sure you can see it from your angle." He walked back, picked up the applesauce. "You gonna eat this?"

I shook my head and he ate it standing up.

"You know those golf clubs?" Tim asked, touching his head, but indicating mine. "Phae got them for my birthday. She said she'd been thinking about doing it since we met." He smiled, as if the memory were equally pleasant for both of us. "I guess we were all there that first night, huh? At dinner. You know, she even took up golf for a bit. Can you imagine? Phaedra, golfing." He chuckled. "She wasn't half bad either. Well, you know how she is when she sets her mind to something—" He pretended to line up a shot and swung his arms at an imaginary golf ball on the floor. It made me physically ill to watch. "Anyway," he straightened up, "she's sorry she couldn't come. Though who could blame her, right? To wake up and catch your ex-husband leaning over you like that. It's gotta be terrifying."

I had no idea why he had come, maybe just to drive home the point that, in this battle of wills, one of us was ready to go all the way.

A doctor rapped on the door and walked in. He looked startled to see Tim.

"Ahh, sorry. Didn't know you had visitors," he said.

"Oh, I was just leaving," Tim said. He tossed the applesauce into the trash can like it was a three-point shot. He flashed me a smile and squeezed my foot through the blanket. "Feel better, Neil."

I watched him walk out the door and disappear down the hall. Even after he left, I could feel his presence.

That night, I thought of my father on the drive home from the hospital. In the driver's seat, he clicked his Zippo lighter open and lit his cigarette. One arm hanging out the window as those fields flew past, now in the opposite direction. My father caught me looking at him in the rearview mirror. I looked away too late and he smiled, tossed the pack of cigarettes back to me, then the Zippo lighter.

I didn't even want to smoke, but I could feel him watching me in the mirror. I lit one and inhaled, then coughed a dry, hacking cough, which made my father laugh. I was eight years old.

Next to me in the backseat, Ethan was watching. I could feel his eyes on me, staring, always staring. I slugged his shoulder as hard as I could. Ethan pulled away, pressing himself against the car door, as far from me as possible. My father laughed in the front seat. In a hospital somewhere behind us, his own father was dying, maybe dead already. Outside, autumn was just coming on.

CHAPTER 30

LUCIA

Then

In a way, the most compelling thing about Micah was his disinterest in me in every regard except sex. He didn't ask what year I was in school. What I studied. Where I lived. If I had a boyfriend. He was interested only in the game we were playing.

I told him I'd chosen a safe word, and his eyes brightened.

"Light," I said.

He looked disappointed.

"That's not really a safe word. A safe word is more like, I don't know, 'red' or 'mercy' or something."

Who made these decisions? What constitutes a good safe word? I decided to stick with *light*.

While sex with Micah became more frequent, Naseem and I had stopped altogether. On our one-year anniversary, we cooked dinner, climbed into bed, and reached for each other under the covers. Only, we didn't have sex. Instead, we curled our bodies into one another. Something we'd done a thousand times.

Only, it felt different. Like the end of something. A shift in the tectonics of our love.

I stand by Rilke when he writes, "Loving does not at first mean merging, surrendering, and uniting with another person." That's not the love Rilke is after. Instead, love is an inducement "to ripen . . . to become world." I'm not bullshitting when I say, I felt closer to Naseem now that he wasn't my lover; our love became a form of granting space, not possession.

***

In the beginning of November, Michelle called me, crying. She and Nurit had broken up—again. We met on campus, and I pulled her into my arms. We didn't say a word. Later, at the library, I watched her. She was skinny and twitchy and unfamiliar.

After an hour, her phone rang. She stepped away, but answered before she reached the hallway, and I could hear her yelling into the phone. I imagined Nurit at the other end, yelling right back. Their passion seemed frightening. Set against the quiet celibacy of Naseem and me, Michelle and Nurit were a tornado that smashed everything in its path. By week's end, they were back together.

One day, Michelle called me.

"Found your girl," she said. I could hear Nurit humming something in the background.

"What girl?"

"Weren't you asking me about Sara? Whatever, Lotus?"

I went quiet.

Michelle continued: "I guess her mom called my mom, who talked to Jas, who called me. Nobody knows where she is. She's a ghost. No one can get in

touch with her. She's not talking to anyone in her family. Just up and disappeared."

In fact, I had not been looking for Lotus. I hadn't even thought about Lotus
since the summer. But now that Michelle said it, everything coalesced. Because
what was Lotus if not a living memory of that night? A witness. Proof that it
happened. That it was real.

"You found her?" I asked.

"Yeah, dude. She's working at a fucking coffee shop. How weird is that?"

I couldn't picture it. Lotus, pulling the lever on an espresso machine as
impatient customers waited for their drinks. Warming up their croissants in a
microwave.

"Where?"

Some bakery across town.

***

That afternoon, I went to Reinhardt's. And there was Lotus, standing behind
the counter, her hair a deep burgundy, framing her pale face. I'd never seen her
in such bright light, always the dim red of the Dionysus hallway. She steamed
milk and wiped her hands down the front of her apron, and I couldn't take my
eyes off her. How incongruous she looked in that place.

It felt powerful to sit there and watch her. In the face of Jack's denial, in the
face of my own withering, Lotus was an anchor to the truth. Even if no one else
knew, Lotus knew—that I had been there, that he had been there. An event had
occurred. She brought everything back, made it present again. I felt hungry to
be around her. When she finally looked up and saw me, her expression was one
of horror. That, too, felt like a kind of power. I didn't exchange a word with
her.

***

Afterward, I went to Micah's apartment. His walls were bare. He had a mattress on the floor. Only a few pieces of clothing in the closet. Nothing in the medicine cabinet. I know because I checked. No photographs, but there were books everywhere. When he was in the bathroom, I swiped one. *The Odyssey*. Later, when I was reading it, I actually laughed out loud. There on the page were the Lotus-eaters. The lure of forgetting. I scribbled the word "Reinhardt" in the margin. A way to bring the night back.

That day, Micah pulled out a shopping bag full of sex toys he'd purchased. Handcuffs, a leather harness with cutouts and metal bindings, bondage rope, a riding crop, a choker studded with ball bearings, something else that looked painful to insert.

Micah beamed.

"Looks expensive," was all I said.

He had researched online and thought he knew everything there was to know. He thought he knew me. He spoke quickly, fingered the sex toys, used words he had learned. *Bottoms* and *scenes* and *power exchanges*.

"Yeah, okay," I said, because I wanted him to stop talking.

I pulled off my shirt and slipped off my pants.

Micah wanted there to be rules, not to slow things down, but so we could take things further. I would have to use the safe word if I wanted him to stop. He wanted descriptions of the pain, humiliation, and discipline. All I wanted was his hands around my neck. The dizziness and lightheadedness, the sudden rush of feeling when he released his fingers and life came surging back.

I slept at his house the entire night. I didn't even check my phone. I had driven Naseem's car, and it was parked in Micah's driveway. I let him do what he wanted to me. I tried to use the riding crop, but it felt silly and staged; I couldn't find the thread of our performance. Halfway through, Micah looked bored. He must have measured his expectations against reality and found reality lacking.

***

In the morning, I left and drove to Naseem's. I crawled into bed next to him and fell asleep. When I awoke, he was staring at me. Cold and distant.

"Naseem?" I said.

He lunged at me, closed his fingers around my neck. He was on top of me, pushing me down, closing off my airway.

"Is this what you want?" He was shouting, shaking me. "Is it? You want *this*? This fucked up shit?" Tears spilled down his cheeks. I clawed at his fingers, trying to pry them off.

"Naseem," I tried to say. "You're hurting me. Stop!"

But he didn't stop. He tightened his grip.

"You're hurting me."

Now I was crying, too.

"Isn't that what you want? To be hurt?!" he shouted. He was pressing me into the bed by my throat. "I don't know what else to do. What can I do?" I was kicking my legs out beneath him. Fighting, struggling. "What can I do? Tell me, Lucia. What do you need?"

Right then, his hands released, and he crumpled forward. His body, limp and trembling. Both of us, shaking. He collapsed onto my ribs. I wrapped my arms around him. He felt like a child, terrified and alone.

Light, I wanted to tell him. My safe word is *light*.

Only, Naseem didn't know it.

CHAPTER 31

NEIL

Now

Graduation came and went. I didn't attend. Throughout the city, families filled up hotels, ate five-star meals, gifted their graduates overseas airplane tickets and fancy luggage. I sat in my office and moved things around aimlessly.

I was leaving campus on Friday afternoon when I saw Lucia's boyfriend, Naseem Bashir, crossing the street from the tennis courts to the student parking lot. When he pulled out in his car, I slipped in behind him. I told myself that I wasn't following him. I made up an excuse for why I turned left when he turned left—*I needed to swing by the grocery store, make a quick stop at the mall.* Yet, all the while, I knew what I was doing.

We carried on this way until he turned off in a fancy part of town where upperclassmen who could afford it lived in single-family homes with their friends. Elm trees out front, beer kegs in the backyard.

I watched him park in one such driveway and idled my car out front, trying to decide what to do. Finally, I threw it into park. There were a million reasons not to do what I was about to do, but what did it matter at this point? Might as well take this thing all the way to the end of the line.

The front door itself was open, only a screen to keep the mosquitos out. I could hear music coming from the back of the house. I knocked at the edge of the screen door, which rattled under my fist. After a moment, Naseem appeared. He didn't open it, just stood there, studying me.

I saw his eyes flick to my head, where I still wore a bandage from Tim's attack.

"Hi, Naseem," I began. "I'm not sure if you remember me—"

"I remember you. From the tennis courts."

"Right."

He held a tangle of computer cords in his hand.

"What do you want?" he asked.

"Just to talk."

"What happened to you?" He nodded at the bandage around my head, still not opening the door.

I could have lied right then. It would have been easy to say that I had been in a car accident or taken a bad fall. But I was so tired of lying.

"I broke into my ex-wife's house," I said. "Her husband hit me with a golf club."

Naseem's face was impassive. He waited a moment, then pushed the screen door open. I followed him into the house. There were cardboard boxes everywhere, stacked one on top of the other. You had to step around them to cross the room.

"You moving out?" I asked.

He sidestepped a box and sat down on the sofa. I took the blue armchair across from him.

"Going home for the summer," he said.

"Are you coming back?"

"I haven't decided yet. It's not—the best place for me right now."

"Because of the police?"

"Because of everything."

I tried to imagine what his life must look like now. The stares on campus. The whispers behind his back. I wondered how many times Detective Waters had dragged him into that small interrogation room.

"At least the cops are letting you go," I said. "That's a good sign, right?"

Naseem shrugged. "They don't have anything on me. But my lawyer says they don't have anything on anyone else either, so they keep coming back around. And I keep telling them, I don't know anything, I've got nothing new to say. When it all happened, my dad flew out, canceled all his patients. He made me get this lawyer." Naseem took a breath. "But the thing is," he continued, "I don't even care."

"About what?"

"I don't care if they question me. I don't even care if they arrest me." He leaned back on the couch, folded his hands behind his head. "For them, it's just this mystery. Another case to be solved. For me, it's everything. She was everything."

Although it was an entirely different situation, I felt I understood something of what he was going through. To go to bed thinking about someone, wake up thinking about them. Stand in the shower, and a memory comes flooding back, or a song they used to like. To forget that you can't just pick up the phone and call. Everything, rewritten in an instant.

Naseem clearly wanted to talk, so I kept my mouth shut and listened.

"You know what the cops said?" he asked. "They said, 'Any guy would have the right to be pissed.' They said, 'If my girlfriend was doing the stuff Lucia was doing, any guy would snap.' That's what they told me." He stood up, like his body was too amped up to sit. He paced to the window, then sat back down. "I'm not an idiot. I know what people said about her. The cheating, the lying. I'm not stupid. And this detective is like, 'Oh, we understand. People snap sometimes. You didn't mean to hurt her. Things just got out of hand. Blah, blah, blah.' And I'm looking at him, and I swear to God, I feel like I'm about four seconds from smashing his face."

Naseem ran a hand through his hair.

"Did you know?" I asked finally. "About the infidelities?" It was a risky tact, but it was a sincere question. Not because he was a suspect, but because I had been there.

"Of course, I knew."

"You didn't care?"

"Of course, I cared." He looked at me with stony eyes. "But I cared more about her." He sank back against the pillows on the couch. "It's not like I expect anyone to understand, but I don't have to explain myself."

"No, you don't," I said, looking at him. "But I do understand."

For a long moment, he was quiet.

"Lucia was just—she had this way about her. Like you could tell she had been through shit. That she was on the edge of something and, at any minute, she could fall. She could fade away. But it's like, she knew it. That's the thing. She wrote about it. She was a good writer."

Naseem got up and walked to one of the boxes. He started rummaging around, looking for something.

"She was pretty much living here. Also, with her parents. But she left a lot of stuff here. Her phone, her clothes."

Finally, he found what he was looking for. A stack of papers. He pulled them out and handed them to me.

"Here, look," he said. "You can see for yourself. She just had this way of putting things into words. Even her essays, they have this—I don't know how to describe it—feeling of an ending."

I looked at the papers he had just handed to me.

"You're not giving them to the cops?" I asked.

"Why would I? They're just essays. For classes and stuff." He glanced at them in my hands. "To be honest, I barely understand them. The economics stuff, yeah, fine. But all this other stuff—the poetry and philosophy—half the time, I don't know what she's talking about."

I looked down and tried to focus on the essay on top, but my head had started throbbing; my vision was blurry, and it was making it hard to concentrate.

"She's a good writer," I said, because Naseem was watching me, and I felt the need to say something.

"You should see all the cards and stuff," he said. "And the letters. There are tons of letters. I have all of it. There's nothing about her death in there, but all these words, they must mean something, right?"

He suddenly seemed too young to be going through this. To be dealing with any of this.

"I'm sorry she's gone." And I was, truly. Though I'd only ever had that one exchange with her, Lucia seemed like someone worth knowing. "I imagine you've thought about this a lot, but do you have any idea who'd want to hurt her?"

"I think about it every minute of every day," he said. "I go through every single memory, searching for some clue. Something I missed. Or the cops missed. Or her sister missed." Naseem shook his head. "And I start accusing every single person I know. In my mind, I'm plotting revenge. Against my roommates. Her old roommates. Michelle, who still hasn't turned up. I think about jealous girls she might have met in the hall. Old friends. Lovers. But there's not a single face that stands out. It's just—it's everyone."

I cleared my throat and lifted the essays.

"Would you mind if I took these home for a few nights? Just to see if I can make any sense of them. I could bring them back before you leave."

His eyes were narrow and dark. It was a huge ask, and I couldn't tell what he was thinking.

"I leave tomorrow," he said.

"Ahh, I see." Reluctantly, I handed the essays back to him. I stood to go, but I had one more question. That night at the bar, Lotus had said something that stuck with me. Once, she'd seen Lucia in the coffee shop with a friend. I wanted to know what Naseem thought of it. I wondered, were there any girls she had been close with?

He scrunched up his face.

"I mean, she didn't exactly have a lot of friends. Michelle maybe," he said. "But honestly, they hadn't hung out in a long time."

I knew it wasn't Michelle. Lotus knew Michelle and would have recognized her.

"For what it's worth, I believe you," I said.

He made a huffing sound.

"Yeah? Well, you're the only one."

After that, I walked to my car and got in. I had just started up the ignition when I saw him trotting out after me. I lowered my window, and he shoved Lucia's papers at me.

"Whatever," he said. "Keep them. I barely understand them anyway."

***

Lucia's papers sat on the passenger seat of my car for an entire night. I couldn't bring myself to read them. I'm not sure why exactly, except that it would be the first and only time I could really hear Lucia in her own voice. Maybe I wasn't ready.

On Saturday morning, before going out to my car to retrieve them, I texted Jack and asked him to meet me for lunch.

We met at a cafe near campus. A small Thai restaurant with five tables inside and the best pad see ew in the city. Jack and I sat in the corner and loaded noodles onto our plates.

He asked about my work, about my article. I didn't bother pretending. I told him it had been rejected and that, at this point, I wasn't expecting tenure. It crushed me to say it. It felt like a final pronouncement on my being. A judgment on my ability to pick myself up and lift myself out of the darkness. An existential verdict had come in, and the answer was, *no*.

"Well," he said, trying to cheer me up, "if you're leaving anyway, might as well go back to that bar and talk to that waitress."

I laughed out loud.

"Yeah, maybe," I said, though I knew I wouldn't.

"Although, you may want to wait until the bandages are off," he said, motioning to my head.

He had waited this long to broach the topic of my break-in.

"So—a golf club, eh?" he said.

I touched the bandage.

"The guy has a killer swing. I'll give him that," I said.

Jack smiled.

"Do I dare ask how it happened?"

"Probably better not to, no. You'll be shocked to learn that it doesn't paint me in the best light."

He smiled. Then said, "I suppose it was bound to happen at some point. Maybe not with a golf club."

"Probably true." I took a bite of the pad see ew, a sip of Singha. "Tim went to the Dionysus, you know." I had planned a thousand ways to broach this topic, but in the end, it just came out. Jack froze, mid-bite. I took another sip and watched him. "Phaedra said he learned about it from you."

Jack looked appalled.

"Like hell he did!" There was a vein that ran vertically down the front of his forehead, and I could see it pulsing. He leaned forward and lowered his voice. "I didn't talk to *any*body about it. Why would I? Least of all to Tim."

"I don't know. Phaedra said it was at one of those Christmas parties. Everyone was drunk. Tim mentioned ayahuasca, so you told him about the club."

Jack's face became very still. A quiet kind of rage.

"Look, I don't pretend to understand your ex-wife," Jack said. "But either Tim's lying to her, or she's lying to you. I didn't say anything to Tim. There is no scenario in this universe—drunk or sober—in which Tim Janek and I are discussing the *goddamn Dionysus*." He mouthed the last two words, rather than say them out loud.

"I believe you," I said. But already, the brief interlude of our goodwill seemed to fizzle out. It was shocking how ready I was to destroy this friendship over and over again. We finished our meal and parted ways.

***

Afterward, I drove to a park in the center of town. On the weekends, they held small jazz concerts on the grass. There were cocktail tables set up, and you could purchase food and wine. In the early days, Phaedra and I had come here to sit and listen. At the time, we were new to the city, and everything was full of promise.

That afternoon, the music was a trio. An upright bassist, a drummer, a guitarist. There were kids sitting on the lawn and adults hovering around the tables. I could feel people staring at my bandages as I walked by.

In my hands were Lucia's papers. Five of them total. I found a vacant table and sat. The musicians were playing an upbeat tune, fingers flying up the frets of the guitar. Their music filled my ears as I began to read.

The first essay was a short one. An economics piece on predatory lending and racial injustice. Lucia's voice was clear, but it lacked precision—the kind of short response students write when there's a party going on and they need to get it done before going out. Next was an essay on the relationship between urban and rural economies and how incentives shape the fabric of society. It was totally average.

Her writing came alive, however, when she turned to other subjects. Poetry and philosophy. There was an essay on Rilke that she had written for Jack's class. It was very good. Then another one about Virginia Woolf's novel, *To the Lighthouse*. She focused on the middle section of the book, where Woolf writes about the death of the mother. The death itself is conveyed within brackets, a seemingly simple parenthetical. Lucia wanted to know why Woolf would write about the death of the central figure of the novel in this way.

It was her final essay, though, that I found myself unable to put down. A piece on our cultural fascination with the dead female body. It was eerie. "Dead girls make for good stories," Lucia wrote, and it sent chills running down my spine.

I was nearly to the end of the essay when I saw a note in the margin.

Her professor had underlined a passage and written, *Citation?* Lucia, it seems, had quoted something from a book without including any bibliographical reference.

I read the page from top to bottom.

When I arrived at the underlined passage, the blood drained from my face. My ears rang, my heart pounded. For that instant, the entire world stopped.

CHAPTER 32

LUCIA

Then

The aquarium was Anne's idea. Instead of meeting at the hiking spot, where we usually met on Saturdays, she asked me to meet her there. I told her I'd never been.

"Aren't you from here?" she asked.

"Exactly," I said.

That Saturday, I arrived at the aquarium early. It was a large metallic building that reflected the afternoon light in moody shades of gray. Inside was a balcony that peered down over an open atrium. There were children running everywhere, their parents trying to corral them. Families and elderly people, babies, and employees. A woman in a wheelchair trying to maneuver into the elevator before the door closed.

In the midst of all that, I saw Anne. A singular light moving across the lobby, pushing a lock of hair behind her ear. I watched her for a moment before calling out to her.

"Anne!" I shouted. But she didn't turn around. To be fair, it was loud, all those voices ricocheting off the walls. I called out again. Again, she didn't turn. Finally, she looked up, a quick flick of her eyes followed by a wave of her hand.

"You came," she said when we made our way toward each other.

We still hadn't exchanged numbers; she still called me Elena.

"Of course, I came. Where else would I go?"

"Good," she said. "C'mon."

"Where are we going?"

"You'll see." Anne led me down a hallway where a tunnel of water surrounded us on all sides. There were schools of fish in red and gold, a manta ray moving in a sleek, ghost-like glide.

"There!" she said.

I looked up.

At first, I didn't see it. It moved so slowly. An enormous beast, swimming silently through the water. When it came into view, I found myself unable to move. I had never seen anything like it. The sheer size of it. Everyone in the corridor watched with reverence.

"It's a whale shark," Anne said. "They put veterans in there with them. For PTSD."

I looked at her aghast.

"In there?"

"It's true," Anne said. For a moment, I thought of Michelle's brother, Manny, stationed overseas. "They're carrying all this trauma. And they get in with those sharks. It does something. On a deeper level."

I looked up at the shadow of that enormous fish.

"It's beautiful," I said. When I turned back, Anne was staring at me, smiling.

"What?"

"You ready?" she asked.

"Yeah." Then: "Wait, ready for what?"

Two hundred and fifty dollars. That was the cost of swimming with a whale shark. Anne had purchased our tickets online. I was incredulous that she'd done it. That she'd paid so much. No one had ever bought me anything that expensive before.

After I regained my composure, I asked, "What if I didn't show up?"

In the waiting room, we had to fill out paperwork before getting in the water. I wrote my sister's name in the blank space.

For the swim itself, Anne had brought me one of her own bathing suits. A red one-piece.

"I wasn't sure it would fit," she said, handing it to me in the locker room.

It was an intimate loan, wearing another woman's bathing suit. I put it on, then stepped into my assigned wetsuit and made my way down the plank.

A group of us sat on the edge, snorkels in hand, our legs dangling in the water. Below us, schools of fish moved about. But we were looking for one shape in particular.

The hardest part was getting in. I kept my eyes on Anne, who kept hers on me. If she was scared, she didn't show it.

Almost immediately, I spotted the whale shark, making its way toward us. That impossibly large form that defies comprehension, white dots along the length of its body like a million stars in a gray-black night. Its movements were long and slow, a presence you could feel in your bones.

I knew there were other people in the water. Somewhere down there with me was Anne. I had caught a glimpse of her hair fanned out around her. But when the whale shark came, everything else disappeared. There was a quiet unlike anything I have ever experienced. A moment of calm that seemed to issue from deep within me. Or from the shark. Or perhaps created in the water between us.

I felt like I was in the presence of grace. They say that animals are healing. People bring dogs to nursing homes and airports. Prisoners help raise them in jails. But this went beyond anything I could comprehend. I don't know how to explain the impossible juxtaposition of feeling utterly vulnerable and perfectly safe.

In that water, something suddenly became clear. In a way, it defied language, but it made me think of reading Kierkegaard with Jack in his office. The holding of two seemingly contradictory ideas. On the one hand, I knew that my fear and rage and loneliness were true, were part of me; but so was transcendence. I could see my own small shadow alongside that animal. And rather than make me insignificant, it made me essential. In that fleeting instant, I mattered. Everything mattered. All around us, there was possibility, like we were all flecks of light against the darkness.

In total, we were only in the water for half an hour, but it seemed like more. Afterward, we changed back into our normal clothes, but the afterglow remained. Then we were pulling on our shoes, moving through the aquarium, and stepping outside into the late afternoon.

"Where'd you park?" Anne asked.

"I took the bus," I said, still dazed from the experience.

"Why? What's wrong with your car?"

"Oh," I said. "It's not my car. I just borrow it sometimes." It felt like an opening, a chance to come clean.

Thus far, I had told Anne very little about my real life. I had told her about the Dionysus, that I had worked there on two occasions, but nothing about the men I serviced. Nothing about Jack. She didn't know my real name or that I was a student. She didn't know that I had a boyfriend or that I had been sexually assaulted. Looking back, it's astonishing how little information you can share with someone and still build something that resembles a friendship.

"I could give you a lift back to your house, if you want."

"How about a coffee?" I asked. "I know a good place."

***

I don't know why I took her there, but right then, those two pieces of my world felt like they belonged together. On the ride to Reinhardt's, Anne and I didn't speak about the whale shark, but it permeated everything. Maybe I was afraid that talking about it would contaminate it. That I would lose something it had given me, even if I couldn't name it. I think Anne felt it, too.

When we arrived, Lotus was behind the bar. I saw her stiffen at the sight of us. I found a table where I could sit across from Anne and see Lotus working the counter behind her. Anne sipped her coffee and told me about an article she'd recently read. Apparently, in the Dominican Republic, they'd found a piece of amber. Entombed inside the amber was a 20-million-year-old flea. And on the flea's proboscis, a single drop of dried blood. Inside that blood, fossilized bacteria, bubonic plague.

"How astonishing is that?" Anne said. "Black Death, captured in amber."

I looked at her. I suppose in some ways we were very similar. Two women who let each other get close while also holding one another at a distance.

And suddenly, urgently, I wanted to know. I wanted a kind of honesty that felt appropriate to the experience we'd just shared.

"Why do you really go to those meetings?" I asked.

She looked surprised by my question.

"Why do you?" she parried back.

Until then, I had only spoken of Giancarlo in the vaguest of terms. I took a breath. For the first time in my entire life, I was prepared to say it. To lay it all bare. Anne would be the one and only person to know, and that felt like a powerful kind of intimacy.

But before I had a chance to answer, she said, "I once took a bunch of pills."

The admission startled me. I'd known people who had tried to kill themselves—or knew of them, at least, but no one I was close to. Friends of friends, always whispered about behind their backs. No one who ever admitted it in plain language. Anne was the first person who ever said it out loud to me.

"When?" I asked.

"A long time ago," she said. "I was young. And stupid. And probably a little bored."

"What happened?"

"Nothing. I shat the bed. Ended up in the hospital for a bit. That was it."

Now, behind her, I could see Lotus looking at me. Her eyes narrowed, her jaw set. What was I trying to prove sitting there, making her stir?

I looked at Anne. "I'm glad it didn't work," I said. "The pills, I mean."

"Me, too," she said and smiled. "Most of the time. But I'm glad I did it. It's important to make choices, even regrettable ones."

That evening, Anne offered to give me a ride home, but I wanted to walk. I wanted to be outside, where the wind slipped inside my coat, where I could think about everything that moved around me. The shark and Anne and Naseem and Jack.

CHAPTER 33

NEIL

Now

Sara didn't work on Sundays. That's what the boy said when I called. I could hear a microwave ding in the background. "She's in tomorrow," he said and hung up.

So, on Monday morning, I drove to Reinhardt's. It was a beautiful, sunny day. The coffee shop was mostly empty. Streaks of yellow light came in through the large windows. It smelled like butter and hot coffee. The only other patrons were a group of bicyclists in spandex shorts and clippy shoes, laughing and drinking iced coffees.

I had taken the bandage off my head, and the bruises around my eyes had faded from purple to a jaundiced yellow. When Sara lifted her eyes from behind the counter and saw me walking toward her, she bristled. I had to wait seven minutes before she was able to sneak away into the back hallway. We stood, looking at each other. She held the trash bag in her hand, her eyes darting to the place on my forehead where the bandage had been.

"Did he do that to you?" she asked under her breath. She looked terrified.

I touched my head. It took me a moment to realize who she meant.

"Leon? No! God, no—"

"Don't say his name," she whispered. "Please."

I think it truly hit me right then how far apart our worlds were. She was running for her life. I was running aimlessly.

"So, who did it?"

"Long story," I said. "But right now, I need to talk to you."

"I'm done talking," she said.

"Just one more question. That's it. Then I'm gone."

"You sound like her, you know."

"Who?"

"Salomé. *One more then I'm gone.* That's what she said." I knew she was talking about Lucia. "But I'm done answering."

I had brought Lucia's essays with me into the coffee shop. I was afraid to let them out of my sight. They were tucked beneath my arm. I could feel the underlined passage burning off the page. There was only one thing I needed to know.

"Please. One more question."

"Jesus, fuck! What do you want?! I already told you everything I know."

I pulled out my phone. She looked impatient as I scrolled through.

"Haven't we done this already?" she asked.

"It's not about him," I said, referring to Tim.

When I found what I was looking for, I hesitated for a moment.

"C'mon, then," she said. "I have to get back to work."

I steadied myself.

"Remember last time, you said that Lucia came in with a friend. And she just sat here, watching you?"

"Yeah, so?" Her lips were drawn. Her eyes, large and impatient.

"Right. So, it's that friend I want to ask you about."

"I told you, I have no idea who she was. I never saw her before."

"But you'd recognize her?"

"No, I wouldn't. Her back was to me. She had wet hair. That's it. That's all I remember. They both had wet hair."

"Wet hair? Like they'd been swimming?"

"Maybe they took a fucking shower. How should I know?"

She folded her arms across her chest. I could feel myself stalling. Wanting to know and not wanting to know. My hand was shaking; Sara saw it. She looked up at me.

"Go on, then," she said. "Just show me."

I turned my phone toward her. Sara leaned in, squinted her eyes.

In the photo, Phaedra was dressed up. It was a picture from six years ago, the professional shot we had taken when we'd first started working. Her hair was longer. She wore a suit jacket with a collared shirt underneath.

Sara shook her head.

"No," she said, and I felt everything in me relax. "This girl had shorter hair." She motioned to her shoulders. Despite myself, I scrolled to a new picture. This time, I found one that looked most like Phaedra now. T-shirt and jeans. Cropped blonde hair. Smiling at the camera, red lipstick. I turned my phone around again.

A heavy silence seemed to settle. Adrenaline coursed through me as I studied Sara's face.

"Is that her?" I asked.

Sara didn't respond; she didn't have to. I saw it. The quick retreat. She might not understand what it meant, but she was a smart girl. She knew it meant something.

"Whatever this is, keep me out of it."

She pushed past me and stormed down the hall, trash bag in hand.

***

I went back to my car and slumped behind the wheel. I didn't start the ignition, just sat there, staring out at nothing. People moved about their lives. Monday morning. An ordinary day.

But inside my car, the universe had upended.

I looked down at Lucia's papers. On top was the essay with the underlined passage. In the margin, her professor had marked her down because she'd neglected to include a citation. Lucia had quoted a book and forgotten to add the page number. I read Lucia's paragraph again for the hundredth time.

These were the words she'd written:

Loss destroys language. As Phaedra Anne Lewis writes in her forthcoming book, The Crypt at Last Light, *"the work of mourning is always destined to fail. One is marked by the loss of the other from the outset." There is no getting over loss. Loss is the condition of existence.*

I had found Phaedra's one and only reader.

CHAPTER 34

LUCIA

Then

That afternoon, Michelle didn't show. I knew she wouldn't. Abandonment was becoming a theme in my life. Last weekend, Anne didn't show either. For over an hour, I'd waited at our usual hiking spot, but she never came. Never.

Now, I was standing in the student center, waiting for Michelle. I hadn't seen her in over a month, but she'd called and asked if I'd meet her here. The school was hosting a holiday event to assemble gift packages for active service members. Michelle's brother was stationed overseas. I said I would.

In the huge atrium of the student center were makeshift tables covered in donations. There were cheap paperback books, sticks of deodorant, beef jerky, tubs of peanut butter, bottles of hot sauce, coffee tins, bars of soap, toothbrushes, and travel-sized mouthwash. On one table, there were headphones and chocolate bars.

I was getting ready to leave when a middle-aged woman came up to me. "Thanks for coming," she said. She wore an emerald turtleneck that matched her eyes. "It means so much to our service members."

The woman held a flattened cardboard box, which she folded into shape on the table in front of me. She dragged tape across the seam.

"Once you set up your box, you can grab whatever you want. We have all kinds of goodies." I looked around doubtfully. She smiled. "It might not seem like much, but when you're thousands of miles from your family at Christmastime, a tub of peanut butter is a big deal." She nodded to someone behind me who had just come in. "Once you're done, you can take your box over there," she pointed to where other boxes were already stacked. "Oh, one last thing," she said, reaching across the table. She picked up a blank piece of stationery. "It means a lot to get a handwritten note—just to know someone back home is thinking of them."

"What am I supposed to write?" I felt stupid for asking, but she gave me that warm smile again.

"Anything you want, honey. Anything at all. You could tell them about what you're studying at school. Heck, you could write about the weather, and it wouldn't matter. Just something handwritten. It goes a long way."

She handed me the blank card and moved on to the next person. I eyed the goods scattered across the tables. I picked up a set of headphones, the peanut butter, hot sauce, packages of jerky, as many books as I could hold, and dumped them all into the box. Then I turned my attention to the card.

Hey there, I wrote. *You don't know me, and I don't know you. It's December now, the dead time between Thanksgiving and Christmas.* I wondered if I should cross off the word 'dead.' It seemed insensitive. *It's actually my favorite time of year. No man's land. Or I don't know, maybe it doesn't feel that way to you, being so far away.* I lifted my pen. I imagined a boy or girl on the other side of the world opening this. I suddenly wanted to lay it all bare. *As for me, I'm kind of struggling right now. I mean, nothing like what you're going through, obviously. It's just, I don't feel like I can hold onto the thread of it all. Like I can't catch my breath. Shit. Sorry, this is supposed to be a holiday card. (Worst holiday card ever. Haha!) Anyway, I hope you have a nice Christmas, or whatever you celebrate. I wish we had better gifts for you. It's hard to know what you'd want or what you're missing the most. Stay safe and Happy Holidays.* I didn't sign my full name. Only L. I sealed up the box and dropped it off in the corner with the other boxes.

I was heading back to my station when Jack Sheridan walked in. I hadn't seen him since he'd handed me an envelope of money. Now, here he was, chatting with a girl—a student no doubt. They dumped their things on an empty table and stood shoulder-to-shoulder, laughing casually. My fingers were shaking as I tried to fold my next box into shape.

The girl was pretty. Auburn hair with a volleyball player's physique. Jack looked different. His hair was longer. His jacket piled in a heap next to him. I watched them work in tandem. Even from this distance, I could sense that delirious combination of desire and restraint that animated their relationship. It felt so familiar. But unlike with me, he'd never act on it. Which meant it could go on indefinitely. Tension building without ever sputtering out. It made me furious.

I suddenly wanted him to see me. To look me in the face. I weaved my way through the tables until I was standing in front of them. The girl noticed me first.

"Hi," she said tentatively. Jack looked up, and his face went white.

"Hi," I said, looking only at him. I wanted the girl to feel superfluous.

After an awkward silence in which no one spoke, Jack finally said, "This is a former student of mine." He didn't introduce me by name, and the three of us stood there for an eternity. Finally, the girl excused herself and went over to another table where a group of students—apparently friends of hers—were filling boxes.

Jack stared into the cavern of his own empty box. I lifted a package of ramen and handed it to him. He dropped it in. Then a toothbrush, a bottle of mouthwash. He took each item and placed it inside.

"How are you?" he asked finally.

"Fine. You?"

"Okay, I guess."

There was a lull.

"I went swimming with whale sharks," I said.

"Really?" His blue eyes brightened. "How was that?"

"It was good. Great, actually. I guess they, um, they send veterans into the water with them. It's supposed to—I don't know—help with trauma or something." He nodded. "Listen, Jack—" I'd never called him Jack before. Not as myself. Not to his face. He looked at me with fear. "I was just going to say—" I lowered my voice. "I still care about you, about what happened to you when you were younger. Everything you said that night. The car accident, your friends."

I saw him wince.

"What do you want, Lucia?"

"I don't want anything. I just want things to go back to the way they were." He looked bewildered.

"They can't go back. Don't you understand that? They can never go back." There was a sudden coldness to him.

"We could—"

"We can't. Whatever you're going to say, we can't." His eyes were pleading. "You want to go back? I want to go back, too. Every night, I go to sleep thinking about it. Wishing I could go back to that night and just—not go. Just, decide to stay home instead—"

"That's not what I meant. I don't want to undo it." I could feel tears burning behind my eyes. He must have sensed the precarious edge on which we stood.

"No, please. Don't," he said. "Listen, you're a special girl. You know I think the world of you."

His words made me recoil. Giancarlo's words. *You're special. You're different, Cucciola.* "But you know this can't happen. It never could. I'm not trying to hurt you. I'm just asking you, please."

Through the windows beyond the tables, I could see that an ashy gray darkness had fallen. Jack took a deep breath.

"I think it would be best for us not to have any contact," he said. "Like, if you see me in the hallway or walking to class, let's just keep going—"

"You're not who I thought you were," I interrupted. "You pretend to give a shit, but you don't. You're a coward, just like everyone else. It's pathetic!"

I could tell by the way he was breathing that I was getting loud.

"I don't disagree with you, Lucia," he whispered, glancing around the student center. "But I never said I didn't care about you. All I'm saying is that it shouldn't have happened. Not like that."

"Screw you."

He didn't respond. I wasn't sure if people were looking and, at that moment, I didn't care. Jack started loading items into his box. A package of Q-tips, a box of Kleenex. He reached for the tape and was about to yank it across the top.

"You didn't put a card in," I said coldly.

He looked at me, confused.

"We're supposed to put cards in," I said. "Write something for the holidays."

He nodded, reached for a blank card, and scribbled "Merry Christmas" across the front.

I gaped at him.

"That's all you're going to write? This person is risking their life, and all you can write is *Merry Christmas*?"

He looked at me, defeated, then dropped the card in just the same.

I continued: "Might as well write, *Hope you don't die*."

I was being outrageous, but I didn't care. Jack reached for his scarf, then pulled on his hat so his hair was poking out from underneath. I desperately wanted him to stay, but every word out of my mouth pushed him away. He put on his jacket.

"Happy holidays, Lucia," he said.

He didn't take his box to the drop off like he was supposed to, just abandoned it there. The pretty girl he'd come in with glanced up as Jack edged his way around the tables. He didn't look back at her. And I saw it on her face, that familiar flash of disappointment.

***

That night was the first time I ever remember truly wanting to die. The desire felt clean and clear. This feeling of futility, of uselessness so deep there was nothing outside of it.

I slumped down on a bench outside the Philosophy Department as night came on. It was cold; the air bit into my face, cracked the knuckles of my hands. A lonely cloud moved across a black sky, wispy and gray and headed nowhere.

There are moments that change the course of everything, that alter the trajectory of your life because you can't undo them, and you can't forget them. You don't see them coming, but once they arrive, it feels like they were always on their way. How was I to know that one such moment was upon me? That it would come, not with a bang, but with a whisper.

It took the shape of a woman, bundled against the December wind. Leafless trees with their arms outstretched. A woman, dressed in a long navy coat that reached almost to her ankles, her collar turned up, walking with determination, no wasted steps. A woman, passing under a streetlamp that lit up her face.

Blonde hair tousled by the wind. No lipstick on her lips. Not tonight. A woman who walked to the doors of the Philosophy Department and disappeared inside.

Everything that followed happened on instinct. I leaped from the bench and ran after her. Inside the building, I couldn't see her, but I could hear her heels clicking down the hallway and I ran in the direction of that sound.

Around the corner, I saw a door click closed; I knew, without doubt, that she was inside. For a long time, I stood outside that door.

To me, she was Anne, with the office job. A girl who once tried to kill herself by overdosing on pills. Anne with a zoologist mother. Anne who'd hiked with me to a hidden lake in the woods and taken me swimming with whale sharks. Anne, who admitted in a meeting once that she felt nothing at all.

On the wall outside her door was a name plate, white lettering etched on a brown background. I ran my fingers along the indentations.

Dr. Phaedra Lewis, Associate Professor of Philosophy.

CHAPTER 35

NEIL

Now

In the memory, there is my mother. She is slumped on the floor. Blood trickles down her chin and falls onto her chest. I see her there, her head slammed against the dresser, as he moves toward her again. *And me? Where am I?* That is the question that always returns.

I see my father coming toward her, and I have a choice. To enter their bedroom, to intervene, to put myself between them. To become my mother's shield. But I don't. Instead, I turn down the hallway and scurry into my room. I shut the door and put on my headphones to drown out the sound. Nirvana, blaring in my eardrums.

And I swear that I don't have a gun

No, I don't have a gun

Memoria, memoria

And afterward, the quiet. Ethan's stare, shameful and knowing.

I step back, every time the memory comes toward me. I step back and back and back until my mother's screams go quiet, until the memories disappear, until all that is left is the distant sound of waves on a beach in California.

CHAPTER 36

LUCIA

Then

I opened Professor Phaedra Lewis's door without knocking.

Anne looked up at me from behind the desk. I could still smell Jack's aftershave somewhere on my clothes, or maybe I only imagined it.

For a long moment, Anne looked at me as if she couldn't figure out who I was. When she finally did, her face transformed. In that instant, she became the other person, Phaedra Lewis.

I knew, of course, that coincidences existed in the world. Naseem once told me that Stephen Hawking's birthday was on Galileo's death day, and that Hawking's death day was on Albert Einstein's birthday. Or the reverse. I couldn't remember. I had no idea if it was true. But this felt impossible on that cosmic level of magnitude. That the person I had met at a group meeting a million miles from campus not only worked at my school, but in the same department as Jack. All that shit they say about truth being stranger than fiction. And I always doubted it.

"Phaedra." I said her name out loud, just to hear it in my own voice. "It's a nice name."

She kept her eyes glued on me. I stepped inside and closed the door.

I saw her nostrils flare. "Depending on which version," she said.

"Which version of what?"

"Of the name. *Phaedra's* either a cunning, vengeful wife or a victim of the gods." I saw her take a deep breath. "Sit down, Elena. Please."

I sat on the edge of the chair.

"You're upset," she said.

"Not for the reasons you think."

"Because I lied."

"Because you didn't show up. I waited for you at the trailhead. Twice. For two Saturdays. You didn't come."

She brushed her hair off her forehead with the back of her hand. She was wearing a white silk blouse beneath her coat. None of it suited her.

"You have every right to be upset, Elena—"

"Lucia," I interrupted. "My name is Lucia. Elena is my sister."

She seemed to take this in. Two liars, that's what we were.

"Why didn't you come?" I demanded. "You knew there was no way for us to get in touch. And still, you didn't come. Were you ever going to show up again?"

She was quiet for moment, then shook her head no.

"So that was it. Swim with whale sharks, then just disappear?" She let me talk, let me perform my incredulity without interruption.

"It was a natural end," she said. "What more was there for us to share? We entered that water. We had an incredible experience. When we got out, it was time to say goodbye."

"But you didn't say goodbye. You just didn't show up."

Phaedra didn't defend herself. She simply watched me. "Was any of it true?" I asked.

"Was any of what true?"

"You."

She cocked her head to the side and became Anne again. Not this stranger in grown-up clothes, sitting behind her grown-up desk. But Anne, who wore T-shirts with band names on them and didn't give a fuck.

"What is it you want to know?" she asked. "Ask me, and I'll tell you."

"Was your mom a zoologist?"

Phaedra laughed.

"That's what you want to know? If my mom was a zoologist?"

"Was she?"

Her eyes darkened, and she slumped back against her chair.

"My mother was a lot of things. A drunk. An abuser. Mentally ill." She huffed. "And yes, she studied zoology. She never finished college, but she would have become one. If I hadn't come along. Another way I wronged her."

"What about all that other stuff? All those things you told me."

Behind her was a small statue. The torso of a woman, her arms lopped off below the shoulders. A neck that ended without a head. Legs that stopped at stumps above the knee.

"What about the pills? The overdose. Did you actually do that?"

She looked away.

"You're pathetic," I said.

"I wanted to. I wanted to go through with it. I thought about it every day. I planned it out, even got the pills. I was ready to do it. It's just—when it came time," she shook her head, "I couldn't."

"Cause you're full of shit."

"Maybe."

Her answers were no answers at all. Yet I couldn't stop asking.

"Why do you go to those meetings? You just sit there and lie."

"I don't know what to tell you, Lucia. You're looking for simple answers, and I don't have simple answers for you. I started going to meetings when I was in grad school. Partly out of boredom, partly because I was hiding from my husband. Partly because I wanted to be shocked. I don't know. But then it became more than that. Listening to all those people detailing their pain in such exacting ways. My mind gets clear when I go."

"Then why'd you stop?"

"Why did you?" she asked.

I didn't answer.

She shrugged. "I stopped because I always stop," she said. "Because it runs its course. Because it gets tiresome."

"So, you use them. Those women. Their traumas."

"If you're trying to reprimand me, go ahead. I'm sure there are things you're not proud of. You have plenty of your own secrets. No one's forcing them out of you."

I dug the nail of my index finger into the cuticle of my thumb. I could feel it cutting into the skin. I was three beats from a panic attack, and I needed to feel my body.

On Phaedra's desk was a single picture frame. I picked it up and looked at it. In it, Phaedra was standing next to a tall man. He had straight hair and glasses; his narrow mouth was pulled up in a slight grin. He was looking at her, while she looked at the camera. It was her eyes that stole the photo. Challenging. Demanding your attention.

"Is he your husband?"

She was watching me intently.

"He is, yes. Tim," she said. "He's a professor here."

"The one you're hiding from in group meetings."

She smiled. Anne again. Mischievous and playful.

"Not that husband," she said. "I had another husband before Tim—when I was in grad school. Neil."

"Where's he? Still searching for you?"

"In a way, yeah. Actually, he's here, too."

"He also teaches here?" I raised my eyebrows.

"Same department," she said, cocking her head as if to say, *you have no idea*.

"That's weird," I said, placing the frame back on her desk. "Why don't you wear a wedding ring?"

"It's complicated. It was burning a hole through my finger."

"Doesn't sound complicated. Sounds miserable."

Sitting there across from her, I suddenly felt exhausted. There was Jack, still looping through my mind. Now Anne, more unreadable and inaccessible than ever. Up until this moment, the lure of our game—not exchanging numbers, not divulging the details of our lives—had felt like a relief. Now it seemed like a burden. Another lie. Another disappointment. There was nothing for me here.

I stood up, ready to walk to the door.

"Wait a sec," she said. "Where are you going?"

"Home." Though that, too, was a lie. I had no home. There was Naseem's. There was my parents'. Neither of which were mine.

"Can you just—wait a minute? Sit down for a second," she implored. I saw something pass over her face. A subtle shift. There was something she wanted.

She got up and walked to the corner of her office where another chair stood, covered in books and papers. She knelt down and rifled through them, in search of something. When she found it, she lifted it up: a thick stack of papers, collated with a black plastic spine.

"I, um—I'm working on something. It's not finished—not yet. I haven't actually shown it to anyone."

It was the rare inelegance of her speech that revealed to me just how important this was. Anne—Phaedra—out on a limb. "I don't normally share what I
write."

I said nothing.

"Honestly, I don't. I've never done anything like this before. I just—I think
you'll maybe understand it." She looked at me with something like desperation—or as close to desperation as I could imagine Anne ever being. "It sounds
crazy, but I almost feel like you're the reader I've been looking for."

"What is it?"

"Philosophy, mostly. And psychoanalysis. But it's also personal—different
from anything else I've written. It's about loss. What happens to us when we
lose something, or someone."

"Like when someone dies?"

She tilted her head to the side.

"Yes, but not always. We lose all kinds of things. Objects. Fantasies. The
future. The past. Things we can't get back. We lose things we never even had.
We're shaped by those losses. In a way, they belong to us."

She held out the manuscript to me. It looked heavy between her hands, and
I felt like I was at an important juncture.

"Will you read it?" she asked.

I took it from her, looked down at the cover page. *The Crypt at Last Light*,
it read. *Mourning, Melancholia, and the Fracturing of the Subject. By Phaedra
Anne Lewis*. I ran my fingertips across her name.

That night, I walked out of her office convinced I would not see her again. I
didn't care if I had her manuscript in my bag. How easily she had been willing
to walk away. How easily I could walk away in return.

Maybe what Phaedra had said was true: sometimes a thing has simply run its
course.

Maybe it had. Maybe *we* had.

Almost.

CHAPTER 37

NEIL

Now

I planned the exact wording of the text message for three days before I sent it. In the end, all I wrote was: "I found your reader. We need to talk."

I saw the ellipsis of Phaedra's typing appear, disappear, then reappear.

"Tomorrow," she finally wrote back. "I can get away tomorrow."

True to form, Phaedra chose a place where the stakes mattered.

***

I didn't sleep the night before, and at 5 a.m., I finally dragged myself from bed. The sky was a bruised blue-black; the streets, quiet.

After we'd broken up, Phaedra kept most of our camping gear—the two-person tent, the butane stove, the headlamps. I'd taken only my sleeping bag. When I pulled it out, it smelled of damp and rot. I hung it up to let it air out, but the smell clung to it, having seeped into the fibers.

My plan that morning had been to arrive at the trailhead first. But I was having trouble finding it because there was no marker or signage, just a pullout on the road, narrow enough for a few cars. Phaedra's was already there when I arrived.

A morning fog hung low in the trees. When she stepped out of the car, Phaedra was a sudden pulse of specificity in that haze. The pale blondeness of her hair, the navy blue of her shirt. She wore hiking boots and shorts and waved to me like nothing was wrong. From her trunk, she pulled out her gear pack and dropped it in the dirt.

"We're not technically allowed to camp here." She flashed a smile and handed me a second backpack. "Figured you didn't have one." She'd already packed it with items we'd need. I fought the urge to ask if it was Tim's.

In retrospect, camping was a terrible idea. I had come with questions, serious questions. Camping put the power in Phaedra's hands. She knew the trail, she brought the gear; clearly, she had been here before.

For a long time, we walked in silence. Soft pine needles covered the ground and muted our steps. The only sound was from birds high up in the trees. It was still early in the day, but you could feel the humidity and the heat, not as a presence but as a promise.

We went on like that for about an hour until we rounded a bend and entered a small copse of trees. The path was wide enough for us to walk side-by-side, and Phaedra slowed to wait for me.

"Shh," she whispered suddenly, her hand on my arm. She was looking up at a tree. "You see that?" She pointed, and I let my gaze follow her finger. Perched on a limb was a white bird with a black beak.

"Snowy egret," she said. "It's good luck." For a moment, she looked at me, her eyes bright, hand still on my arm, a snowy egret in the trees, good luck in the air. And I suddenly doubted everything I'd come here to ask.

Eventually, we came to an outcropping of rock. Phaedra climbed to the highest point and crouched down to pull a water bottle out of her pack. She took a long drink, then tossed it to me.

"How's your head?"

It was the only comment she would make about the break-in.

"Better."

It was a lie. Just the day before, I'd had a migraine from hell that made me double over until I climbed inside my closet and shut out all the light.

Soon, the trail started to climb. Gentle at first, then steeper. I could feel the burn in my thighs. I'd never been fit, *per se*, but since our split, I'd let myself go. There was a notable softness around my belly, a fleshiness to my muscles. Ahead of me, I could see Phaedra's calves engaging with each step. The taut lines of her body. Her movements were fast and confident, and she had to wait for me many times. She stood at the top of a ridge, watching me.

"What?" I asked.

She shaded her eyes against the sun.

"Nothing. Just, you." She didn't elaborate, simply turned and kept climbing. For long stretches, we'd see no one, then a lone hiker or a couple would emerge, nod, say hello, and keep going.

Close to noon, we found a place to stop for lunch. A slight rise where you could see the city in the distance. The spillage of urban sprawl. But also, small pockets of trees, parks, and woods.

"It's greener from up here," she said, looking out. She'd packed us sandwiches. Ham, cheese, extra mustard. Had Tim been in the kitchen as she prepared them? Would he have asked her where she was going? I felt the moments ticking down. It was time to ask, but I couldn't find the words.

In the end, Phaedra didn't need any questions.

"It'll be crowded here soon," she said. "It used to be that no one came up here. A handful of people at most." She looked at me, took another swig of her water. "But since she died, it's a zoo." Her eyes were steel cut gray. "You know how people are."

My breath caught in my throat.

She rubbed the toe of her shoe in the dirt.

It was almost like she could read my mind, anticipate my questions. On some level, I suppose she wanted to tell me as badly as I wanted to know. But she would do it in her own way. At her own pace. The first thing she said about Lucia was: "I met her by accident."

I felt myself go still. In the city down below, you could almost see the converted warehouse where Phaedra and I had once lived.

"I didn't know she was a student," she said. "Well, not at the beginning at least."

A million questions raced through my mind, but Phaedra packed up the trash from our sandwiches and stood.

"Ready?" she asked.

During our walk, I became aware of the way that certain topics haunted us because we could not speak of them. Her mother, my parents, her sadness over the baby we'd lost, our divorce, Tim, my break-in. We hiked in the shadow of these topics, and I could feel their demands, the way they shaped our speech and our silence. Maybe Lucia would finally break them all wide open.

At 2 p.m., we reached the campsite. I wasn't sure what arrangement Phaedra had in mind. We hadn't slept together for weeks. In any case, I didn't even know what I wanted. My body was so trained to need her, to desire her. But my brain had gone off track. Mostly, I think, I was afraid of her.

I fitted the tent poles together as Phaedra spread a tarp on the ground. She took the poles from me and attached them to the clips of the tent. It felt like old times. The two of us working together. Erecting our shelter. Building a home, however impermanent. Phaedra draped the fly over the tent. I staked down the corners, and something in my chest expanded until I couldn't keep it inside any longer.

"She cited you," I blurted out. Phaedra stopped and looked at me. "That's how I figured it out. She mentioned your book in her paper."

Phaedra picked up the empty tent bag and carried it to her backpack. The air felt charged.

"What did she write?"

I couldn't believe it. That's what she wanted to know? What Lucia had written about her book?!

"Something about loss and language. All mourning being destined to fail."

Phaedra nodded. She pulled her sleeping bag from its sack and tossed it inside the tent. I watched her, waiting for her to say more. But all she said was: "We should get wood for the fire. Before the mosquitoes come out."

So, that's what we did. We gathered wood, sifting through damp pieces to find the dry ones. We collected small leaves and pine needles for kindling. And the afternoon wore on. In the air, you could smell a storm coming. One of those great, momentary downpours that drench the South in a sudden burst of rain, like a release, making room for everything to breathe again.

That afternoon, when the rain finally began to fall, Phaedra and I were in the middle of collecting wood and we took off running, scrambling over branches as the deluge pelted us sideways. A crack of thunder somewhere in the distance. Phaedra reached the tent first and dove inside.

"Your shoes. Your shoes," she said, pulling me in. She was laughing, her eyes bright and excited. I kicked them off in the corner of the tent so they wouldn't track mud all over the sleeping bags. Phaedra's hair clung to her face in damp strands of dark blonde.

What happened next happened so quickly and urgently, I felt as though it were not me, but someone else. Looking back, I blame it on the storm and the building tension of the day. Phaedra and me, needing something to break the stifling air, to give us room to breathe.

We fell onto each other, tugging at our clothes. My shirt, discarded. Phaedra, in only her bra, her elbows tucked against her ribs as she reached for my face. Her hands, her body, drawing me in. The two of us collapsed against the sleeping bags, and we made love as three words looped in my head. *We are okay. We are okay. We are okay.*

***

Once the storm passed, we climbed out of the tent to a different world. We ate dinner, couscous and vegetables from a packet, small metal bowls, cutlery clinking softly. I pulled out a smoke.

Somewhere in these woods, Lucia had died. Somewhere near her body, my cigarette had been found. Phaedra was the answer to every question. She reached over and took the cigarette from my lips, took a long drag, and blew it out smooth and clean. Her eyes never left my face.

"Why don't you ask me what you came here to ask?" she said finally.

I took a breath, but I couldn't make the words come.

"C'mon Neil," she prodded. "Don't back out now, not when you've reached the most important part." There she was, doing what she always did. Challenging me, building me up and diminishing me at the same time. Always pressing me to become greater than myself.

"All right," I said, but the words didn't come.

"Say it."

"Fine!" I took a breath. "Did you do it?"

"Did I do *what*?"

"Jesus, Phaedra. Come on. This isn't a joke."

"Farthest thing from it," she said. The firelight reflected in her eyes, and I could see she was dead serious. "I'm not going to answer anything, unless you find the balls to ask me the question you came to ask."

I stared at her, willing her to answer me honestly, but also, to lie.

"Fine. Did you kill Lucia?"

The release was immediate. Phaedra smiled. Not maniacally, but with relief. She took another drag.

"Don't ever let anyone tell you that you aren't capable of greatness, Neil Weber. You are."

From her backpack, Phaedra produced a bottle of whiskey. She took a swig and then a breath. She passed me the bottle and said, "You want to know if I killed her. But it's not a question with an easy answer."

"That's bullshit. Did you?"

She seemed to consider this. There was a long silence, then she began to recount the story.

"I met her at a meeting," she said. "The details don't really matter, except to say that we formed a kind of friendship. In a way, it was strange—to know someone like that. In all the years I've gone to group meetings, I'd never actually befriended anyone." I hadn't known Phaedra to go to meetings, but I didn't interrupt. "We knew so little about each other—almost nothing about one another's real lives. No phone numbers. We didn't even know each other's real names—not until close to the end. No tether at all. There was something freeing about knowing someone like that."

Phaedra's words hollowed me out. All this time, I'd felt a strange kind of ownership over Lucia. Like she was calling to me, revealing herself to me. But in truth, I knew her least of all. Not like Jack, not like Phaedra.

"So, now you know who my reader was," Phaedra said. "Not my editor. Not Tim. Just this girl, a student. Not even a philosophy student. A no one. I gave it to her back in December, months before the end. I gave it to her, and then I waited. Every day, I expected her to come into my office—to tell me she loved it, or hated it, or didn't understand it. But she didn't come. Not for a long time."

Phaedra took the whiskey bottle back from me. An ember from the fire sent a crackle of light into the darkening sky.

"A few months ago, in March, Lucia finally came back. Just showed up one day out of the blue. She had my manuscript in her hands. I remember it had been raining, and she looked like shit. Tired. Older. Not like a twenty-year-old kid should look. She just barged in and dropped the book on my desk. The pages were all bent, coffee stains here and there."

Night was coming on, and I could feel the critters coming out in the woods around us.

"That day—the day she finally showed up—she wanted me to go somewhere with her. A lake. This lake." Phaedra pointed to the woods behind me. I turned, but in the settling darkness, I couldn't see any lake. I couldn't see anything at all. "Anyway, I told her I couldn't. I had work, other things to do. If I'm honest, I just didn't want to. But that day, there was just this—desperation about her. Like she needed it. So, I said I'd go. I'd meet her here the next day."

In front of us, the fire was burning down to the embers. Phaedra stood and tossed another log onto it. I watched the damp bark smoke and eventually catch fire.

Phaedra explained how, that next day, they didn't meet at the trailhead as they usually did. They met at the lake itself. Lucia was already there when Phaedra arrived.

"The first thing Lucia said to me when I got here was: 'You know what a bunch of ravens are called? An unkindness.' That's what she said. An *unkindness*."

"What happened to her, Phaedra?"

She looked at me sharply. "What happened to her?" Phaedra repeated. She seemed almost dazed by the memory of it. "What happened was that she took off her jacket and her sweater and stepped out of her pants. It was freezing cold. I just remember watching her undress and thinking, how is she not freezing? The angles of her body, her skin all covered in goosebumps. Still, she walked right to the edge of that lake and got in." Phaedra's eyes were glassy. "I'll tell you what, Neil, I felt that water. It was ice cold."

I could feel a dull thudding in my head. The start of a migraine that would soon blot out the sound of her voice. But I fought to listen, to hold it all in my mind.

"When she got out, she was shivering. I wrapped her jacket around her, but she couldn't stop shaking." Now Phaedra stood over the fire with a stick in her hand, pushing at the logs. "She was shaking, and I was holding her jacket around her."

For a long moment, Phaedra went silent. When she spoke again, her voice had a remoteness to it. "She wanted it, Neil."

"Wanted what?"

"To die. She wanted it. She *made* it happen."

"I don't understand."

"She kissed me that night," Phaedra said. "Out of the blue. And afterward, she brought my hands to her neck. Right here." Phaedra lifted her hands to her neck. In the fire, those hands looked pale yellow and old. "Lucia said to me, 'I need your help.' So, I asked her, 'Help for what?' But I knew. I already knew.

She said, 'To not be afraid.' That's what she wanted me for. To help her not be afraid."

Phaedra's expression was inscrutable, and it terrified me. She took a breath and continued.

"At first, I pulled my hands away. But she had this look in her eyes. This pleading look. And it was the strangest thing. I let her do it. Hold my hands there. I could feel her breath. This life force inside of her."

I was having trouble following the thread of the story. From the ravens and the swimming to kissing and choking.

"I don't understand, Phaedra. I don't—"

"At first, I thought she had just passed out. That happens, you know. People just pass out. They aren't dead, they just pass out. But this wasn't that. I waited there. A long time. Watching her body, expecting her to move. I kept waiting to see her chest rise or see her move an arm or a limb." Phaedra was shaking her head. "But there was nothing."

Right then, I thought of Phaedra's article on the Golden Gate Bridge, arguing for the rights of jumpers. The right to kill oneself. The right to regret one's decision. It seemed impossible to me that she would go this far. Surely, the right to take one's own life didn't extent to suicide by proxy. Only, looking at her then, it seemed, perhaps, it did.

"I stood there, terrified. I didn't know what to do. I just remember looking at her, her beautiful face. This thing she wanted. I *knew* she wanted it, but still, I panicked. *What about her phone—what about my phone? What about people who might have seen us? What if, what if . . . ?* But I swear to God, it was like she planned the whole thing from the beginning. We never exchanged numbers. She didn't even bring her phone with her that night. She didn't use her real name . . . not at the beginning. She was Elena. I was Anne. No last names. Nothing. I never met her friends. She never met Tim. It was as if she erased any trace of us before we could even put one down."

I could barely move. My throat was dry and raw. I was afraid. Of what I was hearing. Of what it meant. Of who Phaedra was. Of who I was.

"What about fingerprints? Your fingerprints would have been all over her."

"Fingerprints?" She laughed. A strange, terrible noise that sounded deranged. "What fingerprints? She was out here for so long." She looked at me, her face ugly for a moment, distorted in the shadows of the firelight. "They didn't find anything, Neil, because there was nothing to find. No calls, no texts, no emails. No fingerprints. Not one link between me and Lucia. Not one."

"And the other girl? Michelle Alvarez? What happened to her?"

Phaedra looked at me sharp and focused.

"I have nothing to do with her. I never even heard of her until she went missing." She shook her head. "She's not part of this story."

"And me?" I asked gravely. "Why am I part of this story, Phaedra? How did my cigarette end up here?"

She took a deep breath, and I swear, a slight smile played on her lips. It would take me a long time to realize how complex Phaedra's thinking was.

"It was after the Red Baron," she said. "After they found her. I saw you and Tim outside, smoking. That's when it occurred to me. To drop your cigarette here. Her body had already been removed, obviously, but I knew the detectives would come back, looking for anything they missed. It was stupid to risk it, of course. But once the thought occurred to me—well, you know how I can get.

"So, after we left the Red Baron, I pretended that I forgot my jacket and went back. You were already gone. Everyone was gone. But there was the butt of your cigarette, lying there on the patio. Tim's was in the ashtray. You know, for one second, I considered picking up his instead. But I'm glad I didn't. It would have been all wrong. It's so clear to me now that it needed to be yours. So, I took it, and waited, and when the time was right, I hiked back up here and left it. I knew they'd come back to look, and they did."

I didn't tell her that she'd made one grave mistake. She hadn't factored in the weather. Lucia's body had been soaked in the rain. My cigarette, the only dry thing for miles.

"But why?" I asked. It made zero sense. "Why would you do it?"

My mind slid over possibilities. *To up the ante. To make it a game. Because, to Phaedra, life was an experiment, and more than anything, she wanted to push the bounds, to test its limits.* Still, none of those explanations felt complete. There was something missing.

She seemed to consider the right way to explain it. I watched her face, familiar and foreign at the same time.

"When I was younger," she began, "when my mom would slip into one of her rages, I remember thinking that I was only alive because of my father. He was like a shield that surrounded me, protecting me from her. At the time, that was love. That was the deepest kind of love I could imagine. That quiet protection, a force I couldn't see but knew was there because it altered the world around me. When he left, he took that feeling with him. There was nothing to shield me from my mother, from her anger. Nothing to hold the world at bay. Everything became threatening. If he could leave, then what else was possible? Any horrible thing I could imagine.

"But, you know, you can't live like that without losing your mind. Which I did, for a while. I couldn't go anywhere or do anything without debilitating anxiety. This sense of foreboding around every corner. And for good reason. My mother was unpredictable and ruthless. Loud music could set her off. An unfinished dinner. A tone of voice she perceived as hostile or challenging. But it wasn't consistent. One day she'd react; the next, she'd barely notice. It was like crossing a landmine every single day.

"You know what finally saved me? The realization that I, too, had power. Maybe I couldn't defend myself against her. Maybe I couldn't hurt her. But I could hurt myself. I could end it all. I swear to God, the fact that I could take my own life was the most freeing thought I ever had. That I could say when and where it all ended. It was a breath of fresh air."

Phaedra's profile was illuminated by the fire, and I realized she was the embodiment of all contrasts. Delicate and harsh. Honest and deceptive. Home and danger. I loved and hated her at the same time. Those possibilities did not feel mutually exclusive. On the contrary, they seemed to fundamentally belong.

"In the end," she continued, "the real question was not whether I should take my life or not. It was *how* to live with that truth. What does living mean when death does not exist outside of it, but within it? Not as an end, but as something that animates every moment. How do you approach other people? How do you approach the world?"

She looked at me with urgency. She wanted me to understand. She really did.

"But why *me*, Phaedra? What do I have to do with that?"

"You're not listening to what I'm saying."

"Then say it clearer."

"I'm talking about love, Neil. About love—not as a test of how tightly you hold onto something, but of how much space you grant it. Love without judgment, without imposition. A love that meets another person where they are. A love that's large enough to hold life and death."

"I did love you like that!"

"No, you didn't. You think you did—I believe you believe that. But for you, love has always been proprietary. Possessive and hungry."

I was shaking my head.

"That day, after I lost the baby," she said, "you kept waiting for me to cry. To show some sign of sadness. You kept saying, 'It's okay to cry, Phae. It's okay.' You needed me to be something I wasn't. It's what you've *always* needed. For me to be your lifeline. Your savior. You see in me what you want to see, not what is there. I wanted to claw your eyes out that day. I wanted to scream, 'I'm not sad. I'm fucking rejoicing.' You know why I wanted to buy all that alcohol? Why I wanted to drink myself into oblivion? Not to mute the pain of losing the baby, but to shut you out."

"No," I said. "You were devastated. I saw it. With my own eyes."

She shook her head. "You saw what you wanted to see. Believe me, I was not."

I was stunned. Her words were weapons. In the woods somewhere, an animal scurried through the underbrush. For a long moment, neither of us spoke.

Then, she said, "Can't you see that love looks different to me? It's not your fault. But there are different ways to love."

"Like helping someone die!" I shouted. It felt good to shout. To use my lungs and my voice. I felt rage moving inside of me. "You can't be serious, Phaedra."

"I am. Dead serious. I'm not asking you to understand. I don't think you're capable. The intimacy of something like this. To be the one to actually do it. An instrument of someone else's will. Two bodies, acting as one. Lucia's deep need to quiet the world, my willingness to meet her there."

"Ohmygod, is that what you think you did? Gave her death as a form of love?" It was insane. It was ludicrous. What kind of terrifying logic could bring love and death together in this capacity? "Her parents waited over a month to find her body. Is that love? Her sister—"

"This wasn't about them. And I am sorry they had to experience that, but it was Lucia's right. *Her* choice to decide whether to live or die. Nobody else's."

I gripped my head in my hands. The pain was evolving into something large and terrible. I sat like that until the wave passed, then looked at her with a piercing coldness.

"So, what? My cigarette was what? A punishment? Because I dared to think you might be sad after losing our baby?"

She shook her head, and I could see her deep disappointment. That I still failed to understand.

"It's not a punishment, Neil."

"Then why?"

"So, you'd have to choose."

"Choose *what*?"

She looked at me like it was the most obvious thing in the world.

"To act," she said.

Simple and clear, as if everything up until this moment had been only preparation for this. Phaedra planting my cigarette, so I'd finally have to act.

"You view it as an act of treason," she said. "I see it as a gift. An opportunity. To love differently."

I looked at her aghast.

She continued: "You see, I knew it would tie you to this case. The police would find it, and it would make things real for you. Whatever little game you were playing, this little sleuthing act—talking to her sister and her boyfriend—this would make it personal. You'd have to take it all the way to the end. I believed in you, Neil. Probably more than anyone ever has. I knew you'd find out I did it, and once you did, you would have to make a choice."

"A choice between *what*?"

"Between your conscience and your love," she said bluntly. "Just like I had to do for Lucia. Sometimes love is the braver choice."

There was an odd note in her voice—almost triumphant.

"You now have all the information," she said. "You know what happened to Lucia. You can walk away right now, take it to Detective Waters, tell him everything. You can finally be the hero you've always wanted to be," she said.

"You can be the savior—not just a witness. This is Kitty Genovese. This is your drowning woman on the beach in California. You can quiet it all. Right now." She looked at me. "Or you can choose love. Not love that molds someone to your image, but love that sees the truth and does not look away. That does not flinch in the face of the world's ugliness but embraces it. That takes me as I am."

I heard her words, but I couldn't make sense of them. *Love as witness. Love as sacrifice.* Phaedra, always seeking out and finding the edge of existence. Life as performance. Who else but Phaedra to find herself wrapped up in someone else's suicide?

"Does Tim know?" I suddenly needed to know.

"Does Tim know what?"

"What you did. To Lucia."

"Only you." She smiled at me. "Just like you always wanted. To be the only one."

I looked at her. Was she a monster? A sociopath? Someone so committed to an idea that they would be willing to take another's life? Yes, it seemed. On some level, she was all of these things.

"How did Tim know about the Dionysus?" I asked. Jack had been adamant he hadn't said a word. If not Jack, then who?

"I told him," Phaedra said matter-of-factly.

"You?"

"Lucia told me about it, and I told Tim. Well, she wasn't Lucia at the time. She was Elena. We were right here, in these same woods. She said she'd worked there. I had never heard of it, of course. But it was I who told Tim, though I never mentioned Lucia."

"Why? Why would you tell Tim about it?"

She waited a moment, as if trying to parse her own motives.

"Because I knew he'd find it compelling. Because I trust him to make decisions about his own life."

But even as she said it, I could see through it.

"You were testing him," I said. It all suddenly became clear. What Phaedra thought she wanted was a love that asked no questions, that passed no judgment. Love that embraced ugliness. But I didn't believe that she was capable of giving that love in return. Not to her husband. If she had, in fact, been testing him, then the only way he could have passed the test would have been not to go at all. I took a small delight in breaking the news to her. "Well, take a guess what decision he made? He went. Your trustworthy husband. He's a monster, you know?"

Perhaps Phaedra wanted to ask more. Perhaps she wanted to know what I knew. But she has always been a master of restraint. She would never ask outright. It would seem too weak.

"Then we keep good company," was all she said. She looked at me hard and said: "There's something else you should know. Something I never told you."

In that moment, I felt afraid, but also wide awake. A desire to end the conversation where it was, but also, a yearning to know. I felt that we were on the precipice of something large and important.

"Years ago," she began, "that day we were at your mother's house, she took me into the garden. She wanted to show me the summer squash and green beans she'd planted. You and your brother were sitting at the table. You remember that? You were watching me. Always watching me. I don't remember how it came up, but I said something about your trip to California when you were a child and the woman who drowned on the beach."

I could feel my heartbeat pounding in my chest. I didn't know what Phaedra was going to say, but I desperately did not want her to say it.

"You know what your mother said?" Phaedra asked. "She looked at me, all confused. And without any irony or humor, she said: 'We've never been to California. Neil's dad would never have paid for a trip like that.' I remember feeling so confused. So, I said, maybe I got the location wrong. Maybe it was Oregon or Washington? Somewhere along the coast? And your mom just shook her head. She was adamant. 'Neil never even saw an ocean until he moved away.' That's what she said. I remember, I just stood there, staring straight ahead. This story that you told so many times—the woman on the beach, drowning—it never even happened.

"Right then, your mom must have sensed that she'd ruined something, some kind of equilibrium, and she got real quiet. She put her hand on my arm. I remember it so clearly, the feeling of her fingertips on my arm. 'It was real hard on him,' your mom said. 'Watching his father do what he did to me. Of course, there was nothing he could've done. Neil was just a kid, but that doesn't make it any easier—'"

I listened to Phaedra speak without moving a muscle. My eyes were stinging, my head was spinning. The violence of my past returning to me in full force.

"Did you know," Phaedra asked. "Did you know that you made it all up, or did you actually believe it happened?"

"No! It's not true." I was shaking my head.

"Did you know?" she repeated. "That you never went to California?"

"No, I don't believe you."

"Maybe there was a drowning woman," Phaedra said, "but she wasn't on any beach. She was living right there in your house with you. Your dad, smashing her head against the wall while you watched. That's your drowning woman—your own mother."

"No!"

"Yes, Neil. Yes. It's true. Somewhere inside of you, you know it. That you made it up. I believe that it feels real to you, like you saw it with your own eyes. But you didn't! You created the memory and then claimed it as your own."

"No, no." It seemed there were no other words available to me.

"Then your dad left, and you moved as far away as possible. And you punished them. Your mom and your brother. All that rage and powerlessness you felt. You took it out on them, while telling yourself that you simply didn't have time to call back. You had graduate school. You had life to live. But it wasn't that. It was everything they forced you to acknowledge about yourself. About what you had failed to do. You gave them up so you wouldn't have to confront it."

"You're wrong," I said, though there was no conviction behind those words.

"You're not a kid sitting on a beach, Neil. You're a grown man, and it's time to choose. What's it going to be? Love? The real kind, that sees and accepts without design? That can hold this ugliness, accept me as I am? Or are you the savior? The one who will solve Lucia's mystery?" Her face was suddenly hard and unyielding. "I'm not telling you what to do. But you can no longer do nothing."

***

That night, I slept without sleeping.

Our limbs, touching lightly because there was nowhere else to go. The moon, a pale shard in the sky. The campfire coals, burnt down to nothing. In the morning, I woke early. Phaedra was lying there, but I knew she was awake. We didn't say a word as I climbed out of the tent, packed whatever I could into Tim's backpack, and hiked down the mountain. I left Phaedra's stuff against the front tire of her car.

I pulled away as morning light came up over the ridge.

CHAPTER 38

LUCIA

Then

After leaving Phaedra's office that day, I slipped into a darkness so complete, it was hard to remember what light felt like. That afternoon with the whale shark was already a distant memory. Whatever healing power it had seemed to exert now felt illusory.

What I wanted most of all was to return to the night that I had made love to Jack. To go back to the Dionysus. It wasn't enough to sit at Reinhardt's watching Lotus. It now seemed absurd that I had thought it might be.

One evening after dinner, I put on a dress, grabbed my mask, and borrowed my mom's car. I drove out of the city toward that wasteland of desire where I hadn't been since the previous summer. On the way, I felt a giddiness that resembled life again. Only, when I arrived, there was no snaking line around the building. No bouncer with his Zorro mask. There was no Dionysus at all. Instead, there were the remains of a burned building.

I fell to my knees and wept. What I wanted was to mourn—Jack, my lost friendships, my innocence. I wanted to say goodbye. But in the blackened remains of the Dionysus, I understood that there could be no mourning. It would never be complete. It would always be aberrant, always outstanding. And I would always be chasing it.

Over the next three months, that fact felt like the defining principle of my life. My own failure to mourn. Not even a gravesite to mark the loss. I went through the motions of my life, but I was barely there at all.

Until that Thursday night in March.

We were sitting around the dinner table when my father looked up and said to my mother, "Is the guest room clean?"

My mother paused mid-bite.

"I cleaned it yesterday," she assured him. Her hair was pulled back off her face. When she turned, the light hit her cheeks at a particular angle, and I saw the younger version of her tucked inside the older.

"*Brava*," my father said. "He gets in on Saturday afternoon, so we'll eat here first."

Logistical information. Dates, times. A man was arriving. They would eat here first. The guest room was cleaned. My palms were slick with sweat, as if my body knew.

"Who?" I asked, glancing between them. Elena studied her plate.

"Who?!" my father said. "What do you mean, *who*? Giancarlo is who." He laughed as if I'd just told a joke.

"It's clean," my mother said and refilled her wine glass.

All around me, a symphony of dinner sounds. Fork to plate, fork to mouth, chew, repeat. Throats cleared, small cough. Glasses lifted, tilted, set down again. Napkins used, begin again. Move through a meal, rote and uneventful.

A man was coming to town. A friend. An old friend. The oldest friend. Giancarlo from Brindisi would arrive on Saturday. Would sleep here, in the guest room, cleaned by my mother. One door down from my own room. Share a bathroom. Sit at the table. Laugh with his mouth open. Take me and Elena to ice cream. *Call me Uncle Gianni. Do you like this? You're such a special girl.* The loop of his name. The name that was two names, like it couldn't decide. *Gian.* John. And *Carlo.* Giancarlo. Doubling him, his smell, his mouth, his fingers. The bristle of his mustache against the inside of my thigh. A man I had not seen in over a decade. But also, impossibly, a man who had never left. Who has been here this entire time. With me everywhere. In my classes. At the dinner table, in my dreams, when I sleep, when I wake, at the library, in the bathroom, lying there between me and Naseem, between me and the world. *Ego cogito ergo sum.* I am a thinking thing. I am a mind and a body; and outside, the world. A divide at every step. Wedged into that gap—into every gap—is a name I can't bring myself to say.

"No," I said, slamming my fist on the table. My father looked at me, startled.

"No what?" he said.

No, a word to stop time. To stop the ordinary everydayness of our dinner. Every head lifted, every pair of eyes on me. My mother, my father, Elena.

"No," I said again.

My mother put down her fork.

"Lucia," she said. But I didn't look at her. I kept my eyes on my father.

"He is not coming here," I said.

My mother's quick pull of breath. I felt like I could hear her thoughts. A prayer sent up, *per favore, figlia, don't speak.*

In the sudden stillness of the room, only my father was a moving thing.

"*Scusa?*" he said. His eyebrows knitted together. The dimple in his cheek, my inheritance. "*Cosa vuoi dire, no?*" He said the words very slowly. "Enough, Lucia!"

"No!" I shouted.

He slammed his palm on the table.

"This is *my* house. You do not tell me who comes and who does not come."
He leaned forward in his chair. He did not realize how simple it could have been
in that moment. All he had to do was ask: *Perché? Why? Why do you not want
him here?* But he did not ask. He never asked. He chose not to. "Giancarlo comes
on Saturday," he said. "*Basta*! End of story."

"Then I'll leave," I said.

"Then leave! Why are you even here? You do not live here. What are you
doing here? You don't go to school. You don't work. You don't do anything,
just walk around the house. All day you come and go, and you complain, and I
say nothing. But this—" he jabbed his finger on the table, "*Questa è casa mia.*"
This here, this is my house.

"Pietro, please," my mother said.

"No, Annalisa! No!" He put his hands together as if in prayer and shook
them at her. "*Non dirmelo*! She comes in here and tells me what to do. In my
own house? No! No, no, no. Giancarlo comes on Saturday."

He pushed his chair back from the table, its legs scraping against the wood
floor. He walked to the hallway toward the front door. I could hear the jangle
of his keys.

"Pietro!" my mother called out. "Wait!"

He slammed the door behind him, and I leaped from the table and bolted
after him. I flung the door wide.

"Leave!" I shouted into the night. My father was climbing into his car. I
wanted the neighbors to hear. "Leave, like you always do!" It was true. He was
always coming in late and leaving early. Always looking at his watch like he had
somewhere to be. Always avoiding my mother's touch. And, of course, all those
stories about him and Giancarlo chasing girls in Brindisi. "Leave before your
girlfriend closes her fucking legs!" I shouted and then slammed the door.

It was reckless. Outsized and unkind. Not to my father, but to my mother, still sitting at the table, looking like a discarded thing. Her face was buried in her hands. Her shoulders were shaking with every sob. Elena sat like a statue. And I ran upstairs.

***

The next morning it was raining when I woke. I could hear it rapping against the gutters. I crept into my mother's bathroom and swiped every pill I could find. Then I took the bus to school.

When I arrived outside her office door, my hair was wet, my clothes sticking to my skin. Phaedra Anne Lewis was sitting at her desk, her startled eyes looking back at me, her blonde hair tucked behind an ear. She wore a gray blouse with silk around the collar. Too delicate for her.

I dropped her manuscript on the desk.

She stared at me like I was a wild animal. I had read the book so many times. The corners were folded and curled. Coffee stains on the pages. Phaedra seemed unsure whether to reach for it or to leave it where it was.

"Hello, Lucia," she said.

"I need you to come with me," I said.

She raised her eyes. I knew how to intrigue her. How to hold out the promise of something unexpected. Of something she might not see coming.

"Where?"

"The lake."

Not the exciting answer she was looking for. She shook her head.

"I can't. I'm teaching."

"Tomorrow then."

"Lucia, I—"

"Please."

Maybe it was the way I asked. The urgency packed into the word. She agreed to come.

***

That night, I tossed and turned in the cool darkness of Naseem's room. I thought about swallowing my mother's sleeping pills. It might do the trick, but it would be all wrong. I looked at Naseem, his breathing arrhythmic and fitful. There was so much I wanted to say to him, but every word was insufficient. In the end, I leaned in close to his sleeping face.

"You were perfect," I whispered.

In the morning, I left my phone on the bedside table, plugged into the wall, and walked out the door for the last time. I climbed onto a bus—not going in the direction of campus, but north, toward the lake. I had hours to kill before meeting Phaedra, and I wanted to spend them walking the city. My city. Not beautiful. Not meant to dazzle, but lovely in its ordinariness.

I've never lived anywhere else, but I believe a place knows when you're preparing to leave. Cities dress themselves up for your departure. Like lovers when the end is near.

That morning, it was the small details that broke my heart. The flicker of sunlight on the chrome of a passing car. A bird, standing on a street corner as if it was waiting for the light to turn. A woman pulling a squeegee down the windowpane of a nail salon. Life's final farewell.

In the afternoon, I walked along the road that led to the trailhead. There was no sidewalk; it was not a road meant for pedestrians. The shoulder was a thin stretch of weedy grass. At the entrance to the trail, where Anne and I had met so many times, the shoulder was larger. Enough space for a few cars. That day, none were parked there, and I hiked into the woods alone.

Once inside the trees, I felt my lungs expand. Overhead, restless clouds drifted across a tired sun. Two nights ago, after my father stormed out, I crawled into bed, and Elena came to my room. She sat on the edge of my bed, stroking my hair. Her long, artist fingers moving slow and steady.

"He can't hear it," she said. "You know that, right?" She was referring to our father. "He can't hear it because, if he does, it means it happened under his roof. Under his watch."

I turned to look at her, and the room felt suddenly very small. Giancarlo's presence in every crevice. But foremost in my heart was fury. Because it was clear that she knew. Elena knew. *How long had she known? How long had they all known?* I felt like screaming until there was nothing left inside of me.

"Leave," I said.

"Lucia, I—"

"I'm asking you to leave."

"I just wanted to—"

"Why don't you go back to your basement. Hide, like you always do."

My sister looked at me. For a moment, I thought she might say more, but she didn't. She got up, and the mattress readjusted to the weight of only one body. At the door, I could feel her lingering.

"Did you not hear me?" I shouted. "Leave me alone!"

Now, in the woods, I was pushing through the trees at a clip. Somewhere along the way, I had begun to cry. Tears spilled down my cheeks, but I barely felt them. I was in two places at once. Here, on my way to the lake, and there, in my bedroom, Elena by the door.

That night, I saw the rise and fall of her chest as she took a breath. Then I turned my back on her. She said only one more thing before she retreated to the basement. In my anger, however, I failed to hear, to *really* hear. Only now did I understand.

"You're not the only one he hurt," Elena said.

I didn't respond, and she closed the door behind her. At the time, I assumed she was talking about our father. But now, with startling clarity, I knew she wasn't.

You're not the only one he hurt.

She was talking about Giancarlo.

That night, she had been trying to open a conversation. Words as a form of bloodletting. But for me, the wound had never stopped bleeding. For me, it was too late.

***

I was already at the lake when Phaedra arrived. The sun was setting. I had never been up there in the dark, and the trees looked angrier, like we were trespassers.

I sat on a rock and watched Phaedra scramble over the boulders toward me. She was wearing her regular clothes now. The clothes she wore as Anne, not as Phaedra. A T-shirt, hiking shoes. Somewhere in the woods, a bird call ripped through the trees. A raven. I had studied my animals.

Do you know what a group of ravens is called?

An unkindness.

Watching her scramble toward me, I had a realization. Suicide is not a desire to die. It is the end of every alternative.

I suddenly felt like I couldn't catch my breath. My chest was tight, and my body screamed with anxiety. My clothes were suffocating. In that freezing cold, I stripped them off. In front of me was the water. Icy and black. Never before had I felt the urge to climb in, even when my father did in those early days. I preferred to stand guard. But now, it felt different. There was no one to stand guard for.

I took off my boots and stepped from my clothes. I could feel Phaedra watching me, and her eyes were a kind of protection.

I climbed in, and the water was a thousand blades across my skin. I dunked my head, and it took my breath away. Everything frozen. Everything brightly alive. I got out, and she wrapped my jacket around me. A human body needs warmth.

"We were meant to find each other," Phaedra said. I hated her and I needed her. Mostly, I felt grateful. Which is why I kissed her that night. At the press of my lips, she jumped. I did it again. At first, her hesitation, and then, surrender. She leaned in, and I tasted the warmth of her, the startled pleasure of her hands, reaching cautiously for me. She was contradiction itself. Or she made contradiction into shape: my desire to disappear, my desire to live.

I hadn't planned what happened next. But the moment I did it, I knew it was right. That I had found my way. I brought her hands to my neck. I felt her hesitate for just a moment, then she let me do it. In a way, she was reaching for me all along.

"We need a safe word," I said, "just in case."

"In case of what?" she responded.

***

The neck is comprised of so many different parts. Carotid arteries, the vocal cords, the esophagus, spinal cord, jugular veins, the larynx, the hyoid bone, fascia and muscles. Scalene, trapezius, rectus capitis. There are seven bones. The cervical vertebrae. The atlas where it touches the head, a thinking thing. An atlas, what a beautiful image. The whole world, right there, at the base of the skull.

Somewhere above me, the Pleiades were clustered together. A constellation of seven sisters, turning grief into light, their father, burdened with holding up the sky.

Phaedra's fingers closing tight, nails cut short, utilitarian, no polish. No flair. Nails meant for pounding out words on a keyboard. For filling up pages. Those same fingers, pressing down, cutting off oxygen.

I need you to help me not be afraid, I had said to her. *That is what you came into my life to do. To help me not be afraid.* But there is a limit to what one can do. No one can die your death for you. Her hands on my neck, closing tighter. My bare feet on the earth, my naked back against the wind. I lay down. I am falling, and she is gripping. Giancarlo comes tomorrow. Leaves, branches, and twigs, scraping at my skin. The moonlight, slanting in—disinterested in the small lives of people.

I think of a poem I read in class.

Robert Pinsky's "Shirt." Hart Crane's Bedlamite, standing on the edge of a windowsill as the Triangle Factory fire rages below. The man in the poem helps one woman to the ledge, then another. One woman after the next plunges to her death. By the end of the poem, he does, too. He jumps but does not land. The poem preserves him in midair. Descending, trousers billowing, shirt, cut along the bias of history. A man immortalized in verse.

I close my eyes as Phaedra tightens her grip.

I am a child again, falling asleep upstairs while my parents host a party. Voices rise up from the first floor. Their friends from the neighborhood, casual and boisterous. The orange glow of party light spills up the stairs, coating everything with warmth and safety. A female laugh lifts like a wave and enters my dream. My mother breaks away from her guests to come upstairs and check on me. In that half-sleep, I see the shape of her body, silhouetted in the doorframe. Her breath on my neck as she leans down to kiss me goodnight.

A flicker of light inside me. Dim, but there. I reach up for Phaedra's fingers. *No! No, wait.*

I want to say something. *I am not ready. Not yet. Hold on. Just a minute.*

I reach up and put my hands on her hands. But she does not let up, she tightens her grip.

And the word comes flooding toward me.

"Light," I say, forcing it out past her fingers. "Light. *Please.*"

Her eyes are watching me. Watching my mouth move. Form a single word. "Light!"

But there is only the hard set of her jaw in the darkness, a flash in her eyes. She does not loosen her grip but locks down harder. And I see it. The slight shake of her head. *No*, she is saying to me with her entire body. *No. There will be no more light.*

I struggle against her, but I am so tired.

Light has weight and presence. I can feel it on my eyelids, the moonlight through the clouds.

My mother is reading to me in bed. A nursery rhyme. She is embarrassed by her English. She practices it in front of me, her audience of one. Sitting at the edge of my bed, her eyebrows knitted as she studies each word. The halting, hesitating way she moves forward through a sentence. I correct her at each stumble.

Light, I try to say. *I am so sorry.*

The sound of a piano on a beach. A body in a bed. The things you think right at the end. A pair of my father's shoes, the soles coming away at the toe. The way Elena holds a fork, gently resting it in her fingers, like she's afraid she might cause it pain—

CHAPTER 39

NEIL

Now

The summer came and went in a haze of drawn blinds, haunting shadows moving across the floor, fitful sleep.

My mornings and evenings were indistinguishable because I lived in the non-time of memory. In my mind, I would replay conversations with Phaedra. Or I would fall asleep to the sound of my father's voice, holding my breath without realizing it. And there would be Ethan, my brother, thin, uncoordinated with a football, my scapegoat. In that terrible non-time, it seemed to me that my failure had been one of memory itself. To have denied it—our shared story. I killed it the day I walked out and didn't come back.

In those summer months, I did not see Phaedra. I did not see Jack. I didn't see anyone. I stayed away as much for their sake as for mine.

In September, campus reopened. I wandered its halls, feeling as if I had survived some great, unspeakable disaster. In August, the other missing girl, Michelle Alvarez, had been found. Unlike Lucia, she was alive. Not strangled in the woods but living in an old Victorian house in San Francisco. She did not return to campus. Word was that she'd been sent to rehab. It was none of my business.

As my tenure approached, I went through the motions of being a professor, just as I had for so long. I taught my classes. I went to faculty meetings. I attended judiciary committee. In all that time, I don't remember opening my mouth even once.

Unexpectedly, I did begin to write again. Not for publication, just for myself. The topic that I seemed to circle back to in every piece was the question of California. *What was truth? What had I experienced? Why that beach, that woman, that memory? Could a thing still be true even if it didn't happen?*

In November, the department met to review my case for tenure. By then, I had fully accepted its denial. Both Phaedra and Tim were on my committee, which seems implausible, but true. It was time for me to say goodbye.

On a Wednesday, I finished teaching early, and when I opened the door to leave, Jack was standing in the hallway.

"Lunch?" he offered.

It had been so long since I'd had lunch with someone. We started walking toward the dining hall when he stopped. "Let's go off campus," he said.

We went to a cafe down the block.

I knew that earlier in the day, Jack had attended my tenure meeting. We walked in silence. I didn't ask him anything about it, and he didn't offer.

We sat down and ordered.

"You look good, Neil," he said.

I let out a small laugh. And he tilted his head in concession.

"All right, you look *better*," he rephrased.

The waiter set down our food, and we ate.

"So," he said finally. "The meeting."

"The meeting," I repeated.

I watched little boba balls travel the length of his straw, disappear into his mouth. He chewed, then drank again.

"I honestly can't believe they let Tim stay on the committee," he said. "You'd probably have grounds to appeal just on that fact alone. I mean, to swing a golf club at a man's head and then vote on his tenure—it's not right."

I shrugged. "I did break into his house."

"Fair enough," he said. "All the more reason he shouldn't be on your committee."

Despite the reasons I knew I should leave—the school, teaching, Phaedra—I still felt my stomach in knots. I wanted Jack to just come out and say it either way.

"Even that bitch ex-wife of yours—" Jack said. "Sorry, but she is. There's just no reason for your ex-wife to be on your committee."

"Well, I—"

"Hold on. Let me finish." He flashed a smile. "Which is why it is *completely* fucking insane that you got the votes."

I gaped. The words didn't make sense.

"I got the votes?"

"You got the votes," he said. He raised his arms as if to say, there's no accounting for this unpredictable outcome. "Looks like you're keeping your job, Professor."

I dropped my head forward. Relief, exhaustion, doubt, confusion all swirled together. Jack reached across the table and patted my shoulder.

"Not official yet, buddy," he said. I knew it still had to go through the dean. That I'd be waiting until spring for official word. But at our school, no tenure case had ever been denied once the department committee had voted to keep someone on.

I looked at Jack. He was grinning, offering his sincere congratulations.

I stopped smiling.

"I was a shit friend to you," I said. I found it hard to look him in the face. "I'm not making any excuses. I'm just saying, I'm sorry. You've always been there for me."

"A lot of terrible things happened," he said. "I think there are deep regrets all around."

"You're a better man than I am," I said. "I sure as shit wouldn't be sitting across from you if the tables were turned."

"Of course, you would," he said. "Who else would you sit with?"

His laugh was the first good thing I'd heard in months.

***

On Friday evening, I drove across town.

It had been six months since the night Jack and I went to the bar together. There were only a few people seated when I arrived, and I grabbed the same table we'd had that night back in April.

At first, I didn't see her, and I was about to get up and leave, when Tara stepped out of the kitchen, a tray of glasses balancing on one hand. I watched her move. Jeans and a white tank top. She breezed past me.

"Be right with you," she said. No flash of recognition.

After a long wait, she was back, standing at the head of the table. Her hair was pulled up, her eyes just as bright as I remembered them. She had freckles on her nose and across her cheeks. I hadn't noticed them before.

"Hey! It's you," she said. "I was wondering when you might come back in. Wasn't sure you were alive after that last performance."

My heart did a little skid.

"Not my finest moment," I said.

She smiled. "You waiting on your friend tonight?"

"My friend?"

"Messy hair. Likes the ladies."

"Ah. Jack. No," I said. "Just me tonight."

"Good."

I felt my face flush.

"Actually," I said, "I'm sort of celebrating."

"Oh yeah?" Her eyes shone, a soft brown. "What's the good news?"

"Well, it's not official yet. But it looks like I'll be sticking around here for a while."

"Were you planning to leave?"

I shrugged. "I'd thought about it."

I told her about getting tenure. About keeping my job. That it still had to go through the dean, but things were hopeful.

"Ahh, a professor," she said. "That makes sense. Me and James," she gestured behind her toward the bartender. "We had this bet going when you were in here last time. He guessed lawyer."

"Lawyer! Never!"

She laughed. "Hey, I didn't say it. I guessed computer programmer."

"What?!"

"I don't know. You've got that—" she snapped her fingers, "cool nerd thing going on."

I liked this—this playfulness.

"Not sure how to take that."

"As a compliment."

Up close, she had a beautiful smile. Not Phaedra's, which always seemed to hide more than it showed. With Tara's, you could see everything up front.

"Well, Professor," she said, "what's your poison?"

"Neil," I said, extending my hand. "My name is Neil."

"I remember," she said, shaking it. "I'm Tara."

"I remember. Dealer's choice," I said. She brought me an old fashioned. Honey-colored, a cherry at the bottom.

"This one's on me," she said.

I felt my heart flutter. I couldn't even remember the last time that had happened for anyone other than Phaedra.

That night, my only plan had been to muster the courage to ask Tara out. But over the course of my dinner, the bar filled up with people. I watched her greet every single table with that same wide-open smile, those same bright eyes, until I'd talked myself out of it. So, I paid my bill and left the bar.

Outside, the air was turning cold. Christmas decorations were already up. The same songs on repeat in every store. Soon students would be going home for break. Another year coming to a close. I unlocked my car and sank down inside of it with a deep sense of pointlessness. I sat there but didn't start the car. After a long moment, I threw open the door again and walked back to the bar. Tara was taking a dinner order at a table across the room—a handful of guys, who ogled her without shame.

When she saw me standing there, she came over.

"You forget something?" she asked, glancing back at the table where I had been sitting. A new group was already there.

"Oh. No," I said. "I mean, yes. Well, actually, I was wondering if, maybe, you'd like to have dinner with me one night."

She eyed me with circumspection.

"I don't know," she said. "Are you a Gemini?"

"A Gemini? No. A Virgo."

"Are you a serial killer?"

"What! No, I—"

"I'm just kidding, Neil," she said. "Yes. I would like to have dinner with you." I got her number and walked back outside. Everything felt fuller, more possible somehow. I thought about texting Jack. I even pulled out my phone. I knew he'd be elated for me. But in the end, I didn't.

***

One Saturday morning a few weeks later, I drove to a mailbox—a blue USPS collection box. Three hours away. It was December, and school had let out. On the passenger seat next to me was a manila envelope. I wore gloves. The label was printed in computer ink. It was probably excessive, but I wasn't taking any chances.

Inside the envelope were Lucia's papers, all of them except one. I had shredded the essay she'd written for Jack's class. But all the others were there. The name on the front of the envelope was Detective Jerome Waters. The address was the police station.

In the months since Phaedra had told me about that night, I'd become obsessed with geolocation. Services like SensorVault and others. There was always the possibility that new technology would emerge. That coordinates would, one day, link Phaedra's phone to Lucia's death. But in the meantime, the connection would have to be made in other ways. I hesitated for only a moment, then I dropped the envelope in the mailbox, turned around and drove three hours home.

Sometimes I ask myself what I hope will happen.

The truth is, I don't know.

Maybe, one day, Detective Waters will find the killer. I imagine him receiving Lucia's papers in the mail. Staring at them with confusion, trying to discern what secrets they hold. Maybe he'll tuck them away into a file with her name on it. Or maybe he'll read them with forensic scrutiny, searching for clues that only Lucia's language can offer. For the sake of Lucia's sister and parents, I hope he does. I accept that I am too cowardly to do it myself.

Back at my apartment, I collapsed on the couch. Finally, after all these months, something felt finished. Not that it had come to an end. Not that there was closure. Closure is a fiction I don't believe in. But still, there was quiet, and in that quiet, there was a new kind of space.

I pulled out my phone and dialed a number.

It was not a number I was used to calling. It rang once. Then a second time. On the third ring, she picked up.

"Hello?"

For a beat, I couldn't talk.

"Hello?" she said again.

"Hi," I finally said. I wasn't sure how to navigate this. What it might mean—about the past, about the present. "It's me. It's Neil."

"Neil," she said, and for a long moment, my name hung in the empty chasm between us. I wondered if we could find our way back to each other. "It's been so long."

My mother's voice, clear as day.

***

What does it mean to bear witness, I ask myself. There are thinkers far greater than I who can't seem to come up with any definitive answer. There are those who say that the attempt to bear witness is destined to fail, that truth and presence and singularity are merely a seduction. What can we really offer each other in the end? What do we have to give? I don't pretend to have an answer.

To be honest, answers have never really held much weight for me. Right now, it feels important enough to simply have a question.